TELEPATH

ABOUT THE AUTHOR

Janet Edwards lives in England and writes science fiction. As a child, she read everything she could get her hands on, including a huge amount of science fiction and fantasy. She studied Maths at Oxford, and went on to suffer years of writing unbearably complicated technical documents before deciding to write something that was fun for a change. She has a husband, a son, a lot of books, and an aversion to housework.

Visit Janet online at her website www.janetedwards.com to see the current list of her books. You can also make sure you don't miss future books by signing up to get an email alert when there's a new release.

ALSO BY JANET EDWARDS

Set in the Hive Future

TELEPATH

Set in the Portal Future

The prequel novellas:-

EARTH AND FIRE: An Earth Girl Novella

FRONTIER: An Epsilon Sector Novella

The Earth Girl trilogy:-

EARTH GIRL

EARTH STAR

EARTH FLIGHT

The Earth Girl prequel short story collection:-

EARTH 2788: The Earth Girl Short Stories

Other short stories:-

HERA 2781: A Military Short Story

JANET EDWARDS

TELEPATH

HIVE MIND 1

CHAPTER ONE

Forge and Shanna led our group out of the lift into the forbidden territory of Level 1, the highest of the hundred accommodation levels in our Hive city. I stopped for a moment, dazzled by the splendour of the shopping area in front of us. The Level 1 shopping areas always had the finest decorations in the Hive, but this was the last day of Carnival, the annual Hive festival of light and life, so there were added gold and silver streamers everywhere.

Shanna glanced back at me. "Come on, Amber!"

I hurried to join the others under one of the giant overhead signs that said "Level 1". We automatically formed into a circle with Forge and Shanna standing in the centre. Twenty-two of us, all wearing traditional gold and silver Carnival costumes, and carrying masks. Forge was the one exception, conspicuous for choosing a costume and mask in the red and black colours of Halloween, the ominous Hive festival of darkness and death. Forge had constantly been challenging Hive rules on Teen Level, and wearing a Halloween costume during Carnival was his final act of defiance.

I noticed that a couple of men dressed in the blue uniforms of Health and Safety were standing nearby and watching us. On any other day, the hasties would have been scolding us, telling us that a group of teens had no business in one of the shopping areas reserved for the most important people in the Hive, and sternly sending us back down to Teen Level 50.

This wasn't any other day, because we were eighteen.

Tomorrow the million eighteen-year-olds in the Hive would all enter Lottery. We would be assessed, be optimized, be allocated, be imprinted. The Lottery of 2532 would decide our future lives, what profession we would work at, and whether we would live in luxury on a high level of the Hive or in a cramped apartment somewhere in the depths.

Shanna smiled at the rest of us. "We aren't going to be like all the other teens. We won't split up from our friends after Lottery. Let's promise that we'll all meet up two weeks from today."

There was a muttering of promises in reply, my own among them, but we all knew we were lying. We'd lived on the same corridor on Teen Level 50 for five years, and shared thousands of moments of laughter and arguments. Now the notoriously unpredictable verdict of Lottery would send some of us higher up the Hive and others further down, label some of us a success and others a failure.

Shanna had boundless confidence. She was sure she'd be one of the successes, even be among the elite who lived in the top ten accommodation levels of the Hive. The rest of us felt far more uncertain about what lay ahead. We wouldn't want to meet up again if we were among the failures. I knew I couldn't face the others if...

I fought back against the nightmare doubts. The verdicts of Lottery were unpredictable because of the sheer complexity of the automated decision process, but there was logic behind them. Everyone said I was bright and articulate, and I'd followed all the advice about spending my time on Teen Level doing preparation work. The Level 99 Sewage Technician, butt of all the jokes, couldn't happen to me. Please, not to me.

"Good luck," said Forge. "I hope all of you will be high up."

This time the response was wholehearted. "High up, everyone!" we yelled in unison.

There was a second of silence, and then twin chiming sounds as the doors of the two nearest lifts opened. More groups of teens were arriving, and the watching hasties were waving at us to signal that we couldn't linger here any longer. Forge put on the Halloween mask that transformed his handsome face into something demonic. Everyone else put on the joyful masks of Carnival, and followed him across to the moving stairs in the middle of the shopping area.

We jumped onto one of the handrails of the downway. Forge first, then Shanna, and then the rest of us in turn. Riding the handrail was the classic act of teen rebellion. The hasties usually intervened to stop it, telling us to travel sensibly and safely on the moving stairs instead.

They wouldn't intervene today. This was our last day as teens, and Hive tradition gave us the right to one last act of rebellion, starting to ride the handrail on Level 1 itself and continuing on down as deep into the Hive as we could.

I caught a glimpse of us in the mirrored wall beside me. A proud line of twenty-two masked figures, spectacular in our glittering costumes. As the handrail plunged down from the Level 1 shopping area to the one on Level 2, Forge raised his right hand and shouted the ritual words.

"Ride the Hive!"

"Ride the Hive!" We yelled the words back to him.

The shoppers turned their heads to watch us go by, applauded, and called their good wishes to us. "High up to you."

"Ride the Hive!" We yelled the words each time the moving stairs went down to the next level. We'd never be together again. We'd never be the same people again. Lottery would do more than assess our abilities, optimize our possible professions to give us the one most suitable for us and useful to the Hive, and allocate us our level. It would imprint our minds with all the information needed to do our assigned work.

All our lives we'd known and accepted our minds would be imprinted during Lottery. We'd discussed it dozens of times, eagerly looking forward to being given a wealth of knowledge. Over the last few weeks, the tone of those discussions had changed from joyful anticipation to nervous whispers about exactly what imprinting would do to our minds.

Now Lottery was upon us and we were terrified. The assessment stage lasted between three and five days. By this time next week, we'd all be imprinted and beginning our new adult lives.

We'd no idea if we'd be high or low level. We didn't know what profession we'd be given. We weren't even sure that we'd be the same people after our minds were imprinted. We were facing the black unknown, and we screamed defiance to block out the fear.

I was fifth in line when we started on Level 1. Riding the rail was hard, so two of us had fallen before we even reached Level 5. As the overhead signs told us that we'd hit Level 18, I counted the figures reflected in the mirrored walls. We were down to fifteen now, and I was third in line. The ones who fell down from the handrail onto the moving stairs didn't climb back on the handrail again. Custom decreed that the last ride was over when you fell.

I focused my eyes on the two figures still ahead of me. Tall, heavily muscled Forge, his black hair matching his red and black costume. Slender Shanna behind him, her fair hair cascading down the back of her silver dress. She was perfectly poised and elegant, looking as if she could ride the handrail forever, but then her foot slipped as the rail made the bend to reach Level 46.

Shanna flailed her arms, teetered wildly, and tumbled down onto the moving stairs next to her. She'd barely got time to stand up before the downway reached the Level 46 shopping area, where she stepped off and waved at the rest of us. I heard her final cry come from behind me.

"Go Forge! Go Amber! Ride the Hive!"

I daren't look back as she called my name, but I held up my arm in salute and farewell, and blinked back tears from behind the fake smile of my Carnival mask. Shanna had been my best friend for all my years on Teen Level. I'd lived in her shadow, been alternately grateful to her for being my friend and jealous of her self-confidence, and now I'd never see her again.

There was a faint chance that one of my old friends would come out of Lottery as the same level as me and we could stay in touch, but I knew it wouldn't be Shanna. She was bound to be rated far higher level than someone as ordinary as me.

I concentrated on the red of Forge's shirt ahead of me, and the difficult job of keeping my balance as the rail flattened out, turned, and dived down again at each level change. We were below Level 60 now, I was shaking with the effort of the ride, and my legs stung from scratches as my silver sequinned skirt blew around them.

We were still descending through shopping areas, because all the accommodation levels of the Hive had their shops, but they were plainer here, selling more functional goods. There were no fancy mirrored walls now, but I caught a reflection of us in some glass on Level 63, and saw there were only four of us left. By Level 70, there was no one behind me, and at Level 72 Forge fell and I was left alone.

I kept riding the rail on down, all the way to Level 100 itself. There were no shops or people there, just dusty pipes to salute my triumph as I jumped to the ground, but I'd ridden the Hive.

I only felt the briefest moment of celebration before depression hit me. I'd ridden the Hive, I'd screamed defiance, but it hadn't changed anything. Tomorrow morning, I would enter Lottery, because there was nowhere else I could go and nothing else I could do. There were one hundred and six other Hive cities in the world, but I wouldn't have the right to ask to move to one of them until after I'd been through Lottery.

Even if I could ask for a Hive transfer right now, I wasn't courageous enough, or foolish enough, to take that leap into a darkened lift shaft. I'd no idea what life was like in other Hives. Our Hive news sometimes mentioned their names, but never gave any details about them. The occasional malcontent claimed other Hives were far more luxurious places to live than ours, but they obviously hadn't had enough courage in their convictions to apply to move.

Moving Hive wouldn't help me anyway. My problem wasn't with my Hive, but with suffering the suspense of waiting helplessly while my profession, my level, my whole future life was decided for me. Every Hive would have its own equivalent of Lottery, and it was better to face it here than in an alien place.

I yanked off my mask, turned round, and stepped onto the upway. I stood there, weary and defeated, letting it carry me back towards my sliver of a room on Teen Level 50. It would have been much faster to take a lift, but it somehow seemed appropriate to go back the same way that I'd arrived.

I was on Level 56 when I heard the chanting ahead of me

that warned a telepath was nearby. I was looking forward to changing out of the Carnival outfit that had been chosen by Shanna, and was far too spectacular and revealing for someone like me. I was thinking about packing my bag to take to Lottery. I was planning to have an early night so I'd be well rested tomorrow. There was nothing in my head that was incriminating, but I joined in the chanting just the same.

"Two ones are two."

"Two twos are four."

"Two threes are six."

The upway reached Level 55, and the people in the shopping area here were shouting it.

"Two fours are eight."

"Two fives are ten."

"Two sixes are twelve."

I saw the crowd of shoppers move aside to let through a figure dressed in grey and wearing a matching grey mask. That was the telepath, the nosy, with their escort of four blue-clad hasties following behind to guard him or her.

"Two sevens are fourteen!"

"Two eights are sixteen!"

Everyone was screaming it now, and I was yelling as loudly as any of them. People said that filling your thoughts with numbers stopped a nosy from reading your mind. I didn't know if that was true, but it was worth a try. I didn't want anyone seeing my private thoughts. I wanted the nosies to catch the criminals, to keep me safe, but I hated the idea of someone snooping inside my own head.

The nosy seemed to be looking at me now. The bulging shape of the grey mask, and the hint of strange, purple eyes behind it, showed that the wearer wasn't entirely human. I was grateful that the upway was carrying me to safety on the next level.

Once the nosy and the chanting crowd were left behind, I rode on in silence again. I finally reached Level 50, scurried along a couple of corridors, and made it into my room without seeing any of the people who'd once been my friends. We'd said our goodbyes, and Carnival and our teen life was over. Tomorrow, Lottery would begin.

CHAPTER TWO

I woke the next morning, gasping in panic. I'd been trapped in a nightmare where I'd overslept and got lost on my way to Lottery. I couldn't read any of the signs. I was running along the belts, asking people which way to go, and none of them would help me. When I eventually reached my assessment centre, a man stood blocking the doorway.

"Too late," he said, and handed me a card saying Level 99 Sewage Technician.

I hadn't overslept, it had just been a ridiculous dream, but my taut nerves refused to relax and I could only eat half my breakfast before my stomach rebelled. I threw the remains of the food down the waste chute, with inevitable thoughts about whether I'd be joining the low-level workers who ran the waste system, and then concentrated on getting everything I needed inside the one large bag I was allowed to take to Lottery.

Bag packed, I started hurling the rest of my possessions into the storage locker next to my room. I was aware that someone further along the corridor was loading things into their storage locker too, but didn't turn my head to look at them. I couldn't face yet another pointless conversation of goodbye and good luck.

Once my room was empty, I used its built-in comms system to call my parents. Their faces appeared on the wall, smiling anxiously.

"I'm ready to go," I said.

"You'll do brilliantly." My mother turned to my father. "Won't she?"

"Definitely," he said. "I know it's hard, Amber, but try to relax during the assessment process."

"And we'll still be here for you afterwards," said my mother. "No matter what."

My father nodded.

"Thanks," I said.

I knew they meant what they were saying. The Hive encouraged new adults to make a fresh start after Lottery, breaking free from old teen friendships that would fuel discontent in those that were lower level, but it recognized that it could be psychologically damaging to break close ties between parent and child.

Families keeping in touch whatever the Lottery result was accepted, even encouraged, but many parents would still dump an embarrassingly low-level child. Mine wouldn't. Whatever Lottery decreed for me, whatever new life I was thrown into, I'd have the comfort of one link to the past. My parents would still keep calling me their daughter, and I'd be welcome to visit their home.

They'd have to follow the social conventions though. My Lottery result would decide whether my photos stayed in one of the public rooms of their apartment, or were hidden away privately in their bedroom.

My parents were Level 27. Lottery would have to rank me at least Level 29 for it to be socially acceptable for them to keep my photos on public display for their friends. If my photos vanished, then those friends would know what it meant and do the polite thing. Never ask how I'd done in Lottery, or mention my name again.

If I did very well, the situation would be reversed. The photos would be proudly centre stage, and my parents would glow with pride and talk of my success.

Right now, I had a gut feeling there was little chance of that. My photos were heading for the bedroom.

"Gregas!" my mother called. "Come and wish your sister a good Lottery result."

There was a pause before my brother reluctantly came to join them and muttered something inaudible. He was looking pretty strained himself, and I could understand why. Gregas was thirteen. In four short weeks, he'd be moving to Teen Level.

"Good luck to you too, Gregas," I said. "Moving to Teen Level, living on your own in a small room, will seem strange at first, but you'll soon get over that. There's no more school, you can try out all the activities on offer in the community centres, join any sports team you like, go to parties and have a great time."

He grunted a reply, but didn't seem convinced he was going to have fun. To be honest, I wasn't too convinced myself. It was vital to make friends during your first few weeks on Teen Level, and Gregas wasn't very sociable.

"When you move here," I added, "spend as much time as you can in your corridor community room. Everyone on your corridor will be new like you, and they'll all want to make friends. Remember that it's horribly rude to ask what level they came from, or mention what level your own parents are. Your family background doesn't matter once you're on Teen Level, because all teens are Level 50 and equal."

Gregas grunted again, and I gave up. I'd done my best. I'd told him the right things to do, and warned him of the one social blunder he mustn't make. There was no need to emphasize the point about taking part in activities. Gregas would have had plenty of school lessons about the importance of using your time on Teen Level to prepare for Lottery.

I didn't want to talk about the activity sessions anyway. I'd dutifully attended every type my local community centre had to offer, but failed to discover any especial gift for painting, costume design, or a hundred other things. My instructors had said that wasn't a bad omen for the future, because the activity sessions mainly focused on work involving creative skills. Lottery would test all my innate abilities, and search among tens of thousands of other possible professions in the Hive to find the one that was perfect for me, so I still had every chance of becoming high level.

Back when I was fourteen or fifteen, I'd accepted those

comforting words were true. Now I was heading into Lottery, I found them far less reassuring.

"I've got a long way to go," I said, "so I'd better get started."

My parents nodded. "High up to you," they chorused.

"Thanks." I ended the call.

I gave one final, nostalgic look round the room where I'd lived for five years. Once Lottery was over, I'd come and collect my belongings from the storage locker, but maintenance workers would already be overhauling the room itself by then.

I pictured them painting over every familiar scuff mark and scratch on the walls, eliminating every last trace of my residence here ready for another girl or boy to move in. It might even be Gregas who came to live in this room next. Teens were always allocated rooms in their home area, so the support of parents was just a lift ride away.

I picked up my bag and went outside. My door slid closed behind me for the last time, and I hurried down the corridor. At the first crossway, it met a wider corridor with a slow belt lane. I stepped onto the moving strip and rode it to the nearest major belt interchange.

Once there, I took my folded dataview from my pocket, tapped it to make it unfurl, and checked the instructions I'd been sent. Lottery testing was done in the Teen Level 50 community centres, but teens were always allocated to centres a long distance from their home area to make sure they wouldn't be assessed by a friend of their family. I had to travel all the way from my home area of 510/6120 in Blue Zone, to the area 110/3900 community centre in Yellow Zone. I glanced at the overhead signs, and stepped onto the northbound slow belt, before moving across to the medium, and then the express.

Once I was on the express belt, I put my bag down and sat on it. My old friends would all be riding the belt system too, making equally lengthy journeys to different community centres.

It was like a sad echo of the wild ride yesterday. All the Carnival decorations had been taken down, leaving just the usual amateur wall paintings of Teen Level to brighten the corridors. Everyone's Carnival costumes had been replaced by standard teen outfits too, mostly leggings and tunics emblazoned with the emblems of favourite singers or sports teams, though some of the girls wore the fashionable tops and skirts that Shanna adored.

The eighteen-year-olds dotted the express belt, sitting on their bags like me, while the younger teens stood by the corridor walls and watched us go by. I'd been a watcher myself in previous years, wondering what the travellers were thinking. Now my turn had come, and my thoughts were a confused, dejected jumble. I wished the trip was over, but I didn't want to arrive.

"Warning, zone bulkhead approaching!" A voice boomed from overhead speakers, and red signs started flashing count-down numbers.

On any other level, people would start moving across from the express to slower belts, or even get off the belt system entirely so they could walk across the boundary between the two zones.

This was Teen Level, so we just stood up and picked up our bags. The bulkhead approached, its massive blue and turquoise striped doors wide open as always. I saw the boy ahead of me toss his bag across the narrow gap between the end of the Blue Zone belt and the start of the Turquoise Zone belt, then leap after it. A second later, it was my turn. I braced myself, hurled my own bag ahead of me, and jumped.

The safety bar between the two belts made it impossible to fall down the gap, but there was always a fractional difference in speed between two express belts. I staggered on landing, swayed for a moment, but managed to stay on my feet.

"Eight!" screamed a set of voices from over to my left.

There were always some self-appointed judges giving points on how well you managed the zone boundary jump. I didn't turn my head to look at them, just retrieved my bag and sat down on it again.

The watching younger teens wore clothes decorated with the turquoise emblems of Turquoise Zone sports teams now. I travelled on through more bulkheads, crossing from Turquoise Zone to Green, and Green Zone to Yellow, before changing to a westbound belt.

When I finally reached the community centre in 110/3900, I

double and triple checked I'd got the right number and the right place, then dug my assessment card out of my pocket and slid it into the slot beside the door.

"Welcome, Amber, you are now registered for Lottery assessment," it said, spat the card back out at me, and the door slid open.

The inside looked exactly like the community centre back in my old area. All the chairs were out in the main hall, and some teens were already sitting on them, each with a large bag at their side. The huge display wall at the front of the hall was filled with instructions. I picked a chair as far away from the other teens as possible, sat down, and started to read the text.

"Lottery welcomes the candidates of 2532. You should wait in this hall between tests, but are advised to avoid interaction with other candidates. Do not be concerned if your tests are not following the same sequence as those of others. Every candidate follows an individualized test progression, where the results of each test determine what other tests should follow. There may be a delay at times until staff and facilities are available for a key test."

A banner flashed into life at the top of the main screen. "Ricardo, please go to room 17."

A gangly lad scrambled to his feet, looked at the map of the centre on the side wall, and scuttled off down a corridor. I went back to reading the general instructions.

"Do not be concerned if you appear to perform badly on any particular test. Your weaknesses are not important. You will be allocated to a profession that matches your strengths, with priority going to professions harder to fill and more vital to the Hive."

That was the end of the instructions. I focused my attention on the banner now, getting nervous as the minutes went by without my name appearing. The instructions said there could be delays, but...

The banner was showing my name! "Amber, please go to room 23."

I stood up, checked the map, and headed to room 23. A smiling blonde woman was waiting for me inside what looked like a standard medical room. She asked me to roll up my sleeve, and then held a metal gadget to my arm.

"I'm taking a blood and tissue sample. This will feel cold, but it won't hurt."

I'd had blood and tissue samples taken at every one of my annual medical checks. The next bit was just like an annual medical too. The woman turned on a scanning grid, and I stood inside the field while it made murmuring noises.

"Your medical records show you had an allergic reaction to face paints at age three," she said, "and another allergic reaction to the contraceptive pellet implanted in your arm at age sixteen."

I frowned. Would a history of allergies damage my chances in Lottery? "I haven't had any problems since they changed the pellet to a different type," I said hastily.

"You also have occasional headaches. Any other health problems, Amber?"

"No."

The woman turned off the grid. "That's all for now, Amber."

I went back to the hall and sat down next to my bag. It was a quarter of an hour before my name appeared on the banner again, sending me to room 9. This held a central chair facing a wall covered with randomly moving, glowing clusters of colour. A young woman was studying a small technical display in the corner of the room. She only looked a year or two older than me. It wasn't long since she'd been the one being assessed to decide her future career, and now she was assessing me.

"Please sit down, Amber." She gestured at the central chair.

I sat down, and she gave me the same blandly reassuring smile as the earlier woman. Did the information imprinted on the minds of medical and assessment staff include the correct professional expressions?

"I'm taking baseline brain activity measurements." She came across to position a metal blob on each side of my forehead, and then returned to check her technical display.

I sneaked a look at the display myself. A lot of little lights were bouncing up and down. It meant nothing to me, but my tester seemed happy with it.

"Your records show that you followed the recommendations to try all the introductory activity sessions at least once during your time on Teen Level."

"That's right."

"I need you to watch the colours on the wall now."

I sat back in the chair, and watched the colours floating around. I was a ragged mess of nerves, but there was something about the patterns that was soothing. The colours slowly merged to form an image of someone painting a mural on a corridor wall.

"Did you like painting murals, Amber?" the woman asked.

"I loved it." I hesitated a moment. "I was dreadfully bad at painting though."

"For the purposes of this test, all I need to know is whether you enjoyed an activity or not."

The colours in the image drifted apart, and then reformed to show a man peering into the top of a machine.

"Did you like embroidering?" asked the woman.

I'd been frustrated by the painstakingly slow and detailed stitching. "No."

"How about working with clay?"

I'd disliked the faint smell of the wet clay and the touch of it on my hands. "No."

"Singing?"

I smiled. "Yes."

The woman tapped at her controls. "I've calibrated your responses now, so you can just watch the images without saying anything."

I was bewildered, but obediently watched the glowing colours change and merge, shifting between a series of images. They changed faster and faster, the colours moving, blending, separating...

"Amber, wake up," said a soft, female voice.

I jerked upright, hot with embarrassment and horror. I'd fallen asleep during a Lottery test! "I'm sorry. I didn't sleep well last night. Can we do the test again?"

"You did perfectly well, Amber. The test was supposed to have that effect. You can go now."

I stumbled off in confusion, unsure now if I'd actually fallen asleep or not. When I got back to the hall, it was almost empty. The display on the end wall announced a rest break, and said that refreshments were available in a side room.

I wandered through some open double doors, picked up a tray, and joined the end of a queue. There was a startling range of luxury food available. I'd hardly eaten the previous day, and only had half my usual breakfast this morning, so I was starving hungry. I waited impatiently until I reached the head of the queue, loaded a plate with a spoonful from each of twenty different dishes, added a bread roll and a glass of my favourite melon juice, and found a place at a table to eat.

There were plenty of spare seats, since half of my fellow sufferers had only collected drinks before retreating back to the main hall. Those at my table were obeying the Lottery rules by eating in silence and carefully ignoring each other, but a girl behind us was talking to herself in a ceaseless, barely audible monologue. It was obviously just her way of reacting to stress, but it made me feel uncomfortable.

I'd nearly finished eating, when the boy next to me suffered his own individual reaction to stress by throwing up on the table. I abandoned what food was left on my plate and retreated, feeling queasy, into the hall.

The end wall was displaying the standard instructions again. After a few minutes, my name appeared on the banner, and I was sent to do a test involving putting groups of pins into tiny holes, which I was fairly sure was about dexterity. Next came what seemed like a straightforward running speed test, and then I had a long wait before being sent to room 11. I was greeted by a young man with red hair, whose professional smile kept lapsing into a casual grin.

"Hello, Amber." He handed me an over-sized dataview. "You're going to try to solve some puzzles. Don't worry if a few of them make no sense to you. I'm not sure what half of them are about myself."

I took the dataview and sat down on the chair provided. I saw a sample puzzle and solution appear on the wall opposite me. The first real puzzle followed it, and I selected what I thought was the answer on the dataview. The comedian settled down in his own chair by a technical display, and appeared to fall asleep from boredom.

The first puzzles were reassuringly simple. Little diagrams where I had to choose the odd one out. There was a pause and then I got a new batch where I was supposed to pick the next coloured diagram in a sequence. After that, it got more involved. There were some tests that I understood, so I was confident I'd be choosing the right answers. On others, even the instructions seemed to make no sense at all, and I just picked answers at random.

Eventually, the wall went blank. The comedian gave a yawn, took back the dataview, and connected it to his technical display. "Thank you, Amber, you can..."

He was interrupted by a soft chime and lights flashing on his display. I saw him turn and stare at it. "Please wait here for a moment, Amber."

He went out of the room, and I turned in my chair and stared at the door closing behind him. Something had happened, but I didn't know what. I looked back at the technical display by his empty chair, but it just showed a meaningless jumble of letters.

After long minutes of suspense, an older man entered the room. "Hello, Amber. We don't have the facilities here for your next recommended test, so we're sending you to another centre."

He handed me a new assessment card, and I stared blankly down at it.

"Don't worry," he added. "This is perfectly normal. It's impossible to equip all the centres for every test, so sometimes people are transferred."

There was no point in me asking what had happened in the last test. The Lottery rules stated that candidates should never be told the reason for a test or the results of it. At the end of my assessment, I'd simply be told my assigned profession, and be sent for imprinting with the appropriate information.

I accepted there were good reasons for those rules. It would be hard for someone to live with the knowledge that scoring just a little better on a test could have made them twenty levels higher. I still wished I understood what was happening.

I turned, went out of the door, and headed back to the hall. Everyone stared at me as I picked up my bag and walked out. There were hundreds of eighteen-year-olds at this centre, and I was the only one leaving. That had to mean either something very good or something very bad, and I didn't know which.

CHAPTER THREE

Once I was outside the centre, I had a cowardly urge to run to my parents' apartment and hide in what had once been my bedroom. New arrivals on Teen Level sometimes ran away, returning to the comforting familiarity of home and parents. Counsellors would follow and coax them back, embarrassed and blushing, to face the ordeal of growing up and being their own person. Running away from Teen Level made those who did it look ridiculous. I'd look even more ridiculous if I tried running away from Lottery.

I took a deep breath, and headed for the new community centre. I had another long journey to reach it, and of course it looked virtually identical to the last one. I put my new assessment card into the door slot to gain entry.

"Welcome, Amber, your Lottery assessment registration transfer is now complete."

I noticed the different message and was vaguely reassured. I'd never heard of people being transferred during Lottery, but clearly the system was designed for it. I went inside and found a deserted hall with a screen covered in names and room designations. Everyone must have already left for the night, so I found my name on the list, made a note of where I was supposed to be staying, turned round and went back out of the centre.

My designated room was only a few corridors away. I walked there, still obsessing over why I'd been transferred to a different centre. If it was true the old centre didn't have the facilities for my next test, that surely meant it was an unusual test for an uncommon profession.

Was something astonishingly good happening to me or was this a disaster? Was I being tested for an important, high level profession that would give me a glittering future, or for some hideous work deep in the bowels of the Hive? I alternated between excitement and depression, but depression was winning. Even if I was being tested for something high level, I'd probably fail the test and be sent back to my original assessment centre.

I reached a door with the right number on it, opened it, and took my bag and my uncertainty into an unwelcomingly bare room. I set the wall display to show one of the standard pictures, and brilliant blue cornflowers sprang into three dimensional life. The flowers made me feel a bit more at home, but I still missed having all my old familiar clutter of possessions around me.

I'd lost my appetite, so I didn't bother getting any food from the tiny kitchen unit, just stripped off and showered. It seemed a waste of effort to dress again afterwards, so I activated the sleep field, and then dimmed the lighting. I lay enfolded in the darkness and the cushion of warm air, watching the glowing flowers on the wall.

A million other eighteen-year-olds would be in bare rooms like this one, trying to relax after the strain of their first day in Lottery. I briefly wondered who was in my old room now, then drifted on to picturing my old friends. Margot frowning in disapproval of something. Linnette daydreaming. Shanna anxiously studying her reflection in the mirror. Forge...

I pulled a face at the thought of Forge. I'd been fixated on that boy from the first moment I saw him on Teen Level. He'd looked straight past me at Shanna, never thought of me as more than a random member of the group who trailed round in their wake, but my obsession with him had controlled my life for five solid years.

It had made me become Shanna's best friend. It had made me take up swimming. It had made me spend endless tedious hours at the Level 50 beach, cheering for Forge as he took part in the teen inter-zone surfing competitions.

Having a secret, unrequited crush on someone like handsome, reckless Forge would have been embarrassing but perfectly normal. This didn't seem like an ordinary crush though. I didn't long for Forge's kisses, or want to replace Shanna as his girlfriend. I just wanted to watch Forge's face and know he was pleased and happy.

There was the dream as well. A weird, repeating dream that had been haunting my sleep all through Teen Level. It centred on Forge, but it wasn't the sort of dream I'd expect to have about a boy I found attractive. The dream didn't even make any sense.

The strangeness of my reaction to Forge had bothered me enough at times that I'd considered asking to relocate to a room in another corridor, but I couldn't face being the unwelcome new arrival amongst an existing group of friends.

Well, my time with Forge was over now. Lottery had ended it, like it ended all teen relationships. Once I'd been given my result and imprinted, I'd go to live on my adult level, have my work to occupy my days, and a host of new people around me to make me forget about Forge. As everyone always said, Lottery was both an end and a new beginning.

I closed my eyes and relaxed. As I sank into sleep, the repeating dream about Forge began. The two of us walked together, hand in hand, through a strange park with impossibly tall trees. It was hot, far too hot, and the suns in the ceiling were blindingly bright. I was terrified and desperately looking for the exit door.

"Good girl, Amber," said Forge. "You're a good girl, Amber."

I forgot my fear when he said that. Forge was pleased with me, and pleasing him was the most important thing in the world.

When I woke up, I found I'd had ten solid hours of sleep, and I felt wonderful. That was the good side of having the Forge dream. I always woke feeling blissfully content, with the echo of his words in the back of my mind. The oddest thing was that Forge had never said those words to me outside the dream, and his voice sounded deeper than usual when he said them.

I was in a decisive and optimistic mood about everything now, even Lottery. If the change in assessment centre meant I was being offered a chance at something special, then I'd do my best to grab it. If my best wasn't good enough, then I'd just have to accept it, the same way that most teens had to accept they weren't special or high level. Whatever level I ended up living on, my life would improve. I'd have a proper apartment instead of a teen room, a proper income instead of the miserly teen living allowance, and a proper purpose in life.

I picked out fresh clothes to wear, ate breakfast hungrily, and left my belongings scattered around the room. I'd never managed to keep my old room tidy, and there was little incentive to care for one that would only be mine during Lottery.

Back at the centre, I sat watching the display wall, waiting for my name to appear, keyed up for the magical test where success or failure could mean everything for my future. Five minutes, ten minutes, and my name was there. I had to go to room 4.

I hurried there and found an elderly man with dark skin and receding hair. "We're testing your reaction speed," he said. "You sit at this table opposite me."

I took my seat. There was a partition between us so I couldn't see his hands. In front of me was a row of dimly glowing lights in different colours.

"We've both got matching rows of coloured lights," he said. "I touch one on my side, and that colour brightens on both rows. You have to touch the matching bright light on your side as fast as you can."

I frowned. The unquestioning happiness of the Forge dream aftermath was wearing off now. I didn't understand this test at all. What professions needed special reaction speed? I dismissed that thought as the test started. The reason behind it didn't matter. I had to focus on touching the bright light as fast as possible.

At the end of the test, there was nothing in the man's expression to tell me whether I'd done well or badly, but he didn't send me back to my previous assessment centre. That was good. Probably good.

There was a wait in the hall after that, followed by a session where I wore an electronic armband and sat watching a series of pictures. People working, shopping, talking, arguing, and in one case actually fighting. There were people from all levels. Some in party clothes, some dressed for work. Some tall, some short. Some old, some young.

When the pictures finally stopped, I expected to be asked questions, but there weren't any. I headed back to the hall where the other eighteen-year-olds sat, each in their own isolated bubble of anxiety, but barely had time to sit down before I was called for a very straightforward fitness test where I pushed my hands and feet against cushioned, resisting bars.

There was something relaxing about simple physical tiredness, so I was able to eat lunch during the rest break, though I took my plate back into the hall to avoid the risk of anyone being sick near me. There was another girl sitting only two chairs away from me, but she wasn't eating or drinking, just staring at a holo picture of a fair-haired boy.

After one glance in her direction, I kept my eyes firmly on my plate. Even if I'd dared to break the Lottery rule of silence, I couldn't say anything to help her. The boy in the picture had obviously been her boyfriend. They'd have said goodbye before Lottery, the way that teen couples always did, but she hadn't given up hope that they'd get back together. I pitied her. If they came out of Lottery the same level, they might be reunited, but what were the chances of that happening?

I hoped she wasn't counting on love triumphing over a level difference. Yes, it was theoretically possible if a couple were just a few levels apart, and the higher level was prepared to move down, but how often did that happen outside romantic bookettes? In reality, the higher status partner never made the offer, or the lower status partner was too proud to accept the sacrifice.

The girl should be sensible and accept that teen relationships always ended at Lottery, but I knew that was easier said than done. I'd spent five years trying, and failing, to be sensible about Forge.

My train of thought was interrupted by the display wall coming back to life, showing my name listed for another test. I abandoned the congealing remnants of my lunch, and went to another bewildering session of watching seemingly random images. There was music this time as well, with odd sliding notes that did disturbing things to my nerves. It was followed by a peculiar hearing test, where I sat in pitch darkness, trying to hear faint sounds and work out their direction.

There were several more incomprehensible tests during the afternoon. When I went back to my room, I spent the evening pointlessly wondering what skill they'd been assessing. Was I still following the special testing route that had involved me changing centre, or had I already failed it?

When I went to bed, I dreamed of the hearing test. I was alone in the darkness, hearing strange noises. The dream changed into a nightmare, where I groped my way blindly through a maze of corridors, trying to find the source of the sounds. If I didn't find them, something dreadful would happen.

The next morning, I gave up wondering what my testers were trying to achieve, and abandoned myself to the strange, limbo existence of the Lottery. There were tests. There was a break to eat. There were more tests in the afternoon. I hadn't the faintest idea what was going on, or how well I was doing.

As the last few minutes of the afternoon ticked away, the rows of chairs in the hall gradually filled up with nervous, expectant teens. No one said a word, but I knew the same thought was in everyone's head. Third day. Some would be told their results now, good or bad.

I didn't think I'd be one of them. I'd lost time being transferred, so it would be tomorrow at the earliest for me. Probably. Almost certainly. I couldn't be entirely sure, but...

A new display came up on the end wall. A dozen names were asked to go to specific rooms. My name wasn't on the list.

The rest of us were told to leave and return tomorrow. There was the soft sound of held breath being released. I watched the chosen ones hurry off, and left the assessment centre feeling a mixture of relief and disappointment.

When I got back to my temporary room, I checked the time and hesitated. No, it was far too early. Candidates had to be told their results and imprinted before their new professions were publicly posted. Eight o'clock. I should wait until eight o'clock.

So I ate, tried watching the Hive news, and then a swimming competition between Blue Zone and Yellow Zone, but couldn't concentrate. Once it was eight o'clock, I used my dataview to access the Lottery listings, and started entering each of twenty-one identity codes that were as familiar to me as my own.

Not yet available.

Not yet available.

Not yet available.

Linnette 2514-1003-947. Animal Care Expert. Level 41.

I knew Linnette would like that. She'd always loved all kinds of living things. It was good news. I was happy for Linnette. For some strange reason I was crying.

Not yet available. Not yet available. The same words kept repeating again. I'd saved the most important two identity codes for last.

Shanna 2514-0118-223. Not yet available.

Forge 2514-0253-884. Health and Safety, Law Enforcement. Level 20. ARU77139.

The words danced in front of my eyes. They made no sense. Forge was a rebel, constantly breaking the rules. The hasties had scolded me a dozen times for riding the rail, but Forge had gone far beyond that minor act of teen defiance. I remembered when he was caught crawling through the vent system, and forced to wear a child's tracking bracelet for weeks afterwards, all his male adolescent pride embarrassed at being treated like a baby.

Now Forge was a hasty himself. I turned on the sleep field and lay back on it, laughing at the thought of the rebel Forge dressed in a blue uniform, picturing him sternly lecturing teens on the dangers of riding the handrail.

Somewhere on Teen Level, Shanna would be looking up results just like me. I wondered what she was thinking now. She'd always dismissed the hasties as stuffy prudes who were out to spoil people's fun.

The Level 20 next to Forge's name meant nothing. Everyone assigned to a branch of Law Enforcement, whether high or low level, would live on Level 20, which had a mixture of accommodation from simple to luxurious. If I'd understood the code ARU77139, it would presumably have told me Forge's true level, whether he'd have an important post in Law Enforcement or not, but it was better not to know.

Forge was on the other side of the great divide between hasties and citizens. I could picture him as an anonymous figure dressed in blue, which would help me forget him.

Eventually, I rolled out of the sleep field to eat and undress for the night. Tomorrow would be day four of Lottery, when assessment finished for all but a handful of people. By the end of it, I should know my future profession and level. I'd reached the point where I could accept anything Lottery decreed for me, except a Level 99 Sewage Technician, with gratitude.

I went to sleep expecting the usual dream about Forge, but instead I dreamed about flowers, endless racks of flowers in a huge hydroponics area. Bees hastened between them and their hives at the end of the racks.

I knew these bees well. Striped gold and blue, they flew busily round the parks as well as hydroponics. I'd been fascinated by them as a child, and the way they lived in their own little hives, just like we humans did in our much bigger one. I'd reach out a finger and gently stroke their tiny furry bodies. My parents would watch me and smile. They worked in genetics, and told me how the bees had been bred from their wild ancestors to be good natured, hard working, and without stings.

In my dream, I was one of the bees myself. I gathered the pollen and carried it back to my home hive, crawling through the tunnels inside, listening to the reassuring hum of my companions around me.

I woke up the next morning feeling oddly disoriented, and a sense of unease clung to me all through breakfast, the walk to the assessment centre, and more confusing hours of tests. By the afternoon, I had a splitting headache, like a hammer pounding away inside my skull. I blamed it on the light displays in the morning tests.

I fought to ignore the headache, struggling on until there was yet another session with light displays. The throbbing in my head reached a crescendo. I gave a moan of pain and buried my head in my hands.

"What's wrong, Amber?" asked my tester, an elegant woman of about thirty who'd been giving me several of my most recent tests.

"I'm sorry," I said. "I've got a terrible headache."

"I'm a doctor," she said. "I'll give you an injection that will help the pain, and then you can lie down and rest for a while."

I held out my arm, and she gave me a shot with a pressure jet. I still felt awful, but I couldn't stand these tests dragging on into a fifth day. "I don't need a rest."

"You aren't well enough to continue at the moment." She gave me the standard reassuring professional smile, and uttered the words they all kept reciting. "Don't worry."

Her face seemed to blur and sway in front of my eyes, and everything went black.

CHAPTER FOUR

When I woke up, I opened my eyes, and saw the ceiling above me curved down to meet the walls in a strange way I'd never seen before. I studied it for a bewildered second, then remembered getting ill during the test.

I sat up in panic, found I'd been lying on some sort of couch, and looked around. I was in a long, thin room, with a lot of cushioned chairs set formally in pairs on one side. My couch was on the other. The walls had curious metal plates attached to them at intervals, and the place felt odd. I felt odd too.

The doctor who'd treated me was sitting in one of the chairs. She saw my movement, and turned to look at me.

"How do you feel, Amber? Headache gone?"

"Yes," I said. "My head feels..."

I broke off. I'd been about to say my head felt totally normal now, but there was still something peculiar. I frowned as I tried to pin it down.

"It seems very quiet here." That sounded silly, so I hurried on. "I'm sorry I fainted, but I'm better now and can get back to doing the test."

"You didn't faint, Amber. I sedated you. You've been asleep for twenty-seven hours."

"What?" I shrieked the word before I could stop myself. It was stupid to yell at assessment staff, so I hastily apologized. "I'm very sorry. I was startled. Can I continue my tests now?"

The woman took two drinks from a dispenser, and brought one over to me. "My name is Megan."

I took the drink and sipped it. My favourite melon juice. My throat was dry, so I gulped the rest down greedily.

Megan took the empty glass from me, refilled it, and brought it back. "You aren't at the centre any longer, Amber."

I looked round at the weird room again. "I'm in a hospital?"

"You're in an aircraft. That's a transport vehicle that..."

I knew what an aircraft was. They were used to travel to outlying supply stations or the even longer distances to other Hives. I dropped my glass, and it rolled across the floor spilling a pool of juice. I didn't care.

"I'm outside the Hive?" Everyone knew the dangers of Outside. Truesun could blind you if you looked at it.

"We're not in our Hive any longer, but we aren't Outside either." Megan sat down opposite me. "We travelled while you were sleeping. This aircraft is now inside Hive Futura."

I closed my eyes, covered them with my hands, and listened to my breathing for a moment before looking at Megan again.

"Hive Futura was our seed Hive, founded in the Hive expansion phase, but it doesn't exist any longer. The world population dropped. Most seed Hives were reabsorbed by parent Hives, and now there are only one hundred and seven Hive cities." I recited the familiar facts I'd learnt in school, trying to block off my terror, trying to make sense of things. "We can't be inside Hive Futura."

"Hive Futura wasn't totally abandoned. If our Hive population increases, we may need it again, so basic maintenance is still carried out here."

I stared at her. "But why am I here? I'm supposed to be in Lottery." I was losing the battle against my terror.

"Try to stay calm, Amber," said Megan. "Your Lottery assessment is finished. It finished on the second day."

Nobody ever finished their assessment on the second day, and I'd been having tests for four days already. "This is another silly nightmare, isn't it?"

She ignored that. "On the first day of your assessment, you scored an interesting result on a special test that included questions with no genuine answers. As you reached each of those questions, the tester was instructed to concentrate on thinking of one possible answer. You almost always picked that answer, Amber."

What was she talking about? I remembered the test, but... I thought back to that bored looking tester. He'd seemed to be half asleep.

"There were over a million eighteen-year-olds in assessment," Megan continued. "Thousands of candidates had significantly high scores on that special test. You were all moved to different assessment centres to increase the pressure to do well. You remember the reaction speed test that came next?"

I nodded, still bewildered.

"You chose your colour too fast for human reflexes, Amber. On seven occasions, you chose the correct colour before it even had time to light up. You were reading your tester's mind to see what colour he was going to touch."

I shook my head. This couldn't be happening to me. I couldn't read minds. Everyone knew that telepaths had to wear masks because they weren't quite human, and I was a perfectly ordinary girl. Lottery had made a dreadful mistake.

Megan turned her face away from me. "We knew then we'd found a true telepath. I took a specialist team into the assessment centre to take over your whole testing process. Since birth, you'd been protecting yourself from the hundred million minds around you by blocking your telepathic abilities. Most of the tests we gave you were aimed at lowering your mental barriers and bringing your ability to the surface. When your headache started, we knew you were now hearing nearby minds, and it was time to get you out of the Hive."

"No!" I snapped the word at her in flat denial. "You've made a mistake."

She just kept talking as if I hadn't said a word. "We brought you to Hive Futura so you could learn to control and filter the telepathic input without being overwhelmed by the number of minds. Our pilot has already left in another aircraft, so there are only the two of us in Hive Futura now. We'll remain alone here until you complete the first stage of your training."

"It's a mistake," I repeated. "I'm not a telepath."

She turned to face me again, and her lips weren't moving. "I stopped talking two minutes ago, Amber. You've been pulling the pre-vocalized words directly out of my mind."

There was a moment of blank disbelief before panic hit me. I was a telepath. I was a nosy. I'd spend my days wearing a grey mask, walking through hostile crowds with my bodyguard of watchful hasties surrounding me.

"I can't do this," I said. "I can't be this. I can't be a nosy. Everyone will shout at me. Two ones are two. Two twos are four. Two threes are six. Two fours are..."

"Amber!" Megan spoke aloud this time, interrupting my hysterical chanting. "It won't be like that. The nosies dressed in grey aren't telepaths. They're fakes, decoys, ordinary hasties dressed up to make them look alien and frightening."

This didn't make any sense. "But why?"

"People working in Law Enforcement know the nosies are fake, but everyone else in the Hive believes they are genuine telepaths. They see the nosies everywhere they go, in the shopping areas, the corridors, riding the belts, going through the park. Anyone considering committing a crime is scared that a nosy will spot their guilty thoughts. In most cases that's enough to make potential criminals abandon their plans. The deterrent value of the nosy patrols is massive, but it's all bluff."

I stared at her. She didn't seem to be joking, but she couldn't be serious.

Megan studied my face for a moment before she spoke again. "The bluff works because we do have genuine telepaths, but painfully few of them. Lottery discovers almost a thousand people each year with some level of telepathic ability, but virtually all of them are only capable of random, intermittent glimpses into the minds of people around them."

She paused. "That's enough to make borderline telepaths highly valuable to the Hive in areas such as counselling. The real treasure though is the incredibly rare exception capable of true, consciously controlled telepathy. The exception like you, Amber."

I tugged at my hair. "I'm not exceptional."

"We had four true telepaths to watch over the hundred million people in our Hive and protect them from danger. Now we've found you, so we have five. We won't waste your precious time by dressing you as a nosy and letting crowds of people chant at you."

"Five true telepaths? How can five people watch over a hundred million?"

Megan smiled. "I realize this news is a huge shock. You'll need time to adjust to what I've told you before I explain more details. I expect you're feeling hungry. Shall we go to your apartment so you can eat?"

"I'd rather get on with the imprinting. When I understand what I'm supposed to do, this will... may... be easier."

"We never imprint telepaths," said Megan.

I'd always known that I'd be imprinted during Lottery. As a child, I'd daydreamed about the day I'd be given all the knowledge I needed for my new profession. As I approached Lottery, I'd had last minute fears about the imprinting process, but the idea of not being imprinted was shattering.

"But you have to imprint me," I said. "Everyone is imprinted. If you don't imprint me, then I'll never grow up. I'll be stuck as a teen forever."

"That's not true," said Megan. "Life experiences make you grow and mature as a person. Imprinting only gives you a lot of information very quickly. In your case, it's not worth the risk."

"There aren't any risks. The stories about minds being damaged by imprints are just myths." I pleaded for reassurance that some of the things I'd believed were still true. "They are just myths, aren't they?"

"Imprinting is perfectly safe for other people, but not for you, Amber. There's an obvious genetic factor involved in people becoming borderline telepaths, but we don't understand what makes someone move beyond that and develop into a true telepath. There's a danger imprinting could adversely affect your ability, so we don't take the risk."

Megan stood up. "I'll take you to your apartment now. We'll be staying in Hive Futura until your training is complete. By the time we return to the Hive, your unit will be ready for you."

She opened a door. I looked warily past her, and was relieved to see our aircraft was safely inside a huge, featureless room. I followed her down a short and awkward flight of steps to the ground, and we walked across to another doorway. My mind was still struggling to absorb the fact I wouldn't be imprinted, but I finally caught up with her last words.

"Unit?" I asked. "What do you mean by my unit?"

"You will have a Telepath Unit to assist you with your work," said Megan. "I'm your Senior Administrator, responsible for staffing and the day to day running of your unit. Your Tactical Commander will be in charge of the actual unit operations."

"You told me you were a doctor."

She opened the door ahead of us, and we went into a corridor. "I am a doctor. As your Senior Administrator, I need both administrational and medical skills. Your training, health, and wellbeing are my primary concerns."

As we walked down the corridor, I glanced sideways at the doors we were passing. "This looks like an ordinary housing warren, except that it's totally empty."

"This section is where the maintenance crews stay when they visit to do essential repairs."

"Are we really the only two people here?"

"Yes. When you've completed your initial training, your other three team leaders will come to join us. Remember that you're in charge of your Telepath Unit, Amber. If you're uncomfortable with any of the staff I've selected, or with me, you just have to say so and replacements will be found."

I blinked. "You'd find your own replacement?"

"Two alternate candidates for my post are already on standby."

Megan stepped off the belt. I automatically followed her, and saw a door with my name on it. Megan opened it and led the way inside. I looked round at a large hallway, with cream walls that matched the thick carpet underfoot. Several doors led off it.

"Can I explore by myself?" I asked. "I could use a bit of time alone to... adjust."

"Of course." Megan smiled. "You're in charge."

I'd no idea what I was doing, and I wouldn't be imprinted with any information, but Megan said I was in charge. I just had to say the word and she'd be replaced by someone else. This was ridiculous.

"My apartment is next door," Megan continued. "Just use the comms system to call me when you're ready."

She went back out to the corridor and closed the door behind her. I looked round the hall, and opened a random door into what was clearly a bedroom. I wandered inside and touched the wall to open the storage space. I saw a set of clothes. My clothes.

I'd left those clothes in my temporary room back in our Hive. Some of them had been packed in my bag, others discarded on the floor. The whole lot seemed to have been laundered before being hung up here, and the bag itself was sitting on the floor underneath them. I investigated and found it was empty.

I panicked, looked frantically round the room, and then saw the small cube sitting on a table by the side of the sleep field. I went across to touch it with my hand, needing the physical reassurance that its precious holos were safe. These images were all I had left of my life on Teen Level now. I'd never see Forge, Shanna, Linnette, Atticus, Casper, or any of my other old friends again in real life.

Once I'd calmed down again, I carried on exploring. The second room I entered was a dedicated bookette room, an impressive luxury, but I was more interested in food right now. The third room had a table, chairs, and a staggeringly large kitchen unit. I eagerly called up the menu to see what was on offer. Dishes scrolled seemingly endlessly down the front of the unit, and I selected half a dozen to see if they really were all in storage.

Five minutes later, I was sitting at the table with enough food for several people in front of me. I was hungry, and everything tasted wonderful, but I had a host of worries nagging at me. How could someone as ordinary as me be a telepath? What work would I be doing? Why did I need a unit full of people to help me with it?

A shattering new thought suddenly overrode everything else. My parents and Gregas loathed the grey-clad nosies almost as much as I did. How would they react when they saw my Lottery result? It had been hard to say goodbye to all my friends from Teen Level. I couldn't cope with losing my family as well.

I dropped my fork onto my plate, and used the apartment comms unit to ask Megan to come back. She arrived a minute later, smiling as usual. I saw her glance at the plates of spare food, and hastily gestured at them.

"Please help yourself."

She pulled up a chair and sat down facing me. "I've already eaten," she said, but picked up a pastry anyway.

"Have I been listed as a nosy yet?" I asked. "It'll be a huge shock to my parents. They really dislike nosies."

"The last batch of this year's Lottery results should be posted within the next hour," said Megan. "You'll be included in the results, but not as a telepath. It's essential for the security of the Hive that only approved members of Law Enforcement know the true information about telepaths. Given your parents' attitude to nosies, keeping your telepathy secret from them will be best for your family relationships as well."

I waved my hands in despair. "So what do I tell my parents?"

"The established method of dealing with this situation is to list true telepaths as Level 1 Researchers."

"Level 1 Researcher!" My jaw must have dropped low enough to hit the floor. "My parents will ask me lots of questions. What do I say? What am I supposed to be researching?"

"You just explain apologetically that you aren't allowed to answer any questions because your research is classified."

I considered that. My parents would have a shock all right, but not the horrible shock of finding out I was a telepath. They'd be ecstatic at the news their daughter was a Level 1 Researcher. My photos would be centre front with flashing lights round them. Their friends would get sick of hearing about me.

"If Telepath Units are part of Law Enforcement, does that mean I'll be living with the rest of Law Enforcement on Level 20?"

"No," said Megan. "You and all your staff will be living at your Telepath Unit. You can tell your parents that you have a dedicated Research Unit to assist you in your vital work. Explain that you and your staff need to live there for security reasons, and because some work has to take place at unusual hours."

She paused for a moment. "We can't allow anyone from outside Law Enforcement into the operational section of the unit, but your parents will be able to visit your apartment in the accommodation section if you wish."

I gave a disbelieving laugh. A Level 1 daughter with her own Research Unit. My parents were going to faint from joy. I'd be fainting from joy myself if only it was true.

"We want you to be able to relax and sleep properly, Amber," continued Megan, "so your Telepath Unit will be on Industry 1 in an area surrounded by things like water storage tanks that need minimal maintenance. You'll rarely be troubled by the nearness of unfamiliar minds in the daytime, and never at night."

There were a hundred accommodation levels in the Hive, with Level 1 at the top. Above that were fifty more levels that held all the things like manufacturing centres, air purification, recycling, and hydroponics, which were too messy, noisy, or took up too much space to be on an accommodation level. If my Telepath Unit was on Industry 1, the highest of the industrial levels, then it would be right at the top of the Hive!

I had a sick, fluttery feeling in my stomach. "There's a solid ceiling on Industry 1? Truesun won't be able to get us?"

Megan's expression flickered as if she was struggling not to laugh. "The ceiling on Industry 1 looks exactly like the ceiling on any other level. Above it are some special maintenance areas, then the Hive outer structural shield, and then a thick layer of soil and rocks."

She paused. "Should your parents question the remote location of your Research Unit, you can explain that it's dictated by the nature of your research."

Her words triggered another dreadful realization. As soon as my parents had got over the shock of my Lottery result, they'd try to call me, but they wouldn't get an answer because I was in Hive Futura. They'd think I was ignoring their calls, and jump to the obvious conclusion that their Level 1 daughter was dumping her Level 27 parents.

"Megan, you have to get a message to my parents," I said urgently. "Give them some reason why calls won't be reaching me for a while."

She smiled. "You can call your parents yourself, Amber, or they can call you. We've got a secure link to our Hive, and all calls for you will be automatically routed here."

I gave a sigh of relief.

"You obviously can't tell your parents that you're in Hive Futura," added Megan. "I suggest you tell them you're in temporary accommodation while you're setting up your unit. They'll be able to visit you as soon as you've moved into your permanent apartment. Would you like me to leave you alone until you've talked to your parents?"

I nodded, watched Megan go out of the door, and then reached for my dataview. If I could make calls to people in our own Hive, then I should be able to access information too. I checked to see if the final batch of Lottery results had been posted yet, saw they'd just gone up, and automatically started looking to see how my friends had done. This time I started with the most important one.

Shanna was a Level 9 Media Presenter! She'd made the elite top ten levels of the Hive just as she'd expected. I might see her presenting the inter-Hive news or...

No, I couldn't imagine Shanna presenting the news. It seemed far more likely that she'd be covering social events. Whatever programmes she'd be presenting, Shanna must be thrilled that her Lottery result was such a huge success.

After a few moments imagining what Shanna was doing and thinking, picturing her buying all the high level clothes she'd been dreaming of for years, I moved on to checking my other friends.

Margot was a Level 30 Protein Enhancement Supervisor, which was funny because she'd always been so fussy about her food.

Casper was a Level 61 Restaurant Service Specialist. He'd been born with a genetic condition that affected his ability to learn, but had an enthusiasm and infectious happiness that made him a popular member of our group. He loved helping people, so he'd take pleasure in bringing people their food, and they'd enjoy sharing the warmth of his smile.

Reece was a Level 93 Pipe Technician. I cheered aloud. Reece was a bully who'd grabbed every chance to push people around on Teen Level, especially targeting me, Linnette, and Casper. He could try bullying pipes now, and see how far that got him.

Atticus startled me. Level 3 Physician Surgical. High up! A year or so ago, when I was trying to break my obsession with Forge, I'd had a few dates with Atticus. He was a quiet, serious boy with...

"You have an incoming call," the comms system announced.

I took a deep breath and accepted the call. Holo images of my parents appeared in front of me, looking so real that I could imagine reaching out and touching them. This apartment comms system must be a top model, nothing like the basic one I'd had in my room on Teen Level.

"Amber!" My mother gasped my name. "We saw your Lottery result. When there was no news yesterday, I started getting worried, but this is incredible."

My father just gave me a dazed look, seeming completely lost for words.

"I'm in shock too," I said.

"This is your new apartment?" My mother looked round the room. "Very nice."

"This is my temporary accommodation," I said. "I'll have an apartment at the Research Unit, but setting it up will take a few weeks."

"You won't live on Level 1?" She looked disappointed.

I remembered my cover story. "I need to live at the Research Unit because I'll be working odd hours."

My father finally found his voice. "What sort of research will you be doing?"

"I'm afraid I'm not allowed to tell you any details. It's classified."

"If you're Level 1, you must have an important post at this Research Unit," he said.

"It's *my* Research Unit," I said. "It's being specially set up to help me with my work. That means..."

"Your own Research Unit!" My mother turned to look to her left. "Gregas!" she yelled. "Your sister's got her own Research Unit!"

There was a grunt from somewhere off image. I could tell that Gregas was much less thrilled than my mother. I could see his point. He had a Level 1 older sister with her own Research Unit. Anything he did now, short of inventing the elixir of life, was going to be an anti-climax.

"I'll be wildly busy for the next few weeks," I said, "but once my Research Unit is ready you can come and visit me. I won't be able to show you the unit work areas for security reasons, but you can see my apartment."

"We understand," said my father.

"You'll be tired after the imprinting, so we'd better let you go." My mother's expression suddenly changed to something vulnerable and anxious. "You'll keep in touch?"

"I'll keep in touch." I knew my parents really needed the reassurance of me visiting them in person, but I wouldn't be able to do that for weeks. I thought of something that would please my mother. "I'll need you to advise me about clothes. I've no idea what to wear now I'm Level 1."

"That's a good point," said my mother. "You can't keep wearing your old teen clothes in your new position."

"I've no time for shopping right now," I said. "Could you find some clothes you think would look good on me and mail me the details? I can order some of those to start with, and later we can go shopping together."

"I'd love that," said my mother. "We can go to the 500/5000 shopping area on Level 1. The finest shops in the Hive!"

I laughed at the delight in her face, said goodbye, watched my parents' holo images vanish, and gave a sigh of relief. I'd told them a host of lies, but at least the lies had made them happy.

I went back into the bedroom, and picked up the cube that held all the holos of my time on Teen Level. I hadn't played them since the last day of Carnival. I wanted to play them now, but almost every image of my friends would include Forge. If I watched them again, I'd be taking my teen fixation with him into my new life.

There was only one way to stop myself doing that, so I did it. It was surprisingly hard to smash the small cube. Not just mentally hard but physically as well, because it was a tough little thing, and stubbornly dented rather than breaking in pieces. I had to pound it with a chair for several minutes before it shattered into sad little fragments. I collected them up, cutting my right forefinger on a sharp edge, and dumped the lot down the waste chute.

It was done. I'd made a clean break with the past, and could focus on the future. I'd hoped that Lottery would make me high level, and it had made me Level 1 but a telepath. I wasn't sure if that was a dream come true or a nightmare.

CHAPTER FIVE

"You need to go deeper into my mind," said Megan.

"I can't." I snapped the words at her. We'd been sitting at a table in my apartment all morning. We'd spent most of the previous two days sitting here as well. We didn't seem to be making any progress at all, and I was getting increasingly tired and frustrated.

"You're still just picking up pre-vocalization," she said. Her lips weren't moving, I was taking the words straight from her mind, but effectively she was saying them. "When you pick up..."

"I know," I interrupted. "You keep repeating this over and over. It's not enough to read the words someone is preparing to say aloud. I need to go deeper, and read the level beneath with their private thoughts and plans. You keep telling me what I need to do, but you aren't telling me how to do it."

"I can't tell you how to do it, because I'm not a true telepath," she said, or thought.

"Then why don't you get one of the other true telepaths to teach me? Why haven't you told me anything about them? I don't even know their names."

Megan's thoughts seem to freeze for a moment before starting up again. "The other telepaths are Morton, Sapphire, Mira, and Keith. I worked for Keith as a Deputy Administrator before accepting the position as your Senior Administrator."

"What is Keith like?"

"Giving you more information about the other true telepaths would merely distract you at this stage in your learning process," said Megan. "They can't teach you because they're far too busy to come here, and you can't return to the Hive until you've learnt to control your ability."

"Get a borderline telepath to help me then."

"Borderline telepaths can't help you achieve a telepathic depth and control that they don't have themselves," said Megan. "You can do this, Amber. Try to go deeper into my mind."

"You could at least explain to me why I need to learn these things. I keep asking you questions, and you keep avoiding answering them. What are you hiding from me? What does a Telepath Unit do?"

"I'm not hiding anything from you, Amber," said Megan. "I'm only a Senior Administrator. I could tell you all about the day to day running of a Telepath Unit, all the trivial details of general maintenance and ordering supplies, but you don't want to know about those things. You want to learn about the operational side of a Telepath Unit. Your Tactical Commander will be in charge of that, and it's his decision how best to explain your role to you."

I groaned. "Let me talk to my Tactical Commander then."

"Your Tactical Commander can't give you instructional guidance yet because he hasn't been confirmed in his post. All your team leaders need to come here and be approved by you before their appointments are finalized."

"Then get my Tactical Commander here so I can approve him!"

Megan gave me her maddeningly calm smile. "Contact with too many minds can be dangerous for a newly emergent telepath. Your team leaders can't come here until you've learned to control your ability."

I thumped the palms of my hands on the table. I was tempted to bang my head on it too. Better yet, I should bang Megan's head on the table. Every time I tried to get her to answer questions, I got stuck in one of these circular arguments.

Megan looked down at my hands, and her smile changed to an anxious frown. "Your finger is bleeding, Amber. I should put a protective dressing on it."

I glanced down and saw I'd knocked the scab off the cut on my right forefinger. Given Megan's expression of doom, anyone would have thought it was spurting torrents of blood instead of oozing a single tiny drop.

"I don't need a dressing on a microscopic cut."

"It may be a very small cut," said Megan, "but it's still an open wound that could become infected."

I thrust my hands out of sight under the table. "I've survived eighteen years of cuts and bruises without anyone covering them in protective dressings."

Megan sighed. "Let's get back to work then. Try going deeper into my mind. Look for what's beneath the pre-vocalized thought level. Focus on..."

"It's no use!" I stood up and screamed the words at her. "I've tried a thousand times already."

... need patience to achieve the breakthrough that...

... still can't believe my good luck being offered this. A Senior Administrator position at last, and the fresh start I desperately needed after...

... had to resign. It wasn't just my feelings when I looked at Keith, but his feelings when he looked at me. Constantly reminding him of Dean's death. Constantly reminding him of his failure and...

... his fault, his stupid, arrogant, lazy fault. If Keith had done his job, the Strike team would have known Dean was wounded. They'd have been able to reach him before he bled to death, and...

Dean! He's dead and everything's gone with him. All our plans. The children we'll never have now.

Ashes blowing in the artificial wind of the park.

I'd broken through to Megan's deeper thoughts, but there wasn't just one set of them. I was sucked down into her mind, through layer after layer of thoughts and emotions, feeling her grief and her pain, becoming her instead of Amber.

I don't know how long I was caught there, being Megan, lost in her emotional turmoil, before my survival instincts kicked in. I fought my way back to the surface of her mind, like a drowning swimmer desperate for air. I stared at my face – no, that was Megan's face, not mine – still dazed with shock.

"Judging from your face, you managed it that time," said Megan.

"You didn't feel me in your mind?"

She shook her head. "Not a thing. People can't."

She hadn't felt anything, but I'd felt all her emotions as if they were my own. Megan hadn't warned me that reading deeper thought levels would be like this.

"I'd like to be alone for a while."

She nodded, stood up, and left the room. I waited until the door was safely closed before I allowed myself to start crying. Mourning for my husband, Dean. Grieving for the stupid, senseless loss of his precious life, and the children we'd never have.

I'd thought I needed to be imprinted to grow up. I'd been wrong. I felt a hundred years old.

CHAPTER SIX

After a week of only Megan's mind amid total silence, there were three new people in Hive Futura. I'd been practising controlling my telepathic abilities with Megan over the last few days. Now I could open up my telepathic view of the world to see the shapes of three unfamiliar minds nearby, or pull down a mental curtain to protect myself from them.

In theory, that meant I should be in total control of this situation, but the experience of being hit by Megan's grief had taught me the difference between theory and reality. I'd learnt to avoid the dangerous depths inside Megan's head, and keep in the safety of the shallows just below pre-vocalization, but I'd no idea what new emotional whirlpools might lurk inside these strangers.

"We need you to approve or reject your three operational team leader candidates at this point," said Megan. "They can't start selecting their team members until their own appointments are confirmed."

We were sitting in a room in my apartment, lounging in two of several comfortable chairs. Megan showed me the holos of three people. I studied them anxiously.

"Their names are Lucas, Adika, and Fran," Megan continued.

"Do I really have to read their minds?"

"You must read the minds of everyone in your unit before their appointment is confirmed, Amber. If there's anything in their heads that makes you feel uncomfortable, then it's much better to find out at the start and reject them than have it cause problems later."

I was feeling nervous. My team candidates were probably feeling even more nervous. Their future careers depended totally on my personal whim. I could see that in Megan's thoughts right now. She'd chosen the best qualified team leaders she could, but they were replaceable and I wasn't. I had to be begged, bribed, cosseted, whatever it took to keep me happy and doing what the Hive needed. I could demand anyone should be fired, and they would have to go.

That was what Megan had meant when she told me I was in charge. I would be the notional head of my Telepath Unit, not because I was capable of making any useful decisions, but because true telepaths had to be kept happy. I could throw a childish tantrum, whine, scream, and demand anything I wanted, and people would have to obey.

True telepaths had to be kept happy. I kept hitting that over and over again in Megan's thoughts. The fact was connected to something deeper down in her mind, something she didn't want to tell me. I'd tried investigating it, but whatever Megan was hiding was surrounded by a wall of powerful emotions. There was a lot of fear in there, and grief that somehow merged into her grief for her dead husband. The combined effect of those emotions overwhelmed me whenever I tried to get past them.

"Which of your team leader candidates would you like to read first?" asked Megan.

There were two men and one woman, and I felt another woman's mind would be easier. "I think I'll start with Fran."

"Fran is your candidate for the Liaison team leader position," said Megan. "You may find some initial tension when you enter her mind. She's been highly successful in several similar team leader positions, but she hasn't worked in a Telepath Unit before."

"What does the Liaison team do?" I asked.

"They collect data and co-ordinate unit operations with the rest of the Hive."

That meant nothing to me. The woman in the holo looked as

if she was somewhere between forty and fifty years old. She had an emotionless, professional smile that hardly changed during the short, repeating holo sequence, but Megan had managed to hide all surface signs of her grief behind a similar smile. If I was hit with something equally drastic, and embarrassed myself by crying again, then I didn't want an audience watching it.

"I'd rather see Fran alone," I said.

Megan sighed, but turned off the holo images and left the room.

A minute later, Fran entered. I gestured at a chair opposite me, she sat down, and there was an awkward silence. I forced myself to speak.

"Megan said you hadn't worked in a Telepath Unit before. You understand that I have to...?"

Fran nodded. "I understand there is an initial check."

I reached out to her thoughts. I'd read Megan so often during our training sessions, that her mind had become familiar territory. Fran's mind had a different... sound, taste, texture to it. I hesitated at the surface, adjusting, reading the pre-vocalized words.

I am calm and helpful and have no problem with this. I am calm and helpful and have no problem with this. I am calm and helpful and have no problem with this.

I was startled. Fran was repeating the words, over and over, inside her own head. I wasn't sure if she was trying to convince herself or me, but either way it was obvious they weren't true. It prepared me for the tension I saw on the next level down.

... have to do this or I lose the promotion of a lifetime. Everyone would think...

I moved on to the level below that, and was hit by bitter resentment.

Sneaking, prying nosy!

I recoiled out of her mind. Fran loathed the idea of me reading her thoughts. I didn't know how to react to that. I had to get her out of this room so I could think.

I forced a smile. "Thank you, Fran. You've been very helpful. Please ask Megan to come back."

Fran's face lit up with relief. She believed her ridiculous chant had hidden her resentment, and she'd got the post as my Liaison team leader. I watched her eagerly leave the room, and wondered what I should do now.

The easy way out would be to reject Fran, but I remembered all the times I'd been part of hostile crowds, chanting tables as a grey-masked nosy went by. How could I blame Fran, reject Fran, for feeling exactly the same way that I'd felt myself?

Megan came back into the room. "What did you think about Fran? Was she tense?"

I tried to keep my voice calm as I answered her. "Yes. I suppose that's natural. I won't have to read her again?"

"The only people in your unit that you must read on a regular basis are the members of your Strike team, but the telepath has the right to read anyone's mind at any time. All candidates for Telepath Unit positions understand that and are happy about it."

I didn't believe Fran was happy about it, but if reading her mind wasn't necessary for my work then I wouldn't be doing it. My mood abruptly changed from uncertainty to grim determination. I was going to prove to Fran that I was totally different from the hated, prying nosies that had frightened me as a child. I'd show her that I'd only read minds when necessary for the good of my Hive, and then she'd accept me.

I needed Fran to accept me. My hatred of nosies hadn't vanished when I learned I was a telepath myself. It lingered on as a nagging voice in the corner of my mind, telling me that I was a vile and disgusting thing. If Fran accepted me, then perhaps I could accept myself, and that nagging voice would leave me in peace. I could be happy then, remember all the Hive Obligations and Duty songs we'd learned in school, and celebrate the fact I was Level 1 and valuable to my Hive.

I glanced at the images on the wall. "Adika next."

"Adika is your candidate for the Strike team leader position," said Megan. "When Mira was discovered during Lottery seventeen years ago, Adika came out of Lottery as one of her Strike team members. Ten years later, he moved to become a deputy Strike team leader for Morton."

I didn't ask what the Strike team did. I already knew their work was dangerous, because I'd been seeing that fact every day in Megan's mind. Her husband, Dean, had been a Strike team member in Keith's Telepath Unit. It was barely a month since Dean had been wounded on a mission and bled to death. However much Megan concentrated on training me, there was always a deep part of her mind brooding on her loss.

On a conscious level, Megan believed that true telepaths were incredibly valuable to the Hive and must not be criticized or rebuked. On a subconscious level, she believed that Dean would be alive today if Keith hadn't been so selfishly lazy and arrogant. The two parts of her mind were fighting a constant war.

Megan went out of the room, and a minute later Adika came in. The holo sequence of his dark face hadn't prepared me for just how powerfully built the man was, and the way his presence dominated the room. I couldn't guess his age by looking at him. If he'd been through Lottery seventeen years ago, then he must be thirty-five now, a few years older than Megan.

He sat down, and gave a relaxed nod that seemed to be an invitation to go ahead. I braced myself, reached out to a mind with such sharply defined edges that it could have been carved with a chisel, and tapped warily into his surface thoughts.

... physically ideal, we'll hardly notice her weight carrying her, but how good is she at what really counts? Are you able to read me, Amber? Tell me what I'm thinking now. I was born in Red Zone. I have two brothers. I broke my right arm when I was twenty-three.

I gave a startled laugh. Adika was utterly relaxed about me reading his thoughts. I chanted his list of facts back at him. "You were born in Red Zone. You have two brothers. You broke your right arm when you were twenty-three."

He gave an approving nod. "You're doing well for this early in your training."

Part of Adika's mind was comparing me to his memories of Mira soon after she came out of Lottery. I'd scavenged a scanty few pieces of information about the other true telepaths from Megan's mind, and was eager for more. I focused on Adika's thoughts about Mira, saw his memory of her talking to him, and was startled to see her face had the same distinctive features as those of my friend Casper from Teen Level.

"I didn't know Mira was born with a genetic condition," I said.

"I didn't realize I was thinking about Mira," said Adika.

There was an incomprehensible patch in his thoughts. Something about an extra copy of a chromosome. The word chromosome was vaguely familiar, I thought I'd heard my parents say it, but I didn't know its meaning. I made a mental note that it was possible to read someone's thoughts but not understand them.

"Mira turned out to be an excellent telepath, and always eager to do her best to help the Hive," said Adika. "We just needed to protect her from too much pressure, and make sure she always had the same familiar bodyguards with her."

I listened to the words, but picked up extra details from Adika's thoughts as well. I relived the echo of his old disappointment, when Mira's preferences had put someone else into a deputy team leader spot, and he'd had to wait ten long years for a chance to fill that role for Morton. I resented that for Adika, but he'd never considered it an injustice. He had tremendous respect for how hard Mira worked and how well she did her job. If having someone else as deputy team leader made things easier for her, then that was for the good of the Hive, and...

I realized I'd got caught by that old memory, swept up in the emotional overtones as if it was happening right here and now instead of seventeen years ago. I pulled myself away with an effort.

"Since I can't be imprinted, I'd like to meet the other true telepaths and learn from them."

"That's not a good idea," said Adika. "Mira couldn't help you, Keith would be a very bad example, Morton wouldn't agree, and Sapphire..."

He hesitated for a moment. It was strange reading his thoughts. I could see he was inventing reasons why I shouldn't meet the other telepaths, attempting to convince himself as much as me.

I went a level or two deeper into his mind, and things got even stranger. Adika knew it was important that telepaths should be kept apart from each other, but not why. There were no memories associated to the rule, and there was an odd, impersonal quality to it. I'd met this sort of thing before in Megan's mind, and discovered it meant it was imprinted data rather than something she'd learned personally, but usually rules like this included the reasons behind them.

"Sapphire is far too busy," added Adika finally.

He was thinking that this first meeting had achieved its purpose, and he wanted to leave before I pushed the subject of the other telepaths any further, so I nodded at him. "Thank you."

He stood and went out of the door. I was still linked to his mind as he saw Megan sitting on a chair in the hallway. She stood up to greet him, her short skirt flashing a tempting length of thigh that...

I gasped with shock, and instinctively pulled out of Adika's mind. Waste it! I wasn't attracted to women, and I didn't possess the bit of anatomy that I'd felt responding to Megan.

When she entered the room a moment later, I was deeply relieved to find I reacted to her as myself rather than Adika. Megan must have noticed something strange about my expression, because she frowned at me.

"There's a problem with Adika?"

"No," I said hastily. "He seems perfect for my Strike team leader."

She looked relieved. "Amber, you're clearly finding this difficult and should rest now."

I barely heard her words. I was still thinking through what had happened with Adika. It might have hit me in a different way, but I'd really had exactly the same problem with him as with Megan. Fran too for that matter. Everyone was hurling their emotions at me like missiles.

"I'll tell Lucas that you'll see him tomorrow," said Megan.

I hurriedly shook my head. I didn't want to delay meeting Lucas. He was my Tactical Commander candidate. The person who would give me answers to my host of questions.

"I'm perfectly fine. Different people are... different," I said lamely. "I needed a moment to absorb what I'd learned from reading Adika's mind, but I'm ready to see Lucas now."

Megan hesitated.

"I'll see Lucas now," I repeated.

She sighed and gave in. "Lucas is only twenty-one, but he's by far the best qualified choice for your Tactical Commander. He was deputy leader of Keith's Tactical team."

"You worked for Keith too, so you must know Lucas well."

"Yes. I came out of Lottery with Keith thirteen years ago. Lucas joined us three years ago as a Tactical team member. A person has to be exceptionally gifted to be imprinted for a Telepath Unit position in a year when no true telepath is discovered, but Lucas's Lottery assessment scores were incredible. A year later, the deputy leader of Keith's Tactical team transferred to another post, and Lucas was given the position."

"I seem to be stealing everyone's deputies," I said.

Megan smiled. "You're our big chance for promotion, Amber. Openings as team leader in a Telepath Unit are incredibly rare. Moving from being deputy in a Telepath Unit to being a team leader in another area would be a downwards career move. Telepath Units are the highest prestige assignments in Law Enforcement. Even the team member positions on Strike, Tactical and Liaison teams are rated Level 1."

Megan left, and Lucas walked into the room. He had unruly, light-brown hair, surprisingly dark eyes, and an intense expression that abruptly changed into a grin as he looked at me.

"Are you reading me yet?"

I had to laugh. "Of course not. You've only just walked through the door. You haven't even sat down yet."

He sat down opposite me, and leaned forward eagerly. "I'm sitting down. Please read me now. My chance of becoming your Tactical Commander depends on whether you like what's in my head or not, so I'm desperate for your answer."

"Naturally, anything I see is confidential."

He shrugged, seemingly uncaring about his privacy. "I've no secrets."

I entered his mind, and it was like being in the centre of a whirling Carnival crowd. The thoughts glittered and shone, level upon level of them, racing past at incredible speed.

... is confidential! So different from Keith. The way he teases people...

... still no pattern at all. If there was only...

... of the occipital alpha waves or even the cortical theta rhythm...

... reaction to first reading of Megan was...

... and the parental relationship differs totally from the previous...

... body language looks favourable. Her first impression of me is...

... want this so much! What will her approach be to...

... love her legs, but her physical preference results from Lottery show I haven't a hope of getting into her...

When I first read Megan, I was sucked down against my will into a morass of dark, churning emotions. With Lucas, I was willingly plunging down through the levels of his mind, chasing one shimmering image after another. I finally hit some that were completely indecent, and surfaced, gurgling with laughter. I couldn't be offended when the images were down at the level that was more unconscious emotion than thought. After years of Forge ignoring me, I found it rather flattering that Lucas lusted after my legs and...

I sternly reminded myself that I was supposed to be deciding whether I was happy with Lucas as my Tactical Commander, not nosing round his unconscious fantasies. He was obviously brilliant. His thoughts ran like multi-layered express belts, leaving me sprinting madly in pursuit. Better yet, he was young, friendly, and delightfully unconventional. For the first time, I realized how lonely I'd been since Lottery started.

"You're back out of my mind," Lucas said. "Well? Yes or no?"

I smiled at him. "Yes."

"High up!" He jumped out of his chair, punching the air with one hand, just like an over-excited kid on Teen Level.

I laughed. "Now, if you don't mind, Megan said you were the best person to answer my questions."

Lucas instantly sat down, leaning forward in his chair again, his eyes fixed on me. "Go!"

"What does a Telepath Unit do? What am I supposed to do?"

"Good question. Needs a history lesson. Let's go back in time. People used to live, dotted all over the world, in communities of various sizes. Bigger communities grew into pre-Hive cities. Homes close together, mostly two or three levels. You're following me?"

"Vaguely."

"Imagine the transport issues. Problems providing things like rapid specialist medical care are obvious. People gravitated into larger cities where these things were available. Cities got bigger, buildings taller, closer together. Natural progression into first proto Hives."

He was speaking in partial sentences, as if speech couldn't match the speed of his thoughts. I dipped into his mind to help me keep up, and suddenly what he was saying really was obvious. I could actually watch the process in his head, as humanity clustered together into cities.

"Old lifestyle heavily affected by threat of crime and risk to personal safety. Children watched every second due to perceived threat of abduction and injury."

"What?" I was shocked by a brief, graphic picture in his mind.

"Also major pollution-related health issues and danger from high speed transport vehicles. Anti-crime surveillance measures everywhere. Cameras, facial recognition devices, tracking devices, even automated drones and orbital satellite thermal imaging."

I shook my head in disbelief. Children under ten wore tracking bracelets as a safety precaution, but the thought of adults having their every move tracked and recorded was unbelievable. "People really accepted living like that?"

Lucas shrugged. "People traded privacy for increased safety. Their acceptance of camera surveillance seems strange to us. Current public acceptance of nosy patrols might seem as strange to them."

For eighteen years, I'd believed the nosies were genuine telepaths. I'd hated the idea of them reading my mind, but accepted that nosy patrols were necessary to keep the Hive a safe place. "You're probably right."

"Now!" Lucas startled me by shouting the single word, before babbling on in speed speech again. "First true Hives relatively small, but major impact on society. New enclosed habitat available. All amenities immediately accessible. No pollution. No danger from vehicles. No criminals allowed entry. Hives perceived as superior, safer environment, huge demand to become residents."

I was checking his pre-vocalized thought level now, patching in the missing words that he wasn't saying aloud, to help me make sense of his shortened sentences. "Yes, but..."

Lucas kept relentlessly jabbering on. "Phase of extending prototype Hives to become mega Hives. Design variations. All in geologically stable areas, mainly underground, 70 to 210 levels. Other communities gradually abandoned."

I had another try at interrupting him. "Yes, but I still don't see where I...?"

Lucas raised a hand to stop me. "Approaching that. Hives now sole major environment. Existing undesirable elements not allowed entry, but new ones appear within Hives. Vast numbers of people packed close together, hugely vulnerable to predatory natures. Crime and murder rate soared. Society panic defence response."

I didn't understand the last sentence at all, because he was talking too fast and leaving out too many words. Then something happened. Lucas's pre-vocalized thought level seemed to blur, merge with the images in the level below, and come abruptly back into focus again. Had my mind made an adjustment to read both levels at once, or was it his that had changed? I didn't know, but I could understand what he was saying now without consciously filling in the missing words.

"Hive society responded in panic, instituting oppressive defence measures. Trivial breaches of rules resulted in the offender being classed as a criminal. Children were screened for factors considered a potential danger to society. Undesirable elements were controlled, medicated, even genetically restricted."

Lucas's speed speech wasn't an issue any longer, but there was still a problem if I didn't understand the words in his mind. "What does genetically restricted mean?"

He rephrased it at my intellectual level. "People classed as criminals or socially undesirable were not allowed to have children."

I missed the next couple of sentences while I absorbed that. The implications of it were huge. "Hold on. Go back to the not allowed to have children bit. I've never heard of anything like that happening."

"The policy of genetic restriction proved to have immensely damaging consequences." Lucas pulled a pained face of disapproval. "It resulted in large population drops that seriously weakened Hives. Many valuable qualities were mistakenly labelled as negative. The elimination of diverse characteristics harmed the gene pool. Some Hives suffered horrific epidemics due to their populations having reduced disease resistance. Hives became isolationist, banning all casual travel between Hives as a disease containment measure. Changing Hive, either by individual choice or as part of a Hive personnel trade agreement, became an irrevocable lifetime commitment."

He waved his hands in despair. "Genetic restriction was abandoned two centuries ago. Hives reabsorbed their seed Hives, or merged with neighbouring Hives to restore their populations. New approaches were developed to keep Hives safe. Eighteen-year-olds were tested to assess their abilities, and allocated to professions that were personally rewarding and useful to the Hive."

He smiled. "Qualities previously seen as negative were proven to be highly productive when correctly channelled. The nosy system was instituted to deter criminal activities. Social changes were made to limit conflict with authority arising during the peak danger years of adolescence."

"Social changes," I repeated. "That's why teens all live on Level 50?"

"Yes."

I had a sudden new insight. "We really are bees. Tame bees."

Lucas tipped his head on one side. "We live in Hives, but...?"

"My parents work in genetics. They told me all about bees.

Wild bees have stings. The ones in the parks and hydroponics don't. They were specially bred from the wild bees, to be friendly and hardworking."

Lucas's face lit up, and he clapped his hands. "Yes! Our Hive is full of tame bees. Well fed, comfortably housed, with different types of workers all happily making their contribution. Luxury differentials between levels are carefully limited to avoid fuelling discontent. People are deterred from committing crimes by the nosy patrols, but..."

He grimaced. "Various factors can result in a wild bee appearing. An individual with a potential for harming others. Most get spotted in annual development checks or in Lottery screening, treated where necessary, and channelled by Lottery into being productive members of the Hive. In rare, extreme cases kept securely confined."

"Most get spotted," I muttered, ahead of him for once.

"Some are very intelligent and fake their way through screening. In other cases, behaviour gradually escalates. They're surrounded by potential prey. Imagine, for example, if one of them is a danger to children. In this Hive, children roam freely to the park, to the nursery, wherever they want to play. Hasties keep them safe from accidents, but think of the tempting opportunities for a wild bee. Hence." Lucas pointed his finger at me. "You!"

"I catch the wild bees?"

"Yes. Old style surveillance could only catch a wild bee after they've committed a crime, but a true telepath can catch them before anyone gets hurt. You have a whole unit to help you. Tactical, Liaison, and Strike are the operational teams."

"What do they... I... do?"

Complex sentences involving incomprehensible words flashed through Lucas's mind, but I didn't need to ask him to explain what they meant. He knew I wouldn't understand psychological definitions, and was trying to rephrase them in simple terms.

"The biggest problems come from those who have no concern for the wellbeing of other people. They feel that indulging their own wishes is far more important than the rights, safety, even the lives of everyone else. The only thing limiting their behaviour is their fear of harmful consequences to themselves. They cautiously push the limits, testing how much trouble they can cause without their behaviour being challenged by a nosy patrol. The Liaison team monitors the Hive, feeding information to the Tactical team who analyze it for a whole range of early warning signs. Things like complaints about unsociable behaviour or harassment, patterns of suspicious accidents, or outbreaks of vandalism."

I thought of Reece's behaviour on Teen Level. "Or bullying?"

Lucas nodded. "There's often an obvious guilty party. If they're identified before the behaviour pattern becomes too established, then the Tactical team can simply arrange for a nosy patrol to intercept the culprit and frighten them into better behaviour. More entrenched cases have to be referred to specialist units for treatment."

He paused. "Where there's no clue to the identity of the wild bee, a true telepath is needed. As your Tactical Commander, I'll decide an area needs checking. You'll go out with the Strike team, and identify the target wild bee among all the tame ones. Liaison get data on the area, evacuate bystanders if appropriate, and tell creative lies to cover up what's happening. The muscle-bound heroes of the Strike team go in to collect the target."

He paused again. "The Strike team will divide into two at that point. Chase team will go after the target. Bodyguard team will keep you safe from trouble. Wild bees may fight when cornered. You're irreplaceable, and mustn't be stung. When..."

He broke off, and turned his head to look towards the door. I realized that Megan had come back in and was watching us. She had an odd expression on her face.

"Is there a problem?" I asked.

"No," she said. "It's just that this has been taking a very long time. I came to see if you were all right."

"I'm fine," I said. "Lucas has been explaining how Telepath Units work."

Megan gave me a bewildered look. "But he was just gabbling a list of random words. Divide. Target. Trouble. Irreplaceable."

Lucas laughed. "Megan, you know that I sometimes miss out the obvious, trivial words in sentences to save time."

"Yes," she said bitterly, "but what's an obvious word to you isn't necessarily obvious to other people. As I keep telling you, it doesn't save time if the rest of us don't understand what you're saying."

"But Amber *does* understand," said Lucas. "I tried abbreviating sentences further, and she still understood. I found I could go right down to using the occasional key word to anchor my mental logic train."

He turned to give me a joyous grin. "I've never been able to talk to someone this way before. It's incredible."

I couldn't help grinning back at him. "Surely you could talk to Keith in the same way?"

Lucas and Megan exchanged glances. "The situation with Keith was different," said Lucas.

"So you're happy with Lucas as your Tactical Commander, Amber?" asked Megan.

"Definitely," I said.

"That's good." She gave Lucas an oddly doubtful look, and went back out of the room.

Lucas turned back to me. "You understand what a true telepath does now?"

"Yes, but there are a hundred million people in our Hive, and only five true telepaths. That's twenty million people each."

He nodded.

"What if we miss finding one of the wild bees?"

He looked down at the floor. "If the list of areas that need checking is too long, then we may not get to one before the wild bee injures or kills someone. That means an emergency response, to locate and apprehend the target before more people get hurt."

I shook my head in disbelief. "I've never heard of a criminal hurting or killing anyone. The nosies don't let..."

I broke off. The nosies were fake. There were only five true telepaths. One of those five was me.

Lucas lifted his head again. "Liaison invents unfortunate accidents to cover up such incidents. That's better than having others tempted to copy the actions of a wild bee. Better than having a hundred million people living in fear."

He paused for a moment. "The faster any suspect areas are checked, the fewer emergency runs happen. Once our unit is operational, we'll be able to help ease the strain on the other Telepath Units."

I glimpsed Morton's name flashing by on level three of Lucas's express thoughts. He was thinking about the other telepaths. Eager for more information about them, I chased after that thought train.

... hope I'm not imagining seeing Morton and Sapphire's strength in her. We mustn't lose Amber. Olivia collapsing under pressure was bad enough, but York...

There was more information in other linked thought levels, as well as emotional pain and far too much graphic imagery. I hastily pulled out of Lucas's mind, but I couldn't unsee the things I'd seen.

"Megan's right though," I said, trying to keep my voice under control. "This has taken a long time and I'm getting tired."

Lucas stood up. "We'll continue this conversation another time then. You mustn't overstrain yourself reading new minds at this stage."

I didn't trust myself to answer that, so I kept silent as he walked out of the room, and then buried my face in my hands. I'd thought the Hive had four other true telepaths, but the truth was that there were five and should have been six.

Olivia had come out of Lottery eight years ago, collapsed under the strain of the work, and could barely use her telepathy at all now. York had come out of Lottery thirty years ago, and killed himself a few months later.

This was what Megan had been hiding from me. This was why I was smothered in luxuries, and why my every whim would be granted without argument. True telepaths had to be kept as happy as possible, because they could break under the strain of their work.

CHAPTER SEVEN

I handed a glass of deep red juice to Lucas. He accepted it without taking his eyes from his dataview display. I picked up my own glass of melon juice, went to lounge on Lucas's couch, and watched the cascading thoughts in his head.

I'd spent a lot of time in Lucas's apartment over the last week. I preferred it to my own for two reasons. One was that it wasn't so intimidatingly large and luxurious. The other was that it had Lucas in it. I'd solemnly explained to Megan that studying Lucas's mind was excellent training for me as a telepath, far better than the exercises I was doing with her. She'd politely accepted that verbally, while her mind was filled with protective concern and lurid speculation about what else was going on while the two of us were locked away together.

I frowned as the colour, nature, taste of Lucas's mind abruptly darkened. Baffled, I tried to make sense of the words gabbling away in his mind as he read the rapidly scrolling information, but they were too technical for me.

"What are you reading, Lucas?" I asked.

"The data feed from yesterday's Joint Tactical Meeting. That's when the Tactical teams from all the Telepath Units link up in a conference call to exchange ideas and data on problem areas. My ex boss, Keith's Tactical Commander, wants my opinion on the latest events in Orange Zone."

"Around 600/2600 again?" I knew Lucas was deeply worried

about that area of the Hive. He spent a lot of time thinking about it, desperately trying to find a pattern to the oddities there.

"Yes." The data feed ended. Lucas tapped his dataview to turn off the display, and slammed back into his chair. I didn't need telepathy to sense his mood. I could almost physically feel his frustration.

"Gaius is right," he said. "There's still something wrong about that area. No big trouble in the last two weeks, but far too many minor things, and they're spread virtually evenly across the levels which is highly unusual."

"What's Keith planning to do about it?"

"Nothing!" Lucas said savagely. "Keith says he's checked there twice already. He's found nothing because there's nothing to find. We should quit bothering him with a statistical anomaly."

Lucas thought there was a wild bee in 600/2600. Keith had tried to find him or her, failed, and given up. I believed in Lucas. "When we get back to our Hive, do you want me to go over there and take a look?"

"No, Amber!" Lucas swung his chair round to face me. "We're not staffed yet. You must never go near any suspect area without a full Strike team guarding you, and especially not near this one. The pattern is entirely wrong. There's no obvious motivation factor. It doesn't match a single target or two targets working together. It doesn't distribute like two independent targets. It doesn't make any sense at all, which is why I'm so worried about it."

I sipped from my glass, and put it down on the small table next to me. "When our unit's operational then."

Lucas considered that. "Yes, once we're operational, it would be helpful if our unit takes over responsibility for area 600/2600. Now Keith's decided there's no problem there, it's impossible for Gaius to make any progress with it."

I let the issue of area 600/2600 drop, and asked the question that had been bothering me for days. "Why can't I meet the other true telepaths?"

"Inadvisable," said Lucas.

"Why? Surely they're the best people to teach me how to do my job."

Both Megan and Adika had reacted in confusion to this question. I was curious to see how Lucas would respond. He didn't disappoint me.

"I don't know," he said. "I'm imprinted with the fact, but not the reason. Very strange."

"I can tell it's an imprinted fact, because it has no memories or emotions attached to it. Imprinted facts usually seem to be very impersonal."

"Imprinted facts should *always* be totally impersonal," said Lucas. "The data can include objective reasons and ancillary data, but any private memories and feelings should be strictly excluded. It's horribly easy to cause unwanted emotional side-effects when you use either imprinting techniques or hypnotics. That's why the teens in Lottery are encouraged to avoid contact with each other."

I was startled by this revelation of the reason behind the Lottery custom of silence. "It is? You mean some of the tests use hypnotics."

He nodded. "Those interact with the subconscious, and could escalate a casual flirtation between two of the subjects into something they'd regret after the hypnotics wore off."

That was interesting, but I didn't want to be distracted from my original question. "Megan and Adika don't know the reason why I shouldn't meet other telepaths either. Why would all your imprints exclude it?"

I watched Lucas's mind tackle the issue on multiple levels, the thoughts accelerating to a speed I couldn't follow, before reaching a conclusion.

"To keep the information from telepaths. You can't directly read the imprinted data in our minds, but you can see it in our heads when we think about it. You should try to forget about this issue, Amber."

"You aren't curious about what's being kept secret from us? You aren't going to try to find out what it is?"

"Yes, I'm curious," said Lucas, "but my imprint includes

some very nasty facts. Things that are kept secret from the general population of the Hive to avoid terrifying people. I recommend that you pull out of my mind if you see me thinking about them, because the details are horrific and you don't need to know them. I often wish I didn't know them myself, but I have to be informed about these things to do my job."

He paused. "My point is that the reason you shouldn't meet other telepaths could turn out to be something even worse. Something that both of us would regret learning. Something that could leave either or both of us traumatized. You're a newly emergent telepath, Amber. The next few months will be hard for you. I'm not going to try to learn information that could make your life even more difficult."

I deliberately pulled out of Lucas's mind before I said the next sentence. "You're worried it could increase the risk of me ending up like Olivia or York."

There was a short silence before Lucas spoke. "I thought you must know about them by now. Your staff have to be fully informed about what happened to Olivia, York, and other telepaths in prior centuries, so we can help guard against you suffering similar problems. We can't stop ourselves thinking about them, and you're too good a telepath to miss seeing those thoughts in our minds. You weren't saying anything about it though, and Megan agreed with me that it was best to let you raise the subject in your own time."

"I think this is the time," I said.

"What happened to Olivia and York won't happen to you, Amber."

"You think the Hive can stop me from breaking under the strain by giving me a luxurious apartment to live in and my favourite foods to eat?"

"Of course not. We'll do everything we can to help you be happy and relaxed when you aren't working, but that can only help a little. What will make the real difference is that you have deep reserves of inner strength."

Lucas sounded as if he believed what he was saying. I didn't dare to check his mind to see if that was really true. If Lucas had doubts about my ability to cope, then I didn't want to see them. I had too many doubts of my own.

My dataview chimed with an incoming call. I pulled it from my pocket, tapped it to make it unfurl, and saw who was calling. I pulled a graphic face of despair at Lucas before hitting the accept call button.

"Yes, Megan, what is it?"

"It's nearly time for your next training exercise."

I forced a smile. "We're not due to start the next training exercise for another twenty minutes. Lucas and I have been discussing the latest developments in 600/2600, and whether our unit should take over responsibility for that area once we're operational. I'll join you as soon as we've finished the conversation."

I held the smile while I ended the call, then indulged myself with a faint scream.

Lucas laughed.

"It's not funny," I said. "I understand that Megan's primary role is protecting my physical and mental wellbeing, in the same way that Adika's primary role is protecting me from attack, but she takes it much too far. If I bump my elbow, or cut a finger, Megan acts as if I'm terminally wounded, and just look at the way she's making excuses to get me out of your apartment. Anyone would think she wasn't my Senior Administrator but my mother!"

I was drifting among the top levels of Lucas's mind again now, and caught his amused reaction to my words. "What? Lottery selected Megan to act as her telepath's mother? You may think that's funny, Lucas, but I don't. I'm not letting Megan replace my own mother!"

He cowered at the anger in my voice. "Respectfully point out that you have a strong relationship with both your parents. Many people aren't that fortunate. I've no contact at all with either of my parents."

"Oh." My anger instantly faded, and I pulled out of his mind again while I thought for a moment. "I didn't know that. I'm sorry."

I wondered what had gone wrong between Lucas and his parents. The obvious answer was that Lottery had made Lucas Level 1, and he'd cold-bloodedly dumped his low-level parents. That idea worried me.

"Can I ask why you've no contact with them?"

He groaned. "It's all in my head, Amber. You can just read it."

"It's my job to read minds, so I can't help stumbling across information by accident sometimes, but I shouldn't cold-bloodedly invade your privacy and nose through your secrets."

"I've told you before that I don't have any secrets," said Lucas. "Not from anyone, but especially not from you. My parents felt I was an incomprehensible, emotional mess, and dumped me. Perfectly understandable action."

I wanted to strangle Lucas's parents. "You aren't incomprehensible or an emotional mess."

"Possibly less incomprehensible to a telepath. Getting back to Megan. Lottery selects Senior Administrators to have the ability to act as a substitute parent if needed."

"I'm eighteen years old, Lucas. I'm supposed to be taking on an adult role and responsibilities. I don't need or want someone mothering me in front of everyone in my Telepath Unit."

"Remember that you'll be able to discuss things with Megan that you can't discuss with your own mother."

"Because I have to keep lying to my parents." I sighed.

"Amber, you told Megan that your parents have a strong dislike of nosies. You mustn't risk telling them you're a telepath, or try reading their minds. Doing either of those things could irretrievably damage your relationship with them."

I was silent for a moment. I'd already thought through the fact my parents loathed nosies, and pictured the nightmare consequences of them discovering I was a telepath. Now I imagined reading their thoughts, and being hit by the same disgust of nosies that I'd seen in Fran's mind.

Lucas was anxiously watching my face. "I'd always had a difficult relationship with my parents, but it was still painful to be cut off from them. You'd find the situation even more agonizing.

You've huge amounts to lose and little to gain by telling your parents that you're a telepath. Even if your relationship with them miraculously survived the revelation, you'd still end up lying to them about your work to avoid frightening them."

"You've made your point, Lucas. There's no need to distress yourself by talking about this any longer. I admit that I could, in theory, discuss things with Megan that I can't discuss with my own mother, but I can't imagine me wanting to do that in reality."

Lucas nodded. "Think of Megan as your safety net. You may never need her, but she's there in an emergency."

I knew we were on the brink of discussing Olivia and York again. I didn't want to find out the details of exactly what had broken them and might break me, so I hastily stood up. "I'd better go or my substitute mother will come in here after me."

CHAPTER EIGHT

Two days later, Megan, Adika, Lucas and I were having a meeting in Megan's lounge to discuss my progress with my telepathic training.

"That means Amber has now completed both phase two and phase three of her training," Megan summed up everything she'd said in the last ten minutes.

Adika smiled. "You're progressing very quickly, Amber."

Megan frowned, leaned back in her chair, and lifted her right hand to play with the glittering beads of her necklace. "Possibly too quickly. I'm wondering if we should spend a couple of days reviewing the earlier exercises before moving on to phase four."

"What is phase four?" I asked.

"It covers sensory input," said Megan. "You have to report what someone in another room is seeing, hearing, smelling, touching or tasting."

"When we're chasing someone, those details can help us locate the target," Adika added. "I think Amber is ready to move on to phase four. She's noticed things in my mind that I didn't even know I was thinking about."

"I agree with Adika." Lucas bounced to his feet. "Amber moves on to phase four, which means we can expect to head back to the Hive in about a week."

Megan didn't seem too happy about the decision, but accepted it. She walked us to the door of her apartment. Adika jogged off down the corridor to the right. Lucas and I turned left and walked down the corridor to his apartment.

"Megan's watching us and imagining lurid things," I whispered, as Lucas opened the door.

"How lurid?" asked Lucas.

We went into the lounge and I sat on the couch. "Hugging, kissing, everything up to and including me sharing your bed. She's trying desperately hard not to think about it, because she knows I'll see it in her mind, but that just makes her think about it even more."

There was a short silence. Lucas couldn't read my mind, but he was imprinted with behavioural analysis techniques. I watched his thoughts busily analyzing the fact I'd raised this subject, and saw my own face through his eyes as he studied my expression and body language. He dropped into speed speech.

"Preferable delay discussion topic."

"I don't see any reason why we can't talk about this now. I'm attracted to you, Lucas, and I know you're attracted to me."

I saw his thoughts abruptly turn savage, and instinctively recoiled from them. "Lucas, different levels of your mind are arguing with each other about me. What's going on?"

He sighed, and came to sit on the floor facing me. "Megan has good reason to be concerned about what's happening between us. Lottery divided you from your friends. You spent days being tested, and sitting among crowds of silent strangers. After that, you were alone in Hive Futura with Megan. Once I arrived, someone close to your age, you naturally liked to spend time with me."

"Yes, I was lonely, but it's more than that. I only met you just over a week ago, but the telepathy makes a huge difference. I know you as well as any of my friends on Teen Level, probably much better, and you've become very important to me."

"When I first met you," said Lucas, "I found you desirable. I knew you'd see that in my head, so there was no point in trying to hide it. You seemed to like me in return, I thought that was as a friend, but you're obviously thinking of our relationship developing into more than friendship."

"Yes, I am."

He stared down at the carpet. "In a few days' time, we'll go back to the Hive, you'll meet a lot of male eighteen-year-olds, and you'll find them all far more attractive than me. I mustn't start building expectations on something that's going to vanish from under my feet."

His underlying thoughts startled me. "What? Lottery chose my Strike team to...?"

"It's standard procedure," said Lucas. "The second we locate a telepath, the process of staffing their Telepath Unit begins. Some positions have to be filled by people who've the benefit of actual experience as well as imprinted knowledge, but most of your staff will have been chosen by Lottery. One of the factors considered in their selection is the necessity of providing potential partners for the telepath."

"Lottery has been choosing potential boyfriends for me! Why?"

"Logical option," said Lucas. "Compensation inevitable issues missing optimization."

"I don't understand. Your mind is..." I broke off. His mind was fighting multiple internal civil wars over what was good for the Hive and what was good for him. It was a confusing and extremely unhappy place. "Explain properly. Include all the words."

Lucas pulled a face and painstakingly spelled it out for me. "Teens fear Lottery because they have no control over what happens to them, but the system doesn't blindly hammer square pegs into round holes. With a hundred million people to play with, the optimization phase of Lottery can give people not just necessary work that they can do well, but work they really enjoy. That's better for the people and more productive for the Hive. I was terrified entering Lottery, I didn't see what they'd do with a misfit like me, but I love my work."

I could imagine Lucas as a weird teen entering Lottery. At a different time, I'd have smiled.

"Lottery works," Lucas repeated, "except for the one in a million people who have some ability so vital to the Hive that they never enter optimization phase. You're one of those, Amber. The Hive needs you to fill a dangerously stressful role, whether you're suited to it or not. You know what the pressure of that did to Olivia and York. You know we try to compensate for that by doing everything we can to help you be relaxed and happy outside your work. Part of that is allowing you the possibility of having a relationship with someone."

"I don't mind getting indulged with a huge apartment and luxury food," I said, "but choosing potential boyfriends for me is going too far."

"You'll be living in your Telepath Unit, totally isolated from the rest of the Hive. If potential partners don't exist in your unit, how would you meet them? If you did meet someone, and they worked outside Law Enforcement, there'd be huge security issues."

Lucas paused. "You're already uncomfortable about having to lie to your parents. That problem would be far worse with a partner. You'd be constantly lying about your work, inventing reasons why you get called away unexpectedly, and being embarrassed by bodyguards following you on dates and lurking outside your partner's apartment when you spend the night there."

"I wouldn't need bodyguards if I was going on a date."

"Adika wouldn't agree with that," said Lucas. "If your relationship progressed to the point of you wishing to live with someone, they'd have to move to your Telepath Unit. That would mean you had to tell them the full truth about yourself, and they might not react well to the news you were a telepath."

I thought about myself a few months ago, pictured how I'd have reacted to a boyfriend telling me he was a nosy, and winced. "I suppose it would be difficult."

"Very difficult and potentially even dangerous for you. Lottery tries to avoid these problems by running tests to find out the new telepath's preferred type of partner, and making sure some are included among their unit staff. In your case, it was very simple. You're attracted to men, particularly the sort of athletic, muscled male that makes an ideal Strike team member. All that was needed was to add a few extra constraints to the standard Strike team selection criteria. That candidates should have a certain facial bone structure and black hair."

I shook my head. "Strike team candidates should be chosen because of their abilities, not because I like their hair colour."

"Lottery found thousands of people with the ideal physical and mental characteristics for your Strike team," said Lucas. "Since a Strike team member has to be able to run at top speed while carrying the telepath, most of the possible candidates were male. The female candidates would primarily be considered for either Morton or Keith's Strike teams anyway, because their preference is for female partners."

"The Hive does this sort of thing for Morton and Keith too?"

"As I said, it's standard procedure for all telepaths," said Lucas. "Our unit needs two Strike teams because we must never be in the situation where the telepath is ready to respond to an emergency but the Strike team are not. Adika is already choosing his twenty Strike team members for the Alpha team. When they're trained and operational, he'll pick his Beta team. That's a total of forty Strike team places."

I'd worked out that my Telepath Unit was going to be bigger than the Research Unit where my parents worked. I revised my estimate of its size up even further.

Lucas was still talking. "Lottery will have considered thousands of candidates for those forty places. It will have imprinted a couple of hundred of them, to allow for rejections, sudden vacancies in other units, and because there are a few other Hive roles that overlap with Strike team imprinting. Rather than choose the final two hundred candidates randomly, Lottery chose them to be men that you'd find attractive."

"That's... humiliating."

"Would you prefer to be carried round by men you find repugnant?" asked Lucas. "Think that through, Amber. It's not just being carried. In some situations your Strike team will be physically protecting you with their bodies. That can get very intimate. Keith is heavily built, so it's impossible to make his Strike team all female, but he reacts badly to close physical contact with men. That causes huge problems for his staff."

I waved a dismissive hand. "This is all irrelevant. However good looking my Strike team are, I don't believe that meeting them will change my feelings for you, Lucas."

He didn't say a word, but his answer was laid out for me in

his head. He'd no self-confidence in this area. Girls had never been interested in someone so bewilderingly unconventional and incomprehensibly bright. Lucas had never really tried to overcome that problem. He couldn't see the point when he knew his initial physical attraction to a girl would soon change to boredom anyway.

I was different. The only person Lucas had ever met who could keep up with his high speed conversations. The only girl he'd ever met who fascinated rather than bored him.

"You're afraid that we'll move on from being friends," I said, "and then I'll meet my Strike team and dump you."

"It would be difficult to continue a working relationship after that." His head was busy lining up the stakes involved. The pain he'd feel at investing in a relationship just to have me turn away from him within weeks. The risk of losing not just my friendship but possibly his position as Tactical Commander as well. He couldn't stay in my Telepath Unit if I was uncomfortable with him being there.

I sighed. "We'll do this your way then. Wait and see what happens when I meet my Strike team."

CHAPTER NINE

My mind was focused on my relationship with Lucas, so it took me until the next morning to think of the obvious point. Lottery had chosen my Strike team members to match my preferences in a partner, and Lucas had said something about muscled men with black hair. There was something ominously familiar about that description.

I had breakfast, left the dirty dishes strewn across the table, and headed towards Lucas's apartment. Halfway down the corridor, I abruptly stopped. It would be much simpler for me to get the information I needed from Adika.

His apartment was in the opposite direction, so I turned round, and was just in time to see a girl opening my apartment door. That was Hannah, one of the general staff who worked for Megan. She'd been brought here a few days ago, when the untidiness of my apartment reached crisis point.

It was somehow symbolic of how my life had changed, that Megan hadn't made the slightest complaint about how a pristine luxury apartment had turned into a disaster area. You don't argue with the telepath, tell her to tidy up, or even suggest she stops throwing her clothes on the floor. You don't leave her to live in a garbage heap in the hope she'll eventually clear it up herself. You make no comment about it at all, just bring someone in to clean up after her and deal with her laundry.

My reluctance to have a cleaner invading my private apartment was hugely outweighed by my reluctance to do the cleaning myself, so I'd welcomed Hannah's arrival. As an extra bonus, the girl was fresh from Lottery like me. I'd naively pictured us chatting together, but our first encounter had been horribly awkward. I was feeling uncomfortable about having to read Hannah's mind to approve her appointment. She was utterly overawed to be in the presence of someone as critically important to the Hive as a telepath.

Since then, I hadn't seen Hannah at all. Each day, I'd leave my apartment in chaos and return to find it magically restored to perfect order. I grabbed my chance to talk to her again, hurrying back towards her and calling her name. "Hannah!"

She guiltily swung round to face me. "I'm sorry, Amber. I thought you were going out. I'll come back later."

"No, please don't go." I smiled at her. "I wanted to thank you for cleaning up my apartment. I'm afraid it was in a dreadful state when you arrived."

She flushed nervously. "It was a pleasure. I love tidying up and cleaning places."

I knew that was true. When I was reading Hannah's mind, I'd felt her delight in arranging things, polishing things, and bringing out the natural beauty in rooms. I'd even been inspired to try some cleaning myself, but my second-hand enthusiasm hadn't survived for more than five minutes of throwing rubbish into the waste chute.

"I was imprinted as an office cleaner," Hannah continued, "but working in your lovely apartment is even more satisfying. I..."

A frosty voice interrupted her. "Hannah, you shouldn't be wasting the telepath's precious time with your chatter."

I turned to face Fran. "I was thanking Hannah for tidying my apartment. She's done a wonderful job of..." I broke off as I realized Hannah was scurrying away down the corridor.

"There's no need for you to thank a Level 57 Law Enforcement Office Cleaner for doing her work adequately," said Fran. "Hannah is remarkably fortunate that her discretion and loyalty to the Hive have gained her a position in a Telepath Unit. She'll have accommodation above the standard she'd normally be given, along with many additional privileges."

She didn't give me time to reply to that, just rapidly changed the subject. "I was disappointed to discover that you'd excluded me from yesterday's meeting about your training progress."

"I didn't exclude you."

"You told Megan that you didn't think my presence was necessary."

It was true I'd said that to Megan. I'd known that Fran would hate having to sit smiling through a discussion of my telepathy. I'd thought she would be relieved to be excused the ordeal. I hadn't allowed for the fact that she might be glad not to be at the meeting but still resent not being invited.

"Yes, but..." I tried to think of a tactful answer. "I didn't think you'd be interested in attending since I don't need to work telepathically with my Liaison team."

"You don't *need* to work telepathically with your Tactical Commander either, however Lucas was present in the meeting." From the acid tone of her voice, Fran was obviously aware that I spent a lot of time reading Lucas's mind.

"If you prefer it, you can be included in future meetings about my telepathic training."

"I prefer to be included in all future meetings whatever the subject," said Fran.

I held back a groan. "Then you will be."

"Thank you." Fran gave a stiff nod, turned, and walked away.

I sighed, and headed on to Adika's apartment. I pressed the chime button next to his door, but there was no response. After a second press of the chime achieved nothing, I reached out to Adika's mind and found him watching me on the image from the door camera.

Come in, Amber.

I gave a despairing laugh and opened the door. I was trying to win the approval of both Fran and myself by setting boundaries, rules for when I should or shouldn't read minds. Megan, Lucas, and Adika were all encouraging me to break those boundaries, by pushing me to constantly read their thoughts.

I followed the glow of Adika's mind to the bare empty room he used as a gym. He was weight training, which explained the edge of fatigue in his thoughts. I let him put the weights down before I spoke.

"My first job back in the Hive will be to check your candidates for the Strike team. I thought I could prepare for that now by taking a look at their holos and records."

Adika nodded, his face blank and incurious, and the top level of his thoughts concentrating on the mechanics of getting a data cube and copying the relevant records. Deeper down, his mind was busy speculating.

... spending a lot of time with Lucas, but she surely can't be leaping into his bed when he looks nothing like...

... unshakeable if Amber supports him as well as Megan. Waste it! How can I trust the judgement of a Tactical Commander who acts like a small child? He'll be ordering me and my team into danger and...

The level below that was torn between his wish to tell Megan exactly what he thought of Lucas, and his desire to keep on good terms with her and... I pulled out of that train of thought hastily. I still found it disconcerting to be sucked into male reactions.

Adika's low opinion of Lucas was painfully obvious to everyone. Lucas was deeply amused by it, and mischievously fuelling the poor man's fears by playing the fool in front of him. I considered reassuring Adika that Lucas was brilliant, but that would only convince him that we were a couple. In the current circumstances, it seemed an extremely bad idea.

I kept quiet, accepted the data cube, and headed back to my apartment to start viewing the holos of Adika's twenty preferred candidates for Alpha Strike team. My suspicions were quickly confirmed. The Lottery tests had been affected by my fascination with Forge. The candidates had skin tones that varied from pale to even darker than Adika, but they all had black hair, and there was something subtle about their cheekbones that reminded me of Forge.

I skipped on through fifteen holos, estimating each young man's resemblance to Forge, and was relieved that I felt no compulsion to sit staring at their faces. As far as I could tell, I was merely reacting to them with the natural interest any girl would have in good-looking young men who would be working closely with her.

I stopped watching the holos when I got to number sixteen because there was no point after that. Number sixteen didn't just look like Forge. Number sixteen *was* Forge.

CHAPTER TEN

I sat there, staring blankly at the holo of Forge, telling myself I was a fool to be so shocked by this. I'd known Forge was strong and a natural athlete. I'd known he was addicted to taking risks. I'd even known Lottery had assigned him to Law Enforcement. I should have realized there was a high risk of him showing up on my Strike team. There might be thousands of other candidates just as well qualified, but Lottery had made the final choice based on their resemblance to Forge, so he'd naturally be selected.

I forced myself to turn off the holo, went to my bedroom, and floated in the warm air of the sleep field thinking about the situation. Lottery had weighted the odds in Forge's favour, so he was one of the two hundred or so candidates imprinted for Strike team. The process hadn't stopped then, because Adika had been impressed enough to choose him as one of his twenty preferred candidates for the Alpha team.

It hadn't stopped then, but it was going to stop right now. I could reject anyone in my unit, and I was going to reject Forge. You don't argue with the telepath, so Adika would just accept my decision and replace Forge with a reserve candidate. He'd be surprised though, and might ask what I'd seen in Forge's record that made me reject him.

I could bend the truth, say I'd met Forge on Teen Level and hadn't liked him, but a comment like that from a telepath might hurt Forge's future career. He'd been allocated one of the highest prestige positions in Law Enforcement, and I was going to take it away from him. I mustn't wreck his other chances as well.

Anyway, I daren't admit I'd known Forge on Teen Level. Lucas was already shying away from having a relationship with me because he expected me to dump him for some member of my Strike team. He wouldn't miss the implications of the Lottery results for my physical preferences in men matching someone I'd known on Teen Level.

I'd seen all the rapidly changing moods of Lucas's mind. His excitement as his thoughts raced on a multitude of different levels to solve a work related puzzle. How he'd glow with boundless self-confidence at the moment he found the solution. The way all that brightness could suddenly darken and fold in on itself when he remembered a girl mocking him on Teen Level.

Lucas's ego was very fragile when it came to relationships. At the slightest hint that there'd been something special between me and Forge, Lucas would assume my future was decided, and retreat behind an unassailable wall of his insecurities.

I could keep the past out of this by claiming I didn't like the birthmark on Forge's face. Shanna had kept complaining about that one slight imperfection in his good looks, and I could pretend I felt the same. Surely no one could blame Forge for a telepath disliking his birthmark.

I stood up, my mind automatically reaching ahead of me to where the now familiar shape, taste, sound of Adika's thoughts hung in the black silence, and then sat down again. Adika was with Megan. He was about to make a huge mistake that Megan might never forgive.

I hadn't expected Adika to push things with Megan this fast. I hadn't allowed for the fact he was a Strike team leader, used to acting swiftly and decisively. If I'd realized, I could have stopped this, warned him that Megan was still raw with grief for her husband, so approaching her now would only distress both of them.

It was too late to warn him now, and was I entitled to do that anyway? What were the boundary lines here? Even Megan didn't know that I'd seen her deepest, most private feelings about her husband. I should surely keep that knowledge strictly confidential.

The problem was that I didn't want either Adika or Megan to get hurt. I was relieved that I hadn't known about this in advance, because it would have been hard to stand silently by and let the pair of them walk off an emotional cliff.

... stinging pain on my cheek from Megan's slap. I've just shot myself in the foot. Time to pull back and regroup. I could use a Tactical Commander telling me how to...

I surfaced from Adika's mind, both confused and startled. I hadn't even realized I was inside his head until I felt Megan's slap.

First lesson, it was dangerously easy for me to drift from thinking about a familiar mind to reading it. Second lesson, I didn't just experience other people's feelings as if they were my own, I felt their pain the same way. That was... ominous.

This obviously wasn't a good time to talk to Adika, so I postponed the job of rejecting Forge until the next day. For the rest of the evening, I fought the temptation to play the holo of Forge again. I won that battle, but it was an empty victory. When I went to sleep that night, I had the Forge dream.

It was the first time I'd dreamed it in Hive Futura, and it seemed somehow clearer, brighter, more sharply defined. I could smell the tang of pine on the air, and hear the dry leaves crunching under my feet. My eyes were dazzled by the bright light, it was hot, unbearably hot, and I was sobbing from fear until Forge said the magic words that made everything right.

"Good girl, Amber. You're a good girl, Amber."

I woke up in a glow of happiness, and knew that I wouldn't talk to Adika. If I didn't allow Forge on my Strike team, it would make him unhappy. He wouldn't be pleased. He wouldn't say I was a good girl. I should get rid of Adika instead, and make Forge my Strike team leader. Forge would like that.

No, maybe Forge wouldn't like that. Stray remnants of reason warned me that Forge might be highly embarrassed to be thrust into Adika's shoes, and everyone would ask a lot of awkward questions. At the beginning, Forge would be happier as a Strike team member. Later on, Adika would want two deputy team leaders.

I rolled out of the sleep field, and hurried to check the records on Adika's data cube. Most of the candidates were only imprinted for Strike team member, but five were imprinted for Strike team leader. Kaden, Rothan, Matias, Eli, and Forge!

I smiled. That solved everything. I'd tell Adika to make Forge deputy leader in charge of Alpha team. Adika would do what I told him, just the way Mira's Strike team leader had chosen the deputies she wanted. Later on, when he had enough experience, Forge could take over Adika's position.

The happy haze of imagining how pleased Forge would be lasted for several hours. After that, I started wondering if I'd totally lost control of my own mind. I absolutely must tell Adika to reject Forge. The flaw in that plan was that I was bound to have the dream again. The minute I woke up from it, I knew I'd go dashing back to Adika, saying I'd changed my mind and insisting he should put Forge on the team again.

I had to think carefully before I did anything at all. I needed to make sense of the way I was reacting to Forge. If I couldn't make sense of it myself, then I'd have to ask for help, but I knew exactly how Lucas would react to my story. He was a Tactical Commander, imprinted with information on psychology and behavioural analysis techniques, an expert in taking the clues of odd behaviour and determining the reasons behind them. His mind would work like a machine at the mystery of my reaction to Forge, the same way it had worked on the mystery of why true telepaths shouldn't meet, but his emotions would take it as a personal rejection.

That triggered a new thought. Perhaps those two mysteries were linked. Perhaps true telepaths affected each other in the same way that Forge affected me. As a small child, I'd learnt to block the massed thoughts around me, but the stronger thoughts of another telepath might have been able to get through my defences.

If Forge's thoughts and feelings had been hitting me telepathically when I was on Teen Level, it would explain my fixation on making him happy. Lottery would never have missed discovering Forge if he was a true telepath, but he could be a borderline telepath. Megan kept telling me that borderline telepaths could only get random glimpses into other minds. If Forge's random glimpses had come at the wrong times, the Lottery tests wouldn't have detected him.

I was feeling a lot calmer now. If Forge was a borderline telepath, it would explain everything. I should stop worrying about him being on my Strike team until I was back in the Hive. Once I met Forge again, and read his mind, I'd know if my theory was right.

CHAPTER ELEVEN

A week later, I was stepping back into the aircraft that had brought me to Hive Futura. I was eager to return home to our own Hive, but the thought of the journey was scaring me to death. I fought to hide that, trying to appear calm and collected as I chose a seat and sat down.

"You could be sedated for the journey, Amber," said Megan.

Waste it! My terror must be blatantly obvious.

"It's better if Amber stays awake for the journey," said Lucas. "If she has a problem approaching the huge mind density of the Hive, she can warn us and we can turn back."

"That's true," Megan admitted.

Lucas grabbed the seat between me and the wall, and Adika sat behind me. Megan pointedly sat in front of me to avoid being near Adika, and Fran took the seat next to her. I saw Fran lean across to whisper something in Megan's ear, but couldn't hear what she said, and resisted the urge to read Megan's mind to find out. Since the face slapping incident, Adika and Megan had only had minimal, coolly professional contact with each other, while Fran seemed to be getting increasingly friendly with Megan.

Hannah waited nervously until her superiors were settled, before taking a seat two rows in front of Megan and Fran. I could understand someone who was Level 57 preferring to keep her distance from a group of Level 1 people.

"We could uncover the window and enjoy the view," suggested Lucas.

I glanced at the square metal plate on the wall, shuddered, and shook my head. This aircraft was about to leave Hive Futura. We'd be flying through the air, and on the other side of that thin metal plate would be the terrifying Truesun.

"Lucas! Don't you dare remove any of the window covers," said Megan. "Amber's already nervous about the flight."

There was a faint squeak from in front of me, which told me Hannah was as terrified as me by the idea of seeing Outside. Adika was never going to embarrass himself by squeaking, but I caught the tension in his thoughts too, as he fervently wished that Lucas would shut up.

Lucas sighed. "The environment Outside isn't innately hostile, it's merely unfamiliar. There's an initial agoraphobic reaction due to the increased scale of the surroundings, but that's easily overcome."

"We've no reason to be interested in Outside," said Fran. "The Hive is our whole world and provides everything we need. A few unfortunate maintenance workers may be required to go Outside to perform tasks necessary to the Hive, but the rest of us can shelter within the perfect safety of its walls."

For once, I was totally on Fran's side against Lucas, though her tone of voice reminded me of a disapproving school teacher. Lucas must have been thinking the same thing, because he laughed and spoke in a pretentiously smug voice.

"Now children, let's all sit on the floor in a circle and hold hands while we sing Hive Duty song number ten. 'The Hive Is Our World.'"

Fran swung round in her seat to frown at him. "Lucas, you shouldn't mock the Hive Duty songs. Don't you realize their importance?"

He gave her an unrepentant grin. "I know their importance far better than you do, Fran. My imprint includes full details of the part that school plays in socially conditioning children to be conformist and productive members of the Hive."

"Then why make fun of the Hive Duty songs?" Adika joined in the attack.

"Because that social conditioning may be desirable for 99 per cent of Hive members," said Lucas, "but our role in the Hive puts us in the small minority who need to step beyond the comforting lies and the songs and the myths. Nosies are fakes. The Hive isn't a totally safe place. It isn't the whole world either. We're in a different Hive right now, and as for having no reason to be interested in Outside... Waste it, this aircraft will be flying Outside in a minute!"

I didn't need reminding of that fact. I was already far too terrifyingly conscious of it. I was strongly tempted to order Adika to tie Lucas up and gag him, an order that I knew would be gladly obeyed, but Megan hastily changed the subject.

"We're heading back much too soon. Amber's only spent three weeks training in Hive Futura. Keith was here for far longer."

"The main Hive is a much more secure location." Adika lounged back in his seat, nearly as relieved as me by the new topic of conversation.

I was carefully avoiding reading Lucas's mind, but I dipped into Adika's head and was shocked by what I saw. I'd picked up that Adika was edgy about me being at Hive Futura, but the undercurrent of his thoughts had never explicitly stated why he wanted me back in the security of our own Hive. Now I could see it clearly. He wanted me back there before other Hives learnt about my existence.

"Another Hive might try to kidnap me?"

"There's no need to worry, Amber," said Lucas. "Adika is in charge of unit security, so he's paranoid about protecting you. A Hive without any telepaths might well be desperate, but hardly desperate enough to try kidnapping one. Hive Treaty was set up specifically to prevent problems like territory violations and kidnappings, and no Hive would dare to breach Treaty."

If Adika was paranoid about protecting me physically, Megan was equally obsessed with protecting my health and well-being. She stubbornly returned to her original point.

"Amber has progressed much faster than Keith, but going from being near a handful of minds to being near a hundred million is..."

I interrupted to save time. "If I have a problem, I'll say so immediately and we'll turn back."

The room suddenly began to vibrate and Lucas took my hand. I hung on gratefully, and tried to think about anything other than where I was and what was happening. I was tensely aware of the closeness of the unfamiliar mind of our pilot, and the importance of not reading his thoughts. Our pilot would have been selected by Lottery as capable of coping with the sight of Outside, but I couldn't risk seeing through his eyes.

I warily checked Lucas's mind, and found he'd forgotten about the window and Outside. His thoughts were on our relationship now. He was convinced that I'd have no interest in him once I met my Strike team, and was regretting that I'd listened to him, done things his way, and kept my distance.

Waste it! Better a few days than nothing but too late now. I'll never have another chance with a girl who can really understand what I'm saying.

The vibration eased, but I could feel the room around me moving in a peculiar way. I was Outside in a fragile metal box, hanging in the air below the Truesun. I stared at the back of Fran's head, trying to distract myself from my fear.

The situation with Fran was becoming a serious problem. When I accepted her as my Liaison team leader, I'd believed I would be in total control of my telepathy, picking and choosing what minds I read and when. Now I'd learned that opening up my telepathic view of the world was like opening my eyes on a room full of people. I couldn't choose to see certain faces and not others. Even worse than that, thinking about a familiar person could be enough to link me to their mind.

I couldn't change the way my telepathy worked to suit Fran, and I mustn't even try, because this was what my Hive needed from me. Telepathy had to be as automatic to me as breathing if I was to search through a multitude of minds to find the single wild bee, and I needed to be able to link to the minds of my Strike team members with split-second speed if I was to help keep them safe.

I'd managed to avoid trespassing in Fran's mind so far. I

worked hard at keeping my mental gaze directed away from her, and pulled guiltily away whenever I accidentally touched her defensive surface thoughts. It was a constant struggle though, and caused added problems. Spending so much time with Lucas had trained me to expand people's words by instinctively reading extra details in their head. Communicating with Fran, limited to just hearing words, felt like groping my way along a corridor blindfolded.

I didn't want to give in and fire Fran at this point though. Firing her wouldn't just cause problems for my unit, but give a victory to the part of me that hated telepaths, and strengthen the voices of self-loathing that nagged at me in moments of weakness.

Besides, I was finally seeing some signs that Fran's attitudes towards telepaths, or at least towards me, were shifting. She'd seemed far less antagonistic towards me during the last week, joining Adika in disapproving of Lucas's light-hearted clown act. I guessed that she was being influenced by Megan's attitude to telepaths.

Once we were in my Telepath Unit, surrounded by people who accepted me as a telepath, I hoped that Fran would give in and accept me too. She'd be the lone hater of telepaths in my unit, because I'd learned my lesson. I wasn't going to accept anyone who shared Fran's attitudes.

I was still brooding on the Fran situation, when I sensed a whispering in the distance. Was that our Hive? I closed my eyes to concentrate better, and reached out cautiously to explore it, but the mind mass was too far away to distinguish any details. I watched it slowly grow nearer, bigger, louder.

Megan's voice disturbed my concentration. "Amber, please wake up. You should start sensing the Hive soon. Tell me at once if you have problems."

I opened my eyes. "I wasn't asleep. I've been... listening... to the Hive. It's hard to describe what that's like in words."

"No appropriate vocabulary available," said Lucas.

I nodded. "Exactly. I borrow words from other senses – sight, smell, sound, touch, taste – but none of them are exactly right. Anyway, the Hive mind is like a hundred million conversations blurring into each other. Noisy, but in a way rest-ful, like the waves on Teen Level beach, or a fountain, or the humming of bees."

That reminded me of something. "During Lottery, I had a dream about bees. Their humming was reassuring me. I think I was hearing the Hive mind then."

I closed my eyes again, and listened to the humming grow closer. There was the vibration of the aircraft landing, and the background hum enfolded me like a warm, comforting blanket. I was back in my Hive. I was home. I was safe.

No, I corrected myself. Things were actually the other way round. I'd been safe in Hive Futura, but not any longer. It was now that the real test of being a telepath would begin. It was now that I'd find out if I was like Morton or York, like Sapphire or Olivia, whether I would cope with the challenges ahead of me or break under the strain.

CHAPTER TWELVE

Until I was thirteen, I lived on Level 27 of the Hive. My first clear memory of leaving that level was the school geography trip when I was seven years old. Our teachers escorted a wildly excited crowd of us down in a lift to Level 100, and then we rode the upway through all the accommodation levels to Level 1 itself. I was dazed to discover the world was so big. I'd only ever seen a small part of Level 27, and now I was passing through level after level.

When we finally reached Level 1, we were allowed five minutes to look in awe at the people walking by. Our teachers told us there were fewer people living on the higher levels, and those who were Level 1 were very special indeed, vital to the success and prosperity of the Hive.

After that, we were taken higher up still, riding in an express commuter lift to one of the fifty working levels above Level 1. We paraded in a wide-eyed line through a hydroponics bay, were allowed to pick strawberries to eat, and then rode up in a lift again to Industry 1, the top level of the Hive, the edge of the world. Some of the other children were brave enough to venture outside the lift, but I stayed at the back with the other cowards. We didn't believe our teachers' reassurances that the Truesun couldn't blind us on Industry 1, and kept our eyes firmly closed until the lift headed down to take us home to Level 27.

As a teen, the working levels were forbidden territory. Now I was back on Industry 1 for the first time since I was seven years old. I couldn't cower at the back of the lift with my eyes closed this time. Not when I was supposed to be in charge of this unit.

I forced myself to step out of the lift, and saw a large open area, with corridors running off to either side and directly ahead.

"I'll take you to your apartment, Amber," said Megan. "You'll want to rest and adjust to the background noise of the Hive."

"I'd like a tour of the unit first." I turned to look behind me. The lift we'd arrived in was one of a row of six. A couple of them had unusually large doors.

"Coming back to the Hive is a major step," said Megan. "You need to rest."

I couldn't rest until I'd made sure this place was safe from the Truesun. "I'd like a tour of the unit," I repeated. "I'll find it easier to relax when I know my surroundings."

Megan turned to look at Adika for support, but he'd already grabbed a bag from our luggage trolley and headed off down a corridor.

Lucas laughed as he picked up a bag as well. "Never argue with the telepath, Megan. A brief tour will help Amber get oriented."

He vanished off as well, followed by Fran. Hannah furtively picked up the luggage trolley controller, and stole silently away with the trolley chasing her. Megan and I were left alone.

Megan sighed. "A very brief tour then. This unit was shut down and put into maintenance mode after Claire died a few years ago."

Claire had obviously been another true telepath. I checked Megan's mind, and was relieved to discover that Claire hadn't broken under the strain of using her telepathy, but died of extreme old age.

"Once you were discovered in Lottery, a complete refurbishment was carried out." Megan gestured at the row of lifts. "We have our own dedicated set of ultra express speed lifts, which connect to major belt interchanges on each level of the Hive, enabling you to reach all areas as quickly as possible. Lift 2 is bigger than standard, designed to take the combined Alpha and Beta Strike teams in extreme emergency. Lift 6 is our freight lift."

She walked straight ahead across the open area. I followed her, gradually calming down as I saw the ceilings were reassuringly solid.

"These corridors are our accommodation section," said Megan. "Your family can spend time with you here and in the park, but mustn't enter the operational section of the unit."

Park? We had our own park? Megan had to be joking. I checked her thoughts. No, she wasn't joking.

Megan led me on through security doors into a corridor, and paused at a crossway. "We're now in the operational section. Tactical area on the left. Liaison area on the right."

We walked on past huge offices to the next crossway. "Administration offices are straight ahead," said Megan, "and the right turn leads to the storage and maintenance areas. We'll skip all that, and go left past the conference rooms."

I obediently turned left, my head dazed by the sheer scale of this. By now I'd worked out the number of people on the Alpha Strike team, the Tactical team, and the Liaison team, and allowed for the fact there'd be a Beta Strike team in future. I hadn't absorbed the fact that there'd be a lot of administration and other support staff too, and all these people would need offices and apartments in the unit.

We reached yet another crossway, and Megan paused again. "This area all belongs to the Strike team. Gym, swimming pool, and equipment storage to the right. Ready room, shooting range, and medical area to the left. Ahead is the park."

Gym? Swimming pool? Medical area? All we needed was a shopping area, and this place would be a whole little level of its own. I shook my head in disbelief, and followed Megan through more security doors. The park looked a little unkempt, with faded patches on the blue ceiling, but the suns were on, there was birdsong among the trees, and a rabbit was watching us curiously.

We followed the path alongside a stream, took a side turning through some trees, skirted a lake, and finally reached more doors. "And we're now back in the accommodation section," said Megan. "The community rooms are all on this corridor."

We walked on and arrived back in the open area by the lift. "You and the Strike team all have apartments close to the lifts to allow a fast response to emergency calls," said Megan. "Adika's apartment is directly opposite yours for security reasons."

She left me at the door of my new apartment, clearly assuming I'd want to explore it by myself. I went inside, and was stunned by the size of the palatial hall. I wandered round it, opening doors on a ridiculous number of rooms, a lot of them totally empty. I paused in one to investigate a stack of boxes, which turned out to contain all the clutter I'd left in my storage locker on Teen Level. Eventually, I found the living room, and frowned at the luxury comms system.

I'd faced my worries about being on Industry 1, but now I had to deal with a bigger problem. I was scheduled to meet Forge tomorrow morning. I was nervous already, and I was bound to dream about him tonight.

I called Adika, and a holo of his head appeared in front of me. "Yes, Amber?"

"I know I'm scheduled to interview your Strike team tomorrow, but I'd like to do a few of them today."

Adika gave me a rueful smile. "Megan won't approve, but I understand you being impatient to get on with your job. Do you want to see anyone in particular?"

The only person I wanted to see was Forge, but I didn't want to make that too obvious. "It's sensible to begin by checking your five potential candidates for the deputy team leader positions."

Adika nodded. "I'll get them here as soon as possible. Shall we use one of the conference rooms?"

I closed my eyes for a second to search for Megan's familiar thoughts.

"Megan's roaming the offices," I said, "checking everything has been set up properly, so we'd better use a room in my apartment. I think I remember seeing a meeting room somewhere near my front door. With luck, I may manage to find it again. Why do I have lots of completely empty rooms in here?"

Adika laughed. "The unit is in an isolated part of the Hive because it makes things quieter for you, and because it's easier for us to set up security defences. Your apartment is huge for the same reasons. If we ever had intruders in the unit, then you'd take refuge in your apartment with your bodyguards. Take a look at the thickness of your walls some time."

He paused. "I'll call you when my candidates are here."

His holo vanished. I stared thoughtfully at the empty air where it had been, and then went to examine the front door of my apartment. There was something odd about the wall and the door. They were thicker than standard, and... I rapped on the wall with my knuckles. It felt, and sounded, like I was knocking on a structural pillar.

I stood still for a moment, thinking about the confusing layout of my apartment and all the empty rooms, then went back to nose around the central area that contained my living room, dining area, and bedroom. Yes, this was surrounded by even thicker walls. If any intruders managed to cut their way into my apartment, my Strike team and I could retreat into here.

This seemed an unbelievable arrangement, but I was a rare and precious resource for my Hive, to be strictly guarded and pampered with endless luxuries. The abrupt change from my basic existence on Teen Level was unnerving.

I stopped worrying about security defences, and started worrying about my meeting with Forge instead. I didn't want to wear my old teen clothes for this interview – I'd need all the advantages I could get when I came face to face with Forge – so I headed to my bedroom. I'd passed my mother's suggestions for new clothes to Megan, and a whole array of them were hanging inside the bedroom storage wall.

There were a couple of packages on the shelf next to them. People were permitted to give occasional personal gifts to lower level family members, so I'd got a fashionable beaded necklace for my mother, and a top of the range dataview for my gadget-loving father.

I hadn't got anything for Gregas. He'd probably sulk about that, but the Teen Level equality rules barred teens from being given presents. Everyone, whether their family was high or low level, was supposed to start on Teen Level with the authorized set of basic clothes and possessions, and live on the standard teen allowance after that. I'd known a couple of cases where teens talked their parents into breaking the rules and giving them luxury items. Those teens had ended up deeply unpopular with everyone else, so I wasn't encouraging Gregas to make the same mistake.

I left checking the presents for later, picked out a very official looking onesuit, changed into it, and dropped my old clothes on the floor. I knew that Hannah would sneak into my apartment and tidy up later. I was probably getting a shameful reputation as the untidy telepath.

I'd just arrived in the meeting room, when the comms system chimed and I heard Adika's voice. "We're outside, Amber."

I ordered the front door to open, and replied over the comms system. "Please wait in the hall until I call you in."

I sat down in a chair, took a deep breath, and cautiously lifted the mental curtain that blocked my telepathic view of the world. I guessed the mind of a borderline telepath would be like an even brighter version of Lucas's glowing thoughts. I was ready to be dazzled, prepared to slam down the curtain and blot out a blinding sight, but there was nothing.

I reached out nervously to Adika's mind, and then to the five unfamiliar ones with him. This was ridiculous. I couldn't even guess which of them was Forge. I dipped into one of their minds, touching the top level of thoughts.

... is it. The telepath says yes or no. All or nothing, and no possible appeal.

There was no mental picture of the telepath linked to the words. Adika, obsessed with security, hadn't told them my name or even my sex, let alone shown them a holo of me. I moved on to the next stranger.

... was supposed to be tomorrow. Is the change good or bad, and why...?

I checked the other three minds as well, but still had no idea which of them was Forge. None of them was thinking of their own name, and the levels below pre-vocalization were just a mess of nervous anticipation. I'd learnt exactly nothing, except that Forge was about to have the shock of his life. I peered at the controls inlaid into the top of the meeting room table, and tapped one of them.

"Please send Forge in."

I straightened up in my chair, and tried to look calm and in control as the door opened. Forge entered, looking less confident than on Teen Level, but a lot better dressed. His new clothes suited him, though Forge could wear a sack and still look handsome.

He took one look at me and froze in shock. I was grateful for his moment of utter confusion, because the sight of his face had hit me just as strongly as in the days before Lottery. I instinctively closed my eyes, and the effect was like turning off a light. From the telepath's viewpoint, Forge was nothing special at all. No joyous Carnival of a mind like Lucas. Forge was an indistinct shadow of Adika, without the hard strength of mind that came from years of experience.

"Amber." I heard him murmur the word, and saw his thoughts struggling to adjust to the situation.

...really is her, but how can she be a telepath when...

Her hair is actually tidy for once. Now that's hard to...

The old days on Teen Level. Shanna!

I winced and surfaced. The low levels were a mess. I'd always seen Forge as the master of every situation, but now he was feeling bewildered and uncertain. There was pain too, because seeing me had triggered memories of the past, making him relive his parting with Shanna.

"Hello, Forge." I opened my eyes but kept them firmly fixed on the table. "Please sit down."

I heard the scrape of a chair as he sat down, and then he spoke in a husky, nervous voice. "I'm ready. Go ahead."

"If you mean go ahead and read your mind," I said, "I already did that."

I suddenly relaxed. Forge definitely wasn't either a borderline or true telepath. I still had no idea why his face had such an effect on me, but all I needed to do was close my eyes and read his mind to break the spell. I still didn't understand what was going on here, but I could control it.

Forge had recovered from the initial shock now, and was panicking about how knowing the telepath would affect his chances. He'd lost Shanna, and desperately wanted this job to give him a new focus in life. Had he only got this far because the telepath was his friend?

"You got this on pure merit," I said. "I knew nothing about it until I discovered you were on Adika's list of preferred candidates for his Alpha team."

Forge blinked, startled to have his unspoken question answered. "The others are still bound to think..."

"They don't know we met on Teen Level," I cut into his words. "No one knows, not even Adika, and we don't have to tell them."

"That would be wonderful," he said. "I don't want..."

"I can see it all in your head," I interrupted him again. "No need to spell it out to me. Any hint of favouritism, or special treatment, could mess up your chances of getting selected as a deputy team leader. Adika won't want a deputy who can't cope without having his hand held by the telepath."

Forge gave a gasp of laughter.

"You'd better get out of here now," I said. "If we spend too long on this, Adika will get nosy about the reason."

There was the sound of a chair moving again. "Thanks, Amber. You're being great about this."

I followed his thoughts as he went out of the room, and saw his sudden shock as he remembered something.

... selection criteria include appearance. Does Amber...? Am I supposed to...?

There was a wordless blank for a second, and then he was reassuring himself.

Amber never showed the slightest interest in me except as a friend who likes the same sports as her. She dated Atticus for a while, and he's dark-haired and...

I'd known that Forge had only been interested in Shanna on Teen Level. I hadn't expected him to be attracted to me now, I didn't want him to be attracted to me now, but it was still a slap in the face to see his distaste at the idea of sleeping with me. I gave myself a moment to pull myself together, and then tapped the table controls. "Please send Eli in."

Another dark-haired young man hurried into the room, his eyes widening as he saw me. I took one look at his thoughts and smiled.

"Yes, I look just like an ordinary girl, Eli. No strangely coloured eyes."

He choked and looked at me in horror.

I laughed. "Don't worry. I'm not going to hold that thought against you. I'm finding it hard to shake off my own ideas about nosies."

Eli gave me an engaging smile. "This is all so strange. I can't believe Lottery hit me with this."

I smiled back at him. "How do you think I feel?"

Kaden came next. His parents worked in Law Enforcement too, and would be thrilled if he got a post in a Telepath Unit. He was already daydreaming about impressing Adika, and winning one of the two deputy Strike team leader positions.

Rothan was much calmer than the others. He had ambitions, but was conscious that the wellbeing of the Hive was more important than his personal wishes.

Matias came last. He had the same problem as Forge, his mind shadowed by thoughts of the girl he'd cared for on Teen Level. He'd always known that Sofia's incredible painting talent would make her Level 1. He'd dreaded Lottery, expecting it to assign him to his home zone weightlifting team. That would give him a profession he'd love but end his relationship with Sofia by creating a barrier of 9 levels between them.

Their Lottery results turned out to be even more cruel than that. Sofia was a Level 1 Mural Painter as expected. Matias was Level 1 as well, but assigned to Law Enforcement. The barrier between them now wasn't about levels but about secrecy. Law Enforcement staff knew things that must be kept secret from the rest of the Hive, so they weren't allowed to enter into relationships with ordinary citizens.

I saw Matias's last memory of Sofia. Her straight black hair was nearly waist length. There was a smudge of green paint on her cheek. She'd thrown her arms round his neck, and...

I pulled sharply away from that intimate memory, disentangled myself from Matias's personal pain, sent him out of the room, and tapped the table. "Adika, please come in."

Adika arrived a moment later, and gave me an enquiring look.

"Those five are cleared," I said. "I'm tempted to get the rest of your team in as well. I keep picking up from Lucas that it's important we get our unit operational as quickly as possible. The sooner you can start your training sessions the better."

You never argue with the telepath, except when you think something might harm her ability to serve the Hive. Adika folded his arms stubbornly. "You mustn't do too much today. The rest of the interviews can start at nine o'clock tomorrow."

I groaned and gave in. I was feeling unnatural wearing such formal clothes, so I headed back to my bedroom, changed into an outfit that was a more adult version of the tunics and leggings I'd worn on Teen Level, and then grimaced at myself in the mirror.

I'd seen no sign that Forge was a borderline telepath, and my obsession with him made even less sense now I'd discovered the trigger was purely visual. I wondered if I should discuss this with Lucas after all, then remembered I'd promised Forge not to tell anyone that I'd known him on Teen Level.

Why had I said that? Was it the old compulsion to do whatever would please Forge? I didn't think so. I'd just seen his thoughts panicking about the effect on his future career, and had a natural urge to reassure him the same way I'd want to reassure any friend. Whatever weirdness was going on here, I was totally in control of it. I just needed to close my eyes, look at Forge's mind instead of his face, and the spell was broken. I found it easier to focus on the telepathic view of the world with my eyes closed anyway, so there was really no problem at all.

That night I had the dream again. We walked through the trees and Forge was pleased with me. I was a good girl.

CHAPTER THIRTEEN

I huddled in a ball. Eyes closed, back against the rough bark of a tree, soft prickles of grass beneath me. Five armed men stood tensely round me, but my mind was reaching out past them, past the small, soft thoughts of birds, mice and squirrels, following one particular mind. It was concentrating on running and hiding.

"Down corridor, turning left, still running," I said.

I could hear Adika's voice coming from the crystal unit that fitted snugly in my ear. I could see the world through the eyes of my target.

"He's just reached a crossway with a main corridor. He's planning to ride the belt."

Adika's voice barked instructions to the Chase team in response.

"He's on the belt now. He's planning to jump. Jumping up now. He's caught a ladder. Arms hurt. Nearly fell. Climbing up ladder now."

"Visual on target!" said Forge's voice.

"Visual confirmed!" said Adika. "Chase team are in position. Strike time!"

This was the danger point where the Strike team moved in to capture my target. A cornered wild bee might fight back, so I had to change focus from reporting my target's movements to protecting my Strike team.

I dumped my mental link to the target, opened my eyes, and looked at the display hovering above the dataview in my right hand. Glowing dots and names marked the position of Adika and the twenty Strike team members on a spider network of corridors and levels. Tapping any one of those glowing dots would display the view from the camera extension of their crystal unit. That feature was vital for others, but I never bothered with it. Why depend on cameras when I could enter someone's thoughts and see the view through their eyes?

"Going circuit," I said.

I hit the circuit button on my dataview. The list of the five names of my current Bodyguard team appeared on the left of the display, while the sixteen names of Adika and the Chase team started scrolling up the right side. The names of the Chase team were currently highlighted in one of red, blue, or green, since Adika had them divided into three groups to approach the target from different directions.

I ignored the Bodyguard team list entirely, since I knew those men were safely next to me. I ignored the coloured highlights on the Chase team list too. I didn't care what group a man was in, just whether he was in trouble and needed help.

I chanted each name on the Chase team aloud as I checked the man's mind, tapping the display to send it back down to the bottom of the list as I moved on to the next. "Adika, Matias, Tobias, Rafael, Kaden, Eli..."

I broke off as pain stabbed my left arm. "Eli's hurt!"

"Eli here. I'm fine. Fell off a girder," said an embarrassed voice.

"Caleb, Dhiren..." I worked my way through the rest of the minds. "Circuit complete." I started again. "Adika, Matias, Tobias..."

"Target down," said Adika.

I completed my circuit, then quit checking minds and relaxed.

"Nice run," said Adika. "Eli, what happened with the girder? Are you hurt?"

"A few bruises. A slight scratch." Eli sighed. "I assumed there'd be the standard gap between girders, but two were further apart. I swung and didn't make it."

"Never assume things," said Adika. "Regroup at the park

now. Our volunteer target for the next training run is Keith's Strike team leader, so be ready for absolutely anything."

We gathered together in the park. The Strike team members made a garish group. They'd all been issued with functional outfits in unobtrusive colours, designed to help them blend in with the crowds in any zone or level of the Hive, but half of them were still wearing old training outfits in the colours of different teen sports teams.

Eli's slight scratch turned out to be a sizeable gash in his arm. Adika got out the medical kit and patched him up. This was our sixth day of training exercises, and half of the Strike team were looking battered.

"Matias, you were out of position at the end," said Adika. "You need to move faster. More gym time."

"I'm working at it," grumbled Matias. "I expected Lottery to assign me to the Purple Zone weightlifting team. If I'd known it was going to throw this at me, I'd have done more running training."

I laughed. Most of the Strike team would have expected to be assigned to one or other of their home zone sports teams, but their Lottery results couldn't have shocked them more than mine had shocked me.

"Other than that, it was a good run," said Adika. "Coming together nicely."

The Strike team members started chatting now, with Kaden, Rothan, Matias, Eli, and Forge dominating the conversation as usual. Everyone was well aware that these were the five men imprinted for Strike team leader. Whenever Adika split the Strike team into groups, he'd choose his group leaders from among those five. Whenever he had a difficult task to be done, he'd choose one of them to do it. He was grabbing every chance to test them with varied challenges, to see which of them would be his best choice to fill his two deputy positions.

"You have to be careful of those savage girders, Eli," said Forge.

Eli tugged down his sleeve. "You need to watch those savage walls as well." He pointed a finger in the direction of the spectacular bruise on Forge's forehead, but misjudged his distance and poked it.

"Ow!" yelped Forge.

Forge's cry of protest made me make the mistake of turning my head and looking straight at him. Seeing his expression of pain, I reacted furiously, screaming at Eli. "You hurt him, waste you!"

There'd been several discussions going on between Strike team members, but they abruptly stopped. Startled faces looked at me. Adika's face was deadpan, but his thoughts were frantically speculating.

... how will our clown of a Tactical Commander react if Amber chooses Forge instead of...

I moved on from Adika's thoughts into Forge's head, and found him cursing.

... never going to take me seriously as a potential deputy if Amber protects me like a helpless baby!

I'd upset Forge! I hastily tried to cover my error. "Why can't you fools remember I feel your pain when I check your heads? Waste it, that's why I'm running circuits, to find out if you're in trouble. Being hit by a score of different aches and pains isn't funny, and if you start deliberately hurting each other then I'm going to quit. Understand?"

"Sorry," said Eli. "I meant to point, not prod."

"All right," I said, "but please be careful. I had exactly the same thing happen yesterday, when I was in Dhiren's head and Matias patted him on his dislocated shoulder."

"Sorry," said Matias.

I checked a few minds. They'd all accepted this wasn't about Forge, but about me being overloaded by pain. Adika was yelling at himself for pushing me too hard in the training sessions, wondering if...

"Target ready," said a voice from my ear crystal.

"You're too tired for this, Amber, so we'll finish now," said Adika.

"No," I said. "You've brought Keith's Strike team leader over especially for this, so we'll carry on. I'm just pointing out that you may all be tough and impervious to pain, but I'm not, so stop making it worse for me."

I'd got them all convinced now, so I quit whining and sent my mind out. It was easy spotting a target in this isolated part of the Hive. I'd no idea how I'd manage when we moved somewhere packed full of people.

... kill people. I'm going to kill people in a horribly gory fashion and spread lots of blood around. Waste it, I feel stupid thinking all this stuff. Blood, blood, blood. Death. Blood...

"Target acquired. It's a woman. About six corridors out. Thataway!" I pointed.

"Eli, you're in charge of Bodyguard team," said Adika. "Chase team divides into four groups now. Rothan take red group, Matias take blue, Forge take green, and Kaden take yellow."

The names on my dataview shuffled around and changed colour as Adika spoke. Eli and four other men clustered round me as my bodyguards, while the rest gathered into four groups and headed out on chase duty.

"Target is heading directly away from us," I said. "She's found an express strip. I see numbers. I've got a position. She's on... No, she isn't. She's picturing a sign that isn't really there, lying in her head to try to fool me."

"I told you to be prepared for anything." Adika sounded amused. "You're dealing with an experienced Strike team leader."

"Trying to work out what's real and what's lies. She's circling round us. She's in the vent system, about eight corridors out. No, make that more like six cors. She's circling anticlockwise. I'm feeling a cold wind."

"She's close to an air conditioning unit then," Adika muttered to himself. "There are four possible ones in our area. Any more clues, Amber?"

"She's lower than us. Three, maybe four levels. Still in the vent system. Still circling anticlockwise."

"Only one possible air conditioning unit matches that height. She can't crawl too fast, so we've got speed over her." Adika started barking instructions, getting his net of Strike team members into position.

"She's gone up at least one level," I reported.

"Still in the vents?" asked Adika.

"Yes, it's cramped in there."

"She can't go up a level in the vent system unless... Got her position!" Adika snapped out more instructions.

"Opening a vent cover. Coming out. Ouch, cut a finger. Turning right and running down corridor. Riding belt. Jumping. Climbing a maintenance ladder." I gabbled. "She's level with us now and still climbing. She's thinking about me."

"She isn't going for the dolls," shouted Adika. "She's going for Amber. Bodyguard!"

Five handsome young men pressed up against me, protecting me with their bodies. If this had been a real threat, I'd have been scared to death, but in training it was rather fun.

I wondered how I'd feel if Forge was among the bodyguards piled against me. I hadn't been in that situation yet, I hadn't even had Forge carrying me, because he was never assigned to Bodyguard team. I'd been worried that was because Adika had guessed something was going on between me and Forge, until I caught Adika thinking about physical fitness levels. He kept assigning Forge to Chase team duties because he was one of the fittest men on the Strike team.

I'd been relieved by that. I didn't need the complications of Adika interfering in this. There was the hideous possibility of him ordering Forge to be... friendly... to me. Forge wouldn't like that. I was almost sure I wouldn't like it either. When I looked at the world with my telepathic view, I was fascinated by Lucas's glowing mind, while Forge's thoughts were no more appealing than the rest of the Strike team.

As a telepath, it all seemed very simple, but when I looked with ordinary human eyes everything abruptly reversed. Lucas was attractive, the Strike team were all handsome men, but one glimpse of Forge's face drew me like a magnet. I was in control of the situation, of course I was, but...

I realized I'd let myself be distracted at a key moment in a chase. Stupid, stupid, stupid! I concentrated on my target mind again, and found it somewhere totally unexpected. "She's right above us now, coming through the ceiling!"

"Strike time!" shouted Adika. "Anyone in range, get her now!"

"Going circuit. Adika, Forge, Dhiren, Caleb, Rafael..." I was hearing shouting voices that weren't coming from my ear crystal. I looked up and saw a tangle of bodies landing in the branches of a dwarf oak just ahead of me.

"Target down," said Adika.

I stopped chanting, and watched Strike team members scramble out of the tree and release the target. The startlingly tall, blonde woman dusted off a few stray leaves.

"I got far too close, Adika. You mustn't let a target get anywhere near that close to your telepath."

"More practice, more gym time," said Adika grimly.

I felt horribly guilty. Adika was embarrassed and angry, and my whole Strike team were upset and blaming themselves, but I knew this was my fault. My team depended totally on the information I gave them, and I'd let my mind drift off into thoughts of Forge.

Adika was looking past me now, frowning at something. I turned to see what he was looking at, and saw blood pouring down Forge's face.

"Forge, that's a nasty looking injury," said Adika. "You'd better go to the medical area and get it treated. In fact, you'd all better go there. We'll be heading into more populated parts of the Hive soon. A mob of young men together is unusual enough, without them all having visible cuts and bruises as well. Medical will issue you each with special antiseptic makeup to match your skin tones, so you can make yourselves look respectable."

The Strike team headed off in a depressed group, and Adika started talking to Keith's Strike team leader. I slunk off to my apartment, and sat there brooding on what had happened. Today had just been a training run, but when we were doing this for real... A single lapse of concentration by Keith had led to the death of Megan's husband. If I let myself get distracted, then one of my Strike team could be the next to die.

CHAPTER FOURTEEN

I sat under a maple tree, with a circle of expectant birds around me. I threw a handful of birdseed, and watched them eagerly fly in pursuit. A moment later, the birds scattered as the Strike team ran past me and started their third lap of the park. Adika was in the lead, with twenty figures chasing after him. They were looking a lot less colourful these days, because Adika had insisted they give up their old Teen Level training outfits and wear the officially provided clothes instead.

A park of our own had seemed an indulgence, but it wasn't. The Strike team needed it for training, and the rest of us needed it as a place to relax. The last few weeks had given me a whole new view of not just the park, but the whole Hive. I'd never realized there were interlevels between the proper levels of the Hive, holding vents, waste disposal, plumbing, and all the other services. I'd walked along corridors and never suspected labyrinths of maintenance areas were hidden behind some of the walls. I'd never even worked out the obvious fact that the park on one level took up two levels above it to give the extra ceiling height, and one level below it for tree roots.

I'd been blind, but now I'd seen all these places. I'd climbed ladders, and crawled through interlevels and vents, both as a watcher in the minds of the Strike team, and in person. Adika said it was vital to understand the areas the targets could hide in, and he was right. Once I'd been there myself, it was much easier to make sense of the clues I picked up from target minds. When they left the corridors and entered the bowels of the Hive, visual clues were far less important than things like the feel of maintenance mesh, or the heat of a nearby lighting duct.

I got off lightly compared to the rest of the team. Adika didn't send me down waste chutes, since those were both smelly and dangerous. I only did a small fraction of the physical training they did as well. Adika just wanted me fit enough to run from danger as a last desperate resort.

Lucas strolled up and stretched out on the grass by my side. Fran came a few minutes later, and carefully dusted off a bench before sitting on it. Megan arrived and sat next to her, but with a significantly large gap between them.

The budding friendship between Fran and Megan had ended a few days ago. I'd only seen a glimpse of the crucial argument in Megan's thoughts. She'd been annoyed by Fran saying something insulting about Adika.

I didn't understand Megan's feelings about Adika. For that matter, Megan didn't seem to understand them either. Megan had over a decade more experience than me. I'd thought that would help her know precisely what she wanted in life, but instead it seemed to complicate things. Whenever I saw her thoughts, at least one of the levels would be agonizing over whether she should give in to her attraction to Adika or stay loyal to her dead husband.

Adika spotted us as he finished the third lap of the park, and left his team resting while he came over to sit on the grass facing me. I could see him glance across at Megan, and her dodge his gaze. I wondered if there'd been another clash between them. In theory, a fight between Adika and Megan was none of my business. In reality, it meant I'd be dragged into an emotional whirlpool the next time I had to read Adika's mind.

"Team status report," I said. "Megan?"

"I'm recruiting a few more maintenance people. The unit will be operational soon, so we can't keep calling in outside staff every time we need minor repairs."

"Please," I said. "No more heavily muscled, black-haired men."

I was drowned out by everyone laughing. Everyone except Fran, who gave her usual rigid, artificial smile.

"You'd prefer them slightly skinny, with light-brown hair?" Adika asked, with a fake air of innocence.

I blushed. I'd been right to keep quiet about the Forge issue. My weird fascination with him had vanished like smoke being sucked into an air vent. I'd no idea what had cured it. I could only guess it was the result of me reading his mind so much.

Whatever the reason, Forge was just a member of the Strike team and an old friend now, while Lucas... The fascination of Lucas's glittering Carnival mind, which had as many levels as the Hive itself, could never fade.

Back in Hive Futura, I'd tried to encourage Lucas into a relationship, but he'd shied away, expecting me to fall for one of my Strike team. Since then, he'd been watching closely as I failed to pair off with anyone. As he watched my actions, I'd been watching his thoughts, an amused bystander in his head as he analyzed the situation and considered possible tactics and outcomes.

Three days ago, my Tactical Commander had decided the probability of success, with its projected benefits, now justified taking risks. He'd been blatantly chasing me since then, and I'd been teasing him a little in revenge for his reluctance in Hive Futura.

Lucas, of course, had worked out exactly what I was doing, why I was doing it, and that his target had every intention of being caught in the end. He also knew that I was busily reading his thoughts and plans, and was constantly picturing wicked images to tease me in return.

Lucas grinned hugely in response to Adika's remark. "I hope she does."

Megan made a choking noise and hastily started talking again. I risked one glance at Lucas's dark eyes, saw he was laughing at me, and pointedly turned my face away from him to concentrate on Megan.

"I've got the candidates standing by for when you have time to interview them, Amber."

"I've been wondering about something," I said cautiously. "Normal accommodation levels have decorations and wall paintings, but our unit walls are all plain white. Would it be possible for us to have a resident mural painter to brighten the place up?"

Megan nodded. "Law Enforcement has its own mural painters, the same way it has its own cleaners, electricians, and other general staff. We can easily get one assigned to us. Would you prefer paintings of people, or flowers, or..."

"Actually, I really liked the paintings done by someone on Teen Level," I said. "Her name is Sofia. She's just come out of Lottery as a Level 1 Mural Painter."

Adika had been gazing across at the resting Strike team, but now he turned to stare at me. He obviously knew that Matias was pining for a girlfriend called Sofia. I was relieved when he didn't say anything.

Megan frowned and tapped at her dataview. "Sofia's clearly an incredibly talented artist to be rated Level 1, but she isn't allocated to Law Enforcement."

I gave a heavy sigh of disappointment. "Is there such a big difference in the imprints that it's impossible for her to work here?"

"No, it's purely a security issue," said Megan. "I could get Sofia's personality profile checked to see if she's suitable for transfer to Law Enforcement. That might involve extra tests on discretion and..."

I smiled. "Please ask Sofia if she'd like to be considered for a transfer."

If Sofia agreed and was approved for a transfer, then she and Matias could be happy together here. The other member of the Strike team who was pining for an old girlfriend was Forge, but I couldn't work out how to fit a Level 9 Media Presenter into a Telepath Unit.

I dismissed that thought for now, and turned to Lucas.

"Tactical team is fully operational," he said, "and in continual data exchange with Tactical teams in the other Telepath Units. We're shadowing Keith's team on the suspect area around

600/2600, and getting their full data feeds about it. They want to hand that area to us as soon as the rest of our unit is operational. Keith has said there's nothing wrong there, and it would take a massacre before he'd admit to making a mistake."

Megan made that choking noise again. Even though the deeper levels of her mind felt Keith's negligence had led to her husband's death, she still wasn't comfortable hearing a telepath openly criticized.

"We've been suffering some glitches in getting our research information," continued Lucas, "but we've built up profiles on a large number of areas with low level suspicious signs. We've already discovered about thirty where the guilty party is obvious, and referred them on to be dealt with by borderline telepaths or nosy patrols. Others are on the list to be checked when our unit is operational. We've also got one area that's just plain peculiar. The area 500/5000 shopping area on Level 1 is being plagued by ducks."

We all stared at him. Area 500/5000 was the centre point of the Hive. On any level, the 500/5000 shopping area was the biggest and fanciest. The one on Level 1 was the finest shopping area in the entire Hive. I'd promised my mother we'd go shopping there one day, but so far I'd been much too busy.

Everyone had the same question in their thoughts. Adika gave in and asked it. "Ducks? Real ducks?"

Lucas shook his head. "Pictures of ducks, fancy golden ducks, keep appearing on walls. A practical joker must be sticking them up, but nobody has caught him in the act yet. It's hardly threatening. In fact, people are finding the duck plague so amusing that the shops have started ordering matching toy ducks to sell themselves."

Megan laughed. "I must go shopping over there and buy one."

Adika came next. "Strike team's basic training is nearly complete," he said. "I've got two or three team members who aren't up to Chase team fitness yet. They're working hard, so it's just a temporary issue. In two days' time, we'll be ready to move from training to limited operational status, checking simple suspect areas. A week of that, and we should be ready to go fully operational and handle emergency runs too."

Those words gave me a shiver of nerves. I knew everyone was impressed by my abilities as a telepath, I could read that in their minds, but so far I'd only done training exercises. I'd no idea how I'd cope with reading a genuine wild bee, or even if I'd be able to recognize one. I'd lived for eighteen years as an ordinary girl. I still felt like an ordinary girl. Could I really do what the Hive needed? If I couldn't, people might die. If I couldn't, what happened to Olivia and York might happen to me.

I forced that thought away, and faced Fran. She immediately burst into resentful speech.

"I object to that snide remark from Lucas about glitches in getting research information. Liaison has complied fully and promptly with every request for data."

Lucas sighed. "You've been refusing to accept calls from me for the last two days, Fran. Claiming you've complied with every request for data may be technically true, but since you're blocking me from making the requests in the first place..."

Fran gave him a look of open disgust. "I merely suggested you route all data requests through your deputy, Emili. A necessary measure due to your offensive attitude."

"Yes, you made that suggestion," said Lucas, "though frankly it sounded more like an order to me. As I told you at the time, we can't work like that."

"What's been going on here?" asked Adika sharply.

Lucas sighed again. "During emergency runs, the Liaison team have to evacuate bystanders without creating panic. My team threw a few practice scenarios at them, situations like a dangerous target heading through a medical area, so they could come up with appropriate responses. They did well, inventing some very creative cover stories. I made a light-hearted joke about them being excellent liars. It was meant as a compliment, but Fran was annoyed."

I checked Lucas's thoughts for extra details. His memory showed Fran had been much more than annoyed, startling him with an explosion of anger.

I tried to smooth things over. "Fran, I think you misunderstood Lucas's joke. He was genuinely impressed by your team's response to the practice scenarios."

"It was more than this one incident," said Fran. "Lucas's entire attitude is frivolous and completely inappropriate. I refuse to work with him until he becomes more professional."

"I agree that Lucas can be frivolous," said Adika, "but you can't blankly refuse to work with him. I've just said that Strike team are only two days away from checking genuine suspect areas. Lucas will be the one calling our tactics. At any moment, he may need Liaison to supply extra information, co-ordinate outside assistance, or organize evacuations."

"He'll have to get Emili to make those requests," said Fran.

Adika's face changed from irritation to outright fury with startling speed. "You're seriously suggesting that Emili has to repeat every order from Lucas before you'll action it? During genuine operational runs? Even the simplest check run can turn unexpectedly nasty, and we'll be responding to full emergencies soon. I'm not having your sulking causing delays that endanger my men's lives."

Fran glared at him. "I'm not sulking, I just insist on..."

I stood up and interrupted her. "I've had enough of this, Fran. I'm in notional charge of this unit, with two deputies who do the actual work. Megan is in charge of everyday running of the unit. Lucas is Tactical Commander in charge of unit operations. That means Lucas is your boss, Fran. You have to follow his orders."

Fran stood up too. "Oh yes, we all have to grovel and obey Lucas because he's sleeping with you. I don't know how he can bear to touch a freak like you, let alone..."

"Shut up!" Megan screamed the words at her.

Everyone was standing now, and there was a strange, shocked silence. Even Fran didn't seem to believe what she'd just said, but there could be no denying or forgetting those words. There was only one thing I could do now. The thing I should have done when I first read Fran's mind. I forced myself to speak and did it.

"Fran, you're fired."

She took a step towards me. "Freak!" she yelled. "Ugly mutant freak!"

Adika was between us in an instant. He grabbed Fran's arm with one of his hands, covered her mouth with the other, and dragged her off.

I watched them go, then buried my face in my hands for a moment. I'd thought that Fran shifting her disapproval from me to Lucas was a sign she was learning to accept me. I'd been horribly wrong. She daren't openly show her hostility towards me, so when she realized I cared for Lucas, she'd made him the target of her hatred instead.

When I lifted my head again, I saw Lucas frowning at me. "You didn't know Fran felt like this?"

"The one time I read Fran, she hated it," I said. "I'd loathed nosies myself as a child, so I understood that and instantly pulled out of her head. I didn't know her feelings were this strong."

Adika handed Fran over to the Strike team, and came jogging back to join us. "Fran is being escorted out of the unit."

"I know this is my fault," I said. "I should have read Fran properly, realized her hatred of telepaths was at an uncontrollable level, and rejected her. I messed up."

"Yes, you messed up, Amber," said Lucas savagely. "You let someone into your unit who wasn't just a problem, but a potential danger to you. How could you have been so stupid?"

"Lucas!" Megan shrieked his name.

I was busy reading Lucas's thoughts not hers, but I could see them in her appalled face. You never criticize the telepath. You definitely don't tell her she's stupid. I'd fired Fran, and now I'd fire Lucas as well, and that would be terrible for the unit and the Hive.

The stress of the situation must have been having an odd effect on me, because I shocked everyone, including myself, by laughing. "Calm down, Megan. Lucas is saying those things because he cares about me. He's scaring himself to death right now, picturing what could have happened if I'd been alone with Fran when she lost her temper, imagining her stabbing me and him finding my bloodstained corpse."

I paused. "Yes, I was stupid, but you were all stupid too. I have to check every member of my unit, not just to see if I'm comfortable with them, but to make sure they aren't a personal threat. Why didn't you tell me that at the start?"

Megan shook her head. "Because it isn't true. Nosy patrols are deliberately set up to be frightening, with the nosy appearing inhuman behind their mask. Most people in Law Enforcement will have gone into Lottery with a mild dislike of nosies, but that dislike vanishes once they're imprinted with the facts about nosy patrols being fake, and true telepaths being rare and vital to the Hive. Lottery would never imprint someone with a serious hatred of nosies for any post in Law Enforcement, let alone a post in a Telepath Unit."

"Fran came out of Lottery twenty-five years ago with Sapphire," said Lucas. "She must have gained her prejudices since then."

His mind finally stopped visualizing my bloodstained corpse. "If Fran's imprint covers Telepath Unit Liaison team leader, why wasn't she given a post in a Telepath Unit years ago?"

"Good question," said Adika. "If Fran was imprinted for team leader, it meant she was one of the most able Liaison candidates. She should have automatically been given a post as team member, just the same way that I automatically included everyone imprinted for Strike Team leader in my preferred candidates for Alpha team."

Megan moistened her lips before speaking. "Fran was one of the preferred candidates for Sapphire's Liaison team, but Sapphire rejected her. I didn't think that was a black mark against Fran. Sapphire's notoriously choosy about the people she has in her unit, and rejects lots of candidates."

"Fran had to wait twenty-five years to get her second chance at a Telepath Unit posting," said Lucas. "She's spent all that time hating Sapphire for rejecting her, and that's extended to hating all true telepaths."

"It never occurred to me that someone could put their own grievance ahead of the needs of the Hive," said Megan miserably. "If Fran had a personal issue with telepaths, then she shouldn't have accepted this posting."

"Fran's very ambitious," said Lucas. "She wouldn't want to give up the prestige of a post as team leader in a Telepath Unit."

Megan groaned. "This is my fault. I recruited her. I resign."

I felt like I was drowning in guilt. I'd been given perfectly simple instructions and chosen not to follow them. Now I was watching Megan tear herself apart, seeing the horror in her mind that she'd made a mistake that put a true telepath at risk. She'd lost Dean, all she had to cling to in life now was her work, but she was going to give that up and leave because of my mistake.

"Not you," said Lucas. "Me. Any competent Tactical Commander would have recognized that Fran wasn't just reserved and formal, but fighting to contain her hatred of telepaths."

Chaos, Lucas was blaming himself now and planning to leave as well. I'd have Adika resigning too if I didn't do something quickly. "Oh, shut up!" I yelled at them. "Nobody is resigning, and that's an order!"

They all looked at me in stunned silence.

"I misled you all by letting you think I'd read Fran properly," I continued. "You naturally assumed I'd have mentioned any rabid hatred of telepaths. If I'd read Fran's thoughts properly, or even told you the little I'd seen, she'd have been replaced on her first day."

I turned to Megan. "This was totally my mistake, Megan. I need your help to sort this out."

Megan gave a helpless gesture with her hands. "What? Yes?"

"I've fired Fran. Tactical team is operational. Strike team is in final training phase. We can't handle operational runs without Liaison. What's our best option for replacing Fran?"

Megan ran her fingers through her hair, wrecking her elegant hairstyle. "We either bring in an alternate candidate, or we promote her deputy. Nicole is imprinted for Liaison team leader position. She only had a year's experience at team member level before coming here, but she had very high assessment scores."

I hadn't had much contact with the Liaison staff apart from the initial interviews. I vaguely remembered Nicole. A girl with long, red, flyaway hair and an anxious expression, who used a powered chair to travel round the unit. "Can we make Nicole temporary team leader, see how that works?"

"That's the best solution," said Lucas. "We can't delay going operational while we look for a new Liaison team leader. The current health of the Hive mind means our unit is urgently needed."

I was alarmed by that sentence. "What do you mean, Lucas?"

"Things have been difficult for the last few years since Claire died," he said. "Only four true telepaths. Morton has physical limitations because of his age, Mira finds emergency runs stressful, and Keith has his own particular issues, so Sapphire has been left carrying far more than her share of the load. She's held the line bravely, kept the Hive functioning, but she's gradually losing ground. Any telepath needs a full day of rest after an emergency run or the casualty rate among the Strike team soars."

He pulled a face. "The problem is that too many areas with warning signs aren't being checked before their wild bees hatch. That means the number of emergency runs is increasing. In turn, that means even less time to check areas with warning signs, but once our unit is operational it will swing the balance back in our favour. We'll make progress with check runs again, and the situation will rapidly become more stable."

I delved into Lucas's mind, and was even more alarmed by the thoughts behind the words. I'd always been aware of his sense of urgency about getting the unit operational, but I'd never caught him thinking through the specific reasons for that.

Now he'd laid out everything neatly in his head for me to see. The numbers and patterns of incidents, the grim current statistics, and the logical future projections that were terrifying every Telepath Unit Tactical team.

The simple truth was that four true telepaths weren't enough. The Hive was heading out of control, moving steadily towards the point where the incidents were too many to cover up, the nosies were unmasked as fakes, and we descended into anarchy. The Hive needed me to help stop that happening. It needed me right now.

I pulled out of Lucas's head, and tried to rally my panicking thoughts. The Hive needed me to get out there and chase wild bees, and I didn't even know if I was capable of it. I forced away that doubt. I was capable of it. I had to be.

I tried to look calmly confident as I nodded at Lucas. "We'll make Nicole temporary team leader then."

The meeting ended. Adika went off to inflict more suffering on the Strike team, and Megan and Lucas exchanged glances. Lucas seemed to lose, because he wandered off, leaving Megan looking at me anxiously.

"Amber," she said. "You mustn't be upset by what Fran said."

"I'm not," I lied. Fran's comment about mutants had struck deep, because I'd always thought of telepaths as frightening, inhuman creatures. I had to forget about Fran's words. Forget about the hatred and disgust in her face that was mirrored by part of my own mind. My Hive was in deep trouble and needed my help.

CHAPTER FIFTEEN

I was still deeply asleep at six the next morning, when a warbling sound filled my bedroom and dragged me awake.

"Unit emergency alert," said a calm, computerized voice. "Unit emergency alert. We have an incident in progress. Operational teams to stations. Strike team to lift 2."

Emergency alert? I sat up, gasping in shock. What was happening? Were Adika and Lucas throwing a special training run at us? I reached out past the thoughts of the other people in the unit, to find one familiar mind with glittering express thoughts.

Waste it, this was a real emergency! I rolled out of the sleep field, pulled on my mesh body armour first, then threw clothes on over the top of it. At the last minute, I remembered to put my crystal unit in my ear before sprinting for my front door.

Outside my apartment, I saw people running at top speed, heading for either their work stations or the lift. Mostly the lift, since the Strike team's apartments were clustered protectively around mine.

I was the last to arrive at the lift. Adika started it moving the second I was inside. I gasped as I felt it dropping at higher than even express speed. The lift was rated to hold up to sixty people, but it seemed crowded with tense Strike team members.

"Strike team is moving," Adika said, his words echoing from my ear crystal.

"Tactical ready," the voice of Lucas responded from the Tactical office.

"Liaison team ready," came a shaky, female voice. That was Nicole, speaking from Liaison's operations room. She must be even more shocked than me. Last night, she'd been told Fran had gone and she was acting team leader. Now she'd been dragged out of bed by an emergency alert.

Adika's voice prompted her. "Tracking active, Nicole?"

"Tracking status green for all Strike team," she said.

I remembered I was next on the checklist, and fumbled for my dataview. The glowing dots of the Strike team were packed tightly together, since we were all in the same lift. I tapped my circuit button and checked the scrolling lists of names. Chase and Bodyguard assignments were still set from our last training run.

"Tracking green here too," I said.

The checklist completed, Lucas's voice started briefing us. "This is not a drill. I repeat: this is not a drill. We have a major incident in progress. Sapphire and her Strike team can't take it, because they're already committed following a target. Keith and Morton both had emergency runs yesterday, so their units are in mandatory recovery time. Mira's unit had a bad run two days ago that ended with Strike team injuries, and Mira is still very distressed. That means we're up."

Lucas sounded reassuringly calm, as if he'd done this dozens of times before. Of course he had, though as deputy rather than Tactical Commander.

"Incident location is 480/1877 Level 54," he said. "You can expect one target. Evidence suggests male and armed with a knife. There are two reported stab victims."

Adika glanced round at the Strike team. "Half of you look like you've been in a fight. Cover up those bruises before people see us. We're supposed to prevent panic, not cause it."

Several of the Strike team urgently dabbed makeup on bruises and cuts. Those who'd already remembered their make-up, or had no visible injuries, watched smugly.

"And why has everyone got crystal units on visual?" added Adika. "You may be used to seeing people wearing cameras at the side of their heads, but the rest of the Hive aren't."

Smug looks vanished as everyone, me included, hastily

switched their ear crystals to audio only. The camera extensions folded themselves neatly back into the crystal units, becoming virtually invisible.

"Changing to belt system," Adika said, as the lift doors opened. He led the charge to the express strip. "Setting assignments now. Kaden is in charge of Bodyguard team. I'm taking red group, Rothan takes blue, Matias takes green, Forge takes yellow."

I glanced at my dataview, and saw the Chase and Bodyguard lists had changed to match the new assignments. I had the standard five bodyguards, who went into formation; three ahead of me, two behind. There were four men in each of the Chase team groups.

Any lift we used would be automatically set to priority usage, not stopping to pick up anyone else, but we had to share the belt system with everyone else in the Hive. Bewildered early morning travellers stared at us. We were in casual clothes, bruises were no longer visible and weapons were hidden, but a group of so many heavily muscled men was still an odd sight.

We rode the belt for perhaps ten minutes before Lucas started talking again. "The first stab victim is a boy aged sixteen with severe but non-fatal injuries. The second stab victim is a woman aged forty-eight with minor injuries. We believe that the sixteen-year-old boy was the original focus of the attack. Our target then ran from the scene, stabbing the woman who was blocking his way. We estimate our target's age at sixteen or seventeen. Previous warning signs in this area had only been strength two. This is a sudden, violent escalation to strength five. The escalation has probably been triggered by a personal event, such as a relationship crisis."

Lucas paused for a moment. "Your destination is a small shopping area. The corridors north and east are residential. There's a park to the west, and a hospital one cor south. Medical and hasties are already at the scene."

Nicole spoke, her voice calmer now. "Liaison is securing the shopping area and the park. The hospital is in lockdown. We're issuing local area announcements advising people to stay in their apartments due to a coolant leak."

"Jump belt," said Adika. "Crystal units to visual."

We all followed him off the belt and adjusted our ear crystals. The camera extensions unfolded at the right side of our faces.

"Visual links green for all Strike team," said Nicole.

"Strike team is approaching scene via upway from Level 55," said Adika.

We were going past a notice board with a red border flashing. There was a group of hasties there, but they moved aside to let us through, their eyes turning to me in open curiosity. I was a lone, slightly built girl, conspicuous among the Strike team. What were they thinking about me?

I caught myself reaching out to check their minds, and gave myself a mental slap. I had to focus on doing my job. The Strike team swept me onto the upway with them. I caught a glimpse of another flashing red announcement about a coolant leak as the moving stairway carried us upwards. We went past the blank walls of the maintenance interlevel between Level 55 and Level 54, and then shops appeared around us. We'd arrived.

I stepped off the stairway with the Strike team clustered around me. This was the first time I'd ever seen a totally deserted shopping area. I was reminded of the emptiness of Hive Futura. There was a row of lifts immediately to my left. In front of them, an abandoned bag lay forlornly, its contents scattered across the ground and its handle trailing through a patch of red liquid. Blood!

I felt a sick lurch of panic. Despite everything I'd been told, everything I'd seen in the minds of my unit members, part of me had still been clinging to my old belief that the Hive was a safe and secure world, patrolled by the hasties and the nosies who made sure that nothing bad ever happened. The sight of the blood made me finally let go of that reassuring fantasy. The grey-clad nosies weren't real. There were only five true telepaths. Right here and now, there was only me.

People had already been stabbed, and their attacker was riding the upway or the lifts right now. I had to find him before anyone else was hurt.

I closed my eyes to avoid the distractions of visual images, and reached out to the minds around us, sifting through them. The familiar ones of the Strike team, wound up with tension at their first emergency run. Adika thinking over his first impressions of Lucas in action as a Tactical Commander, and grudgingly admitting the clown might actually be good at his job. Anxious hasties shaken by the unaccustomed sight of blood.

I reached further out to the minds of relaxed people in apartments. So many, many minds. I could feel myself shaking with panic. I had no idea what I was doing. I'd never touched a genuine target mind. I didn't know how I'd recognize one.

Arms were round me, lifting me and carrying me bodily. I ignored them. The standard procedure was for the Strike team to place their telepath in the most easily guarded location possible. I was on the floor now, with what felt like a wall behind me. I was still seeing perfectly normal minds. Someone was in the shower. Someone was eating breakfast. Someone was...

... *hiding in the dark, panting, frightened...*

"About four cors north," I said.

Adika's voice was giving directions to the Chase team. They were moving out, while the Bodyguard team stayed with me, but I felt something was wrong.

"I'm not sure I've got the... It's not the target, it's a victim. A girl. She's hiding. She's afraid of someone. She's afraid of her brother. Her mother left to work early shift as usual, then her brother arrived at the apartment. He was acting oddly. He hit her. She's hiding in a cupboard. I think she's been there some time."

"He must have gone to the apartment before he came to the shopping area," said Lucas.

"Chase team, pull back," ordered Adika.

"Can you get a name for the girl, Amber?" asked Lucas.

"She's very young. She's alone in the apartment. Her father doesn't live there. Why do people never think of their own name? No, wait, she's remembering her brother yelling it at her. Jade. The girl's name is Jade."

"All right, Amber, try searching for the target again," said Lucas.

I left the frightened girl and searched again. I was searching for one mind among a hundred million. One mind that didn't seem right.

"Girl identified as Jade 2524-1873-966," said Nicole. "Target is Callum, Jade's brother, aged sixteen. We've found a report of an argument last week between Callum and the stabbed boy, Samuel. Apparently Samuel had started dating Callum's ex-girlfriend, Willow. We've dispatched Security teams to guard both Jade and Willow."

"Locate and guard any close family members of both Willow and Samuel as well," said Lucas. "Callum must have either chased or lured Samuel to that shopping area. He'll probably head back to Teen Level to find Willow now, but if he can't get to her then he may go for a secondary target."

"Getting my team on that now," said Nicole.

My questing thoughts found a mind that was a different colour, a different brightness, a different texture from the ones around it. I touched it, felt the heady mix of fury and delight, and lifted my red and sticky hand to let my nose savour the rich tang of Samuel's blood.

Samuel got what he deserved for stealing my...

I was deep in the target mind, but I remembered my training sessions and managed to keep speaking. "Target located. He's five cors east, waiting for a lift."

The lift doors opened. I hurried inside, leaned my back against the coolness of the metal walls, and felt the muscles of my face stretch into a triumphant smile.

"Target is inside the lift and heading up."

"Probable destination is Willow's room on Teen Level," said Lucas. "Is she guarded yet?"

"She's not in her room!" The voice of Nicole was shrill with alarm. "Her dataview's there, but she isn't."

I was being carried, but I was still concentrating on that sharp, feral mind. There was the sensation of being in a lift, both in real life and through the mental link.

"Target's lift doors are opening," I said.

... the blue of hasties' uniforms. Back in the lift! Get back in the lift! Go home to Level 100. Hide.

"Callum saw the hasties, he's back in the lift, going down to Level 100."

"Excellent!" Adika's voice rejoiced. I felt the breath of the word against my face. He must be carrying me himself.

"There's only one maintenance team in that area of Level 100," said Nicole. "Pulling them out now." A pause. "They're in a lift, heading up. You should have a clear run."

... stay calm, stay calm. The hasties must have been going to Samuel's room. There wasn't a nosy near the lift, so they can't know I was there or that I'm going home.

"Callum keeps thinking about going home to Level 100," I reported. "That makes no sense. Callum is sixteen, so he must live on Teen Level."

"He's got a hiding place on Level 100," said Lucas. "A nest. He's used it often. Be careful when you reach Level 100, because he'll know the area really well."

"He's still going down in the lift. He's not sure whether the hasties were looking for him or not. Better play safe and hide." I gave the running commentary on my target's thoughts, as I felt myself being passed from one set of arms to another.

"Bodyguard team stay in the lift with Amber," said Adika. "Chase team be ready to move."

"Callum's out of the lift now," I said. "Running north down a corridor. Going past a network of pipes." Part of me felt our own lift stop. Part of me was with the target. "He's undoing a plate on the wall. He's on the same level as us, and five cors east, one north, past the pipes. He's in a tube now. A big tube, curved under his knees, small enough he has to crawl rather than walk. There's a fan on the left, a very big fan."

"Is that a fan, Amber, or blades?" asked Adika.

"He didn't look at it directly. He didn't think about it. Could be either."

"I think he's in the waste system," said Adika. "Still level with us?"

"Still level," I said. "Still moving north."

Adika gave rapid instructions to the various groups of the Chase team.

"He's reached a chamber, about the size of a freight lift," I said. "It's a sort of crossway. There are pipes coming in from four sides, but at different heights. He's entered through one of them. The place is cluttered with stuff. Bits of metal. Clothes. Boxes."

"That's his nest," said Lucas. "He'll stay there for a while."

"I'm positioning men to enter from all four sides," said Adika.

"Position them but don't go in yet," ordered Lucas. "Will he hear them coming, Amber?"

"It's noisy here because of that big fan thing."

There was a pause while Adika got the Chase team in place. "We're ready now."

"Nicole, any sign of Willow yet?" asked Lucas.

"We still can't locate her," said Nicole.

"Waste that!" said Lucas. "Amber, what can you see? What's Callum doing?"

"He's sharpening a knife," I said. "He finds it relaxing. He's looking down at the blade now. Big curved blade. I think it's home made."

"I hope no one was fool enough to forget their body armour," said Adika.

"I just saw Willow!" I yelled. "She's in there with him. Tied up and gagged. Her eyes are open. She's alive."

"Lucas?" asked Adika, the single word screaming impatience.

"Wait," said Lucas. "Callum's got the knife in his hand. If he hears you coming, the girl's dead. Check your guns are on stun and be ready on my command. Amber, is he planning to kill Willow?"

"No," I said. "She dumped him for someone else. He's planning to keep her his prisoner now. They've got food supplies, and he's tapped into a water pipe, so they can stay there a long time. Callum's putting down the knife now. Walking over to Willow. Kneeling down and smoothing her hair out of her eyes."

I looked down into the eyes of my prisoner and smiled at her. She would never leave me again.

"Strike time!" said Lucas.

"Going circuit." I dumped the target mind, and swapped to

checking my team, touching each of their thoughts in turn. "Adika, Forge, Dhiren, Rothan, ..."

"Target down," said Adika. "We stunned him. The girl seems uninjured but terrified."

"Hasties and a medical team are on the way," said Nicole.

I finished my circuit to make sure all the Strike team were safe, and then checked Willow. "Ugh."

"All right, Amber?" asked Adika.

"Yes, but I checked Willow's mind and..."

"Get out of her head, Amber!" ordered Lucas. "Try to forget whatever you saw. Willow probably won't remember it herself after today. The medical staff won't just treat her injuries, but wipe any traumatic memories to help her recovery."

"Nice job, everyone," said Adika. "You've successfully completed your first emergency run."

CHAPTER SIXTEEN

I went back to my apartment and tried to get back to sleep but couldn't. I felt strange, numb, shaky. In the end, I gave up, rolled out of the sleep field, dressed in luxury clothes, drank luxury drinks, ate luxury foods, and then wandered round my luxury accommodation.

My unit was in the mandatory twenty-four hour recovery time after an emergency run. We were all supposed to relax and unwind, but I was failing miserably. I'd just been faced with the reality of my new life. That chaotic emergency run was why I lived in this luxury, why everyone pandered to my whims, and why I was notionally in charge of this unit. It was all to bribe the freak, mutant girl into being carried round like a piece of luggage, eyes closed and mind sharing the thoughts of someone on a killing frenzy.

And I'd done what the Hive wanted me to do. We'd hunted our wild bee, and we'd caught him. I'd been worried that I wouldn't be able to do my job, but I'd succeeded. I'd saved a girl's life, so why did I feel so odd? Why was I trembling?

The comms system chimed. "Amber," said Lucas's voice. "I'm outside your front door. Can I come in?"

I didn't want to see anyone, not even Lucas. I replied over the comms system. "I was planning to catch up on my sleep now, so maybe another time."

"I've nothing else to do, so I'll just sit out here."

I checked the security images from outside my door. Lucas

was sitting on the floor, arms folded, leaning against the corridor wall.

I wandered round my apartment for fifteen minutes, before checking the security images again. Lucas was still sitting there.

I did one more lap of my apartment, cursed all Tactical Commanders, and then told my front door to open. The security images showed Lucas bouncing up to his feet and coming inside. I didn't go to meet him. This was his idea not mine, so I lay on a couch, eyes closed, and let him come and find me.

"Hello, Amber."

I heard the sound of a chair moving. Lucas would be sitting down, facing me, studying me.

"You're not reading me." His words were a statement, not a question. "How are you feeling?"

"I feel I want to be left alone. Go away."

He laughed, which made me open my eyes and turn my head to glare at him.

"I can't go away." Lucas smiled maddeningly at me. "Leaving you alone to brood too long is a bad idea. Someone had to come and talk to you. Normally, it would be Megan, but she and Adika decided to send me."

"I'll fire the lot of you," I threatened without conviction.

He ignored that. "Stunned, dazed, numb. Reduced energy level. Reluctance to discuss the event. Wishing to avoid the people involved in it. Sound familiar?"

I didn't answer.

"It's after the crisis that's most difficult," he said. "When the danger's over, and you come down from your adrenaline high. The first time is always the worst. Lottery selects the Strike team for their job because they have the right personality for it. If you threw that lot at a wall, then they'd bounce right back at you. It's the rest of us that suffer badly from reaction."

He waited for me to speak, but I didn't.

"People on Teen Level could have died," said Lucas, "but the hasties were there ahead of the target. The girl hostage could have died, but we knew exactly when to send in the Strike team. You made the difference, Amber. Focus on that. You saved lives today."

I still didn't say a word.

Lucas sighed. "Reaction can hit people in a variety of ways. If you'd talk to me, I could help you a lot better."

I finally spoke. "I thought you could read my body language."

"Not well enough. You aren't just suffering from reaction like the rest of us. You've been tapping into the mind of a wild bee for the first time. That must be strange."

I made a peculiar noise, the offspring of a laugh and a sob. "You have no idea, Lucas. Absolutely no idea."

"Tell me. Please, Amber."

I tried to explain the unexplainable. "The first time I read Megan properly, below the pre-vocalization level, it was…"

I faltered, and Lucas tried to fill in the words for me. "A shock? Megan said you were deeply affected. She thought you'd still believed you were hearing words until then."

I lifted my head and stared at him.

"Megan was wrong?" he asked. "That wasn't the problem?"

"You don't know? Isn't it obvious? It was Megan's grief."

Lucas frowned.

"One minute, I was a bewildered, eighteen-year-old, desperately trying to do what the Hive wanted of me. The next, I was Megan, grieving for my husband and the children we'd never have now. Of course I was shocked, waste it! Megan hadn't warned me it would be like that."

Lucas was silent for a moment before replying. "You were Megan? You felt her emotions so strongly that you identified yourself as actually being her?"

"Yes. It hadn't been like that reading her pre-vocalized thoughts. The next couple of levels down were just words too, but when I reached the fourth and fifth levels all the emotion hit me."

"Fourth and fifth levels?"

"Thought levels," I explained. "They're multi-layered. How many levels changes depending on the person and their situation. Most people only have a maximum of five between pre-vocalization and the true subconscious, but I've seen you have as many as fifteen, and even your subconscious levels aren't as… amorphous as in other people. I don't mess around in the subconscious very much. The feelings run wild down there. Not just the sexual ones, but other emotions too."

"You go right down to the subconscious?" Lucas was leaning forward, dark eyes wide with excitement. "Keith barely gets the level below pre-vocalization. The other true telepaths can go deeper. I've been told Sapphire can reach three full levels below pre-vocalization, but nothing approaching your description. None of the other true telepaths experience emotions in the way that you're describing either."

I stared at him. "They don't? Do they feel pain?"

Lucas nodded. "I suppose pain screams at all levels of the mind. Can you read me now? Tell me what's happening on the different levels of my mind?"

"I'm not in the mood to read people."

He instantly reined in his eagerness. "Apologies. Self indulgent curiosity. Important issue..."

He broke off. "Apologies again. I should use all the words. The important issue is that you read minds at much deeper levels than the other telepaths, so you encounter emotions. Query. You aren't mourning for Dean now?"

I shook my head. "The grief wore off after a few hours, but the effect of having felt it... It's hard to find words to explain it."

"Feeling that way was a learning experience?"

I grimaced. "Yes."

"Do you feel that way every time you read Megan?"

"No. I try to avoid going into the deeper levels of her mind. It happens by mistake sometimes. Either I'm careless and drift downwards, or the thought level I'm on suddenly merges with a deeper one. The grief flares up then, but I try to distance myself from it."

"How do you do that?"

I waved my hands helplessly. "It's hard to explain. It's like pulling down my mental curtain to block the telepathy, except this curtain is only made of net. I can still see Megan's thoughts and emotions, but they're a lot fainter."

"So, you haven't really felt you were Megan, experienced her emotions as your own, since that first time. What about with other people? What was it like the first time you read me?"

I managed a smile as I remembered that moment. "You were filled with wild, nervous excitement. I was catching those emotions too, but I never identified as being you. I was constantly reminded I was just an observer, because I couldn't keep up with the speed of the thoughts I was reading."

Lucas smiled. "I had a lot to think about on that day. How about with other people? Has the distancing, the blocking, helped?"

"Mostly, but when there's something unexpected, like..." I broke off.

"Yes?" prompted Lucas.

I was thinking of the first time I'd been in Adika's head when he looked at Megan. I chose my words carefully. "Being in a male head when the man catches sight of a woman is occasionally difficult."

Lucas blinked and suddenly grinned. "Male sexual response?"

I nodded. "The emotions jump up a level or two, and can catch me off guard. Feeling that way about someone you wouldn't normally be attracted to is..."

"Disconcerting."

"Extremely. The first time I hit same sex attraction was less confusing. Probably because I didn't meet that until after I'd worked out the distancing technique."

Lucas hesitated. "Please don't answer if you don't wish to, but query. Situation when girl is you?"

"Oddly enough that's much easier. The girl is me, which reminds me the emotions aren't mine, it's just..." I waved my hands in that helpless gesture again. "I get a different view."

"The topic raises numerous questions," said Lucas, "most importantly about this morning's events. Reading a wild bee was disturbing?"

I pulled a face. "Yes."

"You appeared to cope well. You kept giving us information."

"All the training I'd done made that automatic," I said. "I kept saying where Callum was, what he saw, what he was planning to do, just like when we were training, but the emotions were... And it's even worse remembering them."

Lucas tentatively took my hand. "Remembering the emotions now is worse than feeling them this morning?"

"Yes. When I felt them, I was in the target's head and they seemed natural. Now I think of them and…" I shuddered.

"Tell me. Please. They weren't your emotions, Amber. There's no reason you should feel embarrassed or ashamed of what a wild bee was feeling."

"The first time I read him there was fury," I said reluctantly, "but that was fading. He'd stabbed the other boy for stealing his girlfriend, and felt in control and powerful. He was rejoicing about what he'd done, there was blood on his hand and… Oh Lucas, he was smelling the blood!"

I was crying. Ridiculous of me. I used the back of my hand to rub away the wetness from my cheeks. "He was the one feeling those things, doing those things, Lucas, but I felt like it was me. The way he thought about the girl… That was me too."

I paused. "You said that the medical staff might wipe Willow's memories of what happened?"

"Yes," said Lucas. "If they judged her memories would cause long lasting trauma, they'd remove them."

I wasn't sure how I felt about that. "I suppose that would save her a lot of suffering, but it seems wrong to play around with someone's memory."

"Almost everyone in this Hive has information imprinted on their minds, Amber. Does that worry you?"

"Of course not," I said. "Imprinting extra knowledge is very different from taking away someone's personal memories."

"Editing out traumatic memories is a process that mimics one of the human mind's natural defences. In some cases, a person's mind can block out an unbearable event, resulting in a temporary or permanent memory gap. The mind can even add an extra level of defence by entering a temporary fugue state, where it shelters behind a new personality until it's ready to cope with what's happened."

It sounded as if Lucas was quoting from his imprinted data. Normally, I'd have read his mind to help me make sense of his words. I didn't want to read him now. I'd got an approximate understanding of what he was saying, enough to tell me that I didn't like it.

"There's a crucial difference between someone deciding to edit out their own memories, and a doctor deciding to do it for them," I said.

Lucas frowned. "But even when it happens naturally, the person doesn't make a decision about it. The defence mechanism happens on a subconscious level."

"The person is still making their own decision," I said. "The subconscious is as much a part of someone as their conscious mind. Trust me on that, Lucas. I've seen all the levels of your mind, and in all of them, right down into the deepest sub-conscious, you are still Lucas."

He seemed disconcerted. "I can never know minds the way you do, Amber. I don't know much about how the decision to intervene and remove a memory is made either. My job stops when a target is apprehended. Victim trauma treatment and forensic psychology are specialist roles outside my area, usually filled by borderline telepaths."

I was thinking that might make the situation more acceptable, at least it would if the borderline telepath could pick up something of the person's wishes, but then a horrible thought occurred to me. "If my memories of that emergency run gave me problems, would medical staff want to remove them?"

Lucas looked shocked by the idea. "No one would dare to interfere with a telepath's mind. Removing your memories would be even more dangerous than imprinting you. There's no point in removing memories of an emergency run from Telepath Unit members anyway. They'll be replaced by memories of another within days or weeks. We have to learn to cope with our encounters with wild bees."

Both relieved and disappointed, I returned to my original point. "I could cope with remembering the target's triumphant pleasure, Lucas. The problem is remembering my own."

"Those weren't your emotions," said Lucas. "It was the first time you'd met the emotions of a wild bee, and they took you off guard and swamped you. Another time, you'll be prepared and able to distance yourself. The first time you felt Adika lusting after Megan was a shock, but you distance yourself successfully from that now, don't you?"

I gave him a startled look. When I mentioned that example to Lucas, I'd been careful not to mention Adika's name.

Lucas smiled. "I don't read minds, Amber, but I do read body language. Adika's attraction to Megan is blindingly obvious."

"Oh. Well, yes, I'm ready for it now so I can keep a distance."

"It should be the same for the wild bees. The distancing may not work perfectly straight away, and there may be future new emotions that catch you by surprise, but as you gain experience you'll also gain control and separation."

"You're sure? I'm scared that I've caught something from Callum's mind. I've tried testing myself, thinking of things that make me angry, and I feel violent."

"Everybody has things that make them feel angry and violent," said Lucas. "You could equally well claim to have gained violent tendencies from reading your Strike team as from reading your target this morning. They're all as capable of attacking or killing people as him."

"No, they aren't!" I said sharply.

"Yes, they are," said Lucas. "Your Strike team members were selected for their work because they have a potential for violence. They could, in the wrong circumstances, have been triggered into becoming wild bees themselves. Instead, their violence has been controlled and channelled into a role that's needed by the Hive. If necessary they'll kill, either to defend you, or to protect vulnerable members of the Hive from wild bees."

I knew the Strike team carried guns that had both stun and lethal settings. I knew all their training included the possibility of the team being given the kill order. I couldn't take the idea seriously though. Before Lottery, the only violence I'd ever known was the occasional fight between children. Now I believed that wild bees might kill people, but my Strike team wouldn't.

"I don't believe that."

"It's a fact, Amber. Statistics say that almost all Strike team members will kill a target one day."

I shook my head. "I suppose Adika might do that if he had no choice, but I can't imagine Eli killing anyone."

"Adika has killed multiple times already, and Eli will too if necessary."

I blinked. "I didn't know that Adika had killed anyone. I've never seen that in his thoughts."

"You wouldn't," said Lucas. "Adika doesn't agonize over it. Strike team personnel are carefully selected and trained for their work. They do what needs to be done, and then happily carry on with their lives. Problems only arise if a bystander dies and the Strike team feel responsible because of something they did or didn't do."

He pulled a face. "That's when they get tortured by regrets and need help. The extreme case of that would be if something happened to you. If you got even the slightest injury, Amber, it would have a devastating effect on your Strike team. They would have failed to protect you. They would have failed their Hive."

I sat there in silence, worrying about a confused tangle of different things. Getting injured wasn't one of them. Adika would never let anything happen to me.

Lucas watched me for a while before speaking again. "Hunting wild bees will change you, Amber, but not because you catch their violent tendencies. All experiences change people. You've already done things, experienced things, which you'd never even dreamed about before Lottery. You've grown and developed because of them."

"You really think so?"

"Yes. I can see it even if you can't." He paused. "Megan, Adika and I, all think Nicole did well during that run. What do you think?"

"I agree."

"How do you feel about making her permanent Liaison leader? She's suffering badly from reaction. Confirming her in the team leader position now would be good for her confidence, and help to snap her out of the reaction phase."

I felt guilty. Nicole had had so much thrown at her and done brilliantly, but I hadn't spared her a single thought. I rolled off the couch, ran my fingers through my hair, and called her. The holo of Nicole appeared, sitting in an ordinary cushioned chair rather than her powered one, looking tired and strained.

"Nicole, you did a fantastic job this morning. Forget the acting team leader role; you're Liaison permanent team leader now."

Her face lit up. "That's incredible!"

I managed a couple more enthusiastic sentences, then ended the call and slumped on the couch again.

Lucas leaned back in his chair. "Poor Nicole. Thrown into an emergency run on her first day as Liaison team leader."

"How did we end up doing an emergency run anyway? We were supposed to still be in training."

He groaned. "That was my fault. The other Telepath Units couldn't take the emergency. Their Tactical Commanders knew our unit was nearly operational, so they called me and asked if we could help. I hated throwing that emergency at unprepared people, especially you, but what choice did I have? If our unit didn't respond, the hasties would have to handle it alone, and by the time they identified the target..."

He broke off. "Sorry. I'm babbling. That's the way reaction hits me."

I frowned. "It bothers you too then?"

"Yes." Lucas rubbed his forehead. "I didn't expect it to be this bad, but previously I've just been sitting with the others in the Tactical office, feeding suggestions to my team leader. Today I was the Tactical Commander, making a snap decision on whether to rush us into an operational run or leave an unknown number of people to die."

"You sounded so calm."

"A Tactical Commander has to appear totally calm and relaxed. How can other people trust his guidance if he doesn't sound confident himself? Underneath though, I was horribly aware I was sending people in before they'd finished training. Any injuries would be my fault. Any deaths would be on my conscience."

"I'm surprised. I thought you..."

He interrupted me with an impatient wave of his hand. "You've walked through my mind, Amber. You must know I'm human."

I felt guilty again. I'd been selfishly focused on my own problems, but that emergency run had been hard on Nicole. It had been hard on Lucas. It would have been hard on others too. "How are Adika and the Strike team coping?"

Lucas smiled. "It was the Strike team's first ever run, so they were a little shaken afterwards, but as I said earlier, Strike team bounce. Adika lectured them about a dozen things they could have done better, but finished by saying they did quite well for a bunch of clueless greenies. That's high praise by his standards, so they went off feeling far too exuberant to suffer from nerves."

"Adika gave the poor things a lecture! Why? They did amazingly well."

"Adika has no mercy on his Strike team. Anything short of perfection must be improved, because mistakes could get them killed. I got lectured too."

"You did?"

"After Adika finished with the Strike team, he turned on me. He said a few choice words about me sending them on a genuine emergency run, and made some eye watering suggestions about what he could do to me in revenge. The Strike team really enjoyed listening to him."

I laughed.

Lucas changed the subject. "Let's forget all about emergency runs and wild bees now. How about a relaxing game of chess? You can read my mind and beat me."

"I'm not in the mood to read minds."

"You don't have to read me," he teased, "but you know I'll win if you don't."

We played chess. Lucas didn't so much win as completely slaughter me. After the third massacre, exhaustion hit me. I'd totally lost track of time, and was shocked to discover it was almost midnight.

"I must get to sleep."

Lucas nodded. "I think we should do a standard check run tomorrow."

I tensed.

"You're worried about reading the mind of a wild bee again," he continued. "The best way to reassure you is by doing a nice, peaceful check run. We'll have a little stroll round one of our suspect areas, and you can track down the wild bee without any pressure. There's an area with a simple firebug developing. They've only scorched a few walls so far, but we need to get them treatment before anyone gets hurt. How about scheduling the check run for eleven tomorrow morning?"

I wanted to argue, demand a delay, but I was bone tired and desperate to be left alone. "If that's what you want."

I stood up, and waited for Lucas to move. He didn't.

"I'm going to bed," I said pointedly.

"I'm tired too," said Lucas. "I'll camp in your spare room if that's all right."

I'd had plenty of chances to read the details of what happened to Olivia and York in the minds of people around me. I'd shied away from doing that, because I didn't want to know when and how the strain had got too much for them, but now one fact was obvious. Either Olivia or York had been broken by the stress of their first emergency run. That was why Lucas had pushed his way into my apartment, and why he wanted to stay in my spare room. He was scared what might happen to me if I was left alone.

"I'll be all right, Lucas," I said.

He gave me an unconvincing imitation of his usual light-hearted grin. "But I'm really, really tired, Amber. Don't you have a spare room?"

If I forced him into leaving, he'd probably spend the whole night sitting outside my front door, worrying about me. Waste it, if I forced Lucas into leaving, then Megan would arrive and insist on spending the night here. I gave in.

"There's a spare room or six around somewhere. I have everything in this apartment. I wouldn't be surprised to open a door and find my own beach."

"I don't think Megan could manage a full size beach, but she'd arrange a miniature version if you asked nicely." Lucas paused for a moment. "Promise to call me if you need anything."

I sighed. "I promise."

I went into my bedroom, shut the door, peeled off my clothes, and dumped them on the floor. This morning's clothes were still scattered there as well. I'd been barricaded in my apartment all day, so Hannah had had no chance to sneak in and clear up my mess.

I turned on the sleep field, flopped onto it with relief, and then cursed and rolled out again. I stirred the clothes on the floor with one foot, uncovered the thin smooth mesh of my body armour, picked it up and tossed it on a chair. I'd need that for tomorrow's run. If tomorrow's run didn't turn out to be me running away. I didn't think I could face reading another wild bee.

I collapsed back onto the warm air of the sleep field again. I couldn't run away. The security system would notify Adika if I went into a lift, and I'd have the entire Strike team after me.

Jets of air caressed me, turning me gently as I floated in mid air. I wondered if Lucas was asleep, or if he'd stay awake all night watching over me. Megan should have been the one talking to me today, but Adika and Megan had ganged up on Lucas to send him instead. They both knew that whatever Lottery said about my physical preferences in men, I was attracted to Lucas.

Of course I was attracted to Lucas. Physical appearances only mattered when you looked with your eyes. I was a telepath, and when I saw Lucas's mind...

I slept, lost deep in blackness without dreams.

CHAPTER SEVENTEEN

There was a knocking sound and a voice calling me. "Amber?"

It was Lucas's voice. Telling him to go away wouldn't work. He'd just stubbornly sit outside my apartment until I opened the front door.

I groaned. "Come in."

The door opened. "Are you ready to go and... Oops."

I forced myself awake, and opened my eyes in time to see my bedroom door close. "Oops," I echoed, and hastily left the sleep field. "I'm getting ready!" I yelled.

"Clothes are good," Lucas called back through the closed door. "Or not. Depends what you have in mind. Your call."

I checked the time. Waste it, it was nearly eleven! I showered and dressed at express speed, then realized I'd forgotten to put on the lightweight mesh of the body armour under my clothes. I stripped off, dressed again correctly, grabbed my crystal unit from its shelf, shot out of my room, and found Lucas leaning casually against the wall.

"Sorry about that," I said, in what I hoped was a dignified voice. "I was dreaming that you were outside the apartment, so I said to come in."

He grinned. "A psychologist could have a lot of fun with the symbolism of that one."

"Aren't you a psychologist?"

"Partly. My imprint information covers behavioural analysis, tactical information, basic Lottery evaluation, imprinting techniques, and certain areas of psychology. That sounds a lot, but there's a huge amount of common data between the areas, so it condenses down well."

He paused. "Do you want any breakfast before we head out? There's no desperate rush. Adika can always take the Strike team on a few laps of the park while they're waiting."

I'd been distracted by my embarrassment, but now the cold realization hit me. I had to go and hunt another wild bee. I had to read another mind that was torn with alien emotions. I could refuse, but if I refused this time then the next time would be even harder.

"I'm not hungry."

"We'll stop off for something to eat while we're out then," said Lucas.

I stared at him in silent disbelief.

He smiled. "I told you that check runs are much more peaceful. There's bound to be somewhere serving food in the area."

We went out of my apartment and headed for lift 2. Lucas was obviously going to escort me every inch of the way. If I turned round to look behind me, I'd probably see Hannah sprinting into my apartment to clean up. I might as well be in nappies.

Adika and the Strike team were waiting for me in the lift. Adika exchanged rapid glances with Lucas, and didn't seem to like what was communicated to him. Did they have a pre-arranged signal, so Lucas could tell Adika that their telepath was still refusing to read even him?

I put my crystal unit in my ear and went into the lift. When I turned round, I suffered a moment of pure shock. Lucas was in the lift too!

"Strike team is moving," said Adika.

"Tactical ready," responded a female voice in my ear crystal. That was Emili, deputy leader of the Tactical team.

"Liaison ready," said Nicole's voice. "Tracking is..."

"Hold it!" I interrupted. The lift doors had closed but I opened them again. "Why is Lucas with us?"

"I haven't been shopping in ages," said Lucas. "This is my big chance to buy new socks."

I turned to Adika. "I need a private word. Now!"

He followed me out of the lift. I moved us far enough away to be out of ear shot, and we turned off our crystal units. "You can't put Lucas at risk just to babysit me. He's not trained for this."

"I wouldn't want to take Lucas on an emergency run," said Adika, "but routine check runs are totally different. All the research and analysis has been done in advance, so we know exactly what we'll be facing. It's standard practice to bring a member of the Tactical team along to talk us through the situation."

"But what if something unexpected happens? What if it turns out not to be so routine after all?"

"In that case, Lucas knows he's to keep out of trouble and stick with you and the bodyguards. He may be Tactical not Strike team, but he's an excellent shot with a gun and can move fast."

I frowned in frustration. I could insist that Lucas was kept safely back in the unit, but overruling his decisions, dictating how he lived his life and did his work, would wreck any chance of a relationship between us.

"Lucas has already been out on dozens of routine check runs with Keith," added Adika, in a soothing voice. "Lucas isn't a liability, he won't slow us down, and I won't let him get hurt. I know it can be worrying when someone you care about is..."

I turned, stalked back into the lift, and turned my ear crystal back on.

Adika followed me, and closed the lift doors behind us. "Tracking active, Nicole?"

"Tracking status green for all Strike team," she said.

"Amber?"

I checked my dataview and saw Lucas was listed with my Bodyguard team. "Green," I said.

"Everyone, check any bruises are well covered with make-up," said Adika. "Crystal units kept on audio only for this run. You're supposed to be innocent shoppers, blending into the crowd."

I glanced round at the faces of the Strike team, and got a shock when I saw Forge. The whole of his left cheek had been covered with a skin-toned protective plaster since he cut his face open. Now the plaster was gone, the cut beneath had healed, but...

"What happened to your birthmark, Forge?" I asked.

He flushed. "Medical had to do a bit of reconstructive work after that branch ripped my cheek open, so I asked them to get rid of the birthmark at the same time."

"Did you feel it was spoiling your good looks?" asked Adika.

There was a burst of laughter from the rest of the Strike team, and the colour in Forge's cheeks darkened. "No, but an old girlfriend used to suggest I should get it removed, and this seemed the obvious time to do it."

"That reminds me of something," said Adika. "I heard the unit's new mural painter arrived last night. Is she moving in with you, Matias?"

Matias was the one looking embarrassed now. "Sofia will be living in her own apartment. She wants to settle into the unit before taking any important steps in our relationship."

Adika's face twisted in a dubious expression. "Well, I hope it works out for you."

There was silence until the lift doors opened on Level 24. We joined the random crowd of people travelling on the express belt. My bodyguards were split ahead and behind me, while Lucas cheerfully stood beside me and took my arm. The rest of the Strike team were standing in groups of two and three, chatting to each other, trying to look like casual travellers.

Adika's voice in my ear crystal warned me that we were approaching the scene. Ahead of us was a crowded shopping area.

"Chase team, detached contact," said Adika. "Keep Amber and Lucas in sight at all times, but mix in with the crowds. Bodyguard team, stay close to Amber. Brief us on the situation here, Lucas."

"The first incident was behind this shoe shop." A passerby would think Lucas was talking in a low, confidential voice to the girl on his arm, but his words were going out to the whole team.

I glanced at the shoe shop. Its boundaries were defined by

thin plastic partitions. There was a narrow gap between the back of the shop and a structural wall.

"There was some rubbish behind the shop," said Lucas. "It was set on fire, the sprinkler system put it out quickly, and nothing was damaged. It would have been possible, but difficult, for an adult to squeeze in there. We think we're looking for a child."

Lucas showed us two more spots in the shopping area, all in places blocked from public view. "There were three more incidents in the housing warren north of here, but we'd look a bit conspicuous if we all trek round to see where those happened. There were also two incidents in the park to the south, and one in the local community centre."

He led me to a group of seats in the centre of the shopping area. We sat together on one seat, a pair of bodyguards took the next one, and three others stood in a group nearby. The Chase team lurked around the neighbourhood. Adika was with Forge, apparently debating whether one of the jackets on a clothing stall would suit him. It wouldn't.

"The last incident was the worrying one," said Lucas. "Our firebug used an inflammable liquid, and the blaze was much worse than previous ones. That escalated the warning signs from strength two to strength three. The next progression is sabotaging the sprinkler system, which increases the risk of people getting hurt or killed. We're here to stop that happening. Over to you, Amber."

I couldn't dodge things any longer. I closed my eyes and sat there for a couple of minutes, alone in the darkness in my own head, just thinking. I wasn't sure why I was so reluctant to reach out to other minds. Yesterday had been frightening, it made sense that I didn't want to experience the thoughts of another wild bee, but why didn't I want to read Lucas? I liked reading Lucas. I loved the wild ride of swirling along with his thoughts.

And the answer was obvious. I didn't want to read any thoughts, because I didn't want to be a telepath. I wanted to be imprinted, to be like everyone else, so the part of me that hated nosies would leave me in peace, but that was never going to happen.

The situation was brutally simple. I was a telepath and I was urgently needed. I had to help the Hive mind get more stable, or the other Telepath Units would be overwhelmed by too many emergency runs. I had to stop thinking of myself, and think of a hundred million other people. They didn't know it, but they were depending on me to keep them safe.

I remembered the Hive Obligations and the Duty songs I'd learnt in school. The Hive was our world. We served it and it gave us everything we needed. Since Lottery, the Hive hadn't just given me everything I needed, but buried me in luxuries as well.

I had to do my duty in return. The first step was the hardest, so I made it as easy as possible for myself. I reached out to Lucas, and found his mind was layered with frantic, anxious thoughts.

... still not even reading me, and if she won't do that then...

... stupid gamble pushing her into this. Should have given her more time to...

It was going so well. Too well. Everyone has weaknesses and Amber...

... Telepath Unit with a telepath who won't read people is completely useless.

... blocked me along with the rest. Waste it, that hurts. I thought I was special to her.

... she was floating in mid air, with no clothes on. If I'd stayed...

I was six levels deep, and things were getting very personal. I pulled out rapidly, and then let my mind drift out among the people in the shopping area. Nothing, nothing, nothing. As I reached further out, something caught my attention.

Orange, bright, flickering. Coaxing the tiny fire into life, and the excitement building. Can't do it here. It's not safe here. Mum will be back soon. It'll be different when I have my own place. Next year on Teen Level, I'll be able...

"Target is north of us," I said. "Age twelve."

"Male or female?" asked Lucas.

With Lucas sitting right next to me, hearing him speak was enough to make me link back to his mind. Its normal glow had been dulled by anxiety, but now his thoughts flared out, shining dazzlingly bright with exhilaration and relief. I spent a moment basking in the warmth of his delight before forcing myself to concentrate on my job again.

"Target is male. Fires excite him. His name is Perry. He's at home now. Alone at the moment, but his mother is due back soon. I don't think he has any weapons."

"We have a location," said Nicole's voice through my ear crystal. "Five cors north, one west of you."

"Call for medical assistance," said Adika, "and tell them to wait for us at the end of the corridor. Four of us should be more than sufficient to deal with an unarmed twelve-year-old boy. Forge, Caleb, Rothan, come with me. The rest of you stay here."

Adika had drilled it into my head that seemingly simple situations could go horribly wrong. I dutifully ran circuits on the four minds until Adika announced the target was secured, then relaxed and turned to look at Lucas.

"What will the medical staff do with Perry?"

"Probably give him a little therapy to control his fascination with fires during his time on Teen Level. Once he reaches Lottery, he'll be allocated work that involves fire, and his obsession with it will become a useful asset."

I saw an image in Lucas's mind. A man watching a red-hot furnace, where a tangle of discarded metal objects were melting into glowing liquid.

I hesitated for a moment, and then switched off my ear crystal. Lucas raised his eyebrows, but turned his crystal off as well.

"Why are we having a secret conference?" he asked.

"I was just wondering what will happen to Callum."

Lucas shrugged. "A forensic psychologist will study his case, and assess ways of making him into a productive member of the Hive."

I waved my hands in despair. "No one can make Callum into a productive member of the Hive. He stabbed people."

"Callum seemed to believe his wishes were paramount, and he had the right to do anything he wanted to other people," said Lucas. "If that's a long term, deeply ingrained attitude, then treating him may be extremely difficult, however he escalated in behaviour very quickly. It's possible his attitude is a recent development, in which case it may be possible to reset him."

I'd no idea what Lucas meant by that, so I checked his thoughts and gasped in shock. "They'd take away Callum's memories of stabbing people, and send him back to live on Teen Level again!"

"It's much more complicated than that," said Lucas. "I only know the very basics about this, but they'd reset Callum's mind, unravelling his personal experience chain to take him back to the point where his ego problem either didn't exist or could be treated with appropriate medication and therapy. Once he's cured, he can..."

"Who decides he's cured?" I interrupted. "Who decides it's safe to let Callum live on Teen Level again, and what if they're wrong?"

"In a case this serious, either Sapphire or Morton would make that decision," said Lucas. "Eventually, you'll be assessing reset cases too. Patients have been known to fool even a borderline telepath psychologist into thinking they're cured and referring them for telepath assessment. No one can fool a true telepath though."

"Oh." I frowned as I thought that over. "I suppose that might work, but it doesn't seem right that there'd be no consequences for Callum at all. Not even guilt. He stabbed people, he could easily have killed someone, but he'd go back to live on Teen Level without even remembering what he'd done."

"It would be far more difficult to treat Callum if he remembered stabbing someone."

"But if the girl doesn't remember what Callum did either, he could end up dating her again."

"That wouldn't be allowed to happen," said Lucas. "Reset cases are always relocated to a distant area of the Hive, because close contact with someone involved in their past behaviour could trigger remaining fragments of memory."

He paused. "It's better to salvage someone than to waste them. Better for the person. Better for the Hive."

"I suppose so," I said doubtfully. I wasn't sure what I thought about this. I wasn't even sure what Lucas thought about it. How much of what he was saying were his own ideas, and how much came from his imprinted data?

Lucas was studying my expression. "Amber, the reason I don't worry too much about these things is because I know the Hive has no shortage of borderline telepath experts to treat people. The huge problem is it only has five true telepaths to catch wild bees before they hurt people. Yesterday, you saw what happens when we fail to do that. Today, you saw what happens when we succeed. It's better, isn't it?"

I nodded. "Far better."

"Our unit is operational now. If we focus on doing our jobs, and help the Hive get more stable, then there'll be fewer emergency runs. That's the real answer to your concern, Amber. We can make sure there are fewer cases like Callum and more like Perry. We can make sure no one needs their memories of traumatic events removing, by preventing those events from happening in the first place."

That definitely did make sense. "You're right."

Lucas switched on his ear crystal again. "I'm hungry."

I switched mine on as well. "I'm starving."

"The rest of us would like to eat too," said Adika's voice through my ear crystal.

Lucas jumped up. "There's a restaurant over there. After we've eaten, you can help me buy socks, Amber."

My new life was one where chasing knife-wielding wild bees intermingled with buying socks. Lucas grabbed my hand, pulled me to my feet, and towed me into the restaurant. As we sat down at a table, groups of Strike team members strolled in to join us.

A smiling girl arrived and handed us menu cards, before hurrying to deal with her sudden rush of muscled, black-haired, male customers.

Lucas studied the menu. "I'm afraid they don't have melon juice here."

"I can survive on other drinks." I remembered something. "Eight levels."

"What?"

"Your head currently has eight levels between pre-vocalization and the subconscious."

"You're reading me again?" He grinned. "Speeds discussion. Level content?"

"The level seven content is totally unsuitable for an open sound link. Level eight... I'm not even going to hint at level eight."

"Lucas has a filthy mind?" asked Adika's amused voice in my ear crystal. "I'm profoundly shocked to hear that."

"His mind is a slime vat that needs scrubbing out with disinfectant," I said.

Lucas laughed.

CHAPTER EIGHTEEN

I stood outside the gym, furtively watching Sofia work on her latest mural. She'd painted several dazzling flower designs in the accommodation area of the unit. Those had been scanned into the Hive records, to be copied by other mural painters or even traded to other Hives. This mural was totally different, a wickedly accurate caricature of Adika scolding a cowering Strike team.

Sofia took a step back to scowl fiercely at her painting, finally noticed I was there, and waved an impatient paintbrush at me. "Go away!"

I hastily retreated in the direction of the park. Sofia didn't like people watching her working, and had a habit of blobbing paint on people who didn't leave fast enough when ordered, whether they were lowly office cleaners or illustrious telepaths.

Once inside the park, I walked along the path by the stream, listening to the soothing sound of the water while enjoying the warmth of the suns overhead. Our unit had been fully operational for three weeks now, and it felt like three months or three years. We'd done a dozen relaxed check runs, and handled seven tense emergencies.

The old voice of self-loathing that lurked in the corner of my mind hadn't vanished entirely, but it was far quieter now. When I learned I was a true telepath, I'd naively set out strict rules for my future behaviour. I'd broken all those rules by now because they were impossible to keep, but I'd saved over twenty lives already, and I knew I would save many more in future. That had earned me some grudging self acceptance.

The shadows of Olivia and York disturbed me less often too. I thought I'd made it past the main danger points for a new telepath, and the pressure on me and the other telepaths should gradually ease in future. With my unit fully operational and helping the others, there were already signs that the Hive mind's downward spiral into chaos had been reversed.

I just had a couple of minor worries now. It was much harder to arrange for my parents to visit me now that my unit was operational. If they witnessed me heading off on an emergency run, the cover story of me heading a research unit would fall apart. I had to settle for arranging last minute visits during the mandatory twenty-four hour recovery time after an emergency run. I'd blamed the problem on the demands of my mysterious research work, explaining to my parents that I only had free time when a long experiment was running, and so far they'd accepted that without asking too many questions.

The other concern was Forge. The weird effect he'd had on me in the past had vanished without trace. It must have been an ordinary teen crush after all, and had faded away because of my developing relationship with Lucas. Now I wanted to tell everyone that I'd known Forge on Teen Level, but Forge was still nervous of pointing fingers and accusations of favouritism. He wanted to be sure he'd proved himself, to Adika as well as his team mates, before we told them the truth. I hoped Forge wouldn't insist on us waiting for much longer. I didn't feel comfortable hiding things from Lucas.

I sat down on the grass by the stream's edge, and closed my eyes to think of Lucas. It was a couple of months now since he'd walked into that room in Hive Futura, and I'd first seen his amazing mind. Since then, he'd let me roam freely inside his head, and I knew him better than I'd ever known anyone in my life. Lucas had thrown open the door to the apartment of his mind, and told me to explore wherever I liked.

He'd shown me all his memories, good or bad. He'd applied the logic that he was no saint, but no especial sinner either. There was nothing there that was worse than I'd see in any number of other minds, and he trusted me not to judge him harshly. He'd accidentally walked into my bedroom, seen me naked, and the discarded clothes littering the floor. I'd seen much more intimate things about him.

I was a private, defensive person, and the sheer openness of Lucas stunned me even more than his brilliance. He'd told me that he had no secrets and he truly meant it. His feelings for me weren't just constantly in his thoughts for me to read, he was advertising them to the amused audience of the entire unit. I didn't understand how he could put himself at risk of laughter and ridicule like that.

Lucas had been totally and utterly honest with me, and if he found out I...

A warbling sound filled the air and a computerized voice spoke. "Unit emergency alert. Unit emergency alert. We have an incident in progress. Operational teams to stations. Strike team to lift 2."

I jumped to my feet and sprinted for my apartment. Once inside, I left a trail of garments on my way to the bedroom, grabbed the body armour and the set of clothes that Hannah had hung with it, dressed, and snatched my crystal unit from its place on a shelf before running for the lift. When I arrived there, I found the entire Strike team were already inside, including the two who were officially on down time today.

I put my ear crystal in place, and heard the familiar routine start up as the doors closed and the lift headed downwards.

"Strike team is moving," said Adika.

Lucas's voice spoke in my ear crystal. "Tactical ready." He was safely in the office with the rest of the Tactical team.

"Liaison ready. Tracking status green." Nicole sounded tense but calm. She'd settled in well as Liaison team leader.

I checked my dataview. All the Strike team were on my circuit list, including the two who'd chosen to come along with us rather than go shopping or visit family. "Green here too."

Lucas started briefing us. "We have an emergency call about an incident, definitely strength four, potentially six or higher."

I was already tense, but my nerves stretched tighter. Strength six was a death. What was worse than dead people?

"A child is missing," Lucas said. "A girl aged three."

How could you lose a three-year-old? Children were tagged with unbreakable tracking bracelets until they were ten, so parents could always check up on their location. Having your bracelet removed was one of the significant stages in growing up. You got increased privacy, new rights, and the responsibilities that went with them.

"The girl's bracelet is no longer functioning."

Lucas was in briefing speech mode. Explaining clearly, using all the words, his voice calm and relaxed to build his listeners' confidence in our ability to handle whatever crisis was being thrown at us this time. There was something different from previous emergency runs though. He had an unusual edge to his voice as he continued speaking.

"It's possible this was a freak bracelet failure at a bad time, but you should assume the child was abducted and the bracelet deliberately sabotaged by a target or targets. Incident location is 601/2603 Level 80."

Now I knew why there was that odd edge to Lucas's voice. He'd been worried about the area around 600/2600 for months. Keith had been there twice and found nothing. I'd been there once myself, found nothing either, and had another trip planned for next week. That return trip had arrived ahead of schedule.

"Warning signs have been appearing in this area over a long period," said Lucas, "but they have no discernible pattern. You should assume your target, or targets, are extremely dangerous."

Adika started talking. "First priority, always, Amber stays safe. Second priority, finding the child. Group assignments are..."

He rattled out names and groups. I glanced at my dataview, and was startled to see eight names listed to be my bodyguards instead of the usual five. Lucas had infected me with his worries about area 600/2600, and he'd obviously got to Adika too.

"Incident location is a park," said Nicole. "People in the area are getting upset. They're demanding a telepath to help find the child."

"Send in one of the fake nosy patrol groups to calm them down," said Lucas.

I frowned. "Lucas, I can't work with people's minds screaming numbers at me. You remember what happened when I was out last week. A nosy patrol got too close, I lost my target, and it took nearly an hour to find her again."

"People won't be hostile this time," said Lucas. "They want that child found, so the nosy will be welcomed."

"Sending nosy patrol," said Nicole. "There's one nearby. They should be at the location in a couple of minutes."

We were out of the lift, riding an express belt, when Nicole reported again. "The nosy patrol is getting a good reception from the crowd."

"Now ask people to leave the immediate area," said Lucas. "Tell them the telepath is looking for a very small child, who may well be hurt, even unconscious. The young mind will be very weak and hard to hear. The telepath needs people to move out of the area so they can concentrate."

"Making announcement." Nicole was silent for couple of minutes before speaking again. "People are leaving the area. We've persuaded the parents to move to a distance too. Hasties at the scene are trying heat detectors with no success so far."

"Adika, please make your final approach by lift," said Lucas. "We've just asked everyone to leave, so we don't want you seen coming in."

Adika got us to jump belt, then took us into a lift and down a few levels to Level 84. We rode the belt there for a bit more, before swapping back into another lift.

"Approaching scene," said Adika. "Crystal units to visual."

I adjusted my ear crystal so the camera unfolded, and touched it briefly with my fingertips to check it was correctly in position by the right side of my face.

"Visual links green for all Strike team," said Nicole.

My eight bodyguards clustered round me, guns in hand, as the lift opened. They were really tense about this run. I was too.

Chase team left the lift first. When they'd formed a defensive perimeter, my bodyguards hustled me across to a nice solid tree trunk and formed a human wall round me. Something silver caught my eye. I instinctively looked upwards, and glimpsed a silver and gold balloon caught in the branches of the tree above us.

"Amber, you're at the child's last known location," said Lucas.

I forgot the balloon, huddled into a ball, and shut my eyes. Everyone was acting like I was in mortal danger, but I had to ignore that and sit defenceless with my eyes closed. For the first time, I wished I carried a gun like the Strike team, but I wouldn't know how to use one if I did.

I had to forget about the danger. I could trust my team to keep me safe whatever the cost. My bodyguards would die for me. That fact was clear in their heads right now, too strong to miss. They'd kill to defend me. They'd die to save me. I'd never been hit with that so directly before, and I felt a surge of emotion in response. I loved them. All of them. My Strike team were my brothers, my friends, my family. They'd defend me to the death, and I'd care for them in return.

I forced that emotion away, and made myself concentrate on my job. If we were in danger here, then I mustn't waste time. I reached out past the familiar minds, and encountered the thoughts of the nosy squad. They were feeling frustrated that they could only pretend to be useful rather than actually help.

I moved on again, trying to find anyone else in this park. The child. The target, or targets. Lucas had repeatedly used the plural, to emphasize we shouldn't assume there was only one person involved. Some of the inconsistencies around the 600/2600 area might be because there wasn't just one wild bee there, but two or even more.

"I can't find anyone," I said, frustrated at my lack of success.

"You're getting nothing at all?" asked Lucas.

"I itch."

"Itch?" he repeated. "What do you mean?"

"I don't know, Lucas. There's an odd feeling that I haven't felt before. Like an itch deep inside my mind. Add it to the list of weird things around 600/2600. I'm getting absolutely nothing other than that."

"The child could have been taken further away," said Adika, "or already be dead."

"Amber, what mind level are you searching on?" asked Lucas.

"Level 1 through 3." I realized what he was thinking. "I usually start high level, find the right mind, and then go deeper. I'll see if I can reverse that, and search on the subconscious levels."

I wasn't sure I could do this. How did I even start? I picked Forge's tension filled mind, went down a few levels, and saw some stuff about his feelings for Shanna. He'd seen her! Waste it, he'd found out her apartment location on Level 9, gone to see her on his first precious free day, and she'd...

Shanna had been my friend for years, but I could pelt her elegant face with slime balls for treating Forge like that. The fact she'd made us all promise to stay friends after Lottery made it even worse. She hadn't just sneered at Forge for being a hasty, but mocked him for getting his birthmark removed to please her.

The irony of it was that Shanna had been so horrified to find a hasty on her doorstep, so proud of her status as a Level 9 Media Presenter, that she'd driven Forge away before he could tell her anything. If Shanna had learned he was Level 1, that Amber was in charge of his unit and could use her position to give Shanna work there too, then Forge was cynically sure her reaction would have been very different. Oh yes, Shanna would have grabbed the chance to be with him if it meant she could live in Level 1 luxury and dress in Level 1 clothes.

I guiltily realized I was getting sidetracked from my real goal. That was the problem with fooling around on the lower levels. There were so many swirling feelings, that it was hard to avoid being sucked into the emotional morass.

I headed down two more levels into Forge's subconscious mind, and then tried to search without letting myself drift upwards again. I skated past the emotions of the Strike team and nosy squad, and finally found something.

"I might have the child. They're dreaming. I can't judge distance properly on a subconscious level. Direction is hazy too. Can you move me?"

Someone lifted me up. I didn't know who it was. Anyone on the Strike team was strong enough to carry me while running at full speed. It was a pre-requisite for the job.

"Move me forward. Left. More forward." This must look incredibly silly, but the only information I had was whether I was getting closer or further away from the dreaming child.

"Left again," I continued. "No, back again, and try right. Stop. Forward. Stop. Backward. Stop. I think I'm right on top of her now. Still finding no indication of a target."

"No access hatch round here, and no signs of digging," said Adika. "The child must be in a passageway, and the access to it is elsewhere. This is a park. The level below a park is just soil. Maybe she's down on Level 82."

"She seems closer than that," I said, "and it feels damp down there."

"The level beneath a park is earth and rock," said Lucas, "but there must be other things in there, power cables, drainage." His voice became sharp and urgent. "Nicole, we need the rain turned off in that park. It'll be pre-programmed for regular times, and if it starts raining now the girl could drown."

"Working on that," said Nicole. It was only a minute before she spoke again. "The rain controls should be near the largest lift. Access code is..."

My brain skipped over the next bit, as I checked on the sleeping child. By the time I was listening again, the rain had been turned off, and Nicole was explaining the drainage system.

"... they join the main drain, and that leads into the lake."

"It would be simplest to dig," said Adika.

"I've called our own unit park keeper in to advise us," said Lucas. "She says the area around main drains can be unstable due to leaks. If you try digging, there's a risk of the ground caving in on top of the child."

"Digging is a last resort then." Adika sighed so heavily that his crystal unit picked it up with a rustling sound.

"The target must have taken the child in there," said Lucas. "An adult couldn't fit into most of those pipes, so the target must have entered the main drain from the lake end. There'd have been a grating over the end of the pipe, but that could be easily removed."

He paused for a moment. "I'm afraid someone has to go swimming. Amber, you're sure there's no one else down there? If we send someone in through the drains, then he'll be an easy target for anyone lying in ambush."

"I'm as sure as I can be," I said.

"People outside are getting upset again," said Nicole. "A man's shouting that officials don't care about the child because her parents are only Level 80. Can I give them a news update?"

"Tell them the telepath has already located the child," said Lucas. "The girl is alive, but trapped. The rescuers have to work extremely slowly to avoid hurting the child." He gave a humourless laugh. "We're actually telling the truth for once."

"I could use you here, Lucas," said Adika. "You spend a lot of time training in the pool. Is anyone else good enough at swimming to cope with real problems underwater? Remember it's not just swimming down from the lake surface to the drain entrance, there may be a long stretch of flooded drain as well."

"If the target could get in there with the child, then I can get in there too," said Forge.

"You're sure?" Adika sounded doubtful.

"Forge is an expert swimmer," I confirmed without thinking. "He's been surfing for years."

I instantly regretted saying that, but Adika accepted my statement without comment. He'd naturally assume I had my knowledge from reading Forge's thoughts, rather than from standing on a beach watching him surf.

"Ideal then," said Adika. "Forge, see if you can find the underwater entrance to the drainage system. Amber, can you manage to keep track of both the child and Forge, so you can give directions?"

"I'll try. I daren't lose the child, because she'd be hard to locate again. I'll have to stay with her most of the time, while making occasional, split-second dips into Forge's mind."

"All right," said Adika. "It's the best we can do. Sending more than one person wouldn't help. If they hit trouble in a tight tunnel, the person behind couldn't get a clear shot. Forge, I'll want a running commentary as you go in."

"You should use extreme caution and watch for booby traps," added Lucas.

"Booby traps?" Even Adika sounded startled.

"It doesn't make sense to go to all this trouble to take the child into the drainage system, and then just abandon her," said Lucas. "Amber has no indication the child is hurt, and she's getting no target at all. The plan may not have been to harm the child, but to injure her rescuers."

There was a pause while we all thought that over.

"Perhaps we should try digging instead," said Adika.

"If there really *are* booby traps, and one is near the child..." Lucas didn't need to finish the sentence.

"I hope you're being paranoid about this, Lucas," said Adika. "I've no choice but to send a man in, because getting a robot in there would take far too much time. It probably wouldn't function in the conditions down there anyway. Logic tells me a drain is wet and muddy."

"I'll be careful," said Forge.

"If you see anything odd, anything at all," said Lucas, "stop at once. It might be a good idea to take a long stick with you."

"A long stick!" Adika gave way to frustration. "Lucas, are you telling us to use a long stick to poke booby traps?"

"Safer than using your hand," said Lucas.

There was a pause while Forge stripped to just his body armour and attached wristset lights to both his forearms. I still had my eyes closed, focusing on a small faint mind buried in the earth.

"Going underwater now," said Forge. "Can't talk under there obviously."

There was what seemed like a long wait before he spoke again, sounding breathless. "I've located the entrance. There's no grating over it. Going underwater again and inside."

Another long pause. "I'm in the drainage pipe now. Is my camera still working?"

"Yes," said Adika, "but you must have got some dirt on it. The image is a bit grimy."

"I'm not surprised there's mud on the camera," said Forge. "Everything down here is covered in mud, including me. There's no room to stand, but more crawling space than in the vent system. Only the very first section of pipe was flooded. From this point on, there's just a deep layer of wet silt. I can't see any suspicious objects ahead, but there could be anything under the mud and silt."

"Use the stick to check the ground ahead of you," said Lucas.

I held on to my link to the child, and dipped briefly into Forge's head. He was scared, but not nearly as scared as I was.

"Using stick," said Forge. "Moving slowly. There seems to be something lumpy ahead, almost buried in the silt. If I hadn't been warned, I'd think it was just a tree root, but I'll try the stick again."

"Wait!" ordered Lucas. "I can see the suspect object you're talking about on your camera image. At one point, a glint of light reflected off it. Light doesn't reflect off tree roots, mud, or ceramic drainage pipes. Better back off and try shooting it with your gun. Use a stun setting to make sure you don't damage the pipe."

"Backing off," said Forge. "Shooting now."

I dipped into his head. "Eek!"

"Forge?" shouted Adika. "What happened there?"

"The object is definitely made of metal," said Forge. "It's got jagged bits, like teeth. When I shot at the thing, it seemed to jump up out of the mud, and then the teeth snapped shut. If my hand had been in there..."

"Lucas," said Adika, "I love you."

Lucas laughed. "I love you too, Adika."

I managed a nervous laugh myself.

"We're getting nothing but a brown blur from your visual link now, Forge," said Adika.

"Sorry. When the trap went off, I jerked backwards and caught my head on the muddy side of the pipe. I can try wiping the camera." There was a pause before Forge spoke again. "Is that any better?"

"Not in the slightest," said Lucas. "I think we'll have to forget the visual link. What does the trap look like? Is it safe to get past?"

"I think so. It's snapped solidly shut. I'm pushing it aside. Very slowly. Moving on and using the stick to check what's ahead."

"The target must have taken the child in, and then rigged traps on his way out," said Lucas. "He'd know that we'd be looking out for more traps the same as the first one. I expect any remaining traps will be different."

"Thanks for that cheering thought," said Forge.

"He'd have had limited time," said Lucas. "I doubt there'll be more than three traps."

"Another cheering thought." Forge gave a grunt of pain.

"All right?" asked Adika.

"The silt contains some very sharp stones," said Forge. "I see a junction ahead. Left or right?"

"Left," I said.

"Forge, stop well clear of the junction," said Lucas. "Look it over very closely, and describe it for us. By the way, I've got Keith's Tactical team listening in to a direct feed of our conversation, in case they can think of anything helpful. So far, they're just unable to believe this is happening."

"I can't believe it either," said Adika.

"This looks like a standard T-junction of big pipes," said Forge. "I can't see any sign of traps. Do I shoot the junction?"

"Shoot it," said Adika grimly.

"Shooting now."

I checked Forge's head. Shooting the junction did nothing at all.

"I've shot it several times," said Forge. "Using stick again. Still nothing. Advancing cautiously to junction."

"If the target didn't trap the junction," said Lucas, "I'm betting there's a trap immediately you turn left."

"I can see the child!" Forge's voice went a notch higher with excitement.

"Don't move!" shouted Lucas. "Don't even think about moving. The target would expect you to head instinctively towards the child. Check the ground in front of you."

"It looks fine," said Forge.

I checked the view from his eyes. The ground looked fine to me too.

"Give me a minute," said Lucas. "I've got to think. There are three possibilities. The target booby traps the way to the child, or the other way, or both. The target surely can't have had time to trap both directions, and would expect us to do the obvious thing."

Lucas's voice changed from thoughtful to decisive. "Forge, take a look at the right-hand pipe. Shoot it a bit, prod it with the stick, and make sure it's safe. The idea is you go into it a little way and turn round. That should give you a clear shot at the ground just inside the left-hand pipe, while still being a little distance away. You understand me?"

"I understand," said Forge. "Shooting. Prodding. Moving into right-hand pipe. Turning round... with difficulty. Made it. You want me to take a few shots at the ground in the left-hand pipe now?"

"Yes," said Lucas.

"Shooting."

I dipped into Forge's head just as there was a loud noise. I was thrown backwards and my head hurt. No, not my head, Forge's head.

"Something exploded," I said. "Forge got thrown backwards and hit his head on the roof of the pipe. He's dazed."

"I'm... all right," said Forge.

"He's not feeling too good," I said. "The child is still asleep. She must be drugged to sleep through that. The blast didn't seem to hurt her, but water's dripping on her now."

"I'm going in after Forge," said Adika. "If there's just a short section of flooded drain then I can make it. After this, I do more pool time. We all do more pool time."

"No! I'm almost there now," said Forge. "There's only a short distance between the bit I shot and the child. Surely if there were more traps, the explosion would have triggered them."

"I don't think the target would have put a trap right by the child," said Lucas. "If she moved, set off the trap and it killed her, then we'd just dig up the body afterwards. Be careful though."

"Shooting on stun," said Forge, his voice sounding strained. "Careful not to hit the girl. It seems clear. Moving in now. Checking it's safe as I go. Safety rules."

"What?" asked Adika.

"Swapping to Forge now," I said. "He's in trouble." I suddenly realized what was happening. "There's some sort of gas in there! That's why the child is asleep. Forge, grab her and pull back!"

"Amber, you rode the rail," said Forge.

"Forge, hold your breath, grab the girl, move back!" I yelled.

"Carnival."

"Forge is unconscious," I reported. "He got the girl back to the junction."

"I'm inside the drain now," said a breathless Adika. "Heading for Forge. Let's hope he didn't miss any traps."

"Can we get fresh air pumped down to them?" asked Lucas.

"I've already got an inflatable boat, an air supply, and a pump on the way," said Nicole.

"Rothan, get the pump working as soon as you can." Adika was gasping for breath between the words. I checked his head. He didn't seem in difficulties, just breathing hard because of the effort of the underwater swim and crawling along the drain.

"Bringing the child out," said Adika.

"We're launching the boat and coming to meet you," said Rothan.

There was a long pause before Adika spoke again. "Going underwater with the child."

I felt his anxiety, the cold of the water, and the relief when he surfaced and handed the child to the waiting Strike team. Adika took one desperate gulp of air before grabbing an airline from Rothan and swimming down to the drain again. As he surfaced inside the pipe, the pump started, sending a jet of fresh air out of the airline. Adika filled his lungs from that, before dropping the airline and crawling on through the pipe.

After a minute or two, there was a groan from my ear crystal. It sounded like Forge, so I went back to him. "The fresh air must be reaching Forge," I reported. "He's waking up."

"Amber, I fell off the rail," Forge's voice sounded weak and confused. "Keep going. You can make it all the way. Ride the Hive!"

"Forge, I did make it all the way. You're in the tunnel, remember? Crawl back to the entrance. Adika's coming for you."

"I remember."

Forge started crawling, met Adika, and they both headed back towards the drain entrance. I alternated between their minds as they swam up through the chill of the water. They surfaced, and reached for outstretched, welcoming hands that pulled them into the boat. It was over.

CHAPTER NINETEEN

The emergency run was over, but the discussion afterwards dragged on for hours. That didn't just involve my own team leaders, but direct audio links with worried Tactical Commanders from the other Telepath Units as well. None of them had ever had an incident like this, where a wild bee didn't seem to be aiming to harm their original victim, but to use them as bait to lure rescuers into danger.

On the positive side, Forge and the child were both going to be fine. There'd been a lot of excitement on the Hive news channels about the trapped child, but everyone believed the cover story about a freak accident when a drain collapsed. Nosies were, temporarily at least, almost popular.

On the negative side, we hadn't just failed to bring back a target; we hadn't even got a sniff at one. Keith kept sending his Tactical Commander messages, insisting Gaius interrupt the discussion to point that out. I guessed that Keith was feeling sensitive about the fact he'd dismissed area 600/2600 as perfectly safe, and was criticizing us as a way of fending off potential criticism of him.

After Gaius wearily recited the fifth message from Keith – the one that said Amber's failure to locate the target proved she was an inadequate telepath who'd been rushed through training too fast – Adika lost his temper. He said that if Keith sent one more message insulting me, then he'd go over to Keith's unit and personally bang Keith's telepathic head against a wall.

Gaius instantly started defending his telepath, saying that Keith was making valid points. Since Lucas seemed unwilling to argue with either Adika or his old boss, Megan had to intervene and calm things down before it turned into an inter-unit war.

When everyone finally ran out of things to say about the situation in area 600/2600, I took Lucas back to my apartment so we could discuss a more personal crisis. I sat on one couch, and he dragged another across so he could sit on it facing me. His mind was like a room with all the lights off. He couldn't keep me out of his thoughts, but he could do his best to stop thinking except for the top level of pre-vocalization.

"I need to explain about Forge," I said. "We knew each other on Teen Level."

"I worked that out from what he said when he was suffering from the effects of the gas," said Lucas. "You rode the rail together at the end of Carnival. Forge fell off. You made it all the way. You rode the Hive. Congratulations."

Lucas was shutting me out. His words, his thoughts, his body language, all condemned me unheard. Anger hit me.

"I'm not like you, Lucas. I can't put myself, faults and all, on public display. And please, don't point out the double standard that I'm a telepath reading everyone else's secrets, but I can't handle them knowing mine. I'm fully aware of it."

"So what was the fault you were hiding?" asked Lucas. "Forge is handsome and intelligent. Yesterday, he proved he was heroic and tough as well. That's not exactly an ex-boyfriend to be ashamed of, or is the real truth that he isn't your ex at all? I can understand him wanting to prove he has a place on the Strike team on merit, rather than have them thinking he'd only got in because he was the telepath's boyfriend. Well, he's proved that now, so you can stop keeping your relationship secret."

"Forge isn't my ex! He was never my anything at all." I knew I was ranting at Lucas, but I didn't care. "Forge was besotted with my best friend, Shanna, for all our years on Teen Level. I had this weird obsession with him back then, and a peculiar repeating dream about him."

I shrugged. "Forge never knew about that, and he still

doesn't. I never told anyone because I was horribly embarrassed, and then the whole obsession thing suddenly stopped just after I came to this unit. That's all there is to know, Lucas. Enjoy it!"

The lights went on in a sudden dazzling display. Lucas's head was busy analyzing on so many levels that I lost count. I tried to catch the thoughts as they whizzed by, but they were far too fast.

"Apologies for the misapprehension," he said. "Am I fired?"

"I would fire you, but I can't. You're totally maddening but a brilliant Tactical Commander. I'll come up with an alternative punishment."

I paused to rub my forehead. "I know I should have told you all about this when we were in Hive Futura, but I kept coming up with reasons why I couldn't. I think the real truth was that something about my obsession was blocking me, preventing me from talking about it."

I shrugged. "Now the whole weird reaction to Forge is gone, and he's just an old friend. I've been wanting to tell you about this for weeks, Lucas, but you were partially right. Forge was worried people would think he only got on the team because he was the telepath's pet. I promised him I wouldn't say anything until he'd justified his position."

"I think he achieved that on the last emergency run. Tell me more about your weird reaction to Forge."

Lucas had bounced back. He'd gone through rampaging resentment and jealousy, absorbed my explanation, adjusted his feelings, apologized, and moved on to professionally analyzing the situation. Going through that whole gamut of emotion would have taken normal people days. It had taken Lucas a few minutes. He was unbelievable.

I told Lucas the whole stupid story. My arrival on Teen Level, my first meeting with Forge, the repeating dream where we were walking in the park, and the compulsion to keep him happy. Lucas frowned as he listened to it.

"That wasn't an ordinary teen crush," he said.

"I know. Even when I was on Teen Level, I realized my obsession wasn't normal. Now I've learnt far more about teen crushes. Most of the unit have suffered them in the past.

Hannah's got one right now on... Well, never mind that. Half the Strike team have a kind of crush on me as well."

Lucas grinned. "They're fantasizing about heroically saving their beautiful telepath from certain death?"

I laughed. "I'm not beautiful, but yes. There's a lot of exaggeration of my looks. Their own too sometimes. Anyway, my point is that by now I'm rather an expert on crushes, and my fixation on Forge doesn't seem to fit that pattern at all."

"Agreed." Lucas's mind was still frantically working at the problem, even the pre-vocalized thought level lapsing into his speed speech. "No current theory. Any recurrence, especially of dream, tell me immediately."

"It all seems a little silly now. I've been making a fuss about nothing."

"Emphatically untrue, Amber. Anything that affected a telepath so strongly has to be taken seriously. You're vitally important to the Hive. Vitally important to me too."

Lucas paused. "You don't have to be embarrassed about telling me things that happened to you on Teen Level, Amber. My own time there was a total disaster. I was a social introvert, struggling to cope, rejected by the other teens on my corridor. I got some measure of acceptance in the end by playing the clown."

"Did your clown act on Teen Level make you immune to being mocked?" I asked. "Is that how you manage to be so open about everything?"

"The clown act plus my time in Keith's unit. He teases people about their secrets, and threatens to expose them to the whole unit. I decided the best defensive measure was not to have any secrets at all."

I was horrified. "Keith shouldn't treat the people in his unit that way."

Lucas shrugged. "It's not surprising that Keith lashes out at people given the stress of his situation."

"What situation?"

"You don't know about Keith?" Lucas gave me a startled look. "Only the people in his unit, or on the other Telepath Unit Tactical teams, are fully informed about it, but I'd assumed you'd seen it in either my own or Megan's thoughts by now. Keith isn't really a true telepath."

I blinked. "What do you mean?"

"You know that true telepaths have full control over their ability, while borderline telepaths just have random, intermittent glimpses into the minds of people around them. Keith is the only case we've discovered of a telepath who falls somewhere between those two extremes. He can control his telepathic ability most of the time, but it occasionally cuts out for minutes, hours, even a full day."

Lucas pulled a face. "Think how frustrating that is for Keith's operational teams when it happens in the middle of an emergency run. It's even worse for Keith himself."

"Oh." I sat in silence for a moment. "I'd seen the deep parts of Megan's mind thinking that Keith was arrogant and lazy, and brooding on the fact that he could have saved her husband's life if he'd done his job properly. When I saw you thinking about the problems of working with Keith, I thought..."

I let the words trail off. I'd seen Lucas's relief at leaving the problems of Keith's unit behind him, but skipped the details in his mind, assuming I knew them already. I'd been guilty of the telepathic equivalent of hearing someone speak but not listening to what they were saying.

"It's not surprising that Megan blames Keith for her husband's death, at least on the unconscious level," said Lucas. "The real truth is that the poor man was doing his best, but his telepathy cut out at the worst possible time."

I pictured myself on an emergency run, my telepathy cutting out, and one of my Strike team dying. "How did Keith manage to carry on working after that happened?"

"He's always had to struggle against his problems. He can have nine good runs in a row, and then on the tenth his telepathy randomly cuts out and he loses a target. The biggest problem is that his staff can't help thinking about it, Keith sees that in their heads, and takes it as criticism. That's when he loses his temper, hits back by threatening to reveal their secrets, and goes into his arrogant superior telepath act."

Lucas sighed. "Keith's been having an especially hard time lately. Dean's death was a nightmare for him, and then Lottery discovered a new, highly gifted true telepath. Keith naturally feels jealous and resentful of your abilities, Amber. That's why he kept making Gaius interrupt our meeting with those petty messages about you."

Lucas yawned, and slid sideways to stretch out on his couch. "I hope you understand why I didn't want to argue with Gaius over that. He's Keith's Tactical Commander, so he has to do whatever's necessary to support Keith through these problems."

"I do understand. I wish I could help Keith to..."

I stopped talking. The thoughts in Lucas's head had changed tempo and were less crisply defined. He'd fallen asleep. I watched, fascinated, as his thought patterns seemed to drift down a few levels into the subconscious and then started working away again at trying to make sense of my repeating dream. Lucas did analysis in his sleep!

I hesitated, wondering whether to wake him up and send him home, but decided against it. Lucas desperately needed some sleep. I needed sleep too. There'd been the strain of the emergency run, the long hours of discussion afterwards, and it had been emotionally taxing to tell Lucas about the whole Forge business. I headed to my bedroom, undressed, sank blissfully into the embrace of the sleep field, and went to sleep.

I'm not sure how long I slept before I suddenly woke in panic. I itched deep in my head. Something was dreadfully wrong, I didn't know what, but I automatically started running circuits. Dipping into each of the Strike team's heads in turn for a fraction of a second.

Adika was dreaming of running, chasing after...

Forge was dozing restlessly in a room in our medical area, troubled by ghosts of Shanna.

Eli was thinking about girls.

Matias... Matias had been stabbed!

I reached instinctively for the panic button next to my sleep field, and pressed it to open the emergency sound link between my apartment and Adika. "This is Amber," I screamed. "Someone just stabbed Matias!"

The unit intruder alarm started its staccato beat, and Adika's voice responded over the emergency link. "Amber, stay in your apartment. Do you have a target? Strike team, armour, guns, move! Bodyguards to Amber, everyone else with me to Matias's apartment."

My eyes were closed. My mind was searching. Nothing. No strangers, just familiar minds. "I can't find a target."

"Sofia?" Adika made the name into a grim question.

By now I knew only too well that relationships could sometimes turn violent. I searched for Sofia's mind in a blind panic, worried that I'd made a dreadful mistake in bringing her to the unit. Reading her thoughts had told me she was fiercely passionate about her art, but I'd seen no clue that...

I found Sofia's mind. She was alone in her apartment. She'd been woken up by the alarm, and was anxiously picturing Matias searching the unit along with the rest of the Strike team.

"It wasn't Sofia that stabbed Matias," I said.

Fabric mesh touched my skin and Lucas spoke from next to me. "Urgently suggest you put on your body armour, Amber."

"Is that you, Lucas?" Adika asked. "You're with Amber? Bodyguards, don't shoot Lucas!"

I rolled out of the sleep field, opened my eyes, and pulled on my body armour. As an afterthought, I grabbed a random dress and dropped it over my head. Lucas grabbed my crystal unit from its shelf and handed it to me. When I put it in my ear, I briefly heard Rothan's voice before he was drowned out by Adika shouting angrily at someone.

"Get back in your apartment before you get yourself shot!"

Eli's voice came next from my ear crystal. "Full bodyguard team now in position outside Amber's apartment. Amber, open the door."

I checked the minds outside my apartment, and ordered the front door to open.

"Amber, lock the door," said Eli.

I ordered the front door to close and lock itself. Lucas helpfully opened the bedroom door, and stood aside to let my bodyguards run into the room.

"Relax everyone, emergency over." Adika's voice came from both my ear crystal and the emergency link. He sounded much calmer now. "Matias hasn't been stabbed, but he's only semi-conscious and in a lot of pain. I think he's got appendicitis."

Megan's voice broke in. "Medical team on the way."

I felt an utter fool. "Sorry. It felt like a knife was stabbing Matias in the stomach. All my training is about checking for injury, so I never thought about illness. I should have waited and..."

"No!" Adika interrupted me. "You never wait, Amber. When you sense something that may be an attack, you sound the alarm instantly. If we have an intruder, then seconds count. How did you spot Matias was sick, anyway?"

"I woke up. I had the same itching I had on the last run, so I started checking minds."

"A good thing that you did," said Megan. "I'm with Matias now. The problem is definitely his appendix and he needs emergency surgery."

"Well, in addition to getting vital medical help to Matias, this has been a useful emergency drill," said Adika. "Amber, can we have a full unit meeting at nine to go over a few points with everyone?"

"Of course, Adika. Meeting at nine for the entire unit. Goodnight everyone."

My bodyguards said their farewells, and gave speculative glances at Lucas before leaving. I checked the emergency sound link between my apartment and Adika had been shut down, and took my crystal unit out of my ear.

Lucas gave me a worried look and gabbled in his speed speech. "Woken up by intruder alarm, people being attacked, concerned for your safety."

I nodded. "I quite understand why you came into my bedroom."

"Situation possibly gave misleading impression to bystanders."

"Quite possibly, yes."

"Denial potentially worse."

I lay back on my sleep field, and laughed. "Very true. What time is it now?"

"Six in the morning."

I jumped back to my feet. "I need breakfast. How about you?"

"Starving," said Lucas.

Our meals yesterday had only been hastily grabbed snacks, so I ordered us both substantial breakfasts from my kitchen unit. We were in the middle of eating, when I got an incoming call. I glanced at my dataview.

"Waste it! Lucas, hide!"

"Hide?"

"Yes, hide," I said. "I don't care if my entire unit is speculating on you being here at night, but my mother's calling me. Get under the table or something."

Lucas pointed at the food on the table. "Two meals."

"Good point."

I sprinted into the next room to take the call. My mother's sleepy and worried holo image appeared.

"Amber," she said. "Sorry to wake you, but it's an emergency. Gregas just arrived on our doorstep. He's run away from Teen Level!"

CHAPTER TWENTY

At nine o'clock, everyone in the unit gathered in the park. Adika stood on a picnic table to address the crowd, explaining that everyone except the Strike team should stay locked in their apartments during an intruder alert. Liaison team members, cleaners, and electricians shouldn't be roaming the corridors trying to find out what was going on.

Adika felt strongly on this point, and he expressed himself fully and fluently to the offenders for the next ten minutes. When he'd finished, I headed off to deal with my family crisis. I'd decided to take Lucas along with me. My mother wanted me to talk my brother into going back to Teen Level before his absence was noticed. My theory was that Lucas would have a much better chance of achieving that than I did. When it came to dealing with Gregas, Lucas had two obvious advantages over me. He was imprinted as a tactical expert, and he wasn't a nagging Level 1 big sister.

Adika insisted on going with us, and bringing two of the Strike team as well. This seemed an overreaction to me. I was going to visit my parents in 510/6120 Level 27, which was a full four zones away from the suspect 600/2600 area.

Once we were inside the lift, it became clear Adika was planning to make the most of his time on this trip. "Rothan, Eli, since you're both candidates for my two deputy positions, I didn't want to criticize you in front of the whole unit."

Rothan and Eli looked nervous.

"Rothan first," said Adika. "I'm not asking what you were doing in the park when the intruder alert sounded. I'm not asking who you were doing it with either. I approve of the fact you had your body armour and your gun with you, and you made it to Matias's apartment quickly. Next time, however, I suggest you run round the lake instead of falling into it."

"It was very dark," said Rothan. "The park suns don't turn on until seven o'clock in the morning."

"Moving on to Eli now," said Adika.

Eli cringed. "There's no need to tell me. I already know."

Adika intended to tell him anyway. "Very fast response to safeguard Amber, and you remembered your body armour and gun. Minor point. Next time, try to take at least one item of clothing as well. Body armour is a protective mesh. You can see through it."

He paused for a second. "Amber's safety obviously comes above all other considerations, but you had to wait one minute for the rest of the bodyguard team to arrive before she opened the apartment door. You could have used that minute to get dressed before you dashed into her bedroom. You will now apologize to Amber."

"Sorry," said Eli glumly. "When I realized, it was too late to go back for clothes."

"That's all right," I said. "I didn't notice."

They all stared at me.

"I had other things on my mind," I said. "Matias was in agony, and I was searching for a target."

"You didn't notice?" Adika laughed. "Everyone else did. Well, that's put Eli firmly in his place."

"In a crisis, I tend to operate telepathically rather than visually," I said, "so I have my eyes closed most of the time."

Our lift doors opened on Level 27, and I led the way to the nearest express belt.

"Think yourself lucky, Eli," said Adika. "Now, Lucas."

"Me?" Lucas was clearly caught off guard by this attack. "I don't suppose it helps if I point out I'm your boss."

"Not in the slightest," said Adika. "You told me that you were woken up by the alarm and fell off Amber's couch, hitting your head on the floor. That's a very impressive bruise appearing on the side of your face."

"Thank you," said Lucas.

"You then dashed heroically to defend Amber, without your body armour or gun. In future, wherever you fall asleep, your body armour and gun falls asleep with you."

"I'm not Strike team," Lucas pointed out.

"Explain that to any armed intruders you meet," said Adika. "See how well it works. I suggest you pick up a duplicate body armour and gun, and leave them anywhere you might fall asleep regularly. Now, Amber."

I sighed. I'd been encouraging Adika to treat me like a human being, rather than a telepath who was above criticism, because I wanted to know when I made mistakes and learn from them. Adika had adjusted to this approach, but it made Megan extremely nervous, so he didn't inflict his famous sarcasm on me unless she was well out of the way. This was an ideal opportunity.

"Spotting Matias was in trouble was amazing, and you did exactly the right thing by hitting your panic button. Fine so far, but..."

I'd had a feeling there was a "but" coming.

"Your safety is our top priority, Amber. We give you body armour to protect you. Hannah hangs it lovingly in your bedroom, within reach of your sleep field. Why didn't you put it on immediately? Why did a stray tactician have to fall off your couch, come dashing into your bedroom, and hand it to you?"

"I'll try to remember another time. Approaching scene now," I said pointedly, as we got off the belt near my parents' apartment. "We're visiting my parents and my irritating kid brother. Be very careful what you say, because they mustn't find out I'm a telepath. Eli, keep your clothes on."

Eli blushed.

We reached my parents' door and I pressed the chime button. When my mother opened the door, I saw she was wearing the necklace of golden beads that I'd given her. She gave a startled look at the crowd.

"Please come in," she said.

I led the gang into the main living area. My father and Gregas were already sitting there. They seemed stunned by the invasion.

"Hello." I attempted a casual smile. "I'm afraid my unit had a security alert last night, so my Security team leader insisted I bring an escort. This is my Security team leader, Adika. My bodyguards, Rothan and Eli."

I gestured at people in turn, hesitating when I got to Lucas. He smiled hopefully.

"Lucas is another of my team leaders," I said. "I've brought him here to talk sense into Gregas."

Lucas sighed, and there was a ragged exchange of greetings.

"The idea was that we'd have a private family chat." My mother gave me a meaningful look.

"Don't worry," I said. "Their lips are sealed. If word gets out about Gregas running away, I'll demote them all to Level 99 Sewage Technicians."

My parents gazed at me with horrified faces. I didn't need telepathy to tell me what they were thinking. I'd always been a quiet, dutiful daughter, shyly fading into the background when their friends visited. Now I was back in their apartment for the first time since Lottery, an elite Level 1 marching into their home with a whole set of intimidating bodyguards, and casually threatening to demote people to Level 99. I hadn't believed Lucas when he told me I'd changed since Lottery, but now I could see it was true.

"That was just a joke about demoting people," I said hastily, and turned to my brother, who at least looked sulky rather than scared of me. "Gregas, you have to go back to Teen Level. Lucas, you tell him!"

Gregas glared at me first, then threw a bitter look at Lucas.

"Don't mind me, Gregas," said Lucas, "I'm only another team leader. I'd hoped to be a boyfriend, I'd thought I was at least a friend, but it turns out I'm only another team leader."

He flopped into a chair with an exaggerated expression of despair, and my parents gave him bewildered looks.

I held back a laugh. "Lucas, stop playing the clown. You and I and Gregas are going into the next room to have a nice chat."

Lucas gave a long-suffering groan and stood up again.

"I don't want to talk to him," said Gregas. "Even if he is Level 1 like she is!" He gestured resentfully at me.

"Gregas, manners!" said my father.

"I don't want to talk to you either, Gregas," said Lucas. "Your sister is making me do it. I nearly got fired yesterday, but she said she'd come up with an alternative punishment instead. I think this is it."

Gregas blinked at Lucas in disbelief, and followed me into the bookette room without any more argument. Lucas and I sat down, but Gregas remained stubbornly on his feet and stated his position.

"I don't want to talk to you. I don't want to go back to Teen Level. I hate the place. I don't see why teens have to go there."

"Reason implicit Lottery," said Lucas.

"Full sentences, Lucas," I murmured. As far as I knew, Gregas couldn't read minds, so he'd need all the help he could get to keep up with Lucas.

Lucas started again. "Gregas, your time on Teen Level is vital preparation for Lottery. You learn to live alone in a sheltered and helpful environment. You gain social skills. You gradually distance yourself from your parents' level in preparation for being assigned your own level as an adult. You experiment with a host of different sports, crafts, and activities. When you're eighteen, Lottery will allocate you a profession based on the needs of the Hive."

"Which isn't fair!" snapped Gregas.

"It may not seem fair," said Lucas, "but it's the best thing for the Hive, and that's indirectly the best thing for you. Lottery ensures there are never too few or too many workers in any area, and a job is always done by someone talented at it. That means the Hive does well, and we all benefit as a result. We may not get to choose what we do, but the optimization stage of Lottery makes sure that we're given work we enjoy."

Gregas pulled a disbelieving face.

"It's true, Gregas," said Lucas. "I could never have chosen my job for myself, because I didn't even know it existed, but Lottery did and knew it was perfect for me. Lottery will allocate you work that you love too, but it can only do that if you spend your years on Teen Level establishing your own individual likes and dislikes. If you stay living at home, heavily influenced by your parents, then you'll end up being allocated work that they'd like to do but you'll probably grow to hate. Is that what you want to happen?"

Gregas frowned. "No, but I can't go back to Teen Level. I don't fit in with the others on my corridor. They all go off and do things together, and I'm left sitting in my room by myself. You won't understand how horrible that is, but I've been having a dreadful time."

"You're entirely wrong about that," said Lucas. "I understand perfectly. In fact, I'm an expert on the difficulties of not fitting in on Teen Level. You wish to become part of your corridor social group?"

"Of course I do. I've tried my best to make friends, but it's not working."

"I can fix that. From what I've seen so far, you just have the relatively minor problem that you aren't naturally outgoing and get defensive talking to strangers. We'll assess your personality, work out what roles you could fill in the social group, and decide which would benefit you most. Then I'll explain tactics that should get you established in that role within the next two weeks."

Gregas looked at him uncertainly. "Can you really do that?"

Lucas nodded. "Once you've made the initial start, it will be easy to keep going. Group expectations will keep reaffirming you in your chosen role."

Gregas glanced at me.

"You can trust Lucas," I said. "He's an expert tactician."

"I'll need some information from you, Gregas," said Lucas, "but I doubt you'll want your sister listening while I ask personal questions."

"I don't!" said Gregas.

I laughed and retreated to the next room. I found my parents nervously entertaining the Strike team contingent.

"Where's Gregas?" asked my mother.

"He's still talking to Lucas," I said. "They're working out a plan to make Gregas the leading social star of Teen Level."

"Amber, I've just had a message from Megan," said Adika. "Matias has had his operation and is doing well."

"I'm glad Matias will be all right," I said. "I hope this won't affect his team spot."

Adika's eyes flickered towards my parents, and he chose his answer carefully. "With accelerated healing treatment, Matias should be recovered within a week or two. We have to expect illnesses and work round them. Megan said that Forge is cleared fit for duty again, so we won't be too short staffed."

"Forge is an unusual name," said my mother. "That's not the Forge you knew on Teen Level, is it Amber?"

I was telling enough lies to my parents already. I wasn't going to lie about this as well. "It is actually. By pure fluke, Lottery assigned him to my unit."

"I hadn't realized you two were old friends," said Adika. "So that was what Forge meant when he said..."

He broke off. I automatically checked his thoughts to pick up the end of his sentence, and saw him busily speculating on the fact the entire Strike team bore a strong resemblance to my old friend from Teen Level. Given Lucas had been in a foul mood yesterday, but had spent last night in my apartment, Adika had half a dozen exciting theories about what might be going on.

"Drinks." My mother hastily got to her feet. "I forgot to offer you any drinks."

I realized I was reading Adika's mind in front of my parents. I mustn't do that. My parents shouldn't be able to tell what I was doing just by looking at me, but it would be horribly easy to answer a question that Adika hadn't asked aloud.

I pulled out of Adika's head, and offered to help my mother with the drinks. She seemed disconcerted by the idea but I insisted. I needed to reassure my parents that although I was Level 1, with my own unit and a set of bodyguards, my place in the family hadn't changed. I needed to reassure myself as well.

So we handed round drinks, and plates of small savouries. Adika and Rothan seemed uncomfortable about their telepath acting as a waitress, but Eli brightened up at the sight of the food. By the time he'd enthusiastically gobbled down two plates of the savouries, explained to my mother that he'd missed breakfast because of the security alert, admired the necklace I'd given her as a present, and discussed whether he should get one like it for his own mother, the atmosphere had got a lot more relaxed.

After a while, Lucas reappeared with a very thoughtful looking Gregas. "If you have any problems, Gregas, just tell your sister," said Lucas. "I'll get a message to you about the best way to deal with them, and after the first couple of weeks you'll have no trouble at all."

Gregas nodded. "I need to go before anyone misses me. Goodbye." He shot out of the apartment before any of us could reply.

My mother looked gratefully at Lucas. "Thank you so much."

I glanced at the time display on the wall, aware that we were nearing the end of our unit's mandatory twenty-four hour recovery time after yesterday's emergency run. Lucas hadn't planned any check runs for today, but we needed to be ready to respond to emergency calls.

I stood up. "I'm afraid we have to go now. Coming here wasn't a problem, because one of the long experiments is running at the moment, but I need to be back in the unit when it finishes."

"Your work schedule seems very demanding," said my father.

"I'm afraid that's unavoidable," said Lucas. "Our research is only possible because of Amber's unique skills and insight."

My parents looked impressed and proud to hear that. Everybody moved out into the hallway, there was a round of polite farewells, and then I led my party back to the nearest belt. Once I'd stepped on and moved across to the express belt, I realized that Adika had somehow ended up at my side, his bulk meaning everyone else had to either stand in front or behind us. He breathed a barely audible question in my ear.

"There's no trouble between you and Lucas, is there? If Forge is becoming a problem, I can trade him to another unit."

I was silent for a moment, counting to ten to make myself calm down. It didn't entirely work. "Forge is an old friend," I whispered back. "He has never been my boyfriend. Neither of us mentioned we'd met before, because Forge wanted to prove he was on the team on merit. A stupid mistake in Lottery meant the physical preferences for the Strike team were influenced by Forge's looks. I strongly recommend that you don't start gossiping about that unless you want to find a different job."

I realized my voice was getting far too loud, and forced myself to quieten down again. "Lucas was about a day ahead of you at leaping to conclusions. He knows the real situation now. There's no problem, there's no need to trade Forge, and Lucas really was sleeping on the couch not sharing my sleep field last night. Do you need any more information on my love life, or are you happy now?"

"I consider myself severely reprimanded," said Adika. "Sorry, but I had to ask. Forge is a good man, but losing Lucas would cripple the unit."

I peered over my shoulder for Lucas, spotted him standing behind Eli, and shouted to him. "Lucas, get up here."

Lucas bounced up to join me, and Adika retreated to lurk as inconspicuously as possible at the back of the group. Lucas turned to eye him thoughtfully.

"Why is Adika acting like a scolded toddler?"

I groaned. "When you were out of the room, Megan sent us a message about Matias and Forge. My mother asked if that was the Forge I knew on Teen Level."

I watched Lucas's thoughts. He took less than five seconds to work out an approximation of my conversation with Adika.

"Yes, you've got it almost word for word," I said. "Adika offered to transfer Forge."

Lucas gave a shout of laughter and lapsed into speed speech. "Adika toddler in big trouble. Amber hates privacy violation. Amber furious at transfer suggestion."

I couldn't help joining in his laughter. "I know that being defensive about my privacy is hypocritical for a telepath, but I can't help it. Everyone watches me, thinks about me, studies my every move. I can't so much as breathe without them going into huddles to discuss it."

"This is a Telepath Unit, Amber. I'm afraid that means the telepath is a natural focus of attention."

"Yes." I gnawed guiltily at my bottom lip. "I'll have to call Adika later and apologize to him. I'd better call Forge as well, and warn him that people know we were friends on Teen Level."

Lucas shrugged. "You don't need to apologize to Adika. You let him give you orders. You allow him to criticize you when you make mistakes. You've just made it clear that you draw the line at him asking intrusive personal questions, and I can assure you that it's not the first time Adika's been shouted at for doing that."

That was true. Adika was a Strike team leader. If he felt action was needed, he took it quickly and decisively. If he felt information was needed, he asked for it. Only last week, he'd annoyed Megan with a personal question about her dead husband. They'd been on much better terms since the dramatic scene with Fran, I'd been getting quite hopeful about the two of them, but Megan had reacted to the question by verbally ripping Adika to shreds. I was starting to think their relationship was doomed.

"You don't need to give warnings to Forge either," Lucas continued. "He babbled about you riding the rail at Carnival in front of the whole Strike team. He'll know someone will work out what that meant, but he won't be worried about it now. He must realize he's proved that he's more than worthy of his spot on the Strike team."

"I suppose so."

Lucas hesitated before speaking again. "Amber, I know the real reason you lost your temper with Adika was because that visit to your parents upset you. Was that my fault? Given my history with my own parents, I admit I was panicking about meeting yours, so I reverted to doing my clown act from Teen Level."

I shook my head. "It was my fault, not yours. My parents had visited me in my fancy apartment, but they hadn't seen me with a group of hulking bodyguards before, and then I made that stupid joke about demoting people. They looked absolutely terrified of me. I'm so grateful to Eli for chattering away and making things relaxed and comfortable again. I'd hug him, but I suppose that would start Adika asking questions again."

"You mustn't do anything to worry Adika," said Lucas solemnly. "In fact, you should be reassuring the poor man. I suggest a good method would be if we lie entwined on the grass in the park, madly kissing each other, while the Strike team are running laps."

I laughed.

CHAPTER TWENTY-ONE

The next day, Adika announced he wanted to test everyone on the Strike team's swimming ability, and mine as well, before we made any more trips to 600/2600. We all headed over to the unit swimming pool. I went into a changing room, stripped off my clothes, pulled on my swimming costume, studied my reflection in a wall mirror, and wrinkled my nose. The Strike team were going to have a big disappointment. My figure didn't live up to their fantasies.

When I came out of the changing room, the Strike team were already at the pool side in their swimming costumes. They were all very pointedly not looking at me. A quick check of the closest mind told me that Adika had given them a typically unsubtle warning. "Don't ogle the telepath or I'll drop you down a lift shaft!"

I was startled to see Lucas appear from a changing room, wearing a swimming costume and with a towel slung round his shoulders. He came to stand next to me, giving me a blatant inspection.

"Lucas, behave!" I hissed the words at him.

His eyebrows bounced wickedly at me. "Seen you wearing less," he whispered.

Adika came over and looked at him disapprovingly. "Why are you here, Lucas?"

Lucas beamed at him. "Reporting for swimming ability check."

"We know that you're half fish, Lucas," said Adika. "There's no need to prove it."

"I insist," said Lucas. "This is my big chance to show I'm better at something than half the Strike team."

"Oh, all right," said Adika. "If you must humiliate someone then you can humiliate me. We'll go first."

I watched the two of them line up at the pool edge. The watching Strike team, including Forge, were very decorative half naked, but I was far more interested in Lucas. This was the first time I'd seen him in just a swimming costume. Despite his constant comments about the muscle-bound Strike team, he had plenty of muscles himself.

Lucas did a low racing dive, and powered up the pool and back again at impressive speed, while Adika struggled to swim a single, painfully slow length. My Strike team leader could barely swim, but he'd still gone underwater in that lake, and entered a flooded pipe to help Forge. I was awed by his courage.

When the pair of them were out of the water, Adika made a note of their times. "Amber next!" he called.

I strolled up to the pool, positioned myself ready to dive in, but hesitated. The whole of the Strike team knew about my old friendship with Forge now so...

"Forge!" I beckoned him over.

Adika raised an eyebrow, but didn't say anything. After our conversation yesterday, he was probably scared to comment.

Forge lined up next to me, and we exchanged smiles. "Three, two, one, go!"

We chanted the words in unison and went for the racing dives. I surfaced an instant before Forge as always, and swam hard for the turn and the second length. Forge beat me by the normal couple of seconds, climbed out of the pool with one smooth movement, then took my hand to pull me up to join him.

There was stunned silence from the rest of the Strike team, followed by applause.

"High up, Amber!" yelled an excited Eli.

Lucas groaned. "Unfair, Amber. I wanted to show off and impress you."

I smiled. "You did impress me. Your time was faster than mine."

"But there was nothing in your record to show you could swim at all, let alone at competition standard. I was planning to teach you to swim."

Lucas was genuinely disappointed. I thought rapidly, and remembered my feeling of utter defencelessness back in that park. "You can teach me to use a gun instead."

Everyone seemed startled by this suggestion. "Why would you want to learn to use a gun, Amber?" asked Adika. "Your job is reading minds, not shooting people."

I shrugged. "Lucas isn't supposed to shoot people either, but he carries a gun when he comes with us on a run. I'd feel a bit less vulnerable if I was armed too."

Adika frowned. "Well, if it makes you feel more comfortable, I suppose you can carry a gun once you've done the appropriate training. Lucas keeps his gun on stun, and would only use it if things went badly wrong. The same applies to you, Amber. The telepath only pulls a gun as a last desperate resort when everyone else is out of action. Understood?"

"Yes."

Adika turned back to the waiting Strike team. "Anyone else able to swim well?"

Several of the team were able to swim a few lengths at a slow but steady speed. The rest were struggling to manage a width, and Forge had to stand by to rescue anyone who got into trouble. Lucas and I stood watching the show.

"If you can swim that fast, why is there no record of you being on a teen swimming team?" asked Lucas.

"Isn't it obvious? I had that weird fixation on Forge, and he was a keen swimmer and surfer. I took up swimming so I could go training with him, but I'd no interest in competing myself." I paused. "Why do you swim, Lucas?"

"I find swimming soothing," he said. "It helps me relax and think through difficult problems."

Adika blew a whistle, and everyone went quiet to listen.

"We'll replace some of the regular sessions of running in the park with swimming training," he said. "Forge can be our swimming instructor. Lucas, when the Strike team has swimming sessions, you can take Amber over to the shooting range for weapons training."

Lucas smiled.

"We had problems in that park because we'd never expected to have to follow a target underwater," continued Adika. "I've been trying to think of any other environments where we would be especially vulnerable. I think we're already well prepared for anywhere else inside the Hive. That leaves one very obvious weak area. Outside."

There was a startled silence. I froze up. Adika must be joking.

"There are specialist maintenance workers who regularly go Outside," said Adika. "Nicole found one of them to give me some advice. He said that we'll find the huge scale of things Outside startling to begin with, but with time we should all be able to adjust."

He paused. "Does anyone have experience of going Outside?"

Lucas, Eli and Rothan raised their hands.

"That's actually going Outside, not just looking out of an aircraft window," Adika added.

The hands stayed up.

"Well, that's a good start. Why did you go Outside, and for how long?" He looked at Eli first.

"A friend bet me that I couldn't stay Outside for an hour," said Eli. "I won."

Adika nodded. "How about you, Rothan?"

"My family are members of the Ramblers Association," said Rothan. "We regularly go walking and camping Outside."

"What's camping?" asked Adika.

"If you're going to be Outside for more than one day, you take a tent along. That's a shelter made of cloth. You sleep in it at night and it keeps the rain off. Well, most of the rain off." Rothan glanced round anxiously at the audience of open-mouthed people staring at him. "I know any interest in Outside is considered a sign of disloyalty to the Hive, but I'm not disloyal. I just like the views and the..."

"Calm down, Rothan," interrupted Lucas. "Admitting to liking going Outside won't put a black mark against your name. Everyone in the Strike team will have broken the rules of accepted Hive behaviour and explored forbidden places. Lottery deliberately selects Strike team members who are risk takers, attracted to danger."

"Oh." Rothan seemed to relax. "It's just that my parents warned me not to talk about this to anyone outside the Ramblers Association. I did mention going camping once at school. I couldn't bear the silly things the other children were saying about the Truesun, but the way the teacher looked at me..."

He shuddered. "Anyway, there are about fifty thousand of us in the Ramblers Association. We go Outside in groups, for a day, a weekend, or even weeks at a time. There are lots of footpaths out there."

"Incredible," said Adika. "I didn't even know this Ramblers Association existed."

"I did," said Lucas. "A Tactical Commander's imprint includes details of all known subversive or non-conformist groups. The Hive doesn't want its people requesting transfers elsewhere, so it limits information on other Hives and discourages any interest in Outside. The idea is that everyone will literally think of this Hive as being the whole world."

He smiled at Rothan. "That means the Ramblers Association is technically classed as a non-conformist group, but in reality its existence is beneficial to the Hive. It helps those with a psychological need for more space and contact with nature than they can get in a Hive park. It also provides a useful pool of people that Lottery can draw on to supply the Hive with its Outside workers."

"A lot of Ramblers Association members work Outside," said Rothan. "I expected to come out of Lottery as an Outside worker myself."

"The Hive obviously doesn't want the Ramblers Association spreading information about Outside to the general population," continued Lucas. "Members are expected to be discreet about their shameful hobby, and are forbidden from attempting to recruit new members while inside the Hive. Anyone they meet Outside is displaying non-conformist tendencies already, so regarded as fair game. Ramblers Association members have tried to recruit me several times when I was in country parks."

"What are country parks?" asked Adika.

"There are a lot of exits from the Hive that lead to one of the ten areas of Outside parks," said Lucas. "You must have seen the parks out of the aircraft window when we flew to Hive Futura."

"No," said Adika. "You were the one who insisted on uncovering a window. I was down the other end of the aircraft minding my own business."

"Well, my imprint includes details of the country parks as well as the Ramblers Association," said Lucas. "When I came out of Lottery, I was intrigued by the idea of an Outside park, so I went to take a look at one. I've made several repeat trips to admire the sky, especially at night."

He laughed. "If I'm Outside long enough, I get approached by people in clumpy footwear, who whisper furtively about the love of the open countryside and the existence of the Ramblers Association. I keep telling them I like sitting on a bench in a country park, but feel no desire to go tramping through the wilderness."

Adika shook his head. "Well, we're very fortunate to have a couple of people with experience of conditions Outside, but the rest of us have some acclimatizing to do. Since Lucas is familiar with Outside, there's no need for him to join us on our training trips."

"But I'd love to come along," said Lucas.

"I had a feeling you might." Adika finally turned to me. "Amber, how do you feel about coming along on a few training trips Outside?"

"Not keen." What I really meant was that I was utterly terrified, and I'd rather drown in a slime vat than go Outside where the Truesun could get me.

"The Strike team have to be able to cope out there well enough to chase a target," said Adika, "but you could keep your eyes closed the whole time."

I didn't say a word. Keeping my eyes closed wouldn't save me from the Truesun burning me. I was going to stay safely inside the Hive.

Adika seemed to get the idea he wasn't winning this argument, because he turned back to the Strike team. "We'll do some more swimming training now."

I went to change from my swimming costume back into ordinary clothes. When I came out of the changing room, I found Lucas lying in wait for me. When I headed towards my apartment, he walked alongside me, ignoring my unwelcoming body language.

"The idea of going Outside frightens you."

I didn't reply.

"You were fine inside Hive Futura."

"That was inside a Hive, Lucas. Not Outside. I thought you were supposed to be highly intelligent."

"You coped inside the aircraft too," said Lucas.

"Again, that was inside, and it still wasn't easy. Can we stop talking about this now?"

I reached my apartment and went inside. The protein scum, Lucas, followed me.

"Amber, the Hive uses social conditioning to discourage people from going Outside. Schools treat any interest in Outside as shameful, and encourage children to believe the myths about the danger and the Truesun. There's no truth in those myths, any more than it's true the nosies are telepaths. If you try going Outside, or even read my thoughts about it, you'll see it's quite a pleasant place."

I turned on him. "I've been Outside, Lucas! I went Outside when I was a little girl. It terrified me, and I will never go Outside again. Now get out of my apartment or I'll call the Strike team to throw you out!"

I ran into my bedroom, and locked the door.

CHAPTER TWENTY-TWO

Two days later, my team leaders and I were in meeting room four. Lucas was sitting directly opposite me, so I was staring at the table top to avoid looking at him.

After my angry response to the idea of me going Outside, Lucas had told Adika to abandon his plan, and warned everyone in the Unit not to mention Outside to me. That meant nobody was talking about Outside, but it didn't stop them thinking about it.

Lucas was worst of all, constantly worrying about the violence of my reaction, and nosing through my records for any reference to me going Outside. He'd even tried calling my parents to ask them about it, which had triggered the first in a series of spectacular arguments that...

No, I mustn't let myself think about that because I'd only get upset again. I forced myself to focus on the conversation.

"Nothing has happened in 600/2600 since our emergency run," said Lucas. "No warning signs. No oddities. Absolutely nothing."

"We might have scared our target into moving their activities to another area," said Adika.

"Why would the target be scared of us?" Lucas had a bitter edge to his voice. "We got the child back, but no information about who was behind the incident. There's no reason for the target to panic and leave their familiar territory. They're still there, they're giving us absolutely no clue to their plans, but eventually there'll be another incident."

"You think we should go back for a check run then?" I asked.

Lucas didn't say anything, just frowned down at his hands. My Tactical Commander knew we needed to go back to 600/2600, but he was worried enough, both professionally and personally, that he wouldn't give the order to send us there again.

I took a deep breath. "We either go back to check 600/2600 now, or wait to be forced into action by another incident. I don't want another emergency run with a child's life at stake. None of us does. That means we have to do the check run. Agreed?"

Everyone nodded.

"Do we begin at the park?" asked Adika.

"It's the obvious place to start," said Lucas. "If Amber can't find a target there, then we'll try a couple of places on other levels."

"Do we go today or tomorrow?" asked Adika.

A delay would just make me more nervous. "We go right now."

"Do you want me to come with you?" asked Lucas.

"No!" Adika and I chorused the reply.

"We treat this like an emergency run," Adika said firmly. "No debate. No discussion. No towing along a Tactical Commander."

I stood up and headed back to my apartment. Lucas scampered after me, and waited in the hallway while I went to my bedroom and got changed. Body armour, clothes, ear crystal. I was ready.

Lucas and I went back outside the apartment, and there was an awkward, silent moment. Several Strike team members jogged past us heading for the lift. This was a planned run to check an area, not an emergency run, so they weren't sprinting flat out.

"Read me," said Lucas.

I reached out to touch his thoughts. Lucas loved me. He was sorry about the arguments. He was worried about this run. I had to be careful, because I mustn't get hurt. Not just because I was the irreplaceable telepath, but because I was me.

"I'll be careful," I said.

"First kiss moment?"

More of the Strike team went past, some of them carrying

bags of special equipment that included a newly delivered robot. Everyone that went by gave us curious looks. The entire unit knew about our arguments because two of them had happened in public.

I sighed. This wasn't a good time to try to progress my relationship with Lucas. The arguments about going Outside were too fresh in my mind. People were watching us. I was filled with nerves about today's run. "Maybe not. We have to work on the physical contact issue though."

"I'm scared of messing it up," Lucas admitted.

We were both scared of that. I was a telepath. Lucas had an incredible mind. Our relationship had progressed at high speed mentally, but we were both torn between eagerness and fear at the idea of making it physical. There was so much at stake here. We both felt we could never have another relationship like this, and were terrified that it could be wrecked by a disastrous physical encounter.

"I know," I said. "Eventually, we'll have to take the risk."

We shook hands. Lucas ran for his office. I ran for lift 2, and the doors closed behind me.

"Strike team is moving," Adika said, in a deafening voice.

I twiddled my ear crystal to lower the volume.

"Tactical ready." Lucas's voice sounded breathless. He must have just sprinted into the office to join the rest of the Tactical team.

"Liaison ready. Tracking status green," Nicole said.

I checked my dataview. We had a full team, except for Matias who was still on restricted duties while he recovered from his appendicitis operation. "Green here."

Lucas started briefing us. He'd got his breath back now, and his voice sounded reassuringly calm, but I knew his thoughts would be frantic with worry.

"You're going back to the 600/2600 area to check it at several different locations," he said. "First location, back at the park, 601/2603 Level 80. I don't need to remind you about last time. Extreme caution advised. You'll find the park empty, because it's still closed after the incident with the child."

Adika listed eight names to be my bodyguard team, putting Rothan in charge of them, and then the rest of the trip went by in grim silence.

Everyone's nerves were wound up to breaking point when we entered the park. Chase team formed a defensive perimeter. Rothan carried me, and the other bodyguards clustered tightly around us. They put me down by a vaguely familiar looking tree. There was still a silver and gold balloon stuck in its branches. I ignored it. We'd been here before. We'd done this before.

"Checking the area." I closed my eyes and reached out with my mind. There was a tight knot of bodyguards surrounding me, thoughts concentrated on my protection. Spread around the perimeter, the Chase team were equally tense and alert.

"Check the park itself, Amber," said Lucas. "The target might have returned. It's not that hard to get into a locked park."

Only the wordless thoughts of birds and small creatures floated around me. No strangers. "No one in the park. Reaching further. Checking this level first."

Minds. Lots of minds. None distinctive. None with a different taste, smell, shape. I drifted across them, not going deep into any individual thoughts, just checking the feel of each mind as I brushed its surface. Tame bees, working in their hive, absorbed in their everyday lives. No jarring note among the busy hum.

"Nothing on this level. Trying the higher levels."

I was checking the chattering human heads in the area directly above the park, when I became aware of an itch inside my head. I had a sick feeling in my stomach.

"Itch. Going circuit!" I opened my eyes and stared at my dataview, gabbling the names of both Bodyguard and Chase team members as I checked their minds.

"Amber?" Adika's voice asked. "What's happening?"

"She's got an itch." Lucas's voice was sharp and anxious. "Amber had an itch when the child was unconscious. Amber woke up with an itch when Matias was hit by appendicitis. Some-one's in trouble."

"Everyone take cover!" Adika snapped out the order.

My bodyguards covered me. Literally. At least one of them

was lying on top of me. I couldn't see my dataview any longer, but I kept chanting names from memory.

"Eli's down. Unconscious. Dhiren's down. Unconscious."

"They were next to each other on Chase team perimeter north," said Adika. "The recording of their visual links just shows the angle changing as if they slowly sat down. Pity they weren't looking at each other. Kaden, you're closest to them. Can you see anything?"

"I'm in some bushes. I can only see Eli's foot from here. I could sneak out of the bushes and..."

"Stay in cover!" Adika ordered. "Is everyone else all right?"

I paused in my soft chanting of names. "So far."

"Everyone keep hidden," said Lucas. "Amber, can you get anything from Dhiren and Eli's minds? Any clue to what happened?"

I hated quitting circuit, my team were in danger and it was instinctive to keep checking them. Lucas was right though. We needed to know what had happened.

"Stopping circuit," I said. "Checking Dhiren and Eli. They're unconscious. Dreaming. Rose without a thorn. Something about a thorn. I'm getting an image from Eli."

I focused on the image. Eli's dream was replaying in a loop. "Eli felt something sharp stick into his arm. He thought it was a thorn from one of the bushes. He brushed at it, looked down, and saw that some kind of dart had gone straight through his body armour. He tried to speak but couldn't, then he passed out."

"Darts," muttered Adika. "Still no target mind?"

"No target," I said. "There's no one except us in this park. I can't swear the dart thing is right. I'm getting it from a dream sequence, and editing out what is obviously just fantasy."

"Tell us the edited bit as well," said Lucas. "It might mean something."

"There's a winged angel," I told him. "The light angel from the Halloween festival. She's flying above Eli, and she'll save him from the dark hunt."

"Halloween festival," muttered Lucas. "Filled with frightening images. People all dressed as evil creatures hunting prey.

Light angel only exception, only hope of escaping the hunt. Light angel clearly Amber. She'll save Eli from the hunt. Why is she flying? Light angel has wings but isn't normally flying. What exactly does she do, Amber?"

"She looks over her left shoulder at something, and then flies up towards it. The dream sequence starts looping after that. I don't look much like her, Lucas. I wish I did, but I don't."

Lucas was jabbering away, verbalizing his thought trains in abbreviated sentences. "Idealized image. Flying to save Eli. In the air. Something high up. No target mind. Target uses booby traps."

"Back on circuit." I started chanting names. "Rafael's been hit."

...my hand. The slim, black dart sticking into it didn't hurt much, but I was...

"Rafael's unconscious," I reported.

"He was on the other side of Eli and Dhiren." Adika sounded furious. "There's something to the north, and it's taking us down one at a time. Keep under cover everyone. Don't show a hand, a foot, a finger."

I was still running circuits, checking the unconscious minds along with the rest. So far they just seemed to be peacefully sleeping, but if they started feeling sick...

"Nicole," said Lucas, "cut all power to the park."

"Working on it," said Nicole.

"You'll turn out the suns, Lucas," said Adika, "and we won't be able to see. Eli had the bag with the wristset lights."

"There's a device targeting you," said Lucas. "It may be attached to the park power supply, or it may have its own power cell. If it's using the power supply then it'll be turned off with the suns. If it isn't turned off, then it may not be able to detect you in the dark."

"I've got someone on the power supply now," said Nicole, in a panicky voice. Conflicting orders from the Tactical Commander and the Strike team leader were Liaison's worst nightmare. "Do we turn it off or not?"

"Turn it off," said Adika.

Everything went very black. At least, it went black to Forge.

My own eyes were closed, but I was in his head at the second the lights went out.

"Stay still unless told to move," said Adika. "Kaden, you're closest to Eli and you've got the robot. Can you use it to retrieve Eli's bag of wristset lights?"

At the mention of Kaden's name, I automatically swapped to his mind. I found him wishing he'd been shot so he didn't have to tell Adika the bad news. "The robot is broken down into four pieces for transport," he admitted reluctantly. "I've only got three of the pieces. Rafael's got the main section, and he's…"

"Unconscious," Adika finished the sentence himself and groaned. "You'll have to try to get the bag yourself then. Crawl cautiously towards Eli."

"It's pitch black," said Kaden. "I'm not sure where Eli is now."

"I'll guide you," I said.

"Heading off in hopefully the right direction."

I was a passenger in Kaden's thoughts as he left the shelter of his bushes. I could hear the rustle of leaves as he crawled forward, feel the coolness of grass under the palms of his hands, share his tense awareness that whatever weapon had taken down his team mates could be about to shoot him too.

"Turn a bit more to your left," I said.

"I just hit a tree trunk. Going round it. Now I can move left." Kaden crawled onwards in the darkness.

"Straight on now," I said.

"Found Eli!" A pause. "Got the lights. Do I turn one on?"

"Get into the bushes first," said Adika. "Then turn one light on and throw it away from you. See if anything shoots at it."

"Got that," said Kaden. "Throwing now. Nothing happening."

"Good," said Adika. "Now put on one of the wristset lights and turn it on. If anything shoots at you, turn it off again. If nothing happens, crawl round to team members and hand out lights."

"I've been trying to work out the relative positions," said Lucas. "I think the device shooting you was attached to a park safety camera. Those are focused on lakes or anywhere else dangerous for small children, and automatically analyze people's movements. If their internal software decides someone is in trouble, they trigger alarms and release rescue devices."

He paused and added chattily. "I know this from personal experience. I nearly drowned in a park lake when I was seven, but a heat-seeking flotation device snagged me. After that, I crawled out of the lake, got lectured by an emergency response team, and signed up for swimming lessons."

"Now he tells us," Adika said, in a bitter voice. "Lucas, you could have mentioned the heat-seeking flotation devices before I went swimming on our first trip here. I wouldn't have been so worried about drowning."

Lucas ignored this complaint. "My point is those cameras are designed to operate devices. You're quite close to the lake. I think the target has added a dart gun to a lake safety camera. Maybe the sort of dart gun that vets use to fire tranquilizers. It was set up to shoot at moving targets."

"Rabbits," I said, "and I'm getting dizzy doing circuits here."

"Amber's right," said Lucas. "If that dart gun was active earlier, the park would be full of unconscious squirrels and rabbits. The people we sent to dig up the drain and check for evidence would have been shot too. The dart gun has only just been activated. The target was waiting for us!"

I winced at the volume of the last sentence.

"Don't shout so loud, Lucas," said Adika.

"Our target has set up a way to control the camera and dart gun remotely," said Lucas. "I think he or she was using the camera to watch us the first time we were here. When the target saw we'd come back again, they turned on the dart gun."

Lucas made a sound of pure frustration. "The target's been controlling the situation all along. Playing games with us."

"The dart gun seems to be off now," said Adika, "and I want my injured men out of here. Nicole, get us some medical support."

"Already waiting at the nearest exit," said Nicole.

"Forge, Kaden, come with me. We get Eli, Rafael, and Dhiren, and carry them to the exit. Then we get everyone else out of here."

I watched the scene through constantly changing eyes, as faint lights moved around. At one point, I was in Forge's head as he was running for the lift, with Eli slung over his shoulder. I caught his wish that Eli was as light to carry as Amber.

"We'll get Amber out next," said Adika. "Bodyguard team, what's your status over there?"

"Amber's still by the tree," said Rothan. "That's shielding part of her. We're surrounding her, and Caleb's over the top, so a dart would have to get through him to touch her."

"I thought she sounded a little muffled," said Adika. "Are you crushed to death, Amber, or able to move?"

"I'm all right," I said.

"Caleb's crushing me, not Amber," said Rothan, "and I'd appreciate him moving his left hand somewhere less personal."

"I thought I was leaning on your..." Caleb broke off. "Sorry."

"Disentangle the human pyramid, grab Amber, turn your lights on, and run for the exit," said Adika.

One frantic dash and I was outside the park. The world was dazzlingly bright again. A few minutes later, the rest of the team had gathered there, and we headed back to the unit. Lucas was babbling through my ear crystal all the way.

"Ahead of us. Always ahead of us. Next time, we don't do something as stupidly predictable as going back to the park."

"Next time, however brightly lit the place we're in, everyone wears wristset lights," said Adika.

We headed out of the lift into the sanctuary of our unit.

CHAPTER TWENTY-THREE

I sat on the sand and looked out to sea. The opposite wall of the beach, with its craggy cliffs and nesting gulls, was far away across the water. Nothing else in the Hive was on the massive scale of a beach. The ceiling was far higher than a mere park, and the shore seemed to stretch endlessly on either side of me.

I wasn't staring out to sea to admire the cliffs. I was doing it because Lucas was sitting next to me and I wanted to avoid looking at him. We were having yet another fight, partly because we were both frustrated and angry after yesterday's disastrous trip back to the park. It had achieved nothing. Our discussions afterwards had achieved nothing. Lucas had been right when he said the target was in control of the situation and playing games with us.

"I hoped that coming here would help," said Lucas sadly.

I turned to glare at him. "Help what exactly? Help me get used to large places so I'll agree to go Outside?"

"No! You're not going Outside, Amber. It's out of the question. If we'd had the faintest idea it would affect you like this, no one would ever have suggested it."

"So stop talking about it!"

Lucas sighed. "I haven't been talking about it."

"You're always thinking about it though."

"I'm trying not to think about it," said Lucas, with exaggerated patience, "but the strength of your reaction worries me."

I picked up a pebble and threw it savagely into the foaming remnants of the latest wave. "I know. I can read it in your head right now. It's always there. If it isn't on one of the conscious levels, then your subconscious is analyzing it."

"I really can't be blamed for what the unconscious levels of my mind..." Lucas must have realized the pointlessness of trying to defend himself because he abandoned the sentence.

I knew I was being unreasonable lashing out at Lucas this way, but I couldn't help it. I felt like a wounded animal, cornered and under attack by the people who should be defending me.

"There's no record of me ever going Outside," I said. "My parents say I never went Outside. Therefore it never happened. Therefore I'm lying."

Lucas sat up straight. "Don't tell me I've ever thought that, because I haven't!"

"Not in those exact words, but it works out as the same thing. Watching a bookette, hearing someone else talk about their own experience, getting confused and thinking it happened to me. I'm not making this up, Lucas. I'm not imagining it. It really happened, and it happened to me not someone else."

"I accept that."

"So why does your head keep analyzing and worrying about it?"

Lucas buried his face in his hands. "Amber, I suggested a trip to Level 1 beach because yesterday's run was a nightmare. Everyone needed a break to calm down, and I wanted to try to patch things up between us. Can't we stop arguing?"

"We keep arguing because you keep thinking, Lucas. All the time, you're thinking. You think too much!"

I stood up, and brushed damp sand off my swimming costume. My current bodyguards were sitting on the beach, a wary distance away, pretending not to watch me. Adika and the rest of the Strike team were further along the shoreline. Forge had been acting as swimming instructor while they nervously tested their swimming skills in the waves. Now they were having a rest break, and Forge had grabbed his chance to do a little surfing.

He was out at sea now, perfectly poised on his surf board, the embodiment of male beauty as he rode a wave in to shore. I walked down to meet him, and applauded his arrival.

He grinned at me, flushed with pleasure, his head beautifully free of any thought of the world outside the Hive. Forge didn't have all the complications that came with Lucas. Forge didn't perpetually analyze things. He wasn't obsessed with why I panicked at the mention of Outside or the Truesun. If I was in a relationship with Forge, then we wouldn't still be neurotically working on our first kiss. Forge wouldn't just think about sex, he'd make it a physical reality.

"This is wonderful," said Forge. "We've got this whole section of Level 1 beach to ourselves."

I laughed at his pure delight, and at my own thoughts. This was just like the days on Teen Level. I was thinking about Forge, and he was thinking about surfing. For a blissful moment, I was just a kid again, with no worries about hunting wild bees.

"Thank Adika's paranoia for that," I said. "He reserved this whole section of beach because he didn't want crowds of people near his precious telepath."

Forge and I sat down among the knee deep waves, the way we used to do on teen beach. We lay back and relaxed, letting the water float us to and fro. When I lifted my head for a second, I saw both Lucas and Adika were standing watching us. I was dragged back from the past into the present, and had a moment of rebellion.

"Lend me your board, Forge. I want to surf."

His mind instantly snapped back from memories of Teen Level to being Strike team. I was no longer just scruffy Amber, who tagged round after him and Shanna. I was a precious true telepath.

"Better not, Amber. You've barely done any surfing. What if you get in trouble?"

I shrugged, impatient with being kept wrapped in cotton wool. "It's my neck."

Forge hung tightly on to his board, and nodded at where the other members of the Strike team were sitting. "It's not just your neck, Amber. They'd all be in the water after you, trying to help, and..."

I groaned in defeat. "Yes, if I do something stupid, I could drown half of my Strike team. I'm just so tired of the pressure to do what the Hive wants, be what the Hive wants. Lottery was supposed to allocate me an ordinary profession, not anything like this." My simmering resentment broke surface again. "And I'm not going Outside!"

Forge cowered at the mere mention of the word. "Adika told us not to talk about that."

I dipped into his mind and saw the memory there. Adika forcefully lecturing the Strike team. No one was to mention Outside to Amber. Not ever. Inconsistent of me to resent that, but I did.

"It really happened, Forge. I went Outside and it was horrible. I'm not imagining it."

He gave me a pleading look. "Amber, if Adika finds out that I talked to you about this, he'll fire me."

Forge was genuinely scared of losing his place on the Strike team. It wasn't fair to drag him into this.

"I'm sorry," I said. "I'm just angry with the whole world at the moment, and furious with Lucas." I repeated my earlier words, because they summed up my feelings so well. "He thinks too much."

"Lucas cares about you," said Forge cautiously. "He worries. It's not easy to stop thinking about things that bother you. I wish it was. I'd like to forget Shanna, but I can't. Being here on this beach reminds me of the old days. The surf team. The competitions. You and Shanna cheering for me."

I pulled a sympathetic face. I would probably regret offering this, but... "I could try to get Shanna a job in the unit. On the Liaison team perhaps. I can't guarantee anything, but I could try."

"What would Shanna do on the Liaison team? Give everyone fashion advice?" Forge shook his head. "It doesn't matter anyway, because I don't want Shanna back, but getting over the past is difficult. She was such a huge part of my life on Teen Level. Now I know she never really cared for me, it messes up all my memories."

I gave him a hug. "Do you think we could have a swim without creating hysterical panic among the Strike team?"

"Yes, let's swim."

Forge left his board on the beach, and we swam out into the waves. As we turned back to the shore, I could see Lucas was standing there and watching us. I reached out with my mind to touch his thoughts and winced. He'd seen me hug Forge and was thinking... Waste it, he should know better than that.

I swam faster, losing myself in the cold sting of the waves until I was weary and had to head for shore. Everyone threw on clothes over their swimming costumes after that, and we went back to the unit. It was a silent trip. The Strike team were feeling wet, cold, and tired, and were nervous of talking given my mood and Adika's threats. I missed the ebullient Eli, who was still in our medical area along with Rafael and Dhiren, recovering from the sedatives in the darts. Eli would have chatted away however awkward the situation.

When the lift arrived at the unit, Lucas slouched off in depression. I chased after him. It was probably a mistake, we'd just have yet another row, but I couldn't let him walk away like that.

"I'm sorry that I'm oversensitive about the Outside thing," I said, "but it terrified me, and it hurts that you believe I imagined it."

"I don't believe you imagined it." Lucas stopped walking, and spoke each word with paranoid care. "I keep trying to work out what happened, why we can't find any record of it, and all the possible answers keep running through my head whether I believe they're right or not. I can't stop thinking about puzzles. It's what I do, the way I am, the reason Lottery gave me this job. Whatever happened, it must have been when you were very young."

"Lucas, please just accept it really happened and forget it. The details don't matter. Yes, I was very young, and I was terrified when my skin started falling off." I shuddered.

Lucas was frowning. "Your skin started falling off? That's the first time you've mentioned that detail."

I pulled a face. "It didn't happen until a day or two after I was Outside. My skin was peeling off. It was revolting. Let's forget it."

"The sun burnt you. Your skin peeled afterwards. Sunburn!"

"Lucas! What does it take to stop you thinking? I'll get the Strike team to knock you out." I gave a despairing laugh. "No, even that wouldn't work. You analyze things in your sleep, so I'm sure you'd analyze things when you're unconscious as well."

"I do?" asked Lucas. "In my sleep?" He considered that for an instant, and then he was off again. "You got sunburnt. Your medical records mention an allergic reaction to face paints causing a skin rash when you were three years old. Why does your record say it was an allergic reaction if it was sunburn? Why do your parents think you've never been Outside? Why...?"

Lucas broke off, and stared at me. "I'm a fool! We're all fools! We've been asking other people, and we should have been asking ourselves!"

I checked his thoughts and they were like a stampeding mob. I recoiled out of his head before I got flattened, saw Lucas sprinting off towards his office, waved my arms in despair, and ran after him.

I realized after a moment that I'd been wrong. Lucas wasn't going to his own office, but to the Liaison area. By the time I caught him up, he was already shouting at a startled Nicole.

"We did this ourselves. We called sunburn a skin rash. We hid the fact Amber was taken out of the Hive, because it's standard procedure to cover up the actions of a wild bee."

"What?" I stared at him in shock.

Lucas glanced at me and forced his voice back to more normal levels. "You were kidnapped as a child, Amber, and a Telepath Unit covered it up. Just like we did with that child in the park. We don't want people to live in fear, so we pretended she'd been trapped by accident."

I checked his thoughts. Yes, he was serious about this.

"Nicole, check all the Telepath Unit records for fifteen years ago," said Lucas. "You're looking for a three-year-old child who was taken out of the Hive. It should be easy to find. We don't have many incidents as bad as that."

Nicole pulled herself together and started frantically looking things up. "One of Morton's cases. Fifteen years ago. The target took a hostage. A three-year-old girl. Amber 2514-0172-912."

Nicole broke off and gave me a wide-eyed look. Yes, that was me. Name and identity code.

"Time for a team leader meeting," said Lucas. "Call the others, Nicole."

He took my arm and tugged me off to meeting room 4. Lucas sat me down at the table, and took the chair next to mine. "You were quite right to be angry with me. I should have guessed at once."

"Don't be silly," I said. "How could you guess something like this?"

Nicole, Megan and Adika walked into the room together. By now I'd learned that Nicole's health condition varied from day to day, so sometimes she would walk rather than use her powered chair. This was clearly one of her better days.

The minute everyone had sat down, Megan broke into anxious speech. "It's a bad idea for Amber to learn what happened."

"Amber is being affected by the buried, distorted memories of a terrifying childhood experience," said Lucas. "If she learns what actually happened back then, it should help rather than harm her."

"It's a risk." Megan was practically wailing the words. "We could trigger old traumas."

"We've already triggered them, Megan." Lucas's voice was savage now. "We tried to persuade Amber to go Outside, and when she refused we kept worrying about it. Every time she read our thoughts, it must have created havoc in her subconscious. The way Amber has been acting lately, desperately trying to defend herself, was a huge warning signal. I was just too stupid to recognize it."

He slammed his hands on the table in frustration. "We've already done just about all the harm that's possible short of physically dragging Amber Outside."

Megan gestured helplessly. "I'm still not sure we should tell Amber what happened."

"What other option do we have, Megan?" demanded Lucas. "Amber is a telepath. Once we know the details, she'll read them in our minds."

"Do we need to know?" asked Megan.

"Yes!" Adika joined the argument. "If I don't know then I can't do my job properly."

"That's doubly true for me," said Lucas. "Besides, if we don't know what happened, we'll keep guessing, and Amber will be reading our thoughts about it. May I point out that my imprint, Adika's imprint, and the imprints of the entire Strike team include explicit details of everything wild bees have been known to do to children they've abducted. Adika and I are busily thinking about a dozen gory possibilities right now. The more we try to stop ourselves, the more we'll do it."

"Yes, but..."

"No, Megan," I interrupted her. "Lucas is right. I must know what really happened back then."

Adika glanced at Megan. "We've no choice here."

She gave a sigh of what seemed to be reluctant acceptance.

Adika turned back to face me. "I'm sorry, Amber. Your abduction happened years before I joined Morton's team. I had no knowledge of it."

"Nobody knew," said Lucas bitterly. "Not even Amber's parents. Telepath Units cover up incidents too well. The truth is only held in our confidential records. It's the best thing for the Hive, it reduces the chance of future incidents, but it was disastrous in this case."

He shrugged. "Nicole, look up the details for us. Amber, promise me you won't read any of our minds while Nicole explains what happened. If there's something bad, it's much better for you to just hear it as words, without adding the burden of the emotion and images in our minds."

That made sense. I'd already seen some images in Adika's head that sickened me. "I promise."

Nicole gave Megan a nervous look, then tapped the table to make a data display appear in front of her. She looked down at the flowing text, and took a deep breath before speaking.

"There's only the standard report from Morton's unit. It happened during Carnival. Morton and his Beta Strike team were responding to an emergency call, but the local hasties got the situation under control before they arrived. Morton checked they'd arrested the right target, and the team started heading back to the unit, but Morton picked up something strange on the way. He wasn't sure whether it was a real target or not, but they tried following it to be on the safe side. They must have had a problem doing that, because they rode the belts for ages without catching up with the target."

"A chase wouldn't be easy during Carnival," said Adika. "The belts would be packed with people in silver and gold Carnival outfits, most of them wearing masks."

"The problem seems to have been more than that," said Nicole. "Morton knew the target was a man, but he wasn't getting a name or any clues on what he'd do next. He couldn't even tell if the target knew he was being followed. Eventually, they reached 511/6126, and the target went into a park that was running a Carnival event for children. There were thousands of wildly excited small children and just a scattering of adults."

I must have been one of those children. I tried to remember a party in the park back then, but I'd been to a lot of Carnival events as a child. The earlier ones were just blurred, excited memories of dressing up in costumes, playing games, and chasing balloons. The strange thing was that I had no fear of parks at all. It was only the thought of Outside and the Truesun that bothered me.

Nicole pulled a face. "It was a nightmare situation for Morton's Liaison team. Before they could work out how to evacuate the park, Morton said the target was moving again, heading up in a lift, and he had a small child with him. The child was tagged with a bracelet of course, so Liaison got her identity and started tracking her."

Nicole paused, and gave me a nervous look before continuing. "Tactical decided the target knew he was being followed and had taken a hostage. The bracelet signal went straight up in the lift to Industry 1. Since this was Carnival, all the working areas were empty apart from the odd person watching essential systems. Morton's team were preparing to go for the strike, when the target took the child through a maintenance exit and out of the Hive. That caused a major delay."

Adika frowned. "Why? Were the Strike team scared of going Outside?"

"Tactical wouldn't let them go through the maintenance exit," said Nicole. "Morton wasn't getting anything at all from the target now, and the child's bracelet signal was right outside the door. Tactical thought the target had been terrified by finding himself Outside, and was sitting there, frozen in panic. They were worried that if the Strike team charged out of the door after him, then the target might harm the child."

She shrugged. "Eventually, some of the Strike team went out through another exit, aiming to sneak up and take the target by surprise. It took them over an hour to do that. When they finally got there, they just found the child's bracelet, open but undamaged."

"How could the target have taken off a child's tracking bracelet without damaging it?" asked Megan. "Only approved medical staff have access to the codes to unlock tracking bracelets."

Nicole shook her head. "The report doesn't say anything else about the bracelet. Morton's team were concentrating on finding the target and hostage child. They couldn't involve Outside maintenance workers in a search for a potentially dangerous target. The Strike team had to do all the searching themselves, they were struggling with conditions Outside, and running out of time. When the Carnival event ended, the child's parents would discover she was missing. Eventually, the Strike team heard a child crying, found her hiding in some bushes, and took her back into the Hive for medical checks."

"What did the medical report say?" asked Lucas, in an unfamiliar harsh voice.

"The child was terrified," said Nicole, "but completely unharmed. Her only problem was sunburn. It had been a very hot and sunny day Outside. The medical staff treated that, gave her sedatives and a new tracking bracelet, and delivered her back to her parents telling them she'd had an allergic reaction to face paints."

Adika and Lucas seemed to relax slightly. I cheated on my promise a little, telling myself Nicole had finished her explanation, and skimmed the surface of Lucas's thoughts. I didn't just see his relief, but some of the possibilities he'd been braced to hear. I winced, and told myself to forget those dark images. If Nicole was telling the truth, then I hadn't been harmed. I dipped into her thoughts for a moment to reassure myself. Yes, she was telling the truth.

Lucas groaned. "I know the medical staff would have been under time pressure, but they should have given Amber proper psychological treatment after such a traumatic experience. What about the target? Did the Strike team keep searching for him?"

"No," said Nicole. "It sounds like the Strike team had hit their endurance limit. There were no more searches, but they posted hasties at all the Hive entrances in that area for the next week. No one came in from Outside, so they assumed the target had got lost and had an accident. They closed the case after that. If a target had deliberately left the safety of the Hive and got himself killed, it wasn't their problem."

She paused, frowning. "There's one other thing. It must be just coincidence, but Morton's Strike team first started chasing their target in area 600/2600."

CHAPTER TWENTY-FOUR

There was a long silence after that. Oddly enough, I felt quite calm, as if I'd been expecting to hear Nicole say those words, even as if I was glad to hear them. Maybe I was just relieved to have a solid reason for the fear that had had me snapping at people for days.

I glanced round the table. "Area 600/2600 again. Coincidence?"

Nicole looked like a frightened mouse. Adika and Megan seemed unable to speak. I turned to Lucas.

"Extremely unlikely," he said.

I wrinkled my nose at him. "Wrong answer, Lucas. The right answer, the comforting answer, is that it's obviously pure coincidence."

"It's impractical to lie to a telepath."

I checked heads. Lucas was fighting his anger, trying to concentrate on analyzing the situation. Megan's mind was practically hysterical. Adika was lost in grim and dangerous thoughts. He'd always had an obsession with the possibility of his telepath getting kidnapped. The news that she already had been wasn't helping at all.

I sighed, and asked the truly scary question. "You think our current target in 600/2600 is the same man that kidnapped me, Lucas? Despite the fifteen year time gap?"

"Yes. The child in the booby trapped drain was also a three-year-old girl."

I hadn't thought of that. "He chose a girl of the same age both times."

"More than just the same age," said Lucas. "The girl in the drain had the same name as you."

"What?" I shook my head. "I didn't know she was called Amber."

Lucas pulled a face. "We avoided mentioning her name during the run. Talking about two different Ambers was liable to cause confusion, and it didn't seem significant at the time. Now it's clear it is. The target is playing games with us, deliberately picking a hostage who'd remind you of yourself fifteen years ago."

That sounded seriously creepy to me. "So everything that's been happening in area 600/2600 is about me. The target is hunting me again."

"I believe so," said Lucas.

Adika woke from his trance. "There would have been over a million three-year-old children in the Hive back then, and the target kidnapped the only one who would grow up to become a true telepath. That couldn't be random chance."

"It seems highly unlikely to be random chance," said Lucas, "but if it wasn't then the target had a way of identifying future true telepaths at three years old."

"That's not possible," said Megan. "A century ago, there was a trial attempt to test children for telepathic ability at age twelve. The trial failed because the subconscious defensive block on using telepathic ability was too strong to overcome at that age. It would be even harder to identify a true telepath at age three."

"Our Hive's method of identifying true telepaths doesn't work on young children," said Lucas, "but Hives never trade information on telepaths. It's possible another Hive uses an entirely different approach. Brainwave activity goes through significant changes at around age three. There may be clues that indicate if a child is a potential true telepath."

"Another Hive!" Adika's paranoia about threats from other Hives made him leap at that explanation, his thoughts burning with anger. "Another Hive is behind this. How could an agent from another Hive get information on our children's brainwave activity?"

"Annual infant development checks contain baseline brainwave activity measurements," said Megan, in a despairing voice.

"We know the target had the code to unlock Amber's tracking bracelet," said Lucas. "If the target could hack his way into our Hive's central data storage to get the bracelet code, then he could access the development check records and a host of other information as well. Whatever method he used, he discovered Amber was a true telepath, and carefully planned her abduction. Carnival was the ideal opportunity, with all the children being entertained at special events."

"Kidnapping a true telepath is a major violation of Hive Treaty," said Adika. "We have to report this to Joint Hive Treaty Enforcement."

"They'd dismiss the report as wild supposition," said Lucas. "We've got no evidence at all that another Hive was involved in Amber's kidnapping. We don't even know which other Hive to accuse of the crime. All we've got is a plausible explanation of why Amber was kidnapped rather than any other one of a million three-year-olds."

"You believe the explanation is right though, Lucas?" I asked. "Our target is an agent from another Hive?"

Lucas buried his face in his hands for a moment, thoughts racing on every level of his mind, and then lifted his head again. "Yes. There's a limit to what I can accept as random coincidence, and if everything was deliberately planned then the target knows far too much about too many different things. How to find the one true telepath among a million three-year-old children. How to hack into our central data core. How to lure a telepath and her Strike team into a trap."

Lucas made a helpless gesture with his hands. "We have subversive groups in our Hive, but I can't believe any of them could know more about identifying telepaths than the Hive itself. If the target is an agent from another Hive, it would explain a lot of things, including why Morton was having problems reading his mind fifteen years ago. Morton's a skilled telepath, but was probably struggling because of language issues."

I didn't understand that, and I couldn't cheat by reading Lucas's thoughts when they were running at bewildering speed on multiple, interleaved layers. "Explain that last bit please."

"Many Hives speak a different language to us," said Lucas. "The target must have been imprinted with our language, but the top levels of his mind would still be using words from the language of his home Hive. I don't know exactly what that would look like to a telepath, but it must be confusing."

"I've sometimes had trouble when a target is thinking of something complicated to do with their work," I said. "When a thought level is racing along using lots of technical words that I don't understand, it all blurs together into an incomprehensible mass. I usually get round that by skipping to a thought level that's using simpler words, but presumably all the target's thought levels would have the same problem. That's not good."

I bit my lip. If we ever caught up with this target, I'd find his thoughts unreadable. I'd be able to see the view from his eyes, but not warn my Strike team about his plans.

"So the target kidnapped me, planning to take me back to his own Hive," I continued. "He took off my bracelet so no one could track us and hunt us down. What went wrong? Why did he let me go? If Morton's Strike team scared him away, then he should have made another attempt to kidnap me a few weeks or months later, not wait fifteen years before reappearing. It doesn't make sense."

"I agree," said Lucas. "From what the report says, Morton's Strike team never got close to the target. I doubt he even knew they were chasing him. We need to go back to the beginning and work events through logically."

He paused. "Let's start with the base point assumption that the target is an agent from another Hive. Our time line starts over fifteen years ago when the target came to our Hive. How would he have got here? My imprint doesn't tell me anything about other Hives. I know we have border defences, but I've no information on how they work or..."

"My imprint covers border defences," Adika interrupted. "It's a long way to both our coastline and our land borders with the territory of other Hives. An unauthorized aircraft couldn't breach our air space without being detected. We'd launch intercept aircraft in response, and Joint Hive Treaty Enforcement would send in forces as well. The guilty Hive couldn't possibly explain their incursion, because we're nowhere near any of the neutral trading exchange points."

"How do you think the target reached us then, Adika?" asked Lucas.

"Our land border line is a flat concrete strip patrolled by heat-seeking drones," said Adika. "They'd be hard to evade even with stealth technology, and I don't believe the target came from a neighbouring Hive anyway. We're on good terms with our neighbours, and they speak the same language as us."

He pulled a face. "My guess is the target came from our coastline. Our air space extends offshore, so the target must have been dropped into the sea from an aircraft. There are drones patrolling offshore, but a lone swimmer with breathing equipment could make it past them by diving underwater when they approached. Once the target made it to land, he would have had to make a lengthy journey on foot to reach our Hive. It would have taken him several days, possibly longer, to get here."

Lucas nodded. "And the target would have to make the same trip in reverse to get back home."

Megan burst into speech. "The target surely couldn't have been planning to take Amber on a journey like that. She was only three years old. Spending days Outside. Being dragged underwater. It could have killed her!"

Lucas banged his head forcibly on the table top.

"Lucas, stop that!" I said.

He lifted his head and looked round at us. "Everything strange that's been happening is interconnected. Every bit of it. Amber told me she had a vivid, repeating dream through all her years on Teen Level. She was in a weird park, walking through incredibly tall trees with Forge. It was hot, and the suns were very bright. Of course they were. It was a bright, sunny day Outside when Amber was kidnapped. She was frightened in the dream, but Forge told her she was a good girl. He talked to her as if she was a child, because she was a child when it really happened."

"My dream can't have been a memory of being kidnapped by Forge," I said. "We were both only three years old back then."

"Your dream isn't the exact memory, Amber," said Lucas. "Your mind tried to make sense of confusing fragments by relating them to familiar things. You replaced Outside with a park. You replaced the Truesun with the park's lighting. You replaced your kidnapper with Forge."

He paused. "You were kidnapped when you were three years old, but the dreams didn't start until you moved to Teen Level and met Forge. You had a strange reaction to the sight of Forge as well. Those things must have happened because Forge looks like your kidnapper. The sight of him had triggered latent memories."

Megan turned to look at Lucas with an appalled expression. "Lucas, if you're right that Forge looks like Amber's kidnapper, then the whole Strike team must look like him too!"

"Oh, yes," said Lucas. "We didn't just try to take Amber Outside; we surrounded her with men chosen to look like her kidnapper. Amber should be completely hysterical by now, but she isn't. The dreams and the strange reaction to the sight of Forge have stopped as well. When did that happen, Amber?"

"I'm not sure," I said. "After I worked out my reaction to Forge was caused by me looking at him, I tried to keep my eyes closed when he was around and work telepathically. One day, I accidentally looked at him directly, and found I wasn't reacting to him any longer. It was the same with the dream. I suddenly realized I hadn't had it for a while."

"Did you react to Forge after your arrival at the unit?" asked Lucas.

"Definitely. I remember getting hit by it just before a training run. Keith's Strike team leader was going to be our target."

"I remember that day," said Adika sharply. "Forge had a bruise on his face, and someone poked it. Amber started yelling at them, and we all wondered... Wait a minute!"

He broke off and stood up, leaning forward with his hands on the table. "When Forge arrived at the unit, he had a birthmark. An odd red mark on his left cheek. During the training run with Keith's Strike team leader, Forge cut his face badly on a branch. Our medical staff had to do some reconstruction work on that cheek, and Forge got them to remove the birthmark as well. We all teased him about it."

Adika seemed to realize he was standing up, and sat down again.

"And that's why Amber wasn't reacting to the rest of the Strike team," said Lucas. "They may well have the same general appearance as the target, but they don't have birthmarks."

"We can search Hive records for males of the right age group with a similar birthmark," said Nicole.

"The target may not actually have a birthmark, just some sort of mark on his left cheek," said Lucas. "It could be a mole, a scar, a tattoo, anything, and if he really is an agent from another Hive then he won't be in our records."

Lucas's voice was oddly flat and dispassionate, but his thoughts were an incomprehensible whirlpool of analysis mixed with churning emotion. He'd thought of something very bad, and didn't want to tell me about it.

"Whatever it is you've worked out, Lucas, you have to tell me." I quoted his own words back to him. "It's impractical to lie to a telepath."

Lucas groaned. "What Megan said was right. The target couldn't have been planning to take a three-year-old child on the hideously difficult journey back to his Hive."

"So why did he take me Outside?" I asked.

"He took you Outside to imprint you with orders to obey him."

CHAPTER TWENTY-FIVE

It took me a moment to absorb what Lucas had said, and then panic hit me. "No!" I wasn't sure if I'd shouted the word or not. "The target can't have imprinted me."

Lucas looked me straight in the eyes. "It's the obvious answer, Amber. Your recurring dream and your obsession with Forge are precisely the sort of issues that can happen if the imprinting rules aren't followed correctly. The target intentionally broke those rules so your imprint would include a fixation on him, a compulsion to obey him, and a reward of happy emotions when you pleased him. It will also include a set of orders."

He paused for a second. "The target took you Outside to make sure he wouldn't be disturbed during the imprinting process. I think he was taking you back to the Hive entrance, aiming to put your bracelet back on and take you back into the Hive before anyone realized you were missing, when he ran into Morton's Strike team. The target left you to be found by the Strike team, and I think at that point he went back to his home Hive."

"A set of orders," I repeated Lucas's earlier words. "Orders to do what?"

"The target didn't try to take you back to his Hive with him as a child, because he'd got a much better way to kidnap you. Now that you're an adult, he's returned to complete his plan. He's been trying to reach you and activate the orders he imprinted in your mind. Those orders will compel you to request a transfer to his Hive."

I imagined myself a willing puppet requesting a transfer to an alien Hive, asking to go and live among strangers as their slave. I made a soft, gulping sound of horror.

"Shut up, Lucas!" Megan shouted. "You're frightening Amber."

I moistened my lips and forced myself to speak. "No, carry on explaining, Lucas. We all have to understand what's been happening. Especially me. I can't fight what I don't understand."

Lucas studied my face for a moment, then nodded and started speaking again. "The imprint should have remained completely inactive all through Amber's childhood and teen years, so there'd be no clues for us to spot during Lottery, but she met Forge. The sight of him, with a birthmark that reminded her of something on her kidnapper's face, stirred up some of the imprinted orders."

"I was able to control my reaction to Forge," I said. "A little, at least. Now I know I've been imprinted with orders, it should be easier to resist them."

Lucas shook his head. "The birthmark's effect was only a faint shadow of your imprinted compulsion, Amber. Once the target activates your imprint, you won't stand a chance of resisting its orders."

I hadn't had a headache since Lottery, but I could feel one starting now. I rubbed my forehead to try to banish the pain. "Surely our Hive wouldn't just hand over a telepath?"

Lucas's mind was screaming as he pictured what would happen. "Now you're an adult, you have the right under Hive Treaty to request a transfer to another Hive of your choice. Our Hive would try to talk you out of it, bribe you, do everything we could to stop it, but your imprint could make you act in a way that was actively dangerous. If that wasn't enough to make us give in, then the target's Hive could approach Joint Hive Treaty Enforcement."

Lucas gave a shrug of total despair. "They'd complain we'd refused your Hive transfer request. Joint Hive Treaty Enforcement would send in a team to investigate. Without solid proof that another Hive had tampered with your mind, we'd be left with no options at all. We might be able to stall for weeks, even months, but if you insisted you wanted the transfer then we'd have to let you go in the end."

He grimaced. "It's an utterly brilliant plan. If we hadn't found out you'd been imprinted, we'd never have understood what happened."

I tugged at my hair. "Tell me more about Joint Hive Treaty Enforcement. I've only heard vague references to it."

"Hive Treaty outlaws a host of things like theft from other Hives, kidnapping, and territory violations," said Lucas. "All Hives are signatories. Breaching treaty results in severe penalties."

"So failing to allow my transfer would breach Treaty," I said. "What sort of penalties are we talking about?"

Lucas pulled a face. "The offending Hive faces sanctions, and continued defiance can even result in an attack by the combined forces of all the other Hives. Things like war, invasion, kidnapping raids, and other conflicts are always bad for Hives. It's in the general interest to make offences unprofitable. The occasional theft of research information happens because it's easy to claim it was a simultaneous discovery."

I wasn't following the words as much as the images in Lucas's mind. Pictures of our Hive under attack by hostile aircraft. Housing warrens torn apart, with mangled corpses lying in the corridors. There was no choice here. No choice at all.

"If the worst happens, then you have to hand me over, Lucas," I said. "You can't risk our Hive being attacked."

"Not my decision," said Lucas. "Thankfully. Strongly suggest locking me up in that situation."

"It's not going to happen," said Adika. "The target isn't going to activate Amber's imprint, because we won't give him the chance. She won't leave this unit, we'll go into lockdown, and Forge will be confined to his apartment under armed guard."

I frowned at him. "There's no need to lock up Forge. He didn't know a thing about this. I've spent enough time in his head to be absolutely certain of that."

"If Forge was involved," said Adika, "then your imprint might not allow you to tell us. He might even have given you orders to forget it yourself."

I opened my mouth, only to close it again. I couldn't trust my own mind any longer. I could be ordered to do anything, literally anything, and I'd do it. Hideous thoughts ran through my mind. When we were at the beach, I'd had that silly moment, asked to borrow Forge's board and go surfing. He'd pointed out then just how easy it would be for me to drown half my Strike team.

"I hate to say this," said Lucas, "but Forge is innocent of everything except cuddling Amber on the beach. If you want to lock him up for that, then I'm not going to object, but I'm a little concerned what penalties you'll inflict on me if I sleep with her."

I gave a shocked laugh.

"This isn't a good time to play the fool, Lucas," said Adika.

Lucas gave him a pointed look. "It's exactly the time to play the fool and relieve the tension. Look at Amber's face. She's worked out what this means. She could be ordered to do anything, including sending her own Strike team into a death trap, and she'd do it. How would you feel if you knew someone could take total control of your mind and make you shoot your own telepath?"

I saw Adika's face, his thoughts, and felt sick. The unspeakable horror of a Strike team was letting their telepath be harmed or killed. To make Adika contemplate being forced to murder me was brutally unkind. "Lucas, that was cruel."

"No, Amber," said Lucas. "If an eighteen-year-old girl fresh from Lottery can look nightmare in the face, then a Strike team leader with the experience of a thousand emergency runs behind him had better be able to do the same. All of us have to accept precisely how bad this could be, and then work out how to beat it. We've been very, very lucky. We've found out about your imprint before the target managed to activate it."

"You're sure about that?" I asked. "The imprint might be giving orders to my subconscious without my knowledge."

"I'm sure, Amber." Lucas leaned across and took my hand for a second. "The target wouldn't want us to know about the imprint. If it was active, you'd never have told me about the dreams or the sunburn. Equally, if Forge was working for another Hive, he'd never have removed the birthmark that let him give you orders."

I nodded. "All right. That means we just have to put the unit into lockdown while you remove my imprint."

Lucas's thoughts were too fast and too technical for me to understand the details, but the tone of them panicked me.

"You can't remove imprints?"

"It's not totally impossible," said Lucas, "but it's never easy. The larger the amount of imprinted data, the more difficult it is. The longer it's been in place, the greater the resulting mental confusion, because personal memories are linked to the imprinted data. That means those memories are either removed along with the imprint, or become distorted. In your case, the imprint has never been activated, so your only personal memory directly linked to it is the repeating dream."

"So what's the problem removing it?"

"Imprints are controlled by two linked symbols," said Lucas. "One at the start of the imprinted data thread, called the key symbol. One at the end, called the trigger symbol."

He hesitated, struggling for a way to make this comprehensible without using technical terms. "Think of the key symbol as the key to a lock. It can be used to remove an imprint, by unlocking the start of the data thread so it can be unravelled."

I remembered one of the activities I'd tried on Teen Level. "A thread? Like the thread you use in sewing or embroidery? If you make a mistake, put the stitches in the wrong place, you can unravel them and start again."

"It's a very different sort of thread," said Lucas, "but yes, the analogy works. At the end of the data thread is the trigger symbol, the one used to activate the imprint. Normally, that activation is done immediately the imprint is complete, but in your case it wasn't. The target has been trying to reach you to do it now."

He paused. "The problem with removing the imprint is we know the key symbol for our Hive's imprints, but not the key symbol for the one in your head. Without it, we can't remove your imprint."

I thought about that for a moment. "Hives trade people. Only rarely, but there'll be a few people here who were imprinted by other Hives. One of those imprints could have the same key symbol as mine."

"Hives trade people after Lottery but before imprinting," said Lucas. "The new Hive imprints them on arrival."

"But what about people who ask to move Hive?"

"If they've already been imprinted," he said, "then their imprint is removed before they move."

"You said that could cause mental confusion."

Lucas waved his hands in a gesture of helplessness. "They're warned about that. Joint Hive Treaty Enforcement insists on people having their imprints removed before they transfer Hive. If they were allowed to leave with all the data from their old Hive intact, then it would lead to people with valuable knowledge being offered huge rewards to change Hive. There'd be chaos."

Joint Hive Treaty Enforcement's rules seemed barbaric to me, but I had to focus on the imprint issue. "So you can't remove my imprint without the key symbol, and you don't know the key symbols that other Hives use?"

"Exactly," said Lucas.

"But there's got to be some way to remove the imprint without the key."

"No!" Megan stood up.

Lucas glanced at her. "Let me handle this, Megan."

"Amber's health and wellbeing are my primary concern."

"Mine too," said Lucas. "Sit down, Megan."

She shook her head. "Your role and priorities are different to mine."

Lucas sighed. "We're on the same side here, Megan. I'd never risk harming Amber. I'm not just professionally involved, but personally as well."

Megan finally sat down again and Lucas turned back to me. "We can't even find your imprint without the key symbol, Amber. It's like a single grain of sand lost on the vast beach of data in your mind. We don't know what we're looking for. Even if we could locate it, trying to remove the imprint without the key would be like... Like removing some embroidery stitches by cutting a hole in the material. Like smashing down a door instead of opening it."

He pulled an agonized face. "We'd have to wipe everything in that area of your mind, causing huge damage. You might not be a true telepath afterwards. You might not even be able to walk or talk. It's not an option. Not under any circumstances."

"It can't be that bad," I said. "People have traumatic memories removed all the time. Like the girl that Callum stabbed."

"In cases like that, the traumatic memories are removed by rolling back time," said Lucas. "The personal experience chain is unravelled to a point before the incident happened. Everything after that moment, traumatic or otherwise, is lost forever. You were imprinted when you were three years old, Amber. If we reset you to before that point, then you'd lose all your memories and personal development, and become a small child in an adult body. We have to be truly desperate before we try that."

"We have to find the key to my imprint then," I muttered. "What are these keys like?"

"Our Hive uses complex visual symbols for both the key and trigger," said Lucas. "Audible sequences would also be possible."

I took a deep breath. "I have to go Outside."

"What?" Lucas gave a bewildered shake of his head. "Amber, we've already established that you can't go Outside. Your fear of it isn't natural or rational. You were imprinted as a terrified three-year-old, and your terror of Outside and the Truesun became part of that imprint."

"I have to do this," I said. "We know I was imprinted when I was Outside with the target. We need to bring back my memories of exactly what happened back then."

"It's not safe," said Megan. "There could be serious trauma."

I ignored her, keeping my eyes on Lucas. He was my unit Tactical Commander. He was the one I needed to convince. "Is it possible my memories would give you some clues about the key symbol for my imprint?"

"When our Hive imprints someone after Lottery," said Lucas, "it's done in carefully controlled conditions. The person is left with no memory of the key or trigger symbols. Your case is entirely different though."

He pulled a face. "Your imprinting was an incompetent mess, Amber. The target must have broken every possible rule. I think he kept you awake and looking at him during the process, as the simplest way to imprint the fixation with his face and pleasing him. That would explain how your terror of being Outside got included in the imprint."

Lucas hesitated for a second before speaking again. "If I'm right, and you were awake for the imprinting, then yes. It's possible you'd have a memory of seeing or hearing the key symbol."

"In that case, we have to try this," I said. "I have to go Outside. I have to remember."

"Megan's perfectly right though," said Lucas. "Deliberately awakening those memories is dangerous. We've no idea what makes someone into a telepath. It's possible that causing massive trauma on either conscious or unconscious levels of your mind could damage your ability."

"What else can we do?" I asked. "We can't wait for the target to trigger my imprint and make me his personal slave."

"We go into lockdown," said Adika. "We keep you totally isolated so the target can't reach you."

"For how long?" I asked. "The target has already spent fifteen years hunting me. He'd spend another fifteen if necessary, and I'm no use to the Hive while I hide in my unit."

I paused for a moment. "We have to do something, and there are only two options. Either we reset me back to before I was imprinted, or we try to recover my memories of the key symbol."

No one was saying anything. They knew I was right, but they hated the idea of me going Outside. I hated it even more than they did.

"I have to go Outside." I kept repeating the same words in an attempt to convince myself I could actually do this. I knew it had to be me forcing myself to leave the Hive, because no one else would drag the precious telepath Outside against her will. "I'll need you to help me. Make this as easy as possible for me."

Lucas groaned, and I saw his thoughts accelerate as his head started assessing options. He started talking in speed speech.

"Possible restore memories but danger reliving traumatic childhood experience."

I focused on the pre-vocalized words in his mind, so I could see the full sentences and understand properly.

"We might be able to bring the old memories to the surface without you going Outside, Amber, but then you'd be hit with everything at once. Both the traumatic childhood experience, and the terror of being Outside. Your suggestion is probably best. We give you carefully graduated experiences of being Outside to reduce your fear to a level you can handle. Some of your old memories may surface naturally during that process. If not, we can move on to trying to restore them artificially."

He paused. "The Truesun is the focus of your fear?"

I saw an image of the Truesun appear in his head, and instinctively pulled out of his thoughts. I tried to cover up my shudder by making it into a nod. "Yes, I'm very scared of that."

"Then it's logical to begin going Outside at night."

"When the Truesun is turned off?" I asked.

"A slight technical quibble, the Truesun isn't turned off at night, it's on the other side of our planet. Be aware that the moon will be visible at night. Are you afraid of the moon in the same way as the Truesun?"

"I don't think so," I said. "I've been in parks at night when they were running a moons and stars programme. Moons are a lot less bright than suns. That's the same Outside?"

Lucas nodded.

I moistened my lips. "We'll make a start tonight then."

"Not tonight," said Lucas. "It's inadvisable to rush this."

"It has to be tonight, Lucas. We don't know when the target will make his next move and... I have to do this before I lose my nerve."

He sighed. "If you insist."

I felt my stomach churn with tension. I was going Outside tonight!

CHAPTER TWENTY-SIX

A few hours later, I stood in the midst of a battlefield, my armour covered with mud and blood, my exhausted men gathered around me.

"Once more unto the breach, dear friends, once more; Or close the wall up with our English dead," I heard myself shout in a very masculine voice.

"Do you always play the lead male role in bookettes?" asked Lucas.

I hadn't noticed Lucas entering the room. I turned in surprise, and saw a quizzical look on his face. "Bookette stop." The holo battlefield, the weary men, and my fake masculinity abruptly vanished, leaving me standing in a featureless room. "The bookette doesn't have a female role at this point."

"Why are you viewing a historical bookette anyway?" asked Lucas. "You were supposed to be resting before tonight's trip."

I pulled a face. "I tried to sleep but couldn't. I kept worrying about going Outside. I needed a distraction, so I asked the bookette room for something involving people from different Hives speaking different languages. It came up with this, and it's really confusing me. The relevant scene was right at the end, so I thought I'd play some of the earlier stuff to see if it helped me understand what was happening. It didn't. You watch. Bookette restart first entry Catherine."

Now I was a woman, standing in a large room with tapestries hanging on the wall. The bookette had me wearing a peculiar long dress, and I was accompanied by an older woman who seemed to be my bodyguard. Lucas had been automatically designated the part of Henry, and we stood facing each other, with the ancient dialogue appearing to come from our mouths. This was a top model bookette room, so its holos faked our mouth movements beautifully. I let the scene run for several minutes.

"Bookette pause," I finally said. "So, what's going on? Catherine is getting traded between Hives?"

Lucas/Henry smiled. "Effectively, yes."

"But her imprint of her new Hive language is faulty."

His smile widened. "The story is set prior to the availability of imprints. Catherine is learning the language the slow way."

"Can I do that to help me read the target?"

"The slow way is extremely slow. Takes years. Impractical."

I sighed. "This bookette is weird. Hive England and Hive France are fighting. Henry is king of England. What's a king?"

"A leader. Decisions were made by a person, rather than by systems. In this bookette, Henry decides to make war on France to increase his personal power. You can see why we don't let people make that sort of decision anymore."

"So why is Catherine being traded? What job does Hive England need her to do?"

Lucas clearly loved this question. "Her job is to be queen of Hive England, sleep with Henry, and have a child to be the next leader. Shall we order the bookette room to expand this scene to include that point in their relationship?"

"No," I said firmly.

"We could just let the bookette fake our actions, if you preferred not to actually..."

"Bookette stop. Lucas, quit giggling and behave!"

The room returned to being featureless, and regal Henry turned back into Lucas.

"Is it time for us to go now?" I asked.

Lucas nodded, and led the way out of the apartment. I was bone weary and a mass of nerves. I expected him to escort me to the lifts, but he headed for the park instead.

"We're supposed to be going Outside, Lucas."

"Preliminary phase," he said.

I was too tired and nervous for his speed speech. "Sentences, Lucas. Full sentences. Lots of words."

"You're comfortable with parks, so we'll go to the park first. Our park keeper has just got the moons and stars programme working. We'll sit in the night-time park for a while, and then we'll cover your eyes, take you to a Hive exit, and go Outside. When your eyes are uncovered, you should see a similar scene to that in the park. The idea is to ease the transition for you and make it less threatening."

"That makes sense," I admitted.

"Thank you," he said.

Lucas's voice sounded odd. I took a proper look at him, and realized he was exhausted. I linked into his thoughts for a second. He'd been frantically working out the best way to approach this, picking out suitable spots in the park and Outside, arranging for the moons and stars programme to be set up, choosing a nearby Hive exit to be used, and debating security arrangements with Adika.

Alongside all that, he'd been bouncing ideas to and fro with his team, trying to find a clue about what had happened fifteen years ago that would remove the need for me to do this. If we had some hard evidence against another Hive, then Joint Hive Treaty Enforcement would become an ally not a threat, but we didn't. At the moment, all we had was the imprint in my head, and we couldn't even prove that existed without the key symbol.

I felt guilty about the state Lucas was in, but I could hardly postpone our trip until tomorrow and tell him to go to bed. If I did that after all the preparation work they'd done, my own unit members would strangle me. Well, they wouldn't actually strangle me, because I was an irreplaceable true telepath, but there would definitely be a few graphic thoughts floating around.

We entered the park. It had been run down and neglected while the unit was closed, but now our park keeper was bringing it back to life. Every day, new flowers, butterflies, and birds were appearing. At night, it had been pitch black after the suns were turned off, which was how Rothan had managed to fall into the lake, but now the suns were on at moon brightness, and the tiny lights of stars dotted the ceiling. Lucas led me into a grove of trees, and we sat down on the grass.

"I want you to lie back and relax," he said. "Look up at the trees. You should just see dim light through the leaves, but no details of the sky. In a while, we'll move you to somewhere Outside, where your view around and above will also be restricted by trees. What you'll be able to see should seem like a slightly untidier version of this."

That sounded well thought out and reassuring, but I'd still be Outside. I tried to fight off the tension, do what Lucas said, and relax. I lay back, staring up at the canopy of leaves with the faint light behind them. I gave a sudden gasp as I saw something dark flitter across above me.

"What's that?"

Lucas laughed. "A passing bat. Learning its way round its new home, and looking for a feeding station with fruit. We stole a nocturnal animal shipment scheduled for another park. Telepath Unit priority."

"I'm creating a lot of work, and keeping everyone up for half the night. I'm sorry to rush this, but waiting around would just make me more scared."

"I understand," said Lucas.

"Am I stupid attempting this?"

"No." Lucas had been sitting beside me, but now he lay back and relaxed too. "Trying this scares me for lots of reasons, but you're right. We have to do something, and we have to do it quickly. Our target has been in total control of the situation until now. He deliberately lured us to that park on Level 80. He took the child into the drainage system, and arranged the booby traps, to keep us there as long as possible. He was watching and waiting for us to return the second time, and the dart gun was designed to pin us down and keep us there again."

"He did all those things just to make us spend time in that park?"

"He did all those things to make *you* spend time in that park, Amber. The target must have been trying to activate your imprint. Whatever he'd planned obviously didn't work. We can't afford to sit passively waiting for him to make another, possibly successful, attempt. If we find the key to removing your imprint, it would change everything, so it's worth taking risks."

"I've been thinking," I said. "I could make a recording saying I want to stay in this Hive. Then if I ask for a transfer, you could show it to people."

Lucas shook his head. "Recordings can be faked. We'd have to get a deputation from Joint Hive Treaty Enforcement to come here and witness you saying it yourself. Even then, you could claim later that you'd been pressured into saying it or had simply changed your mind. Worse still, it would give away our only advantage, by telling the target that we know about your imprint."

"And even if we convinced Joint Hive Treaty Enforcement, we still don't know which Hive did this," I said. "They'd escape without penalty, and they could do it again, here or at other Hives."

"Exactly," said Lucas.

"If the worst happens, Lucas. If my imprint triggers, and there's no other way to stop me being transferred to the target's Hive, promise me you'll reset me."

He groaned.

"Please, Lucas, I'd rather be free with the mind of a child in an adult's body, and have to grow up again, than be the target's slave."

"If that's what you want, then I promise."

We lay there in silence for a while longer. Finally, Lucas took something from his pocket.

"Time to blindfold you." He sounded amused. "You're wearing your body armour and crystal unit in case of emergency, but you've got the ear crystal turned off?"

"Yes."

"Good. I don't want you worrying about other people hearing anything you say, so we'll both keep our ear crystals turned off during this. Adika and the Strike team will be on guard nearby when we're Outside, but they should stay out of earshot."

He paused. "Read my thoughts if you like, Amber, but don't read those of anyone else. The Strike team have just been told about you being kidnapped as a child, which made them very angry. Now they're making their first trip Outside, which means most of them are also scared. You mustn't be hit by their emotions on top of your own. I want you to focus on me and trust me. Understand?"

"Yes."

Lucas covered my eyes. I was tense, braced for what would happen next.

"We'll wait here a while longer," said Lucas.

"Why?"

"Because your body language is screaming in terror at me. Relax. I got bitten by a rabbit once."

"What? How?"

"I was four years old," said Lucas. "I wanted to take the rabbit home with me. It wanted to stay in the park. It won. I'm still nervous of rabbits. If we meet one, you'll have to protect me."

I managed a giggle.

"That's better."

I felt myself being lifted into his arms. "I can walk."

"Not for this."

I was being carried. I couldn't see anything, but Lucas was holding me close. "I might bite."

"Query?"

"Like the rabbit."

He laughed.

I was used to having my eyes closed and being carried round like a doll by the Strike team. It was oddly different, intimate, being carried by Lucas. I hugged the warmth of him, tried to concentrate on his reassuring presence, but part of me was worrying about where we were going, automatically noting when we went through doors, took a quick lift ride, and travelled on the belt. I had a feeling there were other people not far away, perhaps even standing next to us. Adika. The Strike team.

"Shouldn't the Strike team carry me?"

"I resent that suggestion," said Lucas. "The Strike team may have a few more muscles than me, but I'm not a complete wet lettuce."

I heard a smothered laugh from someone close by. Was that Adika? There was another short lift journey next. Heading upwards this time. I could feel my heart rate speeding up.

"Trust me, Amber," said Lucas, his voice soft, comforting, hypnotic. "You can trust me. You'll feel a little cooler. There'll be a breeze, like in the park, but much more varied. Sometimes gentle, sometimes strong, and the direction may change."

I was carried up some steps, I could hear Lucas breathing harder from the effort, and then there was the sound of a door opening. I felt the breeze. Lucas was right. This was different from the constant air movement in a park.

"How do you feel?"

"Fine," I said shakily.

We stayed there for a few minutes, and then I felt Lucas walking again. We were Outside, and he was carrying me away from the Hive. I reminded myself that it was night. There was no need to panic. The Truesun was turned off and couldn't burn me.

Lucas stumbled, and I held on tighter.

"Sorry," he said. "I caught my foot on a savage tree root. It's very dark out here, and there isn't much of a path."

We moved on a little further before he stopped. "This is where I put you down. The grass isn't up to park standards, so I left rugs here earlier."

Lucas lowered me onto my own two feet, and I cautiously sat down. I felt something warm being wrapped round my shoulders, and Lucas's hand took mine.

"I can tell you're nervous, so my next move is to distract you from your surroundings and help you relax. Read me."

I checked his thoughts. "Lucas!"

"I'm just considering possible ways to distract you while we're alone in a dark wood."

"Alone except for the Strike team watching us."

"I don't mind them watching us if you don't. You wouldn't want to shock your Strike team though. You care deeply about them."

"They care about me, and risk their lives for me every day. I naturally care about them too. That doesn't worry you, does it?"

"Not in general. It's natural for a telepath to develop intense emotional bonds with their Strike team members. It's only the situation with Forge that worries me. You seemed to be having a very nice time with him at the beach. Cuddling up together."

I frowned. "I gave Forge a sympathetic hug, that's all. We were talking about Shanna."

"Really? Forge looked as if his mind was totally occupied with you."

"Well, it wasn't."

"I need some reassurance. A few sympathetic hugs would be nice, but I'm willing to consider most types of reassurance within reason."

"I hope the Strike team can't hear any of this conversation." I risked looking at the images in Lucas's head again. "You're being outrageous."

"I enjoy being outrageous," said Lucas happily. "Ready for me to take the blindfold off?"

"I'm not sure."

"I could be even more outrageous, but I don't want to risk upsetting you. Well, obviously you know that."

Of course I did. Lucas's teasing images were always heavily intermingled with thoughts analyzing my reactions. At the slightest hint I wasn't amused by his game, he would immediately stop.

"Actually," I said, "your mental images are nothing like as bad as the ones I see in the Strike team's minds. Eli has especially inventive ideas."

Lucas laughed. I felt his fingers touching my blindfold, and hastily closed my eyes before he removed it.

"The Strike team is made up of eighteen-year-old males, bubbling with excess testosterone," he said. "I suppose the fantasies are bound to get a little extreme sometimes. Do they bother you?"

I was safe inside the protective darkness of my own eyelids. "They startled me to begin with, but it's not really personal even when the fantasies centre on me. I'm a girl they're guarding, so they think about me a lot. The Strike team try not to daydream during runs, but things occasionally sneak through."

"Ready to open your eyes?" asked Lucas.

"Yes."

I opened my eyes and looked at Outside. It was almost disappointing. At first sight, it really was just like the view in the park. At second sight, it was clear that this was a very untidy park, but...

"Not such a nightmare as you expected?" asked Lucas.

I pulled a face at him. "Stop reading my body language."

He seemed amused. "Why shouldn't I read your body language? You read my mind all the time. We'll stay here a while, see if you're ready to see the night sky or if we just go to bed. We could even combine the two."

I glanced at the graphic image in his head. "What would you do if I said yes to any of these suggestions?"

"Probably have a major argument with Adika. I must admit I'd rather not have the Strike team watching our intimate moments."

"Where are the Strike team anyway?" I looked round at trees and bushes.

"I think Adika is behind that fallen tree," said Lucas. "I could throw something at it if you like and find out."

"You mustn't throw things at Adika."

"How are you feeling now?"

"Like a bit of a fraud. After all the fuss I made, it's not too bad out here."

"Don't get over confident. You've only looked at a few trees so far. All your fears are centred on the Truesun, so the daytime sky is the real issue. Even looking at the night sky may cause you severe problems."

I felt a surge of nerves at the mention of the sky. I stood up. "Let's try it."

Lucas stood up too, and waved at the fallen tree. "We can play at spotting the shaking bushes as the Strike team follow us."

I was much too tense to laugh at the joke. I took tight hold of

Lucas's hand as we walked through the closely packed trees. We were going to see the sky. Not the ceiling in a park, but the real sky. We had to walk very slowly because the ground underfoot was a mess.

"You were right about there not being much of a path," I said.

"There are nice, smooth, gravel paths in the country parks, but there'd be a risk of meeting other people there so I brought us to a wilderness area." Lucas stopped. "I get to carry you again now. Do you want the blindfold, or would you rather just close your eyes?"

"I'll close my eyes."

He lifted me up. "We're coming out of the trees now. There's a clear area where you'll see the sky. I want you sitting down for this, so I've got another rug waiting for us."

"You've put a lot of thought and planning into this."

"Thought, planning, and also a heavy investment in rugs. Have I earned a reward?" He lowered me to the ground.

"Possibly. I'll think about it."

"I'll sit down next to you now, and put my arms round you," said Lucas. "This is a necessary reassuring measure. My enjoyment of it is purely coincidental."

I gave a shaky laugh.

His arms went round me. "Sky time."

I opened my eyes. The sky was deep, and black, and endless. I grabbed hold of Lucas. "It feels like I'm falling up into the sky."

"I won't let you fall," said Lucas.

"It's bigger than a beach. That must sound stupid."

"It's not stupid at all."

"The stars look nothing like the ones in a park," I said. "There's so many of them, they aren't evenly spaced out, and some are a lot brighter than others."

"Read me."

Lucas wasn't playing with suggestive images this time, just thinking about the beauty of the stars. I sheltered in his feelings, and the dark threatening sky above me changed. I couldn't fall down into it. I couldn't fall up into it. It seemed safer now.

I didn't speak for several minutes. "Where's the moon?"

"There are a few clouds in the sky tonight. Those are composed of water vapour. The moon is currently hidden by that cloud over there." Lucas pointed upwards. "See that whiter, brighter area? The moon will come out from behind the cloud in a few minutes."

I watched the moon slowly appear from behind the cloud. It was much bigger than I'd expected, but it didn't feel as if it was burning me. "The moon has dark bits on it."

Lucas nodded. "That's because it has craters. Perhaps another time I'll bring a telescope, and..."

His voice was drowned out by a wild scream from among the trees, followed by the sound of someone crashing through bushes. I instinctively reached out telepathically to find the threat. There was a scattering of sharp, tiny minds of birds and small animals in that direction, all disturbed by the scream. I searched further and found a huddle of four human minds.

Adika was sprawled across someone's chest, his hand gagging their mouth.

Rothan was pinning down the man's flailing legs.

Forge was sitting beside them, gasping in air after being kicked in the stomach.

Kaden was lying face down in the dirt, his thoughts filled with childhood memories of Halloween tales. All the stories told how the hunter of souls and his pack of demonic creatures patrolled the darkness Outside, entrapping anyone unwary enough to venture there. They'd be out there right now, watching us from among the unnaturally tall trees, and choosing their moment to attack. Once they'd tasted our blood, we'd become like them, cursed to always walk the darkness of Outside and...

I gasped in terror, but I knew this was Kaden's terror not mine. Stories of the hunter of souls roaming the darkness Outside with his train of monsters had never scared me as a child. All my fears of Outside were focused on the blindingly bright Truesun.

I fought my way free of Kaden's mind, and became aware of Lucas's arms holding me. His voice was murmuring reassurance in my ear.

"You're safe, Amber. You're safe. You're safe."

I gradually relaxed. "I'm all right."

Lucas ended his litany of comfort, reached a hand to adjust his ear crystal, and spoke in a hard voice that I'd never heard him use before. "Would someone like to explain what happened there?"

Adika's voice answered, coldly furious. "A small animal ran over Kaden's foot and he panicked."

"Do you think you could keep the Strike team from screaming and running away in terror while I get Amber back inside the Hive?" Lucas's voice was bitterly sarcastic now.

"Nobody is going to scream again." Adika's voice carried a threat of hideous consequences for anyone who did.

I opened my mouth to say that there was no need for me to go back inside the Hive yet, but decided there was no point in arguing. Lucas would say that it was time to go back anyway. He'd say we'd achieved the purpose of this trip. He'd say that I was getting cold and tired. He'd be right.

Lucas released me while he stood up, then reached to lift me up again, but I shook my head. "I can walk this time."

We walked back along the path, moving carefully to avoid tripping over tree roots, and reached a hatch-like, open door in the ground. We went through it, down a flight of steps, and I saw half the Strike team waiting outside a lift. I didn't know what lecture Adika had been giving them over their ear crystals, but they were grimly silent.

A minute or two later, Adika and some more of the Strike team came down the flight of steps behind us. Rothan, Forge, and Kaden were still missing, and it seemed a bad idea to ask where they were. Adika ushered us all into the lift and started it moving. It was a very short lift ride, and then we moved to ride a belt.

"Listen carefully to me, Amber," said Lucas. "This is very important. You'll have a reaction after doing this. Going out again will probably be harder than this time. I want you to go out at least once more at night before you even think about trying it in daylight."

When we arrived back at the unit, Megan was waiting by the lifts. She looked me over anxiously before glaring at Lucas.

"Amber's shaking."

I looked down at my hands. Megan was right. I hadn't realized it, but they were trembling. In fact, all of me was trembling.

"The trip went very well," said Lucas, "but it was a strain. Amber needs to rest now."

He ushered me off to my apartment, and we went inside. "I'm staying the night," he stated flatly. "Adika is in a foul mood about Kaden's panic attack. He needs some exciting gossip to distract him."

I looked down at my quivering hands. "I hope Adika isn't too hard on Kaden. The scream didn't really make things more difficult for me."

"Leave Adika to worry about Kaden," said Lucas. "Would you like food, drink, or sleep?"

"A hot drink would be good."

We both had hot drinks, and the warmth of the liquid seemed to ease my shaking. Lucas escorted me to my bedroom, and paused in the doorway.

"I'll be in one of your spare rooms. Just call me if you need me. I can leave a sound link open if you like."

"An open sound link might be nice."

He adjusted the apartment sound system controls. "There you are. Sleep well."

Lucas headed off into the far reaches of my apartment, and I stripped off my clothes and dumped them on the floor. My body armour and crystal unit got better treatment, being hung up and put away respectively. I set the lights down to low, turned on the sleep field, and let its warm air engulf me.

"Goodnight, Lucas."

"Goodnight," said his voice.

CHAPTER TWENTY-SEVEN

I woke, confused and disoriented from a dream, then snapped back to reality. "Lucas!" I yelled.

His voice answered me, blurred and sleepy. "Amber?"

"I think I need you." I rolled out of the sleep field.

"Are we wearing clothes?"

"We're wearing clothes." I was already pulling on a robe. "I was dreaming."

"Tell me." As I heard the words over the sound system, Lucas entered the room. "Get back in the sleep field, relax, and try to remember everything you can."

I did what he said, closing my eyes, and trying to recapture the dream. "I was Outside in the darkness. I was walking along the same path as last night, holding someone's hand, but it wasn't you. There was a balloon, big, golden and burning, bouncing among the tree branches. It was hunting me."

I realized my voice was shaking. "I know that sounds silly, but it was frightening."

"You were holding someone's hand. Describe them."

"It was a huge man. His face was too high up to see."

"Did the man speak?"

"Yes," I admitted reluctantly. "He said I was a good girl, just like in the Forge dream. I'm pretty sure it was the same voice as in that dream too, huskier and deeper than Forge's real voice."

"You were getting fragments of an old memory," said Lucas. "Your three-year-old self was walking with the target. Your mind changed day to night to protect itself, and the balloon represented the Truesun. Do you remember anything else at all?"

"Sorry, nothing."

Lucas sat in silence for a moment. The lights were still on low, but I could see him frowning. I wanted to read his thoughts, but I couldn't. I had to try to remember more of my dream.

Finally he spoke. "It's a bit of a risk, but I can try to improve your memory of the dream. I'll need to use hypnotics."

"Try it."

Lucas took out a closed dataview, tapped it to make it unfold to full size and turn on, and then went across to the wall display controls. "I'll show you some images. I want you to watch them and relax."

The wall display lit up with swirling colours. There was barely audible music too, just on the edge of my hearing range.

"Watch the colours, Amber," said Lucas. "Relax. Let yourself drift with the music."

I watched the colours change, and waited for the dream to return.

"All done," said Lucas briskly.

The wall display had vanished. I turned to look at Lucas. "That was like one of the Lottery tests, where I thought that I'd fallen asleep but I hadn't."

He nodded. "Several Lottery tests use hypnotics. I've talked you through the whole dream sequence. No details of the target. The golden balloon holds central significance. Obvious sun symbolism." He paused. "It's almost nine in the morning, but we didn't get back here until the middle of the night. Do you want to sleep some more?"

"I don't think so." I sat up, and stepped off the sleep field to stand next to Lucas. "Thank you for helping me last night. You asked me then if you'd earned a reward, and I think you have. First kiss moment."

I stepped towards Lucas and lifted my face for the kiss, but he dodged backwards.

"Would love to," he said, "but can't."

I felt like I'd been walking down a corridor, the floor solid beneath my feet, and then found myself falling down a lift shaft. I was disoriented, hurt, and also angry. Waste it, this was the second time Lucas had blocked things between us. I turned my back on him. Lucas could read faces, and I didn't want him reading mine just then.

His voice came from behind me. "I just used hypnotics on you, Amber. You've been influenced to accept my commands without question, so I can't kiss you now. That kiss could lead to other things, and tomorrow you might feel you'd done things you didn't want to do. Even your offer of a kiss may not actually have been made of your own independent free will, but in an effort to please me."

He paused. "Amber? You understand that, don't you? You need a couple of hours to be clear of the hypnotic effects, or I'd be doing the same thing to you that the target did."

I kept my face away from him, and my voice carefully controlled. "Of course I understand."

"Read me."

"I'd like to get myself some breakfast now." My tone was polite dismissal.

"Message understood," he said. "I shall go to my own apartment, and bang my head against a wall."

I listened to him leave, and then stood still for a few minutes longer, nursing my hurt. Lucas made endless sexual suggestions to me in the safety of his own head, but he didn't seem to want those thoughts to become physically real. I'd taken the first step in Hive Futura. I'd taken the first step again just now. Lucas had turned me down both times. Did he enjoy humiliating me? Despite what he said about hypnotics, one kiss wouldn't have mattered.

Or would it? Would it have stopped at one kiss or gone a lot further? Had I given Lucas his signal at this particular moment because I wanted to, or because I was affected by the hypnotics? I thought it was my own choice, but Lucas couldn't be sure of that.

I grudgingly decided I should admire Lucas's principles rather than be angry with him. I'd have to apologize the next time I saw him.

I cursed imprints, hypnotics, and Lottery, ordered breakfast from my kitchen unit, and was busy not eating it when I noticed a package on a side-table. I went over to investigate, and found the package was from my mother. I ripped it open, and laughed when I found she'd sent me a glittering golden duck. I remembered Lucas mentioning the pictures of golden ducks in the 500/5000 Level 1 shopping area, and how a craze for duck toys was sweeping the Hive.

I picked up the duck, and idly examined the ornate, silver and gold pattern on its side. There was an odd sound in my head, like the clink of metal on metal, before a male voice started talking. I knew that voice. It was the voice of the most important person in the world, and he was telling me what I needed to do to please him.

CHAPTER TWENTY-EIGHT

There were two Ambers now. The Amber that was me was trapped in a spherical, crystal cage within my own head. Fleeting images of people and places swirled around my prison. I could hear snatches of conversation, and recognized that some of the words were spoken in my voice. There were moments when I was aware of my body moving, but it wasn't answering my orders.

The imprint had activated, and put the Amber that was three years old in control of my mind and body. She was the one looking through my eyes, speaking with my mouth, and touching things with my hands. I felt her raw, childish emotions ripping through me, changing abruptly from joy to anger and back to joy again. She'd done what Elden wanted. Elden would be pleased with her. Elden would say she was a good girl.

Elden had to be the name of the man who'd imprinted me. What had the child Amber done to please him? Had she harmed the people I loved? Was she already taking me to serve her master in another Hive?

I couldn't tell anything from the random words and bewildering images that reached me. I tried to talk to the child Amber, reason with her, but she didn't seem to hear me, or even be aware that I existed.

Lucas's face appeared outside my prison, his expression utterly exhausted and despairing. I gathered every ounce of strength, tried to control my body for just a second to speak to him, but couldn't. A moment later, he was gone, and then everything outside the crystal cage went black.

Was that blackness because the three-year-old Amber had closed her eyes, or was it because I'd lost the last fragile link to my body? I remembered the Halloween stories of the hunter of souls. The creatures of the pack that followed him were forever cursed to roam the night shadows of Outside. Was I cursed to hang here in darkness forever?

That was the moment when I felt the walls of my cage move closer to me. The imprint had imprisoned me inside this crystal sphere, and now it was trying to crush me out of existence.

Lucas would be working to remove the imprint, and send the three-year-old Amber back into the past. Working to free me from this cage, and give me my body back. I had to find a way to hold on here, forget my fear and fight for my survival, or there wouldn't be anything left of me for Lucas to set free.

I thought of Elden, screamed my anger and defiance at him, and the walls of my crystal prison moved further away. I focused on the anger that made me stronger. I would survive this, I would take my life back, and I would hunt down Elden and destroy him the way he'd tried to destroy me.

CHAPTER TWENTY-NINE

I woke up, opened my eyes, and stared at the ceiling. There was something wrong about that ceiling. This wasn't my bedroom at my Telepath Unit, or my room on Teen Level. I wasn't on a sleep field either, but lying on a solid bed.

"Welcome back, I hope. Do you know me, Amber? What's my name?"

I turned my head, and saw Lucas was sitting in a chair by my bedside. There was a spectacular purple bruise on his left cheek, and he looked desperately tired. I tried to work out what had happened.

"Of course I know you, Lucas. What's happened? Did I faint when we were Outside?" I frowned. "No, I remember we went back to my apartment after that. I had a dream, and I called you and..."

I remembered the kiss thing, and my words trailed off in embarrassment.

"That all happened three days ago," said Lucas. "Do you have any memory of ducks?"

"Three days!" I sat up, shocked. "Ducks? What? No."

"How about a parcel from your mother?"

"Yes, I remember there was a parcel on the side-table. Hannah must have left it there. I picked it up and..."

I broke off. I'd opened that parcel and discovered a glittering duck. That was followed by a blank patch, which must have been the point when my imprint activated. The next thing I remembered was a long period of nightmare images. I'd been trapped in a crystal sphere, fighting to avoid being crushed out of existence.

I'd been determined to survive and get my life back. I'd succeeded. I gave myself a moment to savour the sight of white room walls, the humming sound of an electrical display next to my bed, the coolness of a sheet beneath my hands, and the distinctive background chemical scent that meant I was in a room in the unit medical area.

The world seemed very convincingly real, but I had to be sure. I lifted my right hand to my mouth, and bit at the side of my forefinger. There was a faint taste of blood and the blaringly loud sensation of pain.

Lucas snatched at my hand, pulling my finger away from my mouth. "What are you doing, Amber?"

"The imprint activated and took control of me, Lucas. I'm checking I'm truly awake. Do you remember that we once had a conversation about telepaths feeling pain? You said that pain screams at all levels of the mind. You were right. There's something very real about pain."

I gave a long sigh. I was back in reality, but that meant I had to face the next problem. What had my three-year-old self been doing with my body during the last three days?

Sick with apprehension, I forced myself to ask the question. "What happened while I was under the control of the imprint?"

"When I left you," said Lucas, "things between us were in a bit of a mess. I waited a couple of hours so you'd be clear of the hypnotics, then went back to try to talk to you."

I'd tested my five standard senses, and now it was time to try that vital sixth one. I reached out with my mind, dipped into Lucas's thoughts, and found them startlingly slow and comprehensible by his standards.

"You wouldn't look at me," he continued. "It wasn't because you were angry. There was something very wrong, like part of you was missing. For a horrific moment, I thought it was my fault, that I'd made some dreadful mistake when I used the hypnotics to get more information about your dream."

I flinched at the pain of his memory. "Lucas, I can read you. There's no need to explain."

He was at breaking point from exhaustion, but he kept talking anyway. He'd been waiting for hours for me to wake up, planning exactly what he'd say, and he insisted on saying it.

"I was going to call Megan over and explain the situation. If she didn't kill me on the spot, I'd find myself a nice deep lift shaft and jump down it. Then you told me that you'd filed a request to transfer to Hive Genex."

He dragged his fingers through his hair. "That made everything clear. The target had somehow managed to activate your imprint when you were safely inside your own apartment, in the middle of our unit, behind the strongest security defences in the Hive."

He gave a despairing shake of his head. "You marched out of your apartment. I pulled myself together and went after you. You were heading for the lifts, so I tried to stop you, and you were kicking my ankles and fighting me."

I looked guiltily at his bruised face. "Did I do that to you?"

"No. Someone must have seen us struggling, because Adika and the Strike team showed up and flattened me. Fortunately, I managed to explain before I suffered major injuries."

"Sorry," I said uselessly.

"There were a few awkward minutes after that. You were fighting the entire Strike team and winning, because they couldn't make themselves use physical force on their own telepath. I finally had the sense to paint a fake birthmark on Forge's face, and got him to reason with you. The effect was incredible. You started calling him by the target's name, Elden, and obeyed his every command."

I saw Lucas's memories of me acting like a puppet, constantly watching Forge, adoring Forge, obeying Forge. I felt a wild medley of distress and fury at seeing myself like that, tried to run my fingers through my hair, and discovered I was wearing something on my head.

I took a look at myself through Lucas's eyes. I was wearing my own familiar clothes, but had a tiara on my head, a ludicrously ornate thing smothered in glass crystals. I disentangled it from my hair. "I see my three-year-old self liked sparkly things."

"Yes, with Forge giving you orders, and rewarding you with shiny jewellery, we had the situation contained. You happily told Forge about finding the duck in the parcel." Lucas's hands clenched into frustrated fists. "I was stupid. I should have guessed those ducks were appearing in the 500/5000 Level 1 shopping area for a reason. The gold and silver pattern on the ducks was the trigger symbol that would activate your imprint. Elden was counting on the fact that a telepath was bound to visit the finest shops in the Hive."

"I kept meaning to go there, but I was too busy."

"Elden finally lost patience, and took more direct action, luring us to that 601/2603 Level 80 park. Once we knew what to look for, we discovered a fragment of a gold and silver balloon there."

"I vaguely remember seeing a balloon when we were there. I never really looked at it. I usually have my eyes closed when I'm working." I threw the tiara into the far corner of the room. "You weren't stupid, Lucas. There was no reason for you to think the ducks were important when they first appeared."

"I was incredibly stupid," said Lucas. "I should have realized about the ducks. I shouldn't have assumed personal mail from your family was safe. I should never have left you alone for one single second. If I'd been there when you opened that package, I'd have realized the duck was the trigger symbol. I might have been able to grab it before..."

I interrupted him. "All that matters is that you've got rid of the imprint now. It is gone, isn't it? It can't control me any longer?"

"The imprint is gone, Amber. It can't make you do anything now."

I moistened my lips before speaking again. "And I didn't... hurt anyone?"

Lucas understood the question I daren't ask. "You didn't kill any of your Strike team by sending them into danger, or shooting them, or doing whatever other horrors you've been picturing in your head. They have a few bruises where you kicked them, some of them in very painful places, but they're always covered in bruises anyway."

I sighed in relief. If my three-year-old self had killed someone in her eagerness to please Elden, everyone would have told me it wasn't my fault, but I'd still have spent the rest of my life feeling like a murderer.

I forced that thought away. It hadn't happened, and it wasn't going to happen. My three-year-old self was back in the past, and I was in control again. "How did you get rid of the imprint? The symbol on the ducks was the key symbol too?"

Lucas shook his head. "The key and the trigger symbols mark the start and end of the imprint, so they have to be different."

"You didn't do it without the key? I'm not...?" I could read Lucas, so I was still a telepath, but would I be able to tell if my mind was damaged in other ways?

"Obviously we had to find the key first. You'd told me about the golden balloon chasing you in your dream. The second you mentioned it, I was sure that was linked to the key symbol. Given our personal relationship, it was shockingly unprofessional of me to use hypnotics on you myself, but I had to break the rules. If I'd delayed to get Megan, your dream memories would have faded."

Lucas hesitated. "Once I'd broken safety protocols to get more details of the balloon, I couldn't possibly risk kissing you."

I waved a dismissive hand. "I understand that, but I didn't know you'd worked out the key symbol."

"I hadn't worked it out. I just had a few clues as a starting point. It was like trying to recreate a piece of broken china when all you have is a couple of remaining fragments. There were a huge number of possibilities for the symbol, but at least we could dismiss the incorrect ones rapidly."

I could see the painful process in his head. Seemingly endless attempts at creating the key symbol. All the times when I'd obeyed Forge's orders to look at the symbol but not responded. Finally, after working solidly for three days and nights, Lucas had found the right answer.

"Once we'd found the correct key symbol, your imprint unravelled beautifully," he said. "It should have taken your artificially imprinted fear of Outside and the Truesun with it, but an unpredictable amount of natural fear will remain given your terrifying experience out there as a child."

"The target, Elden, can't control me anymore. I'm free." I took a moment to savour the thought. "Did you get Forge to order me to cancel my transfer request, or do I still need to do that?"

"I'd rather you didn't cancel that yet," said Lucas. "Elden must have access to the low security areas of our central data core to achieve the things he's done. He'll have seen your request and know your imprint has been activated. If you cancel the request, he'll see that too."

I frowned.

"Our best tactical move is to leave Elden thinking he's in total control of the situation," added Lucas. "Of course our Hive won't process your request, but Elden will expect there to be a delay while we try to convince you not to leave. He'll wait patiently for the next few weeks, joyfully imagining you carrying out your imprinted orders, causing havoc, and convincing every-one our Hive is better off without you."

My instinct was to cancel the transfer request immediately, but I gave a grudging nod. "I suppose that's the best plan."

Lucas stood up. "I'll get Forge in to do some tests, just to confirm the imprint hasn't left any lingering effects."

He went out of the room, and returned a moment later with both Forge and Megan.

"Amber, how are you feeling?" asked Megan anxiously.

I stood up and smiled at her. "Calm down, Megan. I'm myself again and I can still read your mind. Removing the imprint hasn't damaged my telepathy."

The frantic tension in her mind abruptly relaxed, and her thoughts sagged into weariness. She was very tired, though not in as bad a state as Lucas. She'd had a couple of hours sleep in the last three hideous days, but Lucas hadn't rested at all.

I made myself turn to face Forge. He seemed embarrassed,

and I didn't dare read him. Eventually, I'd have to face his thoughts about me acting as his obedient slave, but not now. I wasn't being a coward; I just had too many other things to cope with right now. No, it probably was cowardice, but either way I'd leave reading Forge until another day.

"We think Amber's cured, Forge," said Lucas. "Try the puppet thing."

Forge gave me a self-conscious look and coughed. "Sit down, Amber."

I didn't move.

"Wave at me."

I did nothing.

"Kick Lucas."

I winced.

Forge took a deep breath. "You're a good girl, Amber."

"I'm not a good girl!" I snapped out the words in fury. I wasn't angry at Forge for saying them, but at Elden for using me, controlling me, owning me.

Forge breathed out in a soft sound of relief. "It's really you again. When I saw what an agent of another Hive had done to you, turning you into his obedient little doll, I wanted to kill him. I *am* going to kill him."

"We don't just need to deal with Elden," said Lucas, "but bring the wrath of Joint Hive Treaty Enforcement down on Hive Genex too. Our best plan is to keep Elden in his fool's paradise, thinking he's controlling Amber, while we..."

Megan interrupted him. "You shouldn't be making plans for the future now, Lucas. You need to get some sleep."

Lucas frowned. "It's important that I..."

"No, it isn't!" she said sharply. "Amber will be suffering an unknown amount of trauma. You're on the edge of collapse. Everyone else in the unit is exhausted too. We must allow ourselves recovery time before we do anything at all."

I let Megan argue with Lucas, while I closed my eyes and let my thoughts reach out across my unit, briefly touching mind after mind. Megan was right. Everyone seemed exhausted and hovering somewhere between deep depression and total despair.

I could understand the Strike team feeling like that. They cared about me and I cared about them. Their job was to protect me but physical defence was useless against this attack. They'd spent days in helpless suspense, waiting to see if Megan and Lucas could find a way to bring me back to myself.

I hadn't expected to find nearly as much emotion among the Tactical and Liaison team members, and I hadn't expected the maintenance, medical, and other wildly varied general staff who worked for Megan to be worried about me at all. After all, they hardly knew me.

I was wrong. Every mind that I touched was a huddled mass of anxiety. Their thoughts were running in frantic circles, worrying about me as a person, worrying about how much my loss would harm the Hive, and worrying about the threat to their own futures.

Our Telepath Unit had been developing into a tightly knit community. Without me, the unit would be shut down, and my staff scattered across the Hive. All of them would miss the friends they'd made here. Some of them would lose precious budding relationships that crossed the normal divisions between levels and wouldn't survive elsewhere in the Hive. None of them could hope to get as good a position again. It would be years before Lottery found another telepath.

I pulled back from that suffocating fog of anxiety, and broke into the argument between Megan and Lucas. "Megan's right, Lucas. You'll be able to plan far more effectively if you allow yourself to rest. You told me earlier that Elden will wait patiently for weeks before doing anything."

He sighed. "I suppose that's true. Megan can message people to tell them that you've recovered, and then I'll get some sleep."

I shook my head. "Everyone in the unit seems to be scared to death, Lucas. It's not enough for Megan to send them a message that I'm all right. They need to see and hear it for themselves."

I turned to look at Megan. "Please message everyone in the unit. Tell them that Amber is herself again, and is calling an immediate full unit meeting in the park."

Megan gave me a dubious look. "Are you sure you'll be able to cope with that, Amber."

"I'm sure."

Megan took out her dataview and started tapping at it. I didn't wait for her to send the messages, just went out of the door and headed for the park. Halfway down the corridor, Lucas caught me up.

"I'd expected you to be badly affected by memory loss, Amber," he said. "You must have lost most of your personal memories of the last three days because they'd be inextricably linked with the imprint. Aren't you finding that confusing?"

I pulled a face. "I don't remember what my body has been doing for the last three days, but I remember other things very clearly indeed. I'm not confused, Lucas. I'm angry. I'm deeply aware of the damage Elden's done to me, to you, and to everyone in my unit, and he and Hive Genex are going to pay dearly for it."

Lucas didn't speak again until we'd gone through the door into the park. "Do you want to tell me these other things you remember, Amber?"

"Not now. Maybe never. Just accept that I've been in a very dark place of nightmares for the last few days. Now I've escaped, I don't want to dwell on the memories."

We walked on towards the picnic area, and I perched on the edge of a table. The bright lights of the suns burned in the ceiling above me, the artificial breeze was cool on my face, and gentle water sounds came from the nearby stream. A couple of birds flew to perch on a tree branch, watching hopefully in case I had seed to feed them.

After a few minutes, people started arriving and automatically gathering into work related groups. Adika and the Strike team. Nicole and the Liaison team. Emili and the Tactical team. Small clusters of medical, maintenance, administration and cleaning staff. I noticed our park keeper had a pair of tiny black and white monkeys perched on her shoulder and grooming her hair.

Once everyone seemed to be present, I climbed on top of the table and looked out at the crowd. There was dead silence as they waited for me to speak. I'd just been planning to tell them that I was myself again, but standing here like this, seeing the exhausted figures and their expressions of defeat, I knew that I needed to say far more than that.

I remembered the bookette room playing a scene of a holo battlefield, with a king rallying his defeated troops for another charge at the enemy. That was what I needed to do now. I'd never made a speech before, and I'd no script to tell me what to say, but I had to restore the confidence of these people ready for the next round of the battle against Elden.

CHAPTER THIRTY

When I was trapped in the crystal cage, I'd had to fight to avoid being crushed out of existence. Somewhere in that battle, I'd defeated the self-loathing part of me that hated nosies. Perhaps that was because I'd gained that attitude when I was very young, so the feelings belonged to the three-year-old Amber rather than me.

Whatever the reason, I had my life back now, and I was going to live it as my true self. I'd still have to be careful to hide the fact I was a telepath from my parents, but here in my unit I could embrace my right to use the gift I'd been given. I'd worried a lot about what rules I should follow as a telepath, but in the end there was only one rule that mattered, and it was a rule that applied to everyone, telepath or not. I should try to help rather than harm those around me.

I'd never made a speech before, and I didn't have a script to tell me what to say, but I didn't need one. I could read the minds of my audience and see the words they desperately wanted to hear.

I tried to match the ringing tones that I'd heard Henry use in the bookette room. "We've been fighting an enemy and losing every encounter. We've been losing because we were fighting blindfolded and with our hands tied behind our backs. Our enemy was faceless and nameless, with an unknown purpose. He'd been making his preparations for fifteen years. He'd imprinted me as a three-year-old child, writing a set of orders in my mind."

I paused for a moment. "Three days ago, our enemy

activated those orders and took control of me. He expected that to be the devastating blow that utterly defeated us. It hit us hard, but it did not defeat us. Thanks to the efforts of Lucas, Megan, and all of you, I'm my own person again."

I turned to nod at where Lucas and Megan were standing together, and then faced the crowd again. "We know the face, the name, and the purpose of our enemy now. He is Elden, an agent from Hive Genex, and he is trying to steal true telepaths like me."

I shouted the next words at the top of my voice. "Elden's attempt to steal me has failed! This is where everything changes. Elden has been hunting me for fifteen years, but now I am hunting him. *We* are hunting him."

The faces in front of me had lost their dead, defeated expressions. They were looking eager now, and there was a wild yell that had to be from Eli.

"High up!"

There were some more yells from the Strike team, and other people were clapping. I let the noise die down before speaking again.

"All of you will have a part to play in that hunt. Some of you carry guns and chase a target, while others help plan the chase, or make sure innocent bystanders are moved to safety. Some of you treat injuries, order equipment, or make repairs. Some of you make sure the park is a very special place, full of beautiful birds and animals, where everyone can enjoy vital relaxation time."

I looked pointedly at Hannah. "Some of you make sure the telepath doesn't get buried in a heap of her own rubbish."

There was a burst of laughter.

"Whatever your job is," I said, "you're here in this unit because that job is essential and you're one of the best in the Hive at doing it."

I paused to check my dataview. "It's almost noon. This unit is beginning a mandatory twenty-four hour recovery period. Everyone must get some sleep now, because we'll need you all fully rested and alert by noon tomorrow. That's when Lucas will tell us his plans. That's when our new hunt will begin."

I stayed on the picnic table while the crowd drifted away. Megan gave me a hesitant look before turning and walking away too. There was just me and Lucas left here now.

I climbed down from the table. "I told everyone to go to sleep, Lucas. That includes you."

He gave a mock salute, wandered across to where the grass grew thickly by the edge of the stream, and lay down. I went to sit beside him, and watched his mind slowly sink into sleep.

I was the only person in the unit who wasn't physically tired, and I had a lot of thinking to do. Not just about the past, but its effect on the present and the future. I'd been imprinted as a three-year-old child, and burdened with a terror of the Truesun. My time on Teen Level had been dominated by a fixation on Forge, because his appearance and his birthmark reminded me of the man who imprinted me. That fixation had ruled my life for five years, affecting everything I'd done and every decision I'd made.

I felt a nagging fear that I'd never truly made a decision of my own free will in the whole of my life, and was just a doll moulded by Elden's imprint, but I told myself that was silly. Some of what I was, most of what I was, had nothing to do with that imprint. It hadn't made me a telepath. It hadn't made me chronically untidy. It had given me a fixation on Forge, but it hadn't made me fall in love with Lucas.

I sat there for hours, my mind floating through Lucas's dreams and out across the sleeping minds of my other unit members. A handful were awake. Nicole had been woken by her chiming dataview because it was time for her to take her medication. Rothan's lips were curved into a smile as he looked at a holo image of Emili's face. Sofia was working at frantic speed, painting a mural of me standing on the picnic table and giving my speech. Megan was lying in bed, unable to sleep because she was worrying about me.

I groaned, picked up my dataview, and sent Megan a message. I watched her mind relax as she read it, and then she abruptly fell asleep.

Eventually, Lucas became restless, his dreams turning into a nightmare where he couldn't find the key symbol that would return me to my true self. I was wondering whether to wake him, when he abruptly sat up, stared round, and then relaxed.

"Bad dream." He turned to face me.

"I saw it."

"You stayed with me." He smiled.

"I was worried about you. Your thoughts had slowed down to normal human speed."

"You and Megan were right about me needing rest. I'll be able to work better now."

"I absolutely forbid you to do any work before tomorrow morning. If I catch you even thinking about work, I'll kick you on the ankle."

He laughed, then turned serious and went full sentence mode for emphasis. "You have to ignore the imprint, Amber. You must try to forget how it influenced you, either over Forge or anything else. Deliberately acting against any lingering effects makes you just as much a slave as obeying them."

"I've already worked that out, Lucas. Megan was worried I'd fire my whole Strike team because of their looks, and she'd have a terrible problem finding replacements because most of the candidates imprinted for Strike team in the last Lottery were chosen to resemble Forge. I messaged her to reassure her I wouldn't do anything so stupid and unkind. I don't care what my Strike team look like. They're my friends."

I paused. "We need to discuss something else now."

"Yes?"

I took a deep breath, and studied his mind as I spoke. I wasn't risking any more misunderstandings between us. "I was lost in darkness for the last few days, fighting for my existence. That taught me that life is very precious. I'm not wasting mine brooding on the past. I'm living for the future. Removing my imprint must have involved hypnotics or something. There aren't any problems like after the dream are there? We don't need to be careful?"

His mind did a second of lightning, multi-level analysis, and then he grinned. "All protocols strictly followed. Work done by

Megan in a controlled environment. Safety period elapsed before you were allowed to regain consciousness. First kiss moment?"

"Definitely." I pulled a face. "The issue is starting to become..."

"An intimidating psychological barrier," he completed the sentence. "You're the only person I've ever met who could interact with me on a social level, and you're a true telepath. The chance of me finding another telepathic girlfriend is effectively zero."

His logic said that I was literally the only girl in the world for him. It was incredibly flattering that he thought of me that way, but it meant he was terrified of making a mistake and losing me.

I was scared too. I desperately wanted this relationship to work. I hoped it would eventually turn into a marriage, and a lifetime commitment to a man with thoughts that glittered and danced like a Carnival crowd.

"Best get it over with then," I said.

We looked at each other, both hesitated to allow the other to come to us, and then both moved to meet halfway. I was still reading Lucas's thoughts as our lips met clumsily. His nervous excitement mingled with my own, and then his nervousness changed to a different sort of tension that lit a response in me.

I grabbed Lucas, pulling him closer to me. He wasn't a telepath, but he was an expert in reading body language, and couldn't miss what mine was screaming at him. Everything blurred into a wild whirlpool of emotion, as his feelings fed into mine and my response fed back into him. We finally had to break off the kiss to gasp in air, and Lucas stared at me in stunned disbelief.

"I'd expected kissing you to be special, Amber, but that was... What happened there?"

"Feedback loop," I said. "You should have warned me that would happen if I was reading your mind when we kissed."

There was a split second of analysis and then he laughed. "I'd no idea."

"Surely you knew about this from working with Keith."

"Respectfully point out that I've never kissed Keith. I've

never heard him talking about this either. It's possible Keith's never experienced it because he's only interested in his own feelings." Lucas gave me a hopeful look. "Shall we try another kiss?"

"Just a second." I took out my dataview, then left Lucas's mind to search for Adika. I found him deeply asleep, and hesitated. It seemed unfair to wake the poor man up with a call. It wasn't really necessary anyway. I'd been in Adika's mind a dozen times when he was working on the unit security system. I knew how it worked, and remembered his passwords. I worked on my dataview for a moment, and then put it down.

Lucas frowned. "What did you do to the security system, Amber?"

"I locked the park doors." I smiled at him, and linked to his mind again. "We're all alone in here except for an assortment of birds and animals."

Lucas smiled back at me, we kissed again, and lost ourselves in the wild feedback loop.

CHAPTER THIRTY-ONE

"Strike team is moving," said Adika.

I didn't need to read minds to feel the reaction of the Strike team to those words. Their eagerness filled lift 2. While the imprint controlled me, Lucas and Megan had fought a battle for my mind, but my Strike team could do nothing to help. Now their ordeal of useless inactivity was over, and they were back leading the hunt.

Lucas's familiar voice spoke in my ear crystal. "Tactical ready."

Matias had been declared fully fit by Megan, so he was back with the Strike team. I wished Lucas was coming with us too. At the same time, I was glad he was staying safely in the unit. We were heading back to 600/2600. Our last two trips there had gone very badly indeed, and I daren't make any assumptions about this one being different.

The tense voice of Nicole came over the sound link, interrupting my thoughts. "Liaison ready. Tracking status is green."

It was me next. I checked my dataview. "Green here."

Lucas started speaking in his relaxed, briefing voice. "First thing this morning, we held an emergency meeting of all the Telepath Unit Tactical Commanders, as well as representatives from Hive Trade, Hive Security, Hive Defence, and Hive Politics. Capturing Elden, and bringing Hive Genex to justice, is now the top strategic priority for our Hive."

"I should hope so," muttered Adika.

"The other good news is that Hive Security are confident that Elden could only have hacked his way into the low security areas of our central data core," continued Lucas. "He shouldn't have access to the high security areas containing Telepath Unit records, or be able to decipher our encrypted communications."

"He should never have been able to access anything," grumbled Adika.

"There are plans to tighten security on the whole of our central data core," said Lucas, "but we don't want Hive Security to block off Elden's access yet. We need to keep him believing he's still in control of both the situation and Amber while we hunt him down. The other Telepath Units have agreed to deal with all emergency and check runs for the moment. If Elden has a way of checking the status of Telepath Units, he'll see that our unit is labelled as unavailable because Amber needs extended recovery time."

He paused. "That should keep Elden happy, but it means we can't have people seeing you moving round the Hive. We've got you wearing standard brown maintenance coveralls, and you'll be travelling through Level Zero to reach your destination. Level Zero is always packed with maintenance crews, so you'll blend in among all the others."

"What's Level Zero?" I asked.

"Level Zero divides the accommodation levels of the Hive from the industrial levels," said Adika. "It's like a giant interlevel, and holds a lot of special systems."

I groaned. "A whole level of the Hive that I didn't even know existed."

I heard Lucas's laughter through my ear crystal. "Most people won't be aware that Level Zero exists, Amber. Imprints only include knowledge relevant to a person's profession."

The lift stopped. We were on Industry 50 now. I watched, fascinated, as Adika entered a code into the lift controls, and the destination level number changed to zero. The lift moved on a short distance and the doors opened.

Level Zero was huge, over twice the height of a normal Hive

accommodation level. It seemed incredible that I'd not known about a place this large, but the moving stairways only went as high as Level 1, and lifts moved so rapidly that you wouldn't notice the extra distance between Level 1 and Industry 50.

Adika led us across to what looked like a standard belt interchange. Once we were riding along an express belt, I looked around in bewilderment. There weren't any corridor walls, just...

Actually, I had no idea what half these things were. A few large pipes reminded me of Level 100, but there were also weird, vast tanks that must be the size of a park. I could see what seemed to be murky liquid through the inspection windows.

"What are those tank things?" I asked.

"I think they're part of the water recycling system," said Adika.

Lucas started talking again. "My team has been going through all the old records for 600/2600. Nearly sixteen years ago, some oddities started happening there. That must be when Elden first arrived in our Hive, set up a nest in 600/2600, hacked into our central data core, and started stealing supplies and equipment."

"Were any investigations made back then?" asked Adika.

"Sapphire's unit made a check run but found nothing," said Lucas. "Elden was carefully spreading his thefts across all the different levels to reduce the chance of being caught. Once Amber had been kidnapped and imprinted, the oddities abruptly stopped. We think Elden went back to his home Hive at that point. During the next fifteen years everything was quiet in 600/2600. Elden was probably busy making trips to other Hives. A few months ago, the..."

"Stop right there!" I said sharply. "You think Elden may have gone to other Hives and imprinted other true telepaths?"

"From your description of Elden, he couldn't have been more than twenty years old when he imprinted you, Amber. He wouldn't dare to imprint another true telepath in our Hive, because a second telepath requesting a transfer would look far too suspicious, but he might continue his work in other Hives that speak either our language or the language of Hive Genex."

I clenched my fists as fury hit me. There could be others with a secret childhood imprint. Others who could find control of their mind and body stolen from them. Others who could be taken to serve Hive Genex.

"A few months ago, the oddities in area 600/2600 started up again," Lucas resumed his briefing at the point where I'd interrupted him. "Elden was back in our Hive, and working to activate Amber's imprint. Now he believes the imprint is controlling Amber, so he'll have stopped work and gone into hiding in his nest. He'll stay there to wait out the long process of Amber wearing us down into allowing her transfer to Hive Genex."

"He'll have a longer wait than he expects," said Adika.

"Or a much shorter wait if I'm right about where he's hiding," said Lucas. "My team's analysis of the incidents around area 600/2600 suggests that Elden's not just been using the same nest, but crucially the same equipment that he used fifteen years ago. There are very few places in the Hive where Elden's nest and equipment could have remained undiscovered during his fifteen year absence. I believe his nest has to be inside the area 600/2600 structural column."

"What's a structural column?" I asked.

"Hive structural columns add stability and strength to the physical structure of the Hive," said Lucas. "They're vast hollow columns set into bedrock and reaching up to the top of the Hive. A structural column would be an ideal place for Elden to set up his nest, since their last maintenance inspection was in 2500, and they aren't scheduled to have another until 2550."

Lucas paused. "There are only three entry points to allow maintenance crews to inspect the web of girders inside a structural column. One at the bottom on Level 100, one on Level Zero, and one right at the top on Industry 1. I expect Elden's nest to be inside the 600/2600 structural column just above the Level Zero entry point. That's well positioned for accessing both Hive accommodation and working levels, and in emergency Elden has an escape route that leads him straight up to near a maintenance exit to Outside."

Adika made a pained noise. "So if Elden's there, he'll start climbing, and then we'll have to chase him up fifty levels of ladders or maintenance mesh. Lucas, he'll know that route and we don't."

"I'm not sending you chasing Elden up a structural column," said Lucas. "He's almost certainly armed, and could have placed booby traps at intervals, or just have rocks ready for him to drop on your heads. You'll stop near the structural column and send some men up in a lift to guard Elden's escape point on Industry 1. After that, you just have to frighten Elden into climbing up the structural column and walking into our ambush."

"I like that tactic," said Adika. "Rothan will be in charge of the ambush team. He can take Eli, Matias and Caleb with him. Forge is experienced in cliff climbing, so he and I can go into the structural column. Everyone else will be on Bodyguard team. We'll start checking for booby traps as we approach our destination on Level Zero."

The view around us was changing now. We'd left the huge tanks behind us, and there were lots of strange spiky objects coloured bright red. Several maintenance crews were working on them.

Adika spotted me staring at the spiky objects. "Amber, the main safety rule on Level Zero is that things coloured bright red are dangerous. You must never touch them."

We travelled on, passing more mysterious shapes in assorted colours, including the warning red. When we finally neared our destination, we stopped by a lift. I watched unhappily as Rothan, Eli, Matias and Caleb headed off to Industry 1.

"I can't run circuits on Rothan's team with fifty levels of minds in the way," I said.

"Don't worry, Amber," said Lucas. "If Elden starts climbing, then we can get you up to Industry 1 long before he arrives there. However good Elden is, he can't out-climb an express lift."

Adika moved the rest of us on a short distance before stopping again. "We'll begin checking for booby traps now. We look for cameras that shouldn't be there, or devices that have been tampered with. We check anything and everything. Elden played games with us twice in that park. If we let him beat us again, then we all resign and go stir protein vats!"

The Strike team had been keyed up already, but they went up another notch of tension at Adika's savage tone. They brought out electronic devices, and started scanning the area. I let them get on with their job, while I did mine, closing my eyes and searching for a mind that thought in words I didn't understand.

Somewhere to the north, a maintenance team were working, cleansing relay points. I didn't linger in their minds long enough to find out what a relay point was. Up above my head, a hydroponics unit was working at full stretch in harvest phase. Below me was a community centre packed with children making Halloween costumes and masks.

I'd lost track of time, and forgotten we were getting close to Halloween. I thought back to Carnival. It was months ago, a lifetime ago, that I'd ridden the rail with Forge and the others, plunging into an unknown future.

I reached out to the south, drifting across the minds of ten thousand shoppers, registering a blur of trivial excitement and indecision. Arms went round me, picked me up, and carried me. I ignored them. I had my eyes closed, so my bodyguards knew I was working. They wouldn't expect me to comment or respond as they moved the luggage of my body to a more convenient location.

"We're at the entry point to the structural column now," said Adika. "Amber, is there any sign of Elden?"

"No," I said, trying to keep my frustration out of my voice. "All the minds in this area are perfectly readable and innocent."

"I expected Elden's nest to be just above the entry point," said Lucas, "but he could be much higher than that. Rothan, are your team in position?"

"We're just outside the Industry 1 entry point to the structural column," said Rothan, "hiding behind some convenient notice boards. When Elden arrives, we'll all fire stun shots on my command."

"Make sure you let him get out of the column first," said Lucas. "If he falls down a hundred and fifty levels of the Hive, then he won't be answering any questions afterwards."

He paused. "Adika, you can open the access hatch now and

take a look inside. Be very careful. There shouldn't be any power conduits or cabling inside the column, just bare girders. Stop the second you see anything suspicious."

Long, nervous minutes went by as the hatch was removed. I opened my eyes for a second to see Adika and Forge peering through the hole, their lights probing the dark interior of the column, then went into Adika's head and saw his view of things as he stuck his head inside.

"No ladder or maintenance mesh here," he said. "How are maintenance crews supposed to climb up the structural column to make their checks without them?"

"The structural column plans show a standard series of ladders on the wall to your left," said Nicole.

"The structural column plans are wrong," said Adika.

"We've definitely found Elden's nest then," said Lucas. "He must have removed the first couple of ladders to deter any maintenance staff from getting nosy about what was inside a structural column. Presumably Elden manages to get up there without ladders, in which case..."

Adika gave a faint groan. "In which case, we should be able to get up there too. There are lots of criss-crossing girders, so it's a relatively straightforward climb apart from the darkness and the one hundred level drop beneath us."

Forge's voice spoke for the first time. "We'll rope up then, and make sure we anchor ourselves to the girders at regular intervals. I can go first."

I was with Adika's thoughts, and felt his reluctant acceptance as he replied. "That's the best approach since you're the climbing expert. Remember that when we find Elden, we mustn't shoot him. We just take cover and let him climb up the column."

"Understood," said Forge.

"If you haven't found Elden by the time you've climbed up ten levels then stop," said Lucas. "Amber and the bodyguard team can go up in a lift so they're on the same level as you, and then Amber can have another search for Elden's mind."

There was another minute or two of preparations involving lights, harnesses, and ropes. I moved across into Forge's mind as he entered the great, hollow column, feeling his satisfaction as he balanced easily on one girder, while reaching up to clip a rope to another. This was a golden chance to demonstrate his skills and his worth to Adika.

A second later, he was climbing, swinging himself effortlessly upwards from one girder to the next. Pausing to let Adika catch up. Rejoicing in the response of muscles that had never been this strong before the hard regime of Strike team training. This was what he'd been born to do. This was his perfect life.

Forge swung up to the next girder, then abruptly stopped. "I can see a ladder above me, and a sort of platform across a couple of girders."

"Elden's nest," said Lucas. "He would have built a platform so he could store things and sleep. Still no sign of him, Amber?"

I left Forge's mind and reached higher up, searching. Someone was thinking about production run figures. Someone was running her hand over the soft down of young fledgling birds. Someone was cursing over the foul stench of a failed batch in a protein vat.

"Elden's not there." I tried not to let my voice show my bitter disappointment. "Do we wait for him to come back?"

"If Elden's gone then I doubt he's coming back," said Adika grimly. "He'll have seen Amber's transfer request four days ago. He must have decided his work here was done and headed home to Hive Genex."

Lucas's voice sounded surprisingly untroubled. "Climb up and take some images of the platform, Forge, but don't touch it."

The platform turned out to be made of several sections of flooring, wedged into place on the girders and bolted together. There were three sealed boxes on it, as well as a weird object with glowing lights.

"Is that a bomb?" asked Forge.

"Bodyguard team, get Amber clear of this area!" snapped Adika.

Arms snatched me up. I was being carried at a flat-out run. I kept my eyes closed and my mind linked to Forge.

"Bodyguard team evacuate to Yellow Zone using the express

belts but not the lifts," said Lucas calmly. "Adika and Forge, get out of that column and follow them. Liaison, we need an electronics expert to take a look at those images."

"Do we evacuate that area of the Hive?" asked Nicole, her voice rising in panic. "The evacuation protocol for a possible structural column failure is massive, Lucas. We'd have to evacuate all ten million people from Orange Zone, and close all its bulkhead containment doors to seal it off from the rest of the Hive!"

"There's no need to start a general evacuation yet," said Lucas. "Elden came here with an elaborate plan to steal a telepath. I could believe he's planted a small booby trap device to destroy his nest if it was discovered, but it doesn't make sense for him to set up a bomb on a scale that could damage a structural column and cause massive destruction. It doesn't make sense for him to go back to Hive Genex before our Hive agrees to Amber's transfer either. He might need to give Amber extra orders."

Forge was dropping down from one girder to the next, pausing to help Adika. I tried to stay with their thoughts, but my group was on an express belt now. The distance, and more importantly the number of minds, between me and Forge kept increasing until I lost him. I finally heard the familiar recorded voice from overhead.

"Warning, bulkhead approaching!"

I felt the lurch as whoever was carrying me made the jump from the Orange Zone express belt to the Yellow Zone express belt. A couple of minutes later, we left the belt system, moved into a secluded area between two storage tanks, and my bodyguards gathered round me.

"Bodyguard team are now at a defensible location in Yellow Zone."

That was Kaden speaking. At the sound of his voice, I automatically linked to his mind, and was caught in a fog of grief.

... my last run with the Strike team. I'd hoped this would be the run where Elden was captured, hoped to leave with something good to cling to, but there's nothing but failure to take with me to...

... if Adika would just let me go Outside again, give me the chance to prove...

Waste it, how can I tell my parents that I was fired from the Strike team for cowardice? My father will...

I fought my way out of Kaden's mind just as Adika spoke. "Forge and I are out of the structural column," he said. "Bodyguard team, wait at your current position for us to regroup. Rothan's group, come and rejoin us too."

"We've got expert information on the device now," said Nicole. "It's not a bomb, but some sort of communications relay."

"Which explains everything," said Lucas bleakly. "Elden's done exactly what we expected, gone into hiding to wait for us to agree to Amber's transfer, but he's not using his nest in 600/2600. He's set up a device to relay information to him, and gone Outside."

There was dead silence for the next thirty seconds.

"Waste it!" said Adika. "Why did Elden go Outside? If he has to wait around for weeks while Amber's transfer is processed, he'd surely be more comfortable inside the Hive."

"Remember that Elden's done a lot of travelling Outside," said Lucas. "He's used to the conditions, and could always come back to the Hive if he needs to do something to progress Amber's transfer. I suspect there's an extra incentive for Elden to do his waiting Outside. He's expecting Hive Genex to send an aircraft to collect Amber, and hoping it can pick him up on the way home and save him a long swim."

"Hive Defence can try to hunt Elden down," said Adika, "but searching a vast area of countryside is nothing like patrolling a concrete border strip. The second Elden sees our aircraft or drones on a search pattern, he'll know we've discovered his plan and are chasing him."

He made an exasperated noise. "Elden will have been imprinted with all the ways to beat heat sensors. He may even have a stealth cloak, designed to block his body heat and camouflage him into near invisibility. He just has to stay hidden while the search pattern passes over him and then make a run for the coast. Once he's made it offshore and called Hive Genex to send an aircraft to pick him up, we'll have no evidence to give to Joint Hive Treaty Enforcement."

I opened my eyes, wriggled out of Kaden's arms, and stood up. "We can't let Elden escape. If he's gone Outside, then we have to go there after him. He may be able to hide from heat sensors, but there's no way for him to hide from a true telepath."

"What are you suggesting, Amber?" asked Lucas. "That we send you Outside in an aircraft to search for Elden?"

"No. Even if I could work from an aircraft, Adika's right that Elden would start running the moment he saw the aircraft hunting for him. I'm thinking of us going Outside to search for him on foot. We could pretend to be one of the rambler groups that Rothan mentioned."

Lucas sounded startled. "You can't have thought this through, Amber. Elden could be anywhere between our Hive and the nearest stretch of coastline. Hunting him down would take days or even weeks."

"You said that my imprinted fear of the Truesun has been removed. The natural fear that remains should be easier for me to overcome. If I can't manage that, then I've already coped with being Outside at night. I might be able to shelter somewhere when the Truesun is out."

"That would mean doing all the travelling after dark," said Lucas, "which would be very difficult."

"It would be virtually impossible," Rothan's voice joined in the conversation. "Once you're away from the country parks, Outside is a complete wilderness, with narrow winding tracks that are often overgrown with stinging plants and brambles. The further away from the Hive you get, the worse the conditions become. We couldn't travel at night without using lights on a scale that Elden would see from a huge distance away."

"Perhaps one of the other telepaths would be willing to try going Outside," said Adika.

"Sapphire might be able to handle both the physical and mental demands of hunting Elden Outside," said Lucas, "but we can't put the Hive in the situation where only Morton, Mira and Keith are available to handle emergency runs."

"Amber could help with..."

Lucas interrupted Adika before he could finish his sentence. "If Sapphire was away hunting Elden, then Amber couldn't help with emergency runs or anything else. Remember that Elden's still able to eavesdrop on our Hive using his communications relay. If he spotted any indication that our Telepath Unit was still operating, he'd know he'd lost control of Amber and run for the coast."

Adika groaned. "I suppose that cutting off his communications would send him running home too."

I took a deep breath. "Then it has to be me that hunts down Elden. We can do some test runs Outside and see how well I cope with daylight."

"You can't try facing the Truesun yet, Amber," said Lucas. "You've been through a huge amount in the last few days and need time to recover."

"If we're going to stand any chance of catching Elden, then we have to do this now," I said. "We'll only have two or three weeks before he gets suspicious, and we could need all that time to locate him Outside."

There was a moment of silence before Lucas spoke. "I admit that's true. You're quite sure you want to try this, Amber?"

I didn't want to try it. I had to try it. "I can't just sit around and let Elden escape after everything he's done. I can't let his Hive carry on kidnapping other true telepaths. I have to try to hunt him down. If the only way I can do that is to go Outside and face the Truesun, then that's what I'll do."

CHAPTER THIRTY-TWO

The next evening, everyone else in the unit seemed to be incredibly busy, but I was under orders to rest, sleep if possible. The plan was that there would be a meeting just before midnight, followed by another trip Outside.

I couldn't sit still, let alone sleep. My mind was overloaded with thoughts and emotions, nervously anticipating tonight's trip. We would be staying Outside until dawn, when I'd find out how much of my old fear of the Truesun remained. I didn't know if I'd just be scared, or be hit by total blind panic. Whatever I felt, I had to control it if I was to have any chance of capturing Elden.

I walked three times round my apartment, and then headed to the shooting range. I'd begun my weapons training by firing at stationary targets with a genuine gun. Now I'd graduated to using holo guns in the bookette style, friend or foe scenarios. I had to explore randomized locations and kill enemies before they killed me, while trying not to shoot my own team or innocent bystanders.

Today's scenario had me navigating the vent system, and I ended up scoring an abysmal 21 per cent. When the friend or foe programme shut down, the holo of the vent system vanished, leaving just a featureless hall around me. I was surprised to find Adika standing in the doorway, watching me critically.

"You're incredibly slow on the friend or foe decision," he said, "which is why you're scoring so badly, but your accuracy is good when you finally decide to shoot. Of course there's the point that you can't read the minds of holo targets. You'd have a huge advantage over a genuine human opponent. We should try you in some duels."

"What are those?"

He smiled. "Two of you in there, trying to get a kill shot on each other. I'm betting you could take down half the Strike team. I'm hoping we never need you to fire a gun in reality, but it would be excellent practice for my team. Let's give it a try ourselves."

"But..."

He took a holo gun from the rack, and made some adjustments to the scenario control panel. Our surroundings suddenly changed to be a park at night. The moons and stars programme was running, providing just enough light for me to see the shadowy outlines of trees. I took one wild look round and dived into the nearest bush.

"I wanted a chat with you about the unit security system," said Adika, from somewhere in the darkness. "After your speech in the park, I went back to my apartment to rest. While I was asleep, someone used my passwords to access the system."

I could feel myself blushing. "I just wanted to lock the park doors for a few hours. It didn't seem worth waking you up for that."

"Another time, I'd prefer to be woken up."

I slipped into Adika's mind. He was in amongst some trees, with his back to one of them. He was amused by me locking the park doors, but he didn't want me messing with the unit security system again.

"I apologize," I said. "I'll always call you in future."

Adika accepted my promise, and moved on to another issue. "You've also blocked my request for Kaden to be transferred out of the unit. You're too kind sometimes, Amber. You didn't reject Fran and look what happened."

"Keeping Fran was a mistake. This isn't."

"Kaden has to go. I admit he seemed an excellent Strike team member, I was seriously considering him for one of the two deputy positions, but I can't keep him on the team after that screaming incident Outside."

"I'd like you to let Kaden come Outside with us tonight," I said. "Give him a second chance to prove he can face the conditions there."

Adika had been listening to me talk, worked out my location, and was moving through the trees to get a clear shot at me. "The primary purpose of the Strike team is to protect the telepath. I can't have a man on the team who is afraid to go where you go, Amber."

I rolled sideways, reaching the refuge of a holo rock just before Adika shot the bush where I'd been hiding. "Yes, the Strike team protect me, and I protect them in return. I don't want to discard Kaden over one moment of weakness. You've just said that he's been an excellent Strike team member. When you found out how fast I could swim, you didn't fire all the men who couldn't keep up with me in the water."

Adika knew I was behind the rock, and was working out his best way of outflanking me. "The men just needed to have extra swimming training to be able to deal with that situation. Giving way to fear, having a panic attack, is a very different issue. It's completely unacceptable in a Strike team member."

"I've seen the whole of the Strike team thinking about this. Most of them were scared when they were Outside in the dark, remembering all the frightening childhood stories of the hunter of souls. Kaden was just unlucky that the mouse or rabbit or whatever it was ran over his foot while he was lying in the bushes. A lot of the others know that they'd have screamed too if it had happened to them."

Adika started creeping along the ground, invisible to my eyes but glaringly obvious to my mind. His aim was to circle round to my left while I was busy arguing with him, and then shoot me.

"Rothan has been pleading Kaden's case to me as well," he said.

"The others daren't talk to you directly about this. Rothan can. He's been going Outside all his life, so you know he isn't scared of anything out there."

Adika didn't reply. He was approaching his destination point, and didn't want to give away his position.

I shuffled further round my rock to keep it between me and Adika. "You're worried that you'd have screamed yourself in Kaden's situation."

Adika was silent for a moment. "You're telling me that I've been trying to hide my own fear of Outside by being brutally harsh to my men, so they're taking their problems to Rothan instead of me?"

I really didn't need to reply to that. "The Strike team weren't selected or trained for going Outside. They have to learn to cope with conditions there just as they had to learn to swim. I'd very much appreciate you giving Kaden a second chance."

Adika was huddled behind a tree, brooding over the twin difficulties of either catching me by surprise or arguing with me when I was reading his mind. "All right, but Kaden's no longer a contender for one of the two deputy positions. I can't ask men to trust his leadership after they've had to pin him to the ground to stop him screaming."

"Accepted," I said.

"Eli's a good man, but he's been playing the comedian too much for me to make him a deputy. Humour can be useful to a leader, I use it myself to calm the team down when the tension gets too much, but Eli's misjudging the balance."

"Also accepted."

"Matias was unlucky getting appendicitis," continued Adika, "but I'd already decided he was more interested in his girlfriend than his career. That boy needs to get his hormones under control. They all do. I've got Eli having angel fantasies about you. I've got Rothan meeting his secret love in the park after dark. I've got Forge going round mourning for some girl he was involved with on Teen Level. They need to stop thinking about their love lives and concentrate on their work."

"You aren't doing too well at stopping thinking about Megan."

Adika hastily moved the conversation on. "I'd like to appoint my two deputies now, so I can work with them on choosing candidates for our Beta Strike team. Things will be much easier when we have two fully trained teams. I'll be able to give my men proper rest breaks, and assign temporary cover for injured personnel."

He was moving rapidly through the trees towards my rock now. He'd worked out that keeping quiet didn't hide his position from me, and was trying to use speed instead. I scurried furtively away through the bushes.

"My preference is to put Rothan in charge of Alpha team, and Forge in charge of Beta team," said Adika. "That would flag Rothan as my second in command and eventual successor. I'm aware that Forge is your friend though."

"Forge is my friend," I gasped, "but I agree that Rothan is the better leader. He's won the confidence of the men, and should take charge of Alpha team."

Adika heard me speak, and turned to fire at my location. I saw the thought in his head, and rolled sideways so his shot just missed hitting me. I ran through more bushes, sending a holo rabbit running wildly, and dropped to the ground. The poor holo rabbit got shot, and I struggled to my knees and fired back at Adika. An instant later, I was hit right between the eyes.

"Excellent!" shouted Adika. "You winged me!"

The programme ended, the fake park vanished, and the scores flashed up on the wall. "You have a superficial arm wound, but I'm dead," I pointed out.

"I've had seventeen years practice at this." Adika gave me a smile of delight. "You're definitely ready to wear a gun when you're out with the Strike team. There isn't time for another duel before the meeting, but we must do this again soon."

We walked across to the meeting room together, and found Lucas, Megan and Nicole there ahead of us. There was a stranger too. I took one look at the man's mind and took an instant dislike to him. He'd done some research on my team leaders, and was literally putting a price on their heads.

Once Adika and I had sat down, Lucas started talking. "Telepath Unit imprints don't cover external Hive affairs, so Hive Trade has loaned us an expert to assist us with information on Hive Genex. Over to you, Barrett."

Barrett gave up trying to decide how he'd price Lucas on the trading system, and started talking. I forced myself to listen. I found Barrett's mercenary nature unpleasant, and if he'd been suggested as a permanent member of the unit I'd have rejected him, but he was just on loan to give us some vital knowledge.

"There are 107 Hives at the moment," said Barrett. "All Hives are included in both Treaty and the trade system, but our Hive only trades goods with nineteen other Hives. That's partly due to the geographical difficulty in reaching some Hives while avoiding territory infringements. We have little need for physical goods from other Hives anyway, since we've opted to limit imported luxury goods in the interests of maximizing self sufficiency."

He paused. "We trade people with only fifteen other Hives, and where possible with only seven. Those have similar language and social structures to our own, which eases the transition for traded personnel. Adapting to a new Hive can be difficult, as you'll know from personal experience, Lucas."

I gave Lucas a startled look. He surely wasn't from another Hive. He couldn't be. If he was, I'd have seen it in his mind long ago.

"My father is irrelevant to this." Lucas's voice betrayed the fact he was struggling not to lose his temper. "Can we concentrate on Hive Genex, please?"

Lucas's father was from another Hive. That made far more sense. I wouldn't have seen that in Lucas's mind, because I'd never seen him thinking about his parents at all.

Barrett nodded. "The relevance of my comment is that we never trade people with Hive Genex because there would be serious cultural adjustment problems. We don't trade goods directly with Hive Genex either, but we do receive some goods that originated from Hive Genex through secondary trading with other Hives. This means any items left here by Elden can't be used as evidence for Joint Hive Treaty Enforcement. Hive Genex would just claim we'd obtained them through legitimate trading."

He paused. "We could have offered our telepath's imprint in evidence, but unfortunately it has already been removed. It might have been wiser to delay that process for a few weeks, so that a deputation from Joint Hive Treaty Enforcement could be present."

Barrett would have left me trapped in that crystal cage for weeks! How much of the true me would have been left after that? Would there have been anything at all? Before I could put my anger into words, my team leaders burst into simultaneous speech. Nicole was among them, but her shy voice was completely drowned out by three louder ones.

"The risk of brain damage on removal, with consequent loss of telepathic and other abilities, increased with every hour the imprint was active," said Lucas.

"The danger of including so many people in an imprint removal would..." Megan was practically incoherent.

"You think we should have sat around doing nothing for weeks?" Adika was standing now. He placed both hands flat on the table, and leaned across it to bring his face closer to Barrett's apprehensive eyes. "If Amber had got loose with an enemy Hive controlling her, just think how impossibly hard it would be to hunt down a telepath."

Adika's voice had beaten the others into submission now. "Amber wouldn't just have the advantage of knowing our every move before we made it. She's had months to learn all my knowledge of Hive security defences and my passwords. She's familiar with every hiding place in the Hive, she knows the strengths and weaknesses of my entire Strike team, all our tactics, and can move nearly as fast as us."

He paused a bare second for breath. "Amber's utterly deadly with a gun too. She just scored a hit on me in her first ever duel. Only two other people have ever managed to hit me in a duel, and they were both experienced Strike team leaders."

Barrett hunched defensively in his chair. "Clearly there were strong arguments in favour of removing the imprint quickly."

Adika slowly sat down, but still oozed menace. I stared at him for a blank moment. He'd really meant what he said. He thought I could be a more deadly opponent than any of his Strike team.

Barrett pulled himself together and started speaking again in a subdued voice. "We need to capture Elden and submit him as evidence to Joint Hive Treaty Enforcement. Systematic interrogation will force him to confirm our story. Tissue and bone trace analysis will be even more useful, providing a record of his physical location throughout his life. That will prove both his origin from Hive Genex, and the periods of time he's spent in our territory."

Barrett smiled. "Hive Genex could claim Elden's verbal statements were the result of delusion or brainwashing, but physical location evidence is impossible to explain away. Anyone transferring from Hive Genex to our Hive would never have returned home again. Personnel trades and transfers are irrevocable and permanent."

"Would the physical location evidence show if Elden has visited any other Hives?" I asked.

"Yes." Barrett made a dismissive gesture, showing his lack of interest in other Hives.

I nodded. "So those Hives could be warned that Elden might have imprinted their future true telepaths."

"Yes," said Lucas. "Proving our case to Joint Hive Treaty Enforcement would also make them deeply suspicious of any future requests for transfer by true telepaths or other key personnel. Hive Genex wouldn't be able to use this method to steal people in future, and neither would any other Hives."

"Our Hive would benefit financially as well." Barrett's face took on a disagreeable, gloating expression. "We could expect Joint Hive Treaty Enforcement to impose severe penalties on Hive Genex, including making significant payments to our Hive as compensation for their action against us."

Adika's forehead creased. "We have to catch Elden and hand him over to Joint Hive Treaty Enforcement then? We can't deal with him ourselves? I was hoping to do something rather nasty to him."

Lucas pulled a face. "How sadistic were you planning to be, Adika? Joint Hive Treaty Enforcement will put Elden through destruction analysis. If you're thinking of doing anything approaching that bad to him, then you're a sick man."

I sneaked a look at Lucas's thoughts, and wished I hadn't. Destruction analysis meant using every possible technique to get information from someone, regardless of the physical and mental damage it caused. If Elden was lucky, he'd die early rather than late in the process.

"So everything depends on us catching Elden," said Adika. "Are we done here? It's already dark Outside, so we could make a start on our trip now."

Lucas glanced at Barrett, and then stood up. "Are you ready for this, Amber?"

I tried to forget that disturbing insight into what Elden would face if we caught him. I wouldn't wish that agonizing, prolonged death on anyone, but I couldn't let Elden and his Hive do to others what they'd done to me and my unit. "Yes, I'm ready."

"I'll tell the Strike team that we're moving in thirty minutes," said Adika.

I stood up. "One last thing. Nicole, return Barrett to Hive Trade. Tell them I don't want anyone in my unit who forges Hive records to further his personal career."

I didn't bother to look at Barrett's face, just walked out of the room.

CHAPTER THIRTY-THREE

Lucas and I went back to my apartment in total silence. Once we were safely inside the entrance hall, I stopped and gave him a guilty look. "I've just destroyed Barrett's career, haven't I?"

"Definitely," said Lucas. "When Hive Trade get that message, they'll double-check every move the man has ever made. Even if they can't find anything suspicious, they'll never trust him again."

"Do you think I should call Nicole? Stop her sending the message if it's not already too late?"

"Was your accusation true?" asked Lucas.

I sighed. "Yes. When Barrett was thinking about trading personnel, I caught some of his fringe memories. He arranged several personnel trades after the last Lottery, including some complex five and six-way trades, where multiple highly skilled people were swapped around so each Hive in the deal got their vacancies filled. He didn't exactly mess that up, but our Hive didn't do as well as it should have done. Barrett faked the records of the deal to protect his career. He feels threatened because he knows his deputy is better than him at negotiating."

Lucas shrugged. "In that case, you had no option but to warn Hive Trade."

"I know. Telling Hive Trade was the right thing to do, but... I didn't give that order to Nicole for the good of the Hive, but out of personal revenge. I was angry about Barrett saying you should have left me controlled by the imprint for weeks. You worked to exhaustion point to help me, and he dared to criticize you for it."

"Perfectly justifiable anger," said Lucas. "Criminally irresponsible suggestion. Involvement multiple representatives Joint Hive Treaty Enforcement in imprint removal process dangerous in extreme."

I instinctively dipped into Lucas's thoughts to keep up with his gabbled speed speech, and caught him comparing Barrett's suggestion to the destruction analysis planned for Elden. That was an overreaction, but Lucas was even more angry with Barrett than I was.

Lucas smiled and went into full sentences again. "I'm delighted that Barrett will be demoted. Hopefully to protein vat scrubber. He can think himself lucky that Adika didn't rip his head off his shoulders."

I started to laugh, but broke off as I suffered another wave of guilt. Every person in my unit was imprinted with facts about how true telepaths were rare, precious, and must be protected. Those facts influenced everything they thought and did. Barrett's imprint must be all about putting a price on everything and everyone, and that would influence him too.

I shook my head. "I took an instant dislike to Barrett, because of the way he thought of people as if they were just objects to be traded, but anyone doing his job would be the same. Lottery selects them to be like that, and their imprints reinforce their attitudes. Adika might be right after all."

"Query?"

"Adika said I could be deadly. Maybe he was right. My position gives me a lot of power, and I just used it to break Barrett." I moved on to the other thing that was bothering me. "What Barrett said about your father startled me. The only time you've ever mentioned your parents was back in Hive Futura. I've never even seen you think about them since then, so I didn't know your father was traded to this Hive."

Lucas shrugged. "I rarely think about my parents because I've not had any contact with either of them for eight years."

"Eight years?" I stared at him. "I've been assuming the split happened after you went through Lottery."

Lucas groaned. "My parents divorced when I was six years

old. My father failed to maintain contact after that. My mother dumped me at the earliest opportunity too. Understandable. I wasn't an easy child."

I frowned. "If you haven't had any contact with either parent for eight years, then the split with your mother must have happened soon after you moved to Teen Level."

"It happened three days after I moved to Teen Level," said Lucas. "I found the adjustment difficult and ran back home like Gregas. That was an unfortunate error. I found I wasn't welcome at my mother's apartment any longer, not even as a visitor."

"I'm sorry." I was no psychologist, but I thought I understood Lucas's deep seated insecurities a lot better now. That much rejection as a child must leave scars.

"Let's forget about this now." Lucas was obviously eager to move away from a distressing topic of conversation. "You did the correct thing with Barrett, preventing him from causing further harm to the Hive, and we need to get ready for our trip Outside. We'll be wearing special outdoor clothing, because it's supposed to be quite cold out there tonight."

Outside! That word was enough to make me forget everything other than our trip tonight. Lucas went across to a crate in the corner of the hall, pulled out two bags of clothing, and handed one to me.

I checked his thoughts. Outside temperatures varied a lot. At the moment, they were getting colder because of something called autumn. More things I'd never known because I wasn't imprinted.

No, I corrected myself, that wasn't true. I had to forget my old childish idea that being imprinted would tell me everything. Only facts directly relevant to your profession were included in an imprint. Those who worked Outside would be imprinted with information about autumn. Those few who went Outside by choice, like the ramblers, would presumably learn that information for themselves. The rest of the Hive...

I wrinkled my nose. The rest of the Hive was deliberately left in ignorance of everything to do with Outside, so they'd think of it as a terrifying unknown place. Controlling knowledge was a way of controlling people.

I went into my bedroom, stripped off the outfit I'd been wearing, and dressed in my body armour. Once I'd put on the clothes from the bag, I was uncomfortably hot and looked as shapeless as a bread roll. I thought of my old friend Shanna, with her perfect face and hair, and the alluring clothes that fitted her like a second skin. She'd rather die than dress like this.

I sighed, grabbed my crystal unit from its shelf, and went out to face Lucas. I found he was wearing similar clothes to me, but holding the jacket instead of wearing it. He laughed at my disgusted expression.

"I suggest you either undo that jacket or carry it until we're Outside."

I thankfully took off my jacket. We headed for lift 2, and found it was unusually crowded. The Strike team were dressed in similar special clothing to us, and wearing startlingly large backpacks that took up almost as much space as they did.

I gestured at the backpacks. "What is all this stuff?"

"Camping equipment," said Adika.

I remembered Rothan talking about camping Outside. "We're taking tents with us on this trip?"

Adika nodded. "Also food, drinks, and other supplies. If you're able to adapt to the Truesun, then we'll be making a long trip Outside. Rothan is going to help us prepare for that by giving us some camping training."

As always, I felt a throb of panic at the mention of the Truesun. Lucas must have noticed me tensing up, because he took my hand.

"I've made careful plans for tonight, Amber. You'll be totally in control of your exposure to daylight. You can see the Truesun for as little as a second, or not at all. If there's the slightest problem, then you can be back inside the Hive within minutes."

The lift doors closed and it started moving down. I frowned. "Why are we going down?"

"We have to go down to start with because our unit security defences are in full operation," said Adika.

After only a level or two, the lift doors opened, and then we rode a belt for a few minutes. It felt strange to be with the Strike team when my ear crystal was turned off, but Lucas was sticking to the same rule as before. We had to be able to talk in perfect privacy while we were Outside.

We jumped belt and went into another lift. This one took us upwards to the heavy double doors of a Hive exit. I found it difficult to force myself to go through them. The problem wasn't that I was walking into the darkness Outside, but because I'd be staying out there to watch the Truesun rise.

I'd no idea how I'd react to seeing that. Removing the imprint should have reduced my fear of the Truesun, but to what level? Had I been left with just a hollow, powerless memory of past terror, or would I run, screaming hysterically, from a waking nightmare?

Lucas gestured at a strange object in the darkness ahead of us. "Rothan put our tent up earlier today."

When we reached the tent, Lucas bent his head to go through an opening, and tugged me inside after him. It was even darker in there. I heard Lucas struggle with something, mutter something rude, and then call out.

"Rothan! How do I close this thing?"

The shadowy figure of Rothan appeared, there was a whispered exchange, and then something blocked out the faint light from Outside and things went utterly black.

"I'm going to turn a lantern on," said Lucas. "Don't get worried. It's not the Truesun coming up."

There was a sudden burst of light, seeming very bright after the blackness, and I blinked.

"What does this place feel like to you?" asked Lucas.

I looked round at my surroundings, and saw the lantern was hanging from a peculiar sloping ceiling. "It's a very small, very oddly shaped room. Is that the door?" I pointed.

"According to our camping expert, Rothan, that's called the tent flap. I've sealed it closed." Lucas smiled. "We've got our own tiny Hive here, Amber. We can shut out everything. The night sky, the nosy Strike team leader, the muscle-bound Strike team, and the Truesun as well. You'll be safe in here, and in total control."

My tension went down a notch.

"I remember you telling me that you coped in the aircraft coming back here from Hive Futura because that counted as being inside," said Lucas. "Does this count as being inside as well?"

"It does now. I can't be sure how I'll feel when the Truesun appears Outside." I touched one of the tent walls and felt it move under my fingers. "What is this stuff? Rothan said tents were made from cloth, but this doesn't feel like cloth."

Lucas sat on the floor, gestured for me to sit next to him, and put his arm round me. "Rothan has been going on camping trips since he was a small child. Apparently, there are two sorts of members of the Ramblers Association. Rothan and his parents are traditionalists, who use archaic cloth tents and get wet when it rains. They look down on the soft, comfort-loving modernists, who use the state of the art tents made for Outside workers."

He paused for a second. "Despite Rothan's protests, Adika and I have decided the Strike team are going to be modernists. Rothan can bring his own cloth tent if he insists on being uncomfortable."

I forced a laugh and relaxed a fraction more.

"That's better," said Lucas. "This is a flexi-structure tent, which has been specially modified for us. The usual material has been bonded to an inner layer of two thicknesses of the mesh used to make body armour. Adika's idea, naturally. In theory, the entire Strike team could shoot at this tent for an hour and it wouldn't bother us in the slightest. The downside is it makes the tent much heavier, but I'm planning to let the Strike team do the hard work of carrying it."

My laughter was genuine this time.

"We'll go Outside while it's still dark," said Lucas, "and watch a little of the dawn. The second you get nervous, we'll come back into the tent and shut the tent flap. You'll be in total control."

I nodded, and gave a sudden shiver.

"You're cold," said Lucas. "You should put your jacket on, or try this." He picked up one of a heap of mysterious objects at the far end of the tent, and shook it. Something silver unfurled, like a

Carnival cloak but bigger. "This is a heat sack. You get inside and it traps your own body heat to keep you warm."

I touched the material doubtfully. "It's very thin."

"It works though. I checked out the tent and tested a heat sack earlier today."

I tossed my jacket into the corner of the tent, and tried sliding inside the heat sack. "I was thinking about my old friend, Shanna, earlier. How she'd hate dressing in these clothes and looking like she was wearing a sack. Now I'm wearing a real sack."

"It's highly unlikely that Shanna will ever join the Ramblers Association. The more relevant issue is how Emili will feel about going camping, and whether Rothan will make her suffer in a traditional cloth tent."

I frowned at him. "You know about Rothan and Emili!"

"Of course I know. Emili is my deputy team leader. I'd be a pretty poor behavioural analyst if I couldn't work out why my own deputy keeps mysteriously sneaking off. I don't understand why they're hiding their relationship though. It's not as if the telepath has staked a claim on Rothan, or has she?" Lucas gave me a teasing look.

I stuck my tongue out at him. "Rothan doesn't feel he's good enough for Emili. He's only a novice Strike team member fresh from Lottery, while she's a year older and a deputy team leader. Emili's finding the situation deeply frustrating."

Lucas shook his head. "I don't see what Rothan's worried about. He's got a very mature head on his shoulders, and his expertise in conditions Outside has given him a huge advantage over his rivals for the deputy positions. If Adika hasn't got Rothan lined up to be his deputy in charge of Alpha team, I'll eat the Strike team's camp fire cooking."

"Their what?"

"Rothan is going to teach them to cook food over an open fire. I'm planning to stick to protein bars myself. Much safer."

I laughed.

"Warmer now? Relaxing?" asked Lucas.

"Yes. Surprisingly this heat sack works. The tent floor isn't like a sleep field, or even a couch, but it's a bit soft."

"Another benefit of modern tents over the ones that Rothan favours. Able to read me again now?"

"Yes." I reached out to Lucas's familiar mind. "I know it's stupid, but when I'm scared I tend to huddle away inside my own head."

"I understand. I've been working very hard at using all the words in sentences. Are you relaxed enough for me to share your heat sack?"

"This isn't a good time to..."

"I merely wish to share your heat sack. Nothing more." Lucas gave me a look of wounded innocence. "Respectfully point out that wearing body armour severely limits my actions."

"Doesn't limit your thoughts," I grumbled. "Nothing has ever limited your thoughts. Even the first time I met you."

I shuffled over in the heat sack, and Lucas wriggled in next to me.

"Query? My thoughts the first time you read me?" he asked.

"On the deep levels you were lusting after my legs, and thinking the Lottery information on my preferred partners meant you didn't stand a chance of getting into bed with me."

He gave a shout of laughter. "And you still hired me!"

"I found it quite flattering actually. Remember that I'd spent the whole of Teen Level fixated on Forge and he'd never looked at me. You were the first young man whose thoughts I'd read, and you found me attractive. It was a huge boost to my ego."

I paused to grin at him. "It's the only reason you got your job. You clearly weren't intelligent enough to be a Tactical Commander, and..."

Lucas's kiss silenced me for a moment. "Back then I'd no idea that you could read deep levels of the mind," he said. "I was startled when I found out. I tried to impose control of my thoughts, but decided it was effectively impossible."

"That's true. When I read someone, I automatically try to translate their thoughts into words, but the deeper levels are often just a blur of images and emotion. When you deliberately tease me with suggestive ideas, it's on a higher level controlled by your conscious mind. Very different."

"Fascinating. I wish that I could experience it myself."

We were silent for a few minutes. I felt myself gradually relax as I shared Lucas's reassuring warmth in the heat sack. His thoughts were all about me. A mixture of intellectual curiosity about telepathy, and non-intellectual enjoyment of our closeness.

"This tent material is highly protective," he said, after a while. "Removing our body armour would be a minimal risk."

I sighed. "We'd better be good. Adika would..."

The words triggered a memory. My imprint was gone, but I would never forget my repeating dream and how Elden had told me I was a good girl. I broke off, crawled out of the heat sack, and started stripping.

Lucas raised an eyebrow. "We aren't being good?"

"Lucas, I'm not a good girl!"

His thoughts went into a super speed burst of analysis, then he laughed, and got out of the heat sack to undress as well. We were both extremely bad after that, and lost ourselves in a tidal wave of feedback, before we finally put our body armour back on.

I lay in Lucas's arms afterwards, feeling relaxed, secure and comfortable. It must be late at night now, and I was terribly tired, but I couldn't possibly sleep. Not here, not Outside, not when the Truesun would be rising in a few hours.

I slept.

CHAPTER THIRTY-FOUR

I woke up, and was instantly aware that Lucas's warmth was missing. I looked round in bereft panic, searching with both eyes and mind, and then felt foolish. Lucas wasn't sharing the heat sack with me any longer, but he was literally still within arm's reach, sorting through the heap of equipment at the back of the tent, the odd lighting creating weird shadows as he moved.

He turned to look at me. "Ah, you're awake. Are you hungry? Thirsty? We have protein bars, fruit strips, crunch cakes, and melon juice."

I sat up and rubbed my face. "Megan sent melon juice?"

Lucas took the top off a small container and handed it to me. I sipped it cautiously. Yes, it was melon juice.

"It's ridiculous sending this specially. I could survive without..." I broke off. "It's not dawn yet, is it?"

"It's still fully dark at the moment, but it will be dawn soon. Once you're dressed, I'll open the tent flap."

I crawled out of the heat sack, shivered as an icy draught hit me, groped for my clothes and jacket, and put them on. I was feeling cold, sluggish, and scared, but I had to go through with this. It was vitally important to catch Elden. Not just for the benefit of my Hive, and the unknown number of other telepaths that Elden had imprinted, but for my own peace of mind. If Elden escaped, then I'd always have a nagging fear that he'd return and find a new way to kidnap me.

"I'm ready," I said.

Either Lucas understood the tent flap fastenings better now, or it was easier to open than to close it. I looked out into the darkness, and couldn't see the moon, let alone the Truesun. Lucas went out, waited for me to follow, then let the tent flap fall closed behind us.

The light from inside the tent was blotted out now, and I could barely make out the shadowy shapes of other tents near ours. I hesitated, and Lucas took my hand to guide me to sit on a rug. "Where is everyone?" I asked.

Lucas wrapped a heat sack round my shoulders. "The Strike team are on guard duty in the trees. Are you sufficiently relaxed to try reading some of their minds? None of the Telepath Unit Tactical teams have any data on how well a true telepath can work Outside."

Something in his thoughts grabbed my attention. "If we go hunting Elden, you're planning to come with us."

"Yes. Even if your initial issues with the Truesun are resolved, you may develop problems later, and reading Elden's mind could be very disturbing for you. You must have expert support with you, which means either myself or Megan. My role includes accompanying the Strike team on occasion. Megan's does not."

This wasn't really a surprise. I'd suspected Lucas would insist on coming along, but I'd been trying to avoid thinking about it. "You're only supposed to join us on routine trips."

He grinned at me. "You can't expect me to stay back at the unit while you go wandering round Outside in the company of twenty-one other men."

I checked Lucas's thoughts, and was relieved to see he was joking. I hoped that was a sign he was gaining confidence in himself and our relationship.

"I'll try reading a few minds," I said.

I closed my eyes and reached out with my mind to find the Strike team. They were posted round the camp on guard duty, thinking about the cold night air, the discomfort of hiding in thick undergrowth, and the talks Rothan had been giving them. He'd told them all about the camping trips he'd gone on as a child. Shown them images of himself with his family. Reassured them that he'd never seen any sign of the hunter of souls when he was Outside at night.

Rothan's stories had helped the rest of the Strike team, but they were still very nervous of the darkness, and desperately eager for the Truesun to rise. I was the exact opposite, comfortable with the night but dreading daylight.

I drifted on and found Rothan's mind. Untroubled by any fear of Outside, his thoughts oozed delight on every level.

"Adika's told the Strike team about the promotions then," I said.

"Rothan gets Alpha team?"

"Yes."

"The noble hero, Rothan, has proved his worth and can now claim Emili. That'll be a huge relief to the poor girl."

I laughed.

"Second deputy." Lucas's mind played with probabilities. "Forge has consistently been getting noticed. He gets Beta team. Correct?"

"Correct."

Thinking of Forge made me automatically link to his mind. He was much further away than I'd expected, fighting his way through bushes with Adika and Kaden. Forge was pleased about his promotion to deputy team leader, but the top levels of his mind were worrying about why they were roaming through the wilderness.

Adika had said they needed to try following some paths, to test whether it was possible to travel Outside at night without lights, but Forge believed they were doing more than that. He was sure that Adika had brought Kaden along to see if he could handle being under pressure Outside at night.

Forge hoped he'd been brought along to help Adika if Kaden had another panic attack, but he was nervous that Adika was testing him too. He'd tried to hide his fears of the darkness Outside, but if Adika had spotted them...

I left Forge's anxious mind and dipped into Kaden's thoughts. He was burning with adrenaline, desperate to grab this unexpected last chance to stay with the Strike team, resolved not to show weakness whatever happened.

I moved on into Adika's mind, and found he was testing himself as well as Kaden, pushing both of them to the limit by roaming random paths in the darkness. He'd had to leave Rothan in charge of guarding me, so he'd taken Forge along as his second most reliable man. If he panicked, then Forge would have to take charge of the situation.

There was a sudden burst of high-pitched, inhuman screaming nearby. Adika's mind tensed in response and his hand went to his gun. The minds of the rest of the Strike team were flaring in fear too, filling with tales of the unspeakable horrors lurking beyond the safety of the Hive.

I grabbed for my ear crystal, turned it on, and opened my mouth to say that the screaming was nothing to worry about, but I found Rothan was already talking.

"It sounds like a fox is hunting out there. You'll remember me telling you about foxes. They aren't a threat to us, but they'll eat small mammals."

The Strike team calmed down again, and I heard Adika's voice. "I'm convinced that you're right about it being impossible to travel at night, Rothan. We've completely lost the path we were following, and we're now trying to head back to camp."

I checked Adika's mind, and saw he was satisfied with his own and Kaden's reaction to the screaming. I turned off my ear crystal again, and reached out further with my thoughts. "Lots of animals out there. It's like a vast park."

"You can read animal minds too?" asked Lucas. "Are they less well defined than human minds?"

"It depends. They don't worry about nothing the way humans do. They can have very sharp and well defined thoughts when they're hungry, frightened, or hunting food. They're bliss-fully happy when they're eating."

"Is that why you like feeding the birds and animals in the park?"

I smiled. "Yes. I get a whole wave of happiness coming from them."

"And why you try to help the people around you be happy too, especially your Strike team?"

I pulled a face. "Yes. Adika thinks I'm too kind, but maybe the truth is that I'm dreadfully selfish. I'd rather not be hit by unhappiness every time I'm checking the Strike team's minds. Either way, most of the time I can't do anything to help them. People are very complicated. They can be unhappy because they don't have something, but know they'll be even more unhappy if they get it."

There was a moment of silence before Lucas spoke again. "Are the number of animal minds going to make it difficult for you to find Elden?"

"I don't think so. They're a very different shape, colour, brightness from humans."

I could sense the huge mass of human minds beneath us that was the Hive. A blurred, amorphous hum of thought. The closest of the minds were the familiar ones of people in my Telepath Unit. I caught Megan worrying about how I'd react to daylight. She was jealous of my intimacy with Lucas, and brooding yet again on how she'd rejected Adika. She knew she needed to make up her mind one way or the other, give Adika a clear decision instead of constantly varying the signals she gave him, but...

I realized I'd got sucked into someone else's emotions and problems yet again. I wondered if I'd ever stop making that mistake when reading minds, and forced myself to pull out of Megan's head.

"I've found our unit. It's much easier to reach out through the emptiness, than through corridors crammed with people. My range should be further than it is inside the Hive. Is that enough information for you?"

"It's very helpful and encouraging," said Lucas. "Would you like some food now?"

I opened my eyes. "I'll have a fruit strip."

Lucas munched a couple of crunch cakes, while I nibbled half-heartedly at my fruit strip and looked nervously at the sky. It might be my imagination but it seemed a little brighter. "Is it nearly dawn now?"

"Yes. The Truesun will rise in the east." Lucas pointed directly ahead of us. "There are no corridor signs to tell us directions here, but I'm told that east is that way."

I dropped my fruit strip and focused on why I was out here. Elden had made me his puppet, and I was going to overcome my fear and make him my prisoner. "If I can learn to cope with the Truesun, what are your plans for hunting Elden?"

"We'll head out towards the coast, blending in with the groups from the Ramblers Association as you suggested. Rothan says that it's vitally important for ramblers to help each other with problems, because there's no emergency assistance from the Hive when they're out in the wilderness. That means they're very friendly to each other, totally ignoring level distinctions when they're Outside. We may attract more attention than we'd like from them, but we can let Rothan do most of the talking."

My eyes were fixed on the eastern sky. It was looking brighter now.

Lucas was still talking. "At intervals, we'll stop and let you scan the surrounding area with your mind, looking for Elden. We can put up a tent for you if it helps. I'm hoping it takes days rather than weeks for you to spot him, and then... It'll be like a standard chase, but in highly unusual conditions, and with the added problem that you won't be able to read Elden's plans in his head."

"I'm not sure how I'll pick him out from among the ramblers," I said. "Elden's mind won't be anything like my usual targets. He's a dutiful, tame bee, just one that's following the orders of a different Hive. I suppose we'll just have to chase down anyone with unreadable thoughts and see if they look like an older version of Forge."

"I think you'll find Elden's mind very distinctive," said Lucas. "Hive Genex must have imprinted him with a huge amount of information from several unrelated professions like data systems expert, imprint specialist, and mechanic. On top of that, he'd need a complete imprint of our language, and oddments like techniques for evading our drone patrols and information on booby traps."

Something had been worrying me. I had no choice but to hunt down Elden, but... "Elden must be imprinted with how to detect a true telepath as a child as well. Will our Hive be able to learn the secret from him if we catch him?"

Lucas shook his head. "Elden's imprint must be dangerously

large just to cover the essential information. I can't believe he's been imprinted with expertise in brainwave analysis as well. It would be a totally unnecessary extra burden. Elden must have a way of communicating with Hive Genex to get an aircraft to come and collect him. He could use the same method to transmit data to be analyzed by their own experts."

I wondered what sort of life I'd have had if my Hive had been able to detect telepaths at age three. I felt a traitorous moment of relief that my Hive wouldn't be able to get that knowledge from Elden. Future true telepaths would still be allowed a normal childhood.

"I suspect Elden is hovering on the edge of being imprint overloaded," continued Lucas. "You may see signs of that when you read him."

"There's a limit to how much data you can imprint then?" I asked.

"The limit isn't so much on the amount of data you can imprint," said Lucas, "as on the ability of the receiving mind to handle it. Above a certain point, the mind either ends up unable to access large blocks of the information, or it overloads trying to maintain all the links. Our Hive is careful to keep imprint sizes well inside safety margins. It also avoids the potential issues that can arise with the layering effects of multiple imprints, by only ever giving one imprint at eighteen years old."

He paused. "That means children have to spend some time in school, learning the basics before they go to Teen Level, but school would be necessary anyway. It doesn't just teach children reading and chanting tables, but their duties and obligations to the Hive."

By now I was well aware the main purpose of school was socially conditioning children to become dutiful tame bees to serve the Hive. I wasn't entirely happy about that. On the other hand, I knew exactly how much damage wild bees could do.

I could see the eastern sky was a lot brighter now. "The Truesun is about to rise, isn't it?"

Lucas took my hand. "There'll be some interesting colours in the sky. Don't worry. It's not the world catching on fire or anything. Read me."

I touched his mind. One level of Lucas's thoughts was concentrating on the eastern sky, another on reassuring me, and a third was full of incomprehensible technical details about imprints.

"If I hadn't been a telepath," I said, "Elden wouldn't have kidnapped me. I wouldn't have feared Outside, I wouldn't have had a fixation on Forge, and Teen Level would have been totally different."

I was babbling randomly, as if talking would blot out what was happening in front of my eyes. Memories of Lottery surfaced, and a terrified girl frantically talking to herself. "Why is the sky striped like that?"

"There are some bands of cloud in the sky," said Lucas. "They go different colours at dawn and dusk."

"And Lottery wouldn't have picked me out as being special," I jabbered on. "If I hadn't been a telepath, what job would Lottery have allocated me, Lucas?"

"I've no idea. The minute you tested positive as a telepath, the normal test sequence stopped."

The eastern sky was terrifyingly bright now. I kept suffering the problem of being sucked into other people's emotions, but I could use that to my advantage now. I sheltered in Lucas's emotions, letting them engulf me, and my view of the sky suddenly changed.

The eastern sky wasn't terrifying but incredible, glowing in a rich medley of red, orange, and yellow. I stared at it in awed admiration. Parks just slowly turned up the lights from moon to sun level brightness at dawn, there was nothing like this.

"Can't you make a guess about me?"

"I can't possibly guess what would have happened to you in Lottery," said Lucas. "There are tens of thousands of professions in the Hive. The decision system is far too complicated for any human mind to mimic. Anyway, it's better not to know. It might leave you discontented."

"Well, not if I'd have been a Level 99 Sewage Technician." I saw the amusement in Lucas's thoughts, and screeched in shock. "What? There aren't any Level 99 Sewage Technicians?"

Lucas was struggling not to laugh. "They're an urban myth,

deliberately encouraged by the Hive. Everyone can feel comfortably superior when they joke about the poor Level 99 Sewage Technicians and Waste Handlers living in hovels wedged among the pipes. The truth is that nobody lives below Level 96. Levels 97 to 100 are mostly used for maintenance and storage."

"Gah!" I groaned.

"All Hives aim to be as self-sufficient as possible," said Lucas, "but ours is one of the nearest to being a totally closed environment. We collect a few resources from Outside, trade a little, and have our own sea farm, but for the most part we're independent of the other Hives and Outside. Air, water, food, power, all the main needs are recycled. Our real equivalent of Waste Handlers are Level 1 Ecology Specialists, vital to the wellbeing of the Hive."

I shook my head. "First the whole nosy thing was a bluff, and now there are no Level 99 Sewage Technicians. You have no idea how worried I was that I'd become one."

Lucas couldn't hold back his laughter this time. "It's impossible for me to duplicate the complexity of the Lottery decision process," he gasped, "but I'm absolutely certain you'd have been rated a lot better than Level 99."

He dissolved into laughter again. I cautiously tried separating my mind from his, letting my own emotions take over again. The Truesun's glowing orb was moving above the horizon now, but I wasn't being burnt to death. I wasn't running or screaming either. I felt some nervous fear and tension, but my terror had gone.

I was living in an impossible, incredible new world. The reality of everything I'd known and depended on as a child had shattered into a thousand pieces. My Hive would never imprint me. The grey-masked nosies couldn't read minds. Level 99 Sewage Technicians didn't even exist.

I was Outside, the Truesun was rising, and it wasn't terrifying but glorious. Elden's last hold over me had been broken, and I was free to hunt him down.

CHAPTER THIRTY-FIVE

The next morning, I called my parents so early that they'd barely started eating their breakfasts. "I just wanted to warn you that I'll be extra busy for the next week or two," I said. "My unit is going to be running some especially delicate experiments, so we may have to exchange messages for a while rather than talk to each other."

My parents nodded. My mother and I had a rapid discussion about how Gregas was settling in on Teen Level, while my father just kept giving wistful looks at his breakfast, and then I ended the call.

I double-checked my gun was locked on stun setting, clipped it on to my belt, picked up my crystal unit, slung my jacket over my shoulder, and headed for lift 2. Adika and the Strike team were waiting inside the lift. Lucas was standing outside it with Megan. She'd obviously come to see us off on our hunt for Elden, or more precisely to make a final attempt at stopping us going.

Megan frowned at me. "You've only watched one sunrise and coped with a few hours of daylight, Amber. Leaping straight into this trip on the basis of that, planning to spend day after day Outside, is..." She broke off, unable to make herself say that a telepath was stupid. "Over ambitious."

"We discussed all this in yesterday's meeting, Megan. I'm not scared of Outside or the Truesun any longer. We have to go after Elden now if we want to stand a real chance of catching him."

Megan turned her attack against Lucas. "You must realize

that Amber's been going through far too much lately. That imprint. Your relationship. Going Outside. She shouldn't be rushing off on this trip as well."

"I totally agree," said Lucas. "Leaving immediately is Amber's idea not mine. I'd prefer less precipitous actions, however I can see that she's utilizing her multiple strong emotions to mitigate each other, so leaving now has its advantages."

Megan looked confused.

"Amber's using her anger at Elden to override her residual fear of Outside," Lucas explained helpfully. "She's using her personal relationship with me as a distraction from both those things."

Was I really using those tactics? I supposed that Lucas was right. He was the tactical expert after all.

Lucas spoke deliberately slowly for emphasis. "You won't change Amber's mind about this, Megan. I know. I've tried. Repeatedly. Just look what we're up against!"

He pointed at the wall opposite the lifts, where Sofia had painted her mural of me standing on the picnic table and giving my speech to the unit. I felt that my passionate expression, and my striking pose with both arms raised, owed more to artistic licence than reality, but Megan threw a despairing look at it and groaned.

"Try not to worry too much, Megan," added Lucas. "If Amber's tactics fail, then an aircraft can reach us within minutes and take her back to the Hive."

Megan sighed and retreated in the direction of her office. Lucas and I put our crystal units in our ears, turned them on, and went to join the Strike team in the lift. Adika greeted us with a smile, clearly relieved to have escaped being drawn into the argument with Megan.

"Strike team is moving," he said.

Everyone was carrying backpacks that were even bigger than the ones they'd had yesterday. Lucas and I were the fortunate exceptions, burdened with nothing except our bulky jackets.

Emili's voice spoke in my ear crystal. "Tactical ready."

She sounded worried, and I didn't need telepathy to tell me

why. Lucas was always concerned when he sent me off on an emergency run, and Emili would be even more anxious about Rothan. Lucas knew the entire Strike team would fight to the death to defend me from any threats. Emili knew Rothan's job put him in the forefront of that defence.

The ever anxious voice of Nicole came next. She'd been rushed into being team leader without the standard experience as a deputy. She was doing a great job, but still feeling insecure. "Liaison ready. Tracking status is green."

I'd already checked my dataview. Everyone's signals were there, including Lucas. "Green here," I said.

Lucas started talking in the lecture style he used for briefings. "This is a completely unprecedented run by a Strike team. We're prepared to be Outside for up to a week. Tactical and Liaison teams are organized into shifts to give us round-the-clock support. I can't emphasize enough how important it is for people to rest and sleep when they're off duty. We don't want to be several days into this, hit trouble, and find people are too exhausted to do their job."

"Strike team, that warning is especially relevant for you," said Adika. "I'm splitting you into red group led by Rothan, and blue group led by Forge. Whatever the situation, the group on rest break must try to sleep. Red group is..."

He recited a list of Strike team members, and I watched names changing colour on my dataview.

"Everyone else is blue group," Adika concluded.

Lucas continued his briefing. "We don't want to be seen leaving the Hive, so we'll go all the way down to Level 100, ride an express belt through there, and then take a lift straight up to a maintenance exit near a country park. Liaison have been rescheduling maintenance work on Level 100, so we shouldn't meet too many people there."

Things went quiet until our lift reached Level 100, and we headed out to ride the belt. I stood next to Lucas as we went past seemingly endless mazes of pipes and tanks. Eventually, we jumped belt. Lift 2 at our unit was giant-sized, to allow us to send out the combined Alpha and Beta Strike teams to deal with an extreme emergency. Now we were entering a standard express lift, so it was a tight squeeze for us and all the camping equipment as we made the long ride from Level 100 right up to Industry 1.

When the doors opened, we spilled out into an open area with a flight of steps leading up to a pair of heavy duty doors. Adika held up a hand to stop us, and turned to look at Lucas.

"As we've already discovered," said Lucas, "the terrain Outside can be extremely difficult. Maintenance workers maintain a few paths for access purposes. The Ramblers Association keep some other paths clear for their hobby. We've maps of all available paths, and our expert rambler, Rothan, will be guiding us. If we get lost, blame him not me."

Lucas smiled at Rothan before continuing. "We believe Elden originally came to our Hive from the nearest stretch of coastline. For obvious reasons, our sea farm is at the closest point of that coastline. Elden would want to keep his journey as short as possible, and follow an established path towards our Hive, but avoid the sea farm. That means he'd choose to come ashore at one of two quite small sections of coastline, and follow either the Western or Eastern Coastal Way to reach our Hive."

He paused. "Elden's probably at a nest near one of those two footpaths right now, waiting for Amber's transfer request to be approved. The plan is that we'll head out from the Hive along the Western Coastal Way. If Amber finds no sign of Elden on that route, we'll cut across to pick up the Eastern Coastal Way, and follow that back towards the Hive."

Lucas came to stand next to me, while Rothan and Adika went up the steps and entered the code to open the doors.

"Amber," said Lucas, "if you find your fear of the Truesun returning at any point, say so at once. Rothan can get the tent up within a couple of minutes."

"One minute, forty-five seconds," said Rothan. "We timed it."

The door opened to show an area of unkempt grass and scattered trees. The light Outside was duller than I expected. Some of the more distant trees seemed strangely blurry.

Rothan stepped out of the door and looked around critically. "We've still got some early morning mist. That should clear within an hour, but it looks like we'll have a cloudy day."

"Clouds are good," said Lucas.

I took a deep breath, moved Outside with the rest of the team, and looked upwards. The sky was a uniform greyish white, like a badly painted park sky. I couldn't even see the Truesun. There was a cold edge to the air, so I put on my jacket.

Rothan was staring alternately at his dataview and our surroundings. "We'll have to take a maintenance path down slope and head for Spike 71. Once we're there, we can join the main Hive perimeter path and follow it to the junction with the Western Coastal Way. It may seem like we're going the long way round, but it's much easier and faster than trying to force our way cross-country without a path."

"You're the expert, Rothan," said Adika. "General marching order is that red group go ahead with Rothan, followed by Lucas and Amber in the middle, then Forge and blue group. Cover the flanks when you can. Guns set to stun and hidden under jackets. Ear crystals kept on audio only for now. We're innocent little ramblers going for a stroll."

Rothan led the way along a wide path with an oddly soft surface. I scuffed my feet, and found it was a thick layer of ancient leaves. There were giant trees on either side of us now, towering upwards to a dizzying height.

We mostly walked in silence, though there was the odd joking comment from one or other member of the Strike team. Adika was leaving Rothan to lead, and Forge to act as rearguard, while he lurked near the middle of our party and watched every move I made. I checked his thoughts, and saw that Megan had been lecturing him about the dangers of exposing me to daylight for too long.

I sighed. I understood Megan being especially anxious about this trip, but sometimes I felt like a toddler with an over-protective mother. I allowed myself a brief fantasy about firing her, but knew it was pointless. Any other candidate for Megan's position would be exactly the same, smothering me with care.

I'd learnt a lot about imprints lately. Everyone in my unit was imprinted with identical facts about how telepaths were rare, vital to the Hive, and must be protected at all costs. Everyone except those imprinted for Tactical Commander or Senior Administrator.

Lucas was my Tactical Commander in charge of operations. His imprint had to inform him telepaths were precious, but not overwhelm him with that fact, or he'd never be able to make the decision to send one on an emergency run. That was one of the things that had attracted me to Lucas. Everyone else in my unit looked at me and saw an irreplaceable telepath first and a person second, but Lucas always saw me as Amber.

But if the Hive left my Tactical Commander free to make decisions that put me at risk, it also made sure my Senior Administrator was a balancing influence to defend me. Candidates for Megan's position were chosen to be over-protective by nature, and imprinted with a crippling mass of reasons why a telepath must be kept safe and cosseted.

I pulled a face. I'd once thought that Megan's primary role was protecting my physical and mental wellbeing, in the same way that Adika's primary role was protecting me from attack. That was almost right, but Megan's role also included protecting me from my Tactical Commander. No wonder she was so uncomfortable about me being in a relationship with Lucas.

I realized everyone had stopped moving, and looked round to see why. We'd reached a junction in the path, and Rothan seemed to be conferring with Liaison about which way to go. I sat down on a fallen tree branch to wait, grateful for the rest. I was used to riding an express belt for long distance travel, and what walking I did was along nice level corridors. This path had a habit of sloping upwards and then going down again. Parks weren't totally flat, but they were nothing like this.

I closed my eyes to focus on my telepathic view of the world. Lucas's thoughts flared like a beacon among the rest of our party. Below my feet was the thunderous hum of a hundred million minds. Around us were a multitude of animals and birds. I opened my eyes again.

"Our tracking shows you're definitely at the right junction," said the voice of Nicole.

Rothan peered at his dataview. "This is a four way junction instead of three. The path ahead looks like a temporary one cut by maintenance workers. You get a lot of temporary paths appearing and disappearing out here. We'll turn right."

We walked on and reached a small stream. Adika automatically picked me up and carried me across it.

"If any ramblers see us carrying Amber," said Rothan, "they'll be worried she's been hurt and ask if we need help. We should tell them she's just tripped over a tree root and twisted her ankle."

"Easy enough to injure yourself on paths like this," grumbled Eli.

"That's why we have the special heavy footwear that you've been moaning about, Eli," said Rothan. "The boots protect your feet and ankles, so you're less likely to injure yourself."

When we were across the stream, I did my own walking again. After what seemed a very long time, Megan's voice came over the sound link. "You'll need to give Amber a proper rest break before too long."

"I'm all right so far," I said. "The sky is very cloudy today."

"I was thinking of getting us to the edge of table top, and breaking for a few hours there," said Rothan. "That way everyone will be fully rested for the descent."

"What's table top?" asked Adika.

"It's a rambler term," said Rothan. "When the Hive was first built, a vast, square hole was dug out. Most of the Hive levels were built underground, but the rest stuck up above the surrounding countryside. As we're taught in school, there was just the one zone back then, but over the next century the Hive was gradually extended sideways to add the extra nine zones we have today. The thing they don't mention in school, is that all the spare soil and rocks from extending the hole was used to bury the Hive."

He paused for a moment. "The result is the ground above the Hive is quite flat, like a vast, oblong table top, but when you get to the edge of the Hive there's a very steep slope. Getting down the slope can be tricky, and is best done on an established path."

I wrinkled my nose. I didn't think our current path was all that flat, so how steep would the slope be?

"A break of a few hours sounds good to me," said Lucas. "I'd like us to do our travelling early and late, and give Amber a long rest break inside a tent during the middle of the day."

We walked on through the forest. "If they just piled loose soil on top of the Hive, why are there all these trees?" I asked.

"They planted fast growing conifers to help stabilize the soil," said Rothan. "Other trees grew from random seeds. You mainly get conifers on top of the Hive. Once we're down from table top, you'll find the trees are much more varied."

"How do you know all these things?" asked Eli.

"My parents told me about them," said Rothan. "They do maintenance work Outside, so their imprints have lots of details on the conditions."

The path had been going up, now it went down again. "I thought you said table top was flat?" said Eli. "This feels like a slope to me."

Rothan just laughed.

The trees abruptly thinned out. When we walked past the last of them, we stopped and stood in awed silence. The ground ahead plummeted downwards a terrifying distance. Bushes and the occasional small tree clung on desperately.

"Now *that's* a slope," said Rothan.

"Yes, that's definitely a slope," said Adika, in a thoughtful voice.

Forge casually wandered forward to take a closer look. "I'd be happier if it was even steeper and solid rock. That soil looks dangerously loose to me."

Rothan nodded. "If loose soil and stones start sliding under your feet, then you'll slide with them. If anyone slips at any point, then I advise sitting down, but we shouldn't have any trouble if we stay on the path. It's a maintenance one heading to Spike 71, and should be nice and solid. Rambler paths are a lot more variable."

I advanced nervously to try to see the path heading down, and spotted it zigzagging to and fro across the slope.

"The path takes a very long route," said Eli.

"If you want to save time, you can just jump," said Rothan. "You'll get to the bottom very fast indeed."

Eli gulped. "No thanks."

"Will you be able to cope going down there on foot, Amber?" asked Adika. "I'm not sure it's a good idea to have someone carrying you in case they slip."

I pictured that and winced.

"Would you like me to walk down with you, Amber?" asked Forge.

"That would make me feel a lot safer," I said. "Do you remember the time I tried cliff climbing at Teen Level beach, and got a massive panic attack when I tried their 'C' grade climb?"

"Of course I remember," said Forge. "You froze near the top, and I had to go up and rescue you. This is nothing like a cliff climb though. It's just a steep path, zigzagging downwards. It's wide enough for me to walk beside you on the slope side all the way. You can't possibly fall then."

"That's good," said Eli, "but who's going to stop *me* from falling?"

"I've walked along paths like this since I was three years old," said Rothan.

The rest of the Strike team hastily straightened up and tried to look fearless, but Lucas laughed. "The Strike team may not be scared of a path used by three-year-olds, but I am. I want Rothan to lurk close by, ready to grab me if I slip. I also claim the right to scream in terror at regular intervals. I have to suffer a few hours of agonized anticipation before that though, so can Rothan put up our tent please?"

Rothan turned back from the slope, picked an open area of grass, and took off his backpack. I watched, fascinated, as he rapidly took out, unfolded, and locked together sections of tent.

"Blue group, your job is guard duty and soothing Eli's nerves," said Adika. "Red group, get some more tents up and try to sleep. You'll be on first watch tonight."

Blue group fanned out to take up guard positions. Red group started unpacking more tents. Once Rothan had finished putting up the tent for Lucas and me, I went inside and stretched out blissfully on the floor. Lucas came in after me, took off his ear crystal, and brushed my hair aside to steal mine. He turned them pointedly off.

"Alone at last."

"I'd no idea walking could tire you out so much," I said. It wasn't just the walking. I wasn't going to admit it to anyone, but I still found being Outside quite a strain. It wasn't that it was terrifying me now; it was just so very different from the familiar corridors of the Hive.

Lucas turned on a lantern and sealed the tent flap. "You should have said that you were getting tired, Amber. We don't want you getting exhausted on the first day."

He took out the small package that was a folded heat sack, and shook it out to full size. "Are you hungry, or shall we rest before eating?"

"Rest first."

I watched him taking off the clumpy boots Rothan had given us, sighed, and struggled back into a sitting position to let my own feet out of prison. I wriggled my toes, took off the bulkier layers of outdoor clothing, and slid into the heat sack. Lucas crawled in after me.

"That path looks horribly scary," I said. "I'm a dreadful coward, you know. I gave up surfing after a nasty wipe out. I gave up climbing after that panic attack on the cliff."

"Deeply fortunate." Lucas started talking in speed speech, and I automatically linked to his mind to get the full sentences. "Adika would collapse under the nervous strain of a surfing, cliff-climbing telepath."

"You won't be worried if I cling to Forge on the way down?"

"I shall probably be clinging to Rothan myself. You won't get jealous?"

I laughed. "I'll try not to get overwhelmed by emotion and shoot both of you. I don't want Adika arresting me."

Lucas grinned. "Adika wouldn't arrest a telepath for killing a

Strike team member or a Tactical Commander. Both are replaceable. A telepath isn't. You're above the law, Amber. Untouchable."

"Don't be silly."

"I'm not being silly," said Lucas. "It's in the best interests of our Hive to have a functioning true telepath at all costs. Any aberrations must be tolerated. The slaughter of unit members probably wouldn't be acceptable on a daily basis, but the occasional one..."

I lay back, gurgling with laughter, but abruptly sobered up. "It isn't really funny, is it? However unreasonable I am, everyone has to accept it and humour me. I try not to take advantage of that, but I can't help it sometimes."

"You definitely indulge in some blatant abuse," said Lucas.

"I do?" I gave him a worried look.

He nodded. "Your criminal untidiness shocks the entire unit."

I smiled. "My mother forced me to be unspeakably tidy at home, but my natural slovenliness took over on Teen Level, and now I know Hannah will sneak in and clear up after me... You're right. It's blatant abuse of my position."

"Megan has a theory that your untidiness is a subconscious method of freeing your mind," said Lucas. "She thinks it's the reason you can read deeper thought levels than other true telepaths."

I stared at him. "She does? What do you think?"

"I think it's pure laziness," said Lucas.

I giggled. "I suspect you're right."

"I suggest you make a special effort to be tidy during this trip. Especially if we're going to be sharing this tent on a regular basis. Are we planning to do that?"

I was startled by the question. I'd been assuming that Lucas would be with me at night. If he wasn't... I was shocked by the realization of how alone I'd feel without him. "I'd like that. Would you be happy with it?"

"My options are sharing a tent with Adika or sharing a tent with you," said Lucas. "I'd definitely prefer sharing with you."

There was something oddly anxious about his voice. I finally had the sense to check the deeper levels of his mind, and saw what he was really asking me. Were we just sharing a tent on this trip, or was this the start of something more permanent?

"If sharing a tent works," I said, "then I think there might be space for two people in my apartment."

We lay there in silence for the next few minutes, smiling foolishly at each other, and then I sniffed the air and frowned. "Can you smell something burning?"

Lucas put his crystal unit in his ear, and turned it on. "Are you on fire out there?"

I had my own ear crystal on in time to hear Rothan's cheerful reply. "We're doing camp fire cooking. Want some?"

"No, thank you," said Lucas. "I'm too young to die."

I suddenly felt hungry. "I'll try some."

Lucas groaned. "They're going to poison your telepath, Adika."

"It should be safe," said Adika. "We tested the first batch on Eli and he's still alive."

Lucas wriggled out of the heat sack, and threw on his clothes to open the tent flap and go out. He returned a moment later, and handed me a warm, strangely shaped object. I bit into it cautiously.

"It's a sort of pastryish, breadish thing, with bits of stuff inside it," I said. "It's not bad. Try some."

Lucas shook his head. "I'm sticking to protein bars. I like my food carefully measured and prepared by reliable machines."

"You can't survive for a week on just protein bars, Lucas," said Adika, through our ear crystals.

"Watch me," said Lucas.

I munched my way through my pastry thing, and then dozed for a while until Lucas told me it was time to face the nightmare path. I crawled reluctantly out of the heat sack, and got dressed. When I went out of the tent, I found the Strike team packing equipment and throwing earth on the remains of a small fire. Rothan and Adika were standing near the steep slope down, staring out at something. Lucas and I went to join them.

"What are we looking at?" asked Lucas.

"Spike 71," said Rothan. "The big red and black thing sticking way up above the trees. My plan is to set up camp for the night near there."

I looked at the tall, pointed object. I was finding it hard to judge distances Outside because of the sheer scale of things, but it seemed a very long way away. "What is it?"

"I've no idea," said Rothan, "but there are a lot of them dotted around near the Hive, and they make great landmarks for ramblers."

"They're geothermal energy spikes," said Nicole's voice.

"What does that mean?" I asked.

"I've got a ten thousand word, highly technical description here," said Nicole. "I don't understand a word of it, but I can read it to you if you like."

"Please don't," said Lucas.

"The spikes house geothermal heat pumps," said Eli. "They provide heat and power to supplement the Hive's recycled resources."

We all stared at him in disbelief.

Eli grinned in triumph. "My parents work in Hive Power Resources."

When everyone had stopped laughing, the Strike team finished their packing, and Adika lined us up for the descent. "Forge, you're in the middle taking care of Amber. If she falls off, you're spending the rest of your life scraping scum filters. Lucas, do you genuinely need help, or were you joking earlier?"

"I was deadly serious," said Lucas. "I'm utterly terrified of going down that path."

Adika moved forward to where the path started plunging downwards. "Rothan, take care of Lucas. If he falls off, you get to tidy up after Amber for the rest of the trip. That's probably worse than scraping scum filters." He paused. "Let's do this."

I did a rapid check of minds. Lucas really was scared. So were a lot of the Strike team. A hand on my arm attracted my attention.

"Ready?" asked Forge.

I nodded, and we headed down the path behind Lucas and Rothan. With the solid bulk of Forge between me and the edge, it wasn't as bad as I'd feared.

"When there's heavy rain, water runs down from the table top," said Rothan. "Watch out for ruts in the path."

We progressed slowly and cautiously down the zigzagging path. I hung tightly on to Forge when we reached a point where the path wasn't just rutted, but part of the edge had been washed away.

"I envy your head for heights," I told him. "When I froze on that cliff climb, I was totally rigid with panic, and you had to help move my feet onto the foot holds."

"I get scared too sometimes. That's part of the attraction of things like climbing."

I laughed. "Forge, you're weird."

"I'm weird? You're a telepath, now that's..."

"I hate to interrupt the reminiscences," said Adika, "but remember you're talking on an open sound link. Amber, you can insult Forge all you like, but he can't retaliate."

"Unfair," said Forge happily.

Four more zigzags and the path gradually levelled out. Lucas turned to face me, and gave an exaggerated sigh of relief. "We made it down alive!"

We'd got spread out during the descent. Rothan waited for the stragglers to catch up before speaking. "We'll carry on to Spike 71 and camp there for the night. There's a nice flat area that doesn't flood, and a spring that's good drinking water."

"You expect me to drink the water out here?" Lucas protested. "It runs along the ground. Things live in it. You wouldn't drink out of the park lake!"

Rothan led the way off along the path. "We'll run the water through purifiers so it's perfectly safe to drink."

"You're going to have to drink water, Lucas," said Adika. "We've brought some melon juice, but that's for Amber, not you."

I gave up listening to the argument, and reached out with my thoughts as we walked along. Lucas was in clown mode, exaggerating his fastidiousness about what he ate and drank.

Dhiren was still a mass of nerves after the horrors of the path down the slope. Kaden was happy about being Outside in daylight, but nervous of the night to come. Eli was enjoying himself despite his periodic complaints.

Adika was very aware that Rothan knew these conditions far better than he did, and was letting him take on some of the leader role, studying how his new deputy coped with the sudden responsibility. He was planning to push Rothan hard on this trip, because he saw him as his own eventual successor. It was essential Rothan could cope with anything and everything by that distant future time.

I made a mental note that I should keep an eye on Rothan, and warn Adika if he was overdoing the pressure, then let my thoughts drift out beyond the team. We were leaving behind the mind mass of the Hive, and I could sense the quietness for many cors ahead of us, not that the traditional measuring in standard corridor lengths had much meaning out here.

I felt an arm take mine, and Lucas guided me as I walked away from the Hive, my mind still searching the surrounding countryside. Somewhere in this alien wilderness, my target was hiding.

CHAPTER THIRTY-SIX

"I thought we'd be almost at the coast by now, but I've mis-judged just about everything," said Lucas cheerfully. "I wasn't allowing for the route along the paths being at least twice the straight line distance. I wasn't allowing for walking being so tiring and so slow on uneven ground. I definitely wasn't allowing for us spending a whole day sitting in our tents and watching the rain pour down."

It was our sixth day Outside, and the Strike team were busy with the morning routine of breaking camp. Rothan packed a final section of tent into his backpack, and looked round to check nothing had been left behind.

"I warned you to expect rain, Lucas."

Lucas laughed. "I know you did. I just naively thought the clouds would run out of water after a couple of hours. I was more worried about the Truesun being a strain on Amber, but we haven't seen it for more than five minutes. Well, I am now an older, wiser, and much wetter man."

"Everyone ready to move?" asked Adika.

We formed up in marching order.

"You'll find the path rather muddy after yesterday's rain," said Rothan.

The path turned out to be extremely muddy. We squelched along it for several minutes, and I sensed other minds approach-ing. "Ramblers ahead, coming our way," I warned. "About ten of them."

When the ramblers reached us, they paused for a chat. The Western Coastal Way was one of the main ramblers' routes between the Hive and the coast, so we'd got used to this sort of encounter by now.

"The stream ahead has flooded," said a woman. "The bridge itself is fine, but you'll find the water about ankle deep on the path before you reach it. Once you're over the bridge and headed uphill, you'll be fine through to the quarry."

"Thanks," said Adika.

The other party were looking us over with interest. One of the men turned to Rothan. "You've got a lot of new recruits with you."

Every group we met noticed our matching, brand new equipment, compared it to Rothan's well-worn jacket and boots, and instantly identified him as the experienced leader of a mob of clueless greenies.

Rothan smiled. "I've just come out of Lottery as an Outside maintenance worker. I've talked some of my new work colleagues into trying out camping."

"Don't let yesterday's rain put you off," said another man.

"We won't," said Forge.

"I didn't mind the rain," said Lucas. "It was getting down the slope from table top that terrified me."

The experienced ones laughed. "You'll soon get used to that."

We exchanged waves, moved on, and soon reached the flooding they'd mentioned. As a cosseted telepath, I didn't have to worry about getting my feet wet. Adika picked me up to carry me across, and I automatically closed my eyes to concentrate on doing a proper mental sweep of the area.

Adika had warned me not to neglect the area behind us, so I checked that first. I sensed the group of ramblers we'd just met, and another group much further away. Far beyond them was the distant hum of the Hive.

There were several more sets of ramblers ahead of us, and what I thought must be the minds of the sea farm staff in the far distance. To the east was...

"I may have a target," I said.

The Strike team instantly drew their weapons and gathered round me.

"Relax. The target's a very long way east." I pointed. "It's hard to judge distance, but he's at least a hundred cors away. That's too far for me to get much detail, so I can't be sure it's Elden, but the mind is definitely human, male, and looks unusual."

"How many minds are there in that area?" asked Lucas.

"Just the one man." I concentrated on that elusive speck of thought.

"One person alone out here is suspicious to start with," said Rothan. "Ramblers always travel in groups when they're this far from the Hive."

"A hundred cors away," muttered Adika. "Are you serious, Amber? You're really detecting minds that far away?"

"It's very quiet out here, so my range is much further than inside the Hive. I think I'm already sensing the sea farm ahead of us."

"That's incredible," said Lucas.

"The sea farm is like a tiny smudge of minds," I said. "The Hive is far behind us now, but much louder and quite unmistakable."

Rothan and Adika started checking maps on their dataviews. "There's a major path to the east of us that runs from the Hive to the sea farm," said Rothan.

Lucas peered over his shoulder at the map. "That's the Ocean Path. It's the shortest route between the Hive and the coast, but I assumed Elden would avoid it. He wouldn't want to risk swimming offshore to meet an aircraft anywhere near our sea farm and fishing fleet."

"Elden might not be on the Ocean Path itself." Rothan pointed at his dataview. "There's a minor path that runs between the Western Coastal Way and the Ocean Path."

Lucas nodded. "Elden could have found an isolated place on that minor path to set up his nest."

"If we carry on towards the coast, we should soon reach the junction with the minor path," said Rothan.

We started moving again. About an hour later, we turned onto a narrow, overgrown path.

"This is where we have to start cutting our way through," said Rothan. "We've had an easy time so far, on routes that have a lot of traffic and are well maintained, but not many people use this path."

He took out what looked like a long curved knife. "Matias, come and take the lead with me. We'll hack back the overhanging branches and brambles for the others to get through. It's hard work, so we'll all take turns to lead."

"Cutting the path will slow us down," said Adika. "How long will it take us to reach Elden's area?"

Rothan shrugged. "My worry is whether we can get there at all. It rained a lot yesterday, and we've several water crossings to cope with. We can't expect proper bridges on this path."

He turned and started slashing at branches and brambles. Matias joined him, and the rest of us followed them at a very slow walk.

"Query," said Lucas. "How long does it take the path to get this overgrown?"

"It looks like a full season's growth to me," gasped a breathless Rothan. "Things don't grow so fast in the winter, so it could be anything between six months and a year since anyone came through here."

"In which case," said Lucas, "Elden must have come back to his nest by the shortest possible route, following the Ocean Path until he reached the junction with this minor path, and then cutting his way along it in the opposite direction to us."

"Pity," said Adika. "It would have saved us effort if he'd cut the way through from our side."

"Yes," said Lucas, "but more importantly it means Elden knows several routes between our Hive and the coast. That means he's spent much more time here than we thought, and has explored this whole area. Be aware he'll be familiar with the terrain, and know all the places to hide."

There was a grim silence after that. We moved on painfully slowly, with the Strike team taking turns to hack brambles, and eventually reached a wide stream. The churning water was brown with mud and nearly overflowing its banks. Adika and Rothan exchanged glances.

"That's not jumpable, and the water would sweep us off our feet if we tried wading it," said Adika. "Time to try out the portable bridge."

I was startled. "We've got a bridge?"

"This is going to be interesting," said Lucas. "I vote we send Adika across the bridge first to check it's safe."

Adika ignored him and studied the stream. "We'll use the tree next to me, and the one opposite, as anchor points."

He took a gun shaped object from his backpack, attached the end of a reel of cord, and fired a spike at the tree on the opposite bank. Several of the Strike team took out short rods from their backpacks, and began extending them and snapping them together. I watched them for a moment, before guiltily remembering I should be doing my own job.

I closed my eyes and searched. The mind I'd sensed was closer now and it... I gasped.

"Something wrong, Amber?" asked Lucas.

"I don't know. I think this must be Elden's mind, because I've never met anything like this." I struggled to describe the telepathic view. "His mind is like a net. There are tiny dark patches, holes, everywhere."

"Imprint overload," said Lucas. "They gave him more data than his brain could integrate. You must be seeing the effects of that."

"The surface of Elden's mind ripples." I tried to read the distant thoughts, but they were gibberish. "I don't understand the words on the high levels. That's what we expected. I'll try the deeper levels."

"Be ready to pull out fast, Amber." Lucas sounded worried. "If Elden's in imprint overload, you may find it disturbing."

I traced my way warily down through the gibberish, to where emotions and images whirled in terrifying confusion. I hastily broke contact, and opened my eyes to find Lucas gazing intently into my face.

"That was horrible," I said. "Images melting into each other. A bit like someone having a nightmare, but Elden's definitely awake."

Lucas frowned. "The imprint is breaking down, fragmenting his unconscious thoughts. Reality is mixing with nightmares. I've no idea what techniques Hive Genex used to keep Elden stable this long, but now he's alone out here they're breaking down."

I looked at him anxiously. "Lucas, if imprints can do that to someone, why does our Hive use them? Is it worth the risk?"

"Your body could carry a small stone with no problems, Amber, but not a giant boulder. The mind has limits too. Our Hive keeps imprints to a safe size, and yes they're worth it. Children go to school to learn the basics like reading and numbers. If your team members had to learn their imprinted knowledge in the same way, then they'd have to keep studying through Teen Level and after, until they were about twenty-five or twenty-six years old. They'd need yet more time to gain the knowledge necessary for higher positions. Your deputy team leaders would need to be thirty to thirty-five. Your team leaders nearly forty."

Lucas shrugged. "With the help of imprints, you have Strike team members who are eighteen. That's a gain of at least seven productive years. Look at your team leaders. I had the minimum normal experience before I became your Tactical Commander. I'm twenty-one. Nicole bypassed the deputy experience require-ment entirely. She's nineteen. Megan and Adika had to wait a long time for their team leader openings so they're..."

Megan's voice interrupted him over the sound link. "Careful, Lucas!"

Lucas laughed. "They're a little older. Think of the gain to the Hive in productivity. Because of my imprint, I've gained almost twenty years in my post."

I forced a smile, and nodded my acceptance, but I wasn't totally convinced. As I approached Lottery, I'd been afraid of what being imprinted would do to me. After Lottery, I'd resented being forever excluded from that easy route to knowledge. Now I'd returned, full circle, to fear and suspicion of imprints.

I'd learned from bitter personal experience how imprints could be used to influence emotions, even totally control someone. Our Hive didn't do that, because it was wasteful to change people into blindly obedient automatons, incapable of independent decisions. What it did do was use the Lottery selection process to choose suitable people for a position, and then imprint them with carefully chosen information that would reinforce the attitudes it wanted. It wasn't that the imprint forced people to believe one side of an argument, it just never told them the other side existed.

I was glad I didn't have an imprint. It worried me that Lucas did. I trusted his ability to think for himself, but if that brilliant mind broke under imprint overload... I shied away from that nightmare thought, telling myself it could never happen. Our Hive wasn't a brutal, uncaring place like Hive Genex. Our Hive didn't overload minds or try to steal telepaths.

"The bridge is ready, Amber," said Adika.

I'd forgotten the bridge building. I turned to see a spider's web of rods spanning the raging waters of the stream. Lucas looked at it suspiciously.

"Can that take a man's weight safely?"

"The entire Strike team could stand on it at once," said Adika. "Save your worries until we hit something too wide for the bridge, and have to cross using just ropes."

Forge shepherded me across the bridge, warning me not to look down through the apparently fragile mesh beneath my feet. Rothan followed, keeping an eye on Lucas. Adika waited until everyone was across before speaking.

"Rafael, Caleb, stay here to dismantle the bridge. Given the slowness of cutting a path, you'll have no problem catching us up afterwards."

About half an hour later, we reached another stream, even wider than the first one. I liked sitting by streams in parks, listening to the friendly, soft sound of the water, but this stream didn't sound or look at all friendly. It was ripping threateningly at its banks, and I saw a large branch being carried along with the torrent.

Adika fired a rope across to a tree on the opposite bank. "The bridge should just about be long enough."

"It's the river that worries me," said Rothan.

"What's a river?" I asked.

"A huge stream," said Rothan. "The one here is wider than anything you'd get in a park, but it's just a small stream in full spate after heavy rain. Further ahead, we hit a proper river, and there's a waterfall marked on the map. That's the main reason for the existence of this path. It crosses the river at a ford above the waterfall, and ramblers sometimes go there to admire the views."

Nicole spoke to us over the sound link. "We've accessed the Ramblers Association records, and found some images of the waterfall. Sending them to your dataviews now."

Everyone took out dataviews, unfolded them, and stared at the images. Infinite amounts of water cascading down a cliff face, and then swiftly swirling onwards between two slopes that were even steeper than the descent from table top. I'd seen waterfalls in parks, but nothing like this.

"Waste it!" said Dhiren, in an awed voice. "That's impressive."

"That's... inconvenient," said Adika aloud, though the thought in his head was far more strongly phrased.

The Strike team went back to building their bridge, and I briefly closed my eyes for another check on my target. "Elden's much closer now. I think I can give you a fairly accurate distance. Seven or eight cors ahead of us."

"Which is uncomfortably close to the waterfall." Adika's voice held a note of grim resignation. "Of course Elden would base himself by the river, so he'd have a constant supply of water and fish. If he's on the far bank, then crossing the river using ropes will leave us wide open to attack. Rothan, am I right in assuming that wading across at the ford would be a bad idea after heavy rain?"

"Suicidal," said Rothan.

Adika left the bridge builders to work on their own, and came over to where Lucas and I were sitting. "Lucas, now we've got Elden's position and are sure of his identity, can we just wipe him out with an aerial attack?"

Lucas pulled a face. "Hive Politics would prefer to submit Elden alive to Joint Hive Treaty Enforcement, but his dead body should provide more than enough evidence against Hive Genex. Would we end up with a body?"

Adika groaned. "With so much tree cover here, we'd need to take out the whole area to get him. That wouldn't leave much of a body, or anything else."

I closed my eyes. "I'll see if I can get any clues from Elden. It's frustrating not understanding the conscious levels though."

I reached out to Elden's mind again, and went down to the lower levels where images flashed and emotions burned. "Elden's cold and wet and wants to go home to his nest." I saw a fleeting image. "The nest might be underground. It's definitely somewhere dark and dry."

Adika sighed. "If Elden's got an underground nest, then an aerial assault isn't an option."

I concentrated on Elden's sense of smell and touch. The now familiar forest scent of leaf mould. The sensation of damp clothes slapping against skin. The heavy weight on his hip. No smooth, supportive, slippery feel of... "Elden has a gun, but isn't wearing body armour."

"Amber, you're sure he doesn't have body armour?" asked Adika.

"Quite positive."

Adika smiled. "Excellent news!"

"If he doesn't have body armour, then we should try to get a shot at him before he knows we're here," said Lucas. "Ideally kill him, but aim to at least wound him. If he starts running, we can call in aircraft to take us across the river and help us chase him down. A wounded man shouldn't get far."

The bridge was ready now, so we moved on. This time I made the mistake of looking down at the water beneath me, and saw it flinging itself over jagged rocks. Forge had to tug me forwards to reach the other side.

"We'll leave the bridge in place this time," said Adika. "It won't help us with the river ahead, and we want the option to move back at speed if necessary. Guns accessible. Crystal units to visual."

Everyone clipped their guns to their hips. The camera extensions unfolded for the first time since we'd come Outside.

"Visual links green for all Strike team," said Nicole.

"Forge, Dhiren, Kaden, Rafael, Caleb will be on bodyguard duty," said Adika. "Rothan and the rest are with me on Chase team. Amber, I'm assuming you won't be able to help us with much information from Elden, but we daren't leave you far behind us in this situation. Lucas, stay close to Amber and keep your head down."

Progress was very slow, because those cutting the path were trying to make as little noise as possible. Forge was carrying me, so I closed my eyes and tried to make sense of the bewildering mind of my target.

"Elden's head is like a kaleidoscope of images," I said. "They're disjointed. Flickering. Getting close now. One or two cors ahead and right a bit."

"Bodyguard team drop back and follow us in," said Adika.

We moved on a little further.

"He's one cor ahead, or a little less," I said.

"Across the river then." Adika gave a rapid series of orders. "We're coming up to the river edge now. The ford is directly ahead, and the river goes over the waterfall to our right. Bodyguard team stay in the trees. Chase team crawl from now on, fan out to the left and right and try to spot Elden. If you can get a clear shot, then go for it. Guns on kill. Stunning him is pointless, because he'd regain consciousness long before we got across that river."

I could hear the sound of fast flowing water ahead of me. A sudden clap of wings, loud as a drum roll, drowned it out for a moment. We'd been hearing this periodically for days as we startled birds along our path.

"Waste those pigeons," said Adika. "Freeze everyone. Amber, did that worry Elden?"

"I don't know." I groaned my frustration. "He noticed it but I don't know if he's worried." I sieved through images. "He's high up, looking down at the water."

"If he was above the waterfall, then he'd be level with the water. He's to our right then?" asked Adika.

"No. He's directly ahead."

"But…"

I felt the roughness of bark under my target's hands. "A tree! Elden's up a tree!"

Forge instantly dropped to the ground, taking me with him. A new image flashed in Elden's mind. Men crawling through bushes. Others among trees. One man cradling the slight figure of a girl against him.

"He can see us! He can see me!" I yelled.

Bodies landed heavily on me. My bodyguards throwing themselves between me and danger. I kept focused on Elden's mind. He mustn't escape.

"I have visual!" yelled Eli. "Partial shot. Do I take it?"

"Eli, kill!" Adika ordered.

The sharp note of a kill setting sounded as Eli fired, and I felt flaring pain. "You got his arm."

"Amber, get out of Elden's head!" screamed Lucas from next to me. "You know you have to leave a target's mind the instant the kill order is given."

I'd been stupidly over-eager to help, but I left Elden's mind now. "Going circuit. Adika, Eli…"

I saw the view of the target from Eli's eyes. Elden was high in a tree on the opposite bank, a dark shape among yellow leaves, swinging round to shelter behind the tree trunk.

Eli ran forward to the river edge to get another, clearer shot at him, and fired a fraction of a second before he was hit by a hammer blow to the shoulder. His body armour protected him, but he was caught off balance, staggered and fell. I felt the cold of the racing water engulf him, carrying him on towards the waterfall.

CHAPTER THIRTY-SEVEN

"Eli's hit! He's in the river! Waste it, my leg!"

I screamed in agony as I, as Eli, crashed down the face of the waterfall. I had to fight to force myself to stay with him despite the pain tearing through my, his, body. "Eli's leg's broken. He's unconscious now, caught on some rocks. Cold. So terribly cold."

"There's a path that cuts the corner to a view point," said Rothan. "If we can get downstream of Eli…"

"Rothan, go!" shouted Adika. "Amber, where's Elden?"

I left Eli and searched. "Elden's running away from the river. He's hit, shoulder and arm. Staggering through the trees. No threat to us."

"We've lost Eli's visual link and tracking," said Nicole. "His crystal unit must be smashed."

"Everyone after Rothan!" Adika ordered.

Bodyguards tumbled off me. Forge went off at a frantic sprint, while Kaden grabbed me and carried me along with the main rush of the Strike team. The ground was rocky here, there were no bushes and the sparse trees were stunted. The path was so steep and muddy that we skidded and slid our way down it, but I didn't care.

"Nicole, we need air support now!" Adika gasped the words.

"Aerial one and two are launching," Nicole responded. "Aerial three is holding while medical staff board and will launch in three minutes."

I closed my eyes, hung on to Kaden, and searched for Eli

again. There was agony from his leg, and a sick stabbing in his head and chest, but Eli himself was too far gone to be aware of it.

"We're downstream of Eli now," I yelled. "He's unconscious still. Alive. Just."

There was the sound of the gun that Adika had used to fire ropes across the streams. It fired a second time.

"Eli's been washed off the rocks," I yelled again. "He's coming towards us now!"

"I can't see him." Adika's voice was half drowned by the thundering sound of water.

I opened my eyes. Adika had shot ropes across the river, and he and Forge were wading into the waist deep water. They wore belts that were clipped to the ropes, and were pulling themselves along with their hands, while their legs were being swept from under them by the current.

"He's nearer the other bank. Over there!" I screamed the words, waving my arm frantically at where my mind could see Eli.

Forge glanced at me, then back at the churning water. "I see him now!"

He was just in time to snag the dark tumbling shape that was Eli. Adika joined him, and together they fought against the strength of the river to wind an orange harness around Eli. They got it clipped to the ropes, adjusted it, and slowly dragged themselves and Eli back towards the eager hands of the rest of the Strike team.

Eli was white and motionless when they stretched him out on the riverbank, but I could still sense a sliver of unconscious thought. Adika knelt beside him, pressing rhythmically on his chest to pump water from his lungs, as a roar sounded above us.

"Aerial one requesting target location," said a female voice in my ear crystal.

I closed my eyes and searched. "Target is across the river. Running directly away from it. Three cors away from my position and still moving."

I opened my eyes again, looked up, and saw the impossible sight of something huge and grey hanging in the sky. I stared at it in shock, as it moved across the river, paused to hover above the trees, and was joined by its identical twin.

"Aerial one and two have target on heat sensors," said Nicole. "Aerial three will arrive at your location in two minutes."

"We'll need Aerial three to pick us up," said Adika. "Elden's on the wrong side of the river to us, and Eli's in bad shape. A compound fracture of his left leg and a head injury. What's the target's situation like, Amber?"

"Elden was shot in the left arm and then the left shoulder. He fell out of his tree after that. He's in a lot of pain, but he doesn't seem to care. He's still running through the trees. His mind looked like it was rippling before, but now it's separating into fragments. I can see my own face in the images on the subconscious levels. He's not just in pain from his wounds. There seems to be pain inside his head as well."

"He's seen you and your Strike team hunting him, Amber," said Lucas. "He knows what that means. We've discovered his plan, removed your imprint, and everything he's been through in the last fifteen years has been for nothing. The shock has sent his imprint overload into cascade failure, and his mind is coming apart at the seams. No wonder he's in pain."

"Will he recover from that?" I asked.

"No," said Lucas. "No chance of recovery. No possible treatment. There'll be some remaining rational thought, he'll still be dangerous, but he's broken beyond repair."

There was a roar from overhead. Another massive grey object was above us. That had to be Aerial three. We were by the side of the river with a precipitous slope next to us, so how could the aircraft pick us up?

Then I saw a rigid, man-sized cradle was dangling below the aircraft, and being lowered towards us. Forge and Rothan reached up to grab it and guide it to the ground. They loaded Eli in, careful of his twisted leg, and strapped him in place. He soared up into the air to be taken aboard the aircraft.

A couple of minutes later, Megan's voice spoke. "We have to get Eli back to the Hive immediately."

"Megan, are you in Aerial three?" asked Adika.

"Yes. I've got a full team of doctors with me, and we'll do our best for Eli, but we need to get him into a specialist unit as fast as possible."

I felt sick at the tone of her voice. I'd thought that once Eli was in medical hands then he'd be safe, but it wasn't that simple.

"Aerial three, go!" Adika ordered. "Aerial two, pick the rest of us up. Aerial one, maintain contact with target."

The aircraft carrying Eli suddenly accelerated and shot out of sight beyond the trees. Another took its place. Something was being lowered towards us again, not a one-man cradle this time, but a huge net. Adika caught it, and found an opening.

"Rothan, Forge, Amber, Lucas, Matias, Kaden. You go first."

Rothan and Forge went through the opening, one on each side of the net, using their weight to spread it out and make room for the rest of us. Matias helped Lucas inside, and I gulped and let Kaden lift me in after him.

"Just close your eyes, Amber," said Forge. "Keep them closed until we're aboard."

I closed my eyes, felt the net rock as Matias and Kaden climbed in, and then the world seemed to sway drunkenly as gusts of wind blew around us. I dug my hands into the web of netting and hung on tight, telling myself it was impossible to fall. After a few moments, I felt the netting go slack.

"We're aboard," said Forge. "You can let go of the net, Amber."

I opened my eyes, and saw a stranger, a woman, beckoning us towards a door. I disentangled myself from the webbing, and turned to follow her, catching a sickening glimpse of a hole in the floor with an endless drop below it. I froze, standing staring at it, and Lucas tugged me firmly through a door into a normal looking room filled with seats. He thrust me down into one of them, sat next to me, and the rest of the Strike team gradually arrived to join us, looking either exhilarated or shocked by the experience of riding in the net.

A warm cup arrived in my hands. I looked down stupidly at it for a moment, and then realized it was hot soup. I came out of my trance and drank it greedily.

"Now," said Adika, "we get on the right side of the river and..."

"Aerial one here. We've lost the target," said a voice over the sound link.

"What?" Adika burst out in fury. "How the waste did you lose him?"

"The heat signal just vanished."

"Even if Elden died," said Lucas, "he wouldn't lose his body heat all at once. Three possibilities. He's using stealth technology, he's underwater, or he's underground. Amber?"

I already had my eyes closed, reaching out with my mind. "He's still alive. Still moving. It's dark, and there's a beam of light flashing around. Mud underfoot. Glimpses of rock walls. No, not rock, blocks of carved stone." I felt Elden slip, and instinctively reach out a hand to steady himself. "Cold, hard, gritty, damp walls."

"Underground then," said Lucas. "Rothan, are there any tunnels round here?"

"There's no mention of them on my maps," said Rothan, "but ramblers wouldn't be interested in ancient tunnels. We want to spend time Outside, not underground."

"We're checking the records for tunnels," said the voice of Nicole. There was a pause of several minutes before she spoke again. "We had to go into the archived records to find any mention of tunnels, but there used to be underground express belt links between the Hive, Hive Futura, and the sea farm. When Hive Futura was abandoned, the underground belt links were abandoned too. The ends of the tunnels were sealed off, and now all supplies are sent to and from the sea farm by aircraft."

"Elden must have stumbled across a way into the old tunnel between the sea farm and the Hive when he was exploring this area," said Lucas. "Possibly through an air vent or emergency exit. However he got in there, Elden had a perfect route to our Hive, safe from curious ramblers and aerial surveillance. The belts wouldn't be working, he'd have to walk along them, but that would still be faster than the paths above ground. Why didn't Hive Defence mention these underground tunnels to us?"

Adika groaned. "They probably don't know they exist.

Abandoned express belt links wouldn't be included in anyone's imprinted data."

I didn't say it aloud, because it wouldn't help at this point, but I felt this showed that the Hive's policy of carefully controlling information could sometimes be counterproductive.

"Amber, do you know how Elden got in there?" asked Adika.

"No." I shook my head in frustration. "I can't understand the high levels, and the low levels are a waking nightmare. I just get the odd clue from things he sees, smells or touches. Things he hears too, but at the moment he's only hearing dripping water and his own breathing and footsteps. I'm sorry."

"You're doing brilliantly," said Lucas.

"There's thick forest down there," said Adika. "It could take us days to find a way to get underground after him."

"Elden knows he's failed," said Lucas, "and there's no way for him to get back to Hive Genex. He may still be able to send them a message, but he's too badly wounded to make the swim offshore to meet an aircraft."

"We should increase the coastal patrols on this whole length of coastline anyway," said Adika.

"Contacting Hive Defence about that now," said Nicole.

I was still checking Elden's distant mind for clues. He was sitting on the ground now, back against the tunnel wall, tying up his throbbing wounds and checking his possessions. I caught an angry memory that involved physical movements rather than words. "Elden's lost his gun. He's still got a knife, but no gun."

"No gun?" repeated Adika. "You're absolutely sure about that, Amber?"

"I'm sure," I said. "Elden was high up in a tree next to the river when Eli shot him in the shoulder. Elden lost his grip on his branch, and slithered down the tree, grabbing more branches to break his fall. Somewhere in the middle of that, his gun fell, and was either lost in the river or the undergrowth."

An image appeared in the pain-torn mind. "Elden's planning something," I said urgently. "I just saw him thinking about my brother, Gregas! How does Elden know about Gregas? Why is he thinking about him?"

"Elden will have found out every detail he could about you, Amber," said Lucas. "That would include information on your brother. If he's thinking about him, then..."

I had a shocking thought and interrupted him. "Gregas is another true telepath, and Elden is planning to kidnap him?"

"Your brother has a higher than usual chance of being a borderline telepath," said Lucas, "but it's highly unlikely that he's a true telepath. Elden knows he's failed to kidnap you, and that he can't possibly make it back to his own Hive, so he's going for a revenge killing. He's aware he won't stand a chance of getting through your bodyguards to kill you, so he's aiming to kill Gregas instead. Elden will be hoping that traumatizes you so much that it damages your ability to work for our Hive as a telepath."

I glared at him. "How can you talk about it so calmly? Gregas is irritating, but he's my brother!"

"I can talk about it calmly, because we won't let it happen," said Lucas. "Nicole, we need Gregas guarded until we've captured Elden. Other potential victims as well. Amber's parents obviously. Amber's best friends on Teen Level were Forge and Shanna. Forge can take care of himself, but we'd better put some guards on Shanna."

"That's not good enough," I said. "A few hasties would be no match for Elden. The man's deadly."

I turned in my seat to look at Adika. "I want my brother and my parents safely inside my unit behind the best defences in the Hive."

Adika frowned. "You want your family kept inside our unit for days, Amber? That could cause security problems."

"It won't matter if they find out roughly what our unit does, so long as they don't find out we use telepathy to do it."

Adika sighed. "The girl, Shanna, too?"

Shanna didn't mean much to me these days, but Elden wouldn't know that. "Yes, Shanna too."

"Nicole, get hasties to pick all four of them up and take them to the unit," said Lucas. "We'll fly home ourselves now, and wait for Elden to arrive at the Hive. Even if we could find a way to go underground after Elden, I'm not taking us on a chase along ancient tunnels that could collapse at any moment. It's a totally unnecessary risk when we know exactly where Elden is, where he's going, and what he plans to do when he gets there."

"What if he dies on the way to our Hive?" asked Adika.

Lucas shrugged. "In that case, we'll have to send people into the tunnel to retrieve his body, but I'm betting he'll make it there alive. The man seems indestructible. It should take him at least three days to make the journey, and we know he'll head straight for Gregas's room on Teen Level. We can send Elden's image to every hasty in the Hive, and have them all looking out for him."

"Elden will be conspicuous anyway," said Emili's voice. "He should reach the Hive just in time for the Halloween holiday, and it's trick or treat then. Anyone not wearing a costume is fair game for everyone."

Lucas laughed. "Elden will be pelted with scum balls wherever he goes. We'll need costumes to wear ourselves when we chase after him, because I don't want to smell of algae for days."

"I'll advise Nicole on appropriate costumes," said Emili.

"Aerial one, stay and patrol to make sure our target doesn't double back to the waterfall nest," said Adika. "Aerial two, take us home."

CHAPTER THIRTY-EIGHT

When our lift doors opened back at the unit, we found a crowd waiting to welcome us. Even Sofia had torn herself away from her latest painting to come and meet Matias.

Megan and Emili moved eagerly forward. Emili hugged Rothan, and I noticed Megan was smiling at Adika as well as at me, but the reunion was interrupted by the doors of another lift opening. A gorgeous girl in sparkling party clothes stormed out, followed by my parents, Gregas, and half a dozen blue-clad hasties.

Shanna scowled round at us. "I demand to know the meaning of this outrage!"

She had the same ornate hair and perfectly made up face that she'd had on Teen Level. She was reacting the same way she would have done on Teen Level as well. She hadn't changed a bit since Lottery, while Forge and I were smeared in mud, wearing peculiar, bulky clothes, and openly carrying guns on our hips. It was an utterly surreal moment.

No one answered Shanna, so she tried shouting louder. "I'm a Level 9 Media Presenter. You can't treat me like this."

She expected us to be impressed that she was Level 9. I couldn't help laughing, not because I was Level 1, but because levels hardly seemed to matter any longer. My laughter attracted her attention. She turned to me, wrinkled her nose in disgust, and then blinked in shock.

"Amber! You look ghastly." She marched towards me. "What's going on?"

"You'll be staying here for a few days, Shanna. I suggest you keep quiet and do what you're told."

"I can't stay here. I'm co-host of the special teen Halloween programme on Hive channel 8!"

"They'll cope without you." I threw a glance at my parents and Gregas. They looked stunned at the sight of me wearing a gun, but they had enough sense to wait quietly for instructions rather than make fools of themselves like Shanna.

"I'll tell all my viewers how I was forcibly dragged here by a bunch of ignorant hasties!" screeched Shanna.

I lost patience with her. "Shanna, this is a Level 1 unit that's dealing with a Hive security breach. Since this situation potentially puts you in danger, you've been brought here for your own protection. You'll tell your viewers nothing, you'll forget this ever happened, or you'll spend the rest of your life polishing pipes on Level 100."

I looked round for Forge. "Can you deal with Shanna, Forge? Make sure she understands I really mean that threat."

Forge moved out of the crowd of Strike team members. Shanna didn't seem to have noticed him until now, though admittedly he was almost unrecognizable, still wet and covered in mud after rescuing Eli. Her eyes widened as she looked at him.

"Forge, you're Level 1 as well?"

He didn't say a word, just nodded.

Shanna hesitated for a moment as she absorbed that information, then her face lit up in an encouraging smile. "It's wonderful to see you again. We'll be able to talk about old times on Teen Level, and make plans for the future."

Forge seemed to wince in pain. "We don't have a future, Shanna. You made that very clear the last time I saw you. Your old teen clothes and fashion accessories weren't good enough for you any longer. Neither was I."

"I regretted saying that the moment you'd gone," she said. "We were so good together on Teen Level. We can be just as good again."

Forge raised his eyes to the ceiling for a second. "I used to think we were good together on Teen Level, but now I realize I was stupidly naive back then." He turned to look at me. "Can someone else deal with Shanna, Amber?"

"If that's what you prefer." I nodded at Kaden.

"You can't mean that, Forge. Remember how..." Shanna's words broke off as Kaden grabbed her by the arms, and dragged her unceremoniously away.

My parents had been staring at Sofia's mural of me giving my speech, but now they looked hopefully at me, while Gregas was literally bouncing with excitement. I waved a hand at them.

"I need a minute to check a few things." I turned to Megan. "How is Eli?"

"In the best specialist hands, but they say he'd stand a better chance if they take his leg." Megan gave me a meaningful look. "Eli's unconscious, so they can't ask him for a decision on this."

It took me a moment to take in what she was telling me, what she was asking me. Eli couldn't speak for himself right now. I'd read his thoughts on a daily basis for months, I knew him better than anyone else could ever do, so it was up to me to speak for him. There were those on the Strike team who could accept losing a leg, having a prosthetic limb, moving to a less physically demanding role, but Eli...

I wanted to keep Eli safe, but I had to give his answer not mine. "Eli would want to keep his leg."

I rubbed a grimy hand across my eyes. I was faced with my worst fear. A member of my Strike team, my family, dying.

"You did everything possible, Amber," said Megan. "You stayed with him."

She didn't dare to mention my telepathy with my parents listening, but I knew what she meant. I'd been in Eli's head when he was in trouble. I'd stayed with him despite the pain. I'd told the team what was happening to him, so they had a chance to help.

"Eli knew the risk when he broke cover," said Adika. "He did a great job, but a slightly more accurate shot would have been even better. If the lad lives, he's going to do a lot of target practice."

I had to trust the experts to do everything they could for Eli, while I made sure we caught the man who'd shot him. "Situation status check. Have Hive Defence started the extra coastal patrols yet?"

Nicole nodded. "Joint Hive Treaty Enforcement immediately queried our high level of military activity at our borders. Hive Defence replied that these were temporary defensive manoeuvres in response to another Hive's violation of our territory, necessary while we were gathering evidence to submit a formal complaint. Several Joint Hive Treaty Enforcement aircraft have just arrived to monitor what we're doing."

Adika laughed. "That ties the hands of Hive Genex. They won't dare to send an aircraft to collect Elden from under the noses of Joint Hive Treaty Enforcement."

"So Elden's definitely got no way to escape," I said. "We just have to wait for him to get here."

"The Hive is already on full scale alert," said Lucas, "but he can't possibly get here for another three days."

"Good." I finally turned to my parents and brother. "You've probably worked out by now that I don't run a Research Unit. We're actually a Security Unit, and we're in the middle of dealing with an attack by an agent from another Hive. There was a possibility the agent might take you hostage, so we've brought you here for your protection."

"Enemy agents! High up, Amber!" gasped Gregas.

"This is all highly secret," I continued, "so it's vital you don't tell anyone about it."

My parents solemnly nodded. I knew I could trust them to keep the Hive's secrets. It was my brother that was worrying me.

"Gregas, you understand that?"

He gave an urgent nod. "Amber, when I go through Lottery, can you get me into your unit?"

I wasn't sure what to say, but Lucas stepped forward. "That might be possible, Gregas, but only if you keep totally silent about what you see here. A Security Unit couldn't accept anyone who'd breached Hive secrecy restrictions."

Gregas instantly looked obedient and discreet, a model future member of a Security Unit.

Lucas turned to smile at my parents. "You may remember

me. I visited your apartment. I'm just another of Amber's team leaders."

Lucas turned to give me a teasing look, and I felt myself blushing.

"Mum, Dad, I should have told you this days ago, but I wanted to say it in person rather than in a call. Lucas isn't just a team leader now, but my boyfriend and partner."

My parents looked doubtfully at Lucas, who was just as filthy as the rest of us, and had a clownishly wide smile on his face. I checked his mind. The over-anxious smile was because he knew my parents were important to me, and could cause huge problems if they tried to block our relationship.

There was no need for him to worry. Lucas and I were Level 1. My parents were Level 27, and they'd always been very aware of their place in the Hive hierarchy. The days of them nagging me to tidy my room were gone forever. Their daughter was Level 1 now, always faultless, always right. They wouldn't dream of objecting to my relationship with Lucas.

That was an unnerving thought. I somehow felt alone, abandoned, but of course I wasn't. My parents wouldn't offer advice on my decisions any longer, but they still cared about me as much as ever.

I took Lucas's arm. "I've had a huge amount to cope with since Lottery, and Lucas has been there for me through all of it, helping and supporting me."

My parents nodded again, clearly tongue tied in front of so many high level members of the Hive. I took pity on them.

"Nicole will find you somewhere to stay. I really need to go and clean up now."

My mother gave a single, deeply expressive, look at my clothes and my mud, and said the closest thing to criticism that she'd ever direct at me now. "Yes, I can see that."

Nicole led my parents and brother away, and Lucas and I headed back to the apartment that had been mine and now was ours. There was the luxury of showers and my favourite foods, and then we retired to the blissful comfort of a proper sleep field.

I was exhausted, but could only doze fitfully while watching the wall of our bedroom. Lucas had set it to display the doctors' latest report on Eli's condition in glowing letters, so I just had to turn my head to see it in the darkness. The doctors nearly lost Eli twice before midnight, and it was seven in the morning before the words told me he was stable and they'd saved his leg.

I'd looked my worst fear in the face. One day I'd lose a member of my team, but not this time. I could sleep at last.

CHAPTER THIRTY-NINE

The warbling sound of the alarm came during the first evening of Halloween, summoning us to lift 2. Elden had arrived on schedule, and we were ready and waiting to hunt him. Lucas had insisted on coming with us, so he was among the masked figures wearing red and black Halloween costumes.

The last time I'd worn a mask was for Carnival, months ago, a lifetime ago. Carnival of the silver and gold costumes. Halloween of the red and black. The twin Hive festivals of light and darkness, of life and death.

When the lift doors opened on Level 1, we moved to ride an express belt. I remembered the last day of Carnival. Twenty-two of us from our corridor on Teen Level, all in Carnival costumes of silver and gold except for our leader, Forge, who was breaking tradition by wearing red and black. We'd jumped on the handrail on Level 1, and plunged downwards through the shopping areas, balanced in a proud line and screaming our defiance at fate. Forge's red and black costume had been an act of defiance too.

Now it was Halloween, and Forge and I were back in costume. He was in red and black, and I was in silver and gold, just like before. There was no Eli with us, so nineteen Strike team members, Adika, Lucas, and myself made twenty-two again. Lucas had laughed when he'd seen our costumes, and said Emili had been amusing herself with symbolism when she chose them.

Forge and I were dressed as the twin angels of dark and of light, forever divided by our choices between evil and good. He was the dark angel who had made the wrong choice and fallen. I was in silver and gold, the light angel, the one lone symbol of hope allowed in the grimness of Halloween. Adika was justice, dressed in unrelieved black and carrying a great sword on his back. Lucas was wearing the red-eyed helm of the hunter of souls. The Strike team were in the motley costumes of the members of the pack, the scavengers of darkness.

"Hasties report that Elden has just reached the 510/6100 Level 1 shopping area," said Emili's voice in our ear crystals. "He's cleaned himself up, but he's not in costume, so everyone's shouting at him. He's looking confused, and staggering towards the downway. He must be planning to use that to go down to Gregas's room on Teen Level. The hasties are following."

"Keep the hasties at a discreet distance," said Lucas. "We know Elden has a knife, so we don't want to trigger him into violence in a shopping area packed with people."

"Approaching scene," said Adika.

We stepped off the belt and Forge picked me up. The dark angel carrying the light angel. The crowd looked at us, recognized a full Halloween hunt in professional costumes, and applauded. They thought we were part of the official entertainment.

I closed my eyes, searched for my target, and instantly found him. His mind was blazing like a burning camp fire in darkness, consuming itself. His imprint was tearing apart, the horrors in his subconscious had spread upwards to overwhelm his waking thoughts, and reality was conspiring against him too. He'd come to a Hive that was in Halloween costume. He was surrounded by creatures of nightmare, who were screaming abuse at him.

"Elden's on Level 2 and still descending," I said. "He's totally disoriented, terrified by the Halloween costumes."

"We'll follow," said Adika. "Amber, Lucas, and bodyguards at the back. The crowd will slow us down, but..."

"No!" I wriggled out of Forge's arms to stand on my own feet. "We're the Halloween hunt. People think we're entertainers, so we'll play the roles and the crowd will let us through." I pointed at the handrails of the downway. "Forge, with me!"

I jumped on one handrail and Forge on the other. We

balanced there, riding downwards. Adika cursed my folly and moved to stand on the moving stairs between us. The dark and light angels on the handrails, with justice standing between them. Behind the three of us, on the handrails and the steps, the pack streamed after us. Demons, wolves, and creatures of the night, led by Lucas, the hunter of souls.

"Amber!" Adika shouted above the noise of the crowd. "Get down! You're too conspicuous riding the rail, and you could fall."

"Amber won't fall," said Forge. "We came to this shopping area on the last day of Carnival, and she rode the handrail all the whole way from Level 1 down to Level 100."

I laughed. "I know what I'm doing, Adika. I promise I won't fall or put myself in danger from the target. I know exactly where Elden is. His head's exploding and he's impossible to miss. The crowd is slowing him down, so we'll catch up with him soon."

"If he had any sense," said Lucas, "he'd just take a lift down to Gregas's room."

"Elden's past sense and rational thought, Lucas," I said. "He's broken and in agony. His Hive did this to him. They... they wasted him."

I almost felt sorry for Elden. No, I did feel sorry for him. He'd been loyal to his Hive and done everything it demanded of him, no matter how hard the task or how high the personal cost. If that was a crime, then I was as guilty as he was.

I'd hated Elden, but it was his Hive that was my real enemy, not him. Hive Genex had cold-bloodedly used, broken, and discarded its agent. There was no way to cure what his imprint had done to Elden. He was lost in a tortured existence and worse was to come.

When we captured Elden, he'd be handed over in evidence and destruction analyzed. I'd seen what that inhuman phrase meant in Lucas's head, all the grim details of how a body and mind would be picked apart cell by cell. There would be much more pain before Elden was finally lucky enough to die.

We were on Level 6 when Adika shouted. "There he is!"

I could see him too, the lone figure struggling through the mocking crowd. The people saw us coming, and deliberately blocked Elden's escape, forming a solid wall and laughing at him. Trick or treat. A man was out without costume, the legitimate prey of the Halloween hunt. The mob was holding him for us, so we could pelt him with slime balls or pour fake blood over his head for their entertainment. They didn't know he had a knife. They didn't know he was ripped apart by pain, and might hit out in panic and kill them.

Elden saw the wall of people ahead, turned, and saw the demonic hunt descending on him. He looked at me, at the light angel, at the one sign of hope in the darkness. He'd spent his entire adult life hunting me, but his mind had shattered and he didn't recognize me.

"The Hive wants Elden alive, so guns on stun and take him down as soon as you get a clear shot over the crowd," Adika ordered. "We don't want anyone getting stabbed."

Forge and I were poised on the handrails, looking out over the crowd, and we both drew guns. My Hive wanted Elden alive, but his body was all we really needed to prove our case to Joint Hive Treaty Enforcement. I was a telepath, above the law, untouchable, and I chose to allow myself one moment of rebellion. Elden was a poor broken thing now, and I would grant him the only possible mercy.

Forge's gun was set to stun, but mine was on kill when I shot Elden in the heart. He fell to the ground, and the crowd cheered the dramatic performance by the Halloween entertainers.

CHAPTER FORTY

The warbling sound of the alarm cut into my dreams. I groaned and rolled out of the sleep field.

"Unit emergency alert," said the computerized voice. "Unit emergency alert. We have an incident in progress. Operational teams to stations. Strike team to lift 2."

Adika's voice cut in. "Alpha team, you have the strike."

I grabbed my body armour, pulled it on, and wriggled to get it comfortable before finishing dressing. Over the other side of the sleep field, Lucas was pulling on clothes while simultaneously reading a scrolling display on the wall. I ignored the glowing text. Lucas would brief us on the details later.

We left the apartment together, grabbed a split-second hug and kiss, and then split up. Lucas sprinted for his office, and I ran for lift 2. Adika, Rothan, and the Alpha Strike team were in there already. Forge and the Beta Strike team were standing nearby, and waved cheerfully at me. This wasn't their strike, but Forge still wasn't satisfied with their emergency response speed, so he had them responding to Alpha team alerts for extra practice. I didn't see why he was complaining. They were a lot faster than me. I'd have to sleep in the lift, wearing body armour and full equipment, to get there ahead of either Strike team.

I skidded to a halt in the lift, the doors closed behind me, and the lift started moving. I spotted a familiar mind and figure among the Alpha team, and hugged him in delight.

"Eli! Welcome back to active duty."

He made the most of the hug before releasing me and grinning. "I could have been back weeks ago, instead of being stuck training with Forge and the Beta team greenies."

"We had to be sure your leg was properly healed," said Rothan.

"We certainly did," I said. "We couldn't take silly risks with someone as valuable as you, Eli."

Eli flushed with pleasure and embarrassment.

Adika decided we'd spent enough time giving Eli his welcome back to full Alpha team duty, and started the standard routine. "Strike team is moving."

Lucas's voice spoke in my ear crystal. "Tactical ready."

Nicole came next. "Liaison ready. Tracking status green." She sounded anxious, the way she always did.

I checked my dataview. "We are green."

The warm, relaxed voice of Lucas started briefing us. "We have an emergency call about an incident, strength six. Location is..."

Strength six meant someone had already died. The atmosphere in the lift gained an extra degree of tension as we braced ourselves for the chase. A wild bee was out there on a killing spree. The Strike team were preparing themselves to use deadly force if necessary. They'd been carefully selected by Lottery to be capable of taking instant decisions, and using whatever level of violence was in the interests of the Hive.

I hadn't been like them. I'd been an ordinary girl and should have lived an ordinary life, but it had been a long road from Carnival to Halloween. I wasn't an ordinary girl any longer. I'd read tame minds and wild minds. I'd shared their thoughts and felt their emotions. I'd known the light and the darkness, and walked the thin line between mercy and revenge.

The Hive hadn't let me meet any of the other true telepaths, and now I knew one of the reasons why. Morton, Sapphire, Keith, or even Mira, would have told me the truth. That of all the people in the Hive, only true telepaths were free from imprints and fears of consequences. We would serve the Hive, as everyone did, but we would serve it on our own terms. The Hive didn't want us to know that, but we all learnt it for ourselves in the end.

The lift doors opened, and the Strike team clustered protectively round me as we headed out to defend our Hive.

Message From Janet Edwards

Thank you for reading Telepath. There will be more books in the Hive Mind series. I also have book series set in a very different portal future, where the invention of interstellar portals has allowed humanity to colonise hundreds of worlds scattered across distant star systems.

Please visit my website, www.janetedwards.com, to see the current list of my books. You can also make sure you don't miss future books by signing up to get an email alert when there's a new release.

Best wishes from Janet Edwards

Made in the USA
Lexington, KY
20 January 2018